D1581065

USA TODAY

bes...

CYNTHIA EDEN

"A fast-paced, sexy thrill ride you won't want to miss."
Christine Feehan on *Eternal Hunter*

"Cynthia Eden's on my must-buy list."
Angie Fox, *New York Times* bestselling author

"I dare you not to love a Cynthia Eden book. . . .
Eden's unsurpassed creativity shines once again!"
Larissa Ione, *New York Times* bestselling author

By Cynthia Eden

TWISTED
BROKEN

Forthcoming

SHATTERED

CYNTHIA EDEN

TWISTED

AVONBOOKS

An Imprint of HarperCollins*Publishers*

This is a work of fiction. Names, characters, places, and incidents are products of the author's imagination or are used fictitiously and are not to be construed as real. Any resemblance to actual events, locales, organizations, or persons, living or dead, is entirely coincidental.

AVON BOOKS
An Imprint of HarperCollins*Publishers*
195 Broadway
New York, New York 10007

Copyright © 2015 by Cindy Roussos
Excerpt from *Shattered* copyright © 2015 by Cindy Roussos
ISBN 978-0-06-234964-4
www.avonromance.com

First Avon Books mass market printing: May 2015

Avon Trademark Reg. U.S. Pat. Off. and in Other Countries, Marca Registrada, Hecho en U.S.A.

HarperCollins® is a registered trademark of HarperCollins Publishers.

Printed in the U.S.A.

10 9 8 7 6 5 4 3 2 1

This book is for the lady who inspires me the most . . . my mom. Thanks, Mom, for all that you do.

Acknowledgments

I WANT TO THANK THE WONDERFUL STAFF AT AVON.
My editors work so hard to help me deliver the best
possible book—thank you!

And for my readers—I appreciate all of the support
that you have given me over the years. Thank you for
taking the time to get lost with romantic suspense!

I was so excited to set this book in New Orleans, one
of my absolute favorite towns. I fell in love with this
magical place when I was a teen, and I've been back
countless times. New Orleans is a true city of mystery.
Anything can happen in the Big Easy—and it usually
does.

Happy reading, everyone!

TWISTED

PROLOGUE

WHAT DO YOU SEE FOR MY FUTURE?"

Emma Castille slowly glanced up from the cards that were spread on the table before her. The young girl who sat across from Emma appeared to be barely sixteen. Her blond hair was secured in a haphazard knot at the nape of her neck, her clothes were faded, and her blue eyes were wide with a fear that couldn't be controlled.

Emma didn't reach for the cards on her table. She just stared at the girl, and said, "I see a family that's waiting for you. You need to go home to them."

The girl's chin jerked. "Wh-what if they won't have me?"

"You'd be surprised at what they'd have." Darkness was coming, the night slowly creeping to take over the day. Emma knew that she would have to leave Jackson Square soon. Her time was almost up.

The others around her were already packing up their booths for the day. Psychics. Artists. Musicians. They were a mixed group, one that assembled every day as the sun came out, to capture the attention of the tourists in New Orleans.

Emma wasn't psychic. She wasn't gifted when it came to music or art. But she did have one talent that she used to keep her alive and well fed—Emma had a talent for reading people.

For noticing what others would too easily miss. Too easily *ignore*.

"You're running from someone," Emma said flatly. The girl had already glanced over her left shoulder at least four times while they'd been talking. Fear was a living, breathing thing, clinging to the girl like a shroud.

Emma knew what it was like to run. Sometimes, it seemed as if she'd always been running from someone or something.

"Will he find me?" the girl asked as she leaned forward.

Emma almost reached for the girl's hand because she wanted to comfort her. Almost. "Go back to your family." The girl was a runaway. She'd bet her life on it.

The young blond blanched. "What if it's the family you fear?"

At those words, Emma stiffened.

"Aren't you supposed to tell me that everything will be all right?" the girl asked. She stood then, and her voice rose, breaking with fear. "Aren't you supposed to tell me that I'll go to college, marry my dream man, and live happily ever after?"

Others turned their way because the girl was nearly shouting.

"Aren't you?" the girl demanded.

Emma shook her head. She didn't believe in happily ever after. "Go to the police." She said this softly, her words a direct contrast to the girl's angry tone. "You're in danger." There were bruises on the girl's wrists, bruises peeking out from beneath the long sleeves of her shirt. A long-sleeved shirt in August, in New Orleans? Oh, no, that wasn't right. *What other bruises are you trying to hide?*

The girl stumbled back. "Help me." Now her voice was a desperate whisper.

Emma stood, as well. "I'll go with you—" Emma began.

But the girl had glanced over her shoulder once more. The blonde's too-thin body stiffened, and she gasped. Then she was turning and running away. Shoving through the tourists crowding the busy square. Running as if her very life depended on it.

Because maybe, just maybe, it did.

Emma called out after her, but the girl didn't stop.

Let her go, let her go.

But Emma found herself rushing after the girl, going as fast as she could. But New Orleans, oh, New Orleans, it could be such a tricky bitch, with its narrow streets and secret paths. Emma couldn't find the blonde. She turned to the left and to the right, and she just saw men and women laughing, celebrating. Voices were all around her. So many people.

And there was no sign of the terrified blond girl.

Emma paused, and pressed her hand to the brick wall on her right as she fought to catch her breath.

But the wall was . . . wet. She lifted her hand, and in the faint light, she could see the red stain that covered her palm. A red that was—

Blood.

"OH, JULIA, SWEET Julia, why did you try to run?"

He ran the tip of his knife down Julia's cheek. She was already bleeding, and, before he was done, there would be even more blood.

So much blood.

Behind his left hand, Julia whimpered.

He let the knife slice even deeper into her cheek. "Now I'm just going to have to punish you more. You know that?" His voice was whisper soft because the other woman—the one with the dark hair and too-bright eyes—had followed his Julia. The woman was just steps away, less than five feet. She hadn't realized that they'd ducked into the abandoned bar.

She didn't know that he had Julia in his arms right then.

The woman was looking at her hand.

Ah, did you see Julia's blood?

Because he'd slammed Julia's head into the wall. Stopped her from running.

"You're not going to get away from me," he told Julia, as the other woman crept closer to the bar. The place's windows and doors were boarded up, but he'd found a way inside, a way that gave him perfect access to Julia. "I always keep what's mine."

The dark-haired woman was almost upon them. Through the thin cracks in those boarded-up windows, he could see the shape of her slender body. The long, flowing dress.

He smiled as the thrill of the hunt filled him once more. *"Always . . ."*

CHAPTER ONE

NEW ORLEANS WAS FUCKING HOT. NO OTHER way to describe it. *Fucking. Hot.* On a late-September day, the heat was like a damn blanket wrapping around Dean Bannon. He'd rolled up his sleeves and ditched his tie, but those feeble efforts sure hadn't done any good.

New Orleans was hell, he was convinced of that, and the place was also the site of his latest assignment.

Sixteen-year-old Julia Finney had last been seen in the Big Easy. Her mother was desperate to find the girl, but the local cops weren't giving any of their time to finding the runaway, and he—well, he was one of the agents from LOST who'd been sent down from Atlanta to find the girl.

He made his way slowly down Bourbon Street. The sun hadn't even set yet, and the place was already hopping. Drunk frat boys and drunk sixty-year-old men staggered down the street in near-perfect rhythm. And girls—girls that looked far too young—stood in darkened doorways and waved the men inside.

Ann Finney was worried that her daughter Julia was going to become one of those girls. On the streets, with

no money, no connections . . . what else could happen
to her?

A fucking lot.

Dean lifted the picture of Julia he carried. Showed
it to the girls. But their glassy-eyed stares just passed
right over the image. No one recognized Julia. No one
knew her.

It seemed that no one had ever bothered to *look* at
the girl.

Now he was looking for her, but the clench in Dean's
gut told him that he might already be too late. But he
kept trudging along, kept turning down the streets until
he found himself in Jackson Square.

Street performers were out, some kids playing jazz,
others dancing a fast-and-frantic rhythm on cardboard
boxes they'd brought out as they worked for tips.

The crowd there was huge. So many people. Too
many.

No wonder a sixteen-year-old girl had vanished without a trace.

"Who are you looking for?"

The voice was feminine, low, husky—and very close.
He turned his head and saw her. A woman with a long
cascade of black hair and the bluest eyes he'd ever seen.
She was sitting beneath the shelter of a big blue umbrella. A small table sat in front of her, and a sign by
her said that a "Reading" would be twenty dollars.

His eyes narrowed as he studied her.

She smiled at him, flashing dimples in both of her
cheeks. "Come now, don't be afraid of me, handsome, I
won't bite." Her hand, delicate, tanned, motioned to the
chair across from her. "Come closer."

Why? Did it look like he was some tourist in the mood to be conned? Because that sure as shit wasn't his style.

But if the woman usually worked the square, if she saw all the people coming and going . . . then maybe, just maybe, she'd seen Julia.

Dean ducked his head and slid under the umbrella. But he didn't sit. He leaned over her, and the woman tilted her head back as she stared up at him.

Her smiled dimmed. Those dimples vanished, and Dean had one thought—

Fucking gorgeous.

The woman's face was eerily close to perfect. High cheekbones. Straight nose. Wide, amazing eyes. A delicate chin.

Her lips were full, sexy, and red. Her face might have made her look like an angel, but those lips and that dark mass of hair . . . oh, it made him think of sin.

Not here, not now.

Dean had a rule about mixing business and pleasure. He damn well never did it.

He was there on a case. For Dean, the mission always came first. *Always.*

"Not a cop," she said as she lifted one eyebrow. "But a government agent . . ." Her lips pursed. "FBI?"

Was he supposed to be impressed? He'd been an FBI agent for ten years, working day and night in the Violent Crimes Division. He'd seen enough shit to give most people never-ending nightmares.

Good thing Dean didn't have nightmares. He didn't have dreams, either. When he slept, there was only darkness.

He pulled out the photo of Julia. He noticed that the would-be fortune-teller's eyes fell to the photo, and she tensed, just for an instant.

"I'm betting you see plenty of people come by this way each day."

Her gaze lifted back to his. "I don't work here every day."

He took a step closer to her. She definitely tensed. Dean put the photo of Julia down on the woman's table. As he leaned in even closer to her, Dean could have sworn that he caught the scent of jasmine. He'd grown up on his grandfather's farm, a lifetime ago, and jasmine had been there.

She wasn't looking at the photograph.

"Most people disappear for a reason," she said, staring into his eyes. "They don't like to be found."

Too bad. "My job is to find the lost."

Her head tilted a bit more, and a dark lock of hair slid over her shoulder. She was wearing gold earrings, hoops that moved faintly as she watched him. Those hoops, her hair, her amazing eyes—yeah, they all came together to give her a seductive, mysterious air. He bet the tourists loved her.

But Dean knew there was no mystery about the woman before him. Just another pretty face hiding lies. The woman was a scammer, out there to bilk the people dumb enough to approach her table.

"Look at the girl," he said softly.

Her blue gaze fell to the table.

For just a moment, her eyes widened. "What has she done?"

Interesting question. "Her family wants her home."

Her hand rose. Her fingers slid over the photograph. "She should go home. I . . . told her that."

He caught her hand. Grabbed her wrist in a lightning fast move. "You've seen her." He felt the light ridge of raised skin beneath his fingers. A scar?

She was still looking down at the photograph. "It was at least a week ago. She came here right before sunset." Her full lips curved down as sadness chased over her face. "I'm sorry, but I don't think you'll be finding her."

The hell he wouldn't.

She tugged on her wrist. Dean didn't let her go.

"That girl is sixteen years old," he said. "She ran away from her home in Atlanta, and her mother is desperate to find her. Her mother *needs* her back home."

"I don't think she wanted to go back."

She stood then, moving from beneath the shelter of the umbrella, and she was smaller than he'd thought. Dean stood at six-foot-three, and the woman—she was barely five-foot-four. Maybe five-five. When she tried to slip away from him, he tightened his hold on her wrist.

"Let me go."

He didn't. But his hand slid up her forearm a bit, and he felt more of that raised skin. Just small ridges. Curious now, he looked down as he turned her arm over. Those *were* scars. Faint lines of white that crossed her skin. The marks were at various points on her inner arm, and . . .

His hand pushed open her clenched fist. There were a few more faint scars there, too. Little slices.

A surge of anger caught him by surprise. "Who did it?"

"It's rude to ask questions like that." She actually

sounded as if she was chiding him. "Didn't they teach you a better interview technique at the FBI?"

"I'm not with the FBI."

"Well, not any longer, of course," she said. Her smile flashed, only this time he recognized it for the distraction that it was. Hell, he bet plenty of men got lost in that wide smile.

He wasn't plenty of men.

And he knew better than to fall for a pretty face.

"The girl," Dean gritted out. "Tell me everything you know about her."

Her gaze slid to the left. To the right. And Dean realized that the others close by were watching them.

"You are seriously bad for business," she said, sounding annoyed. "It looks like you're an angry lover who's having some public spat with me. You need to let me go, *now*."

An angry lover? Okay, so he was holding her pretty close, but Dean wasn't backing off. And that sweet jasmine scent was definitely coming from her. "Tell me what I need to know, and—"

"Is there a problem here?" A male voice. Close. Sharp.

He turned his head just a bit and saw the uniformed police officer, frowning at them.

"Ms. Castille? This guy bothering you?"

Dean mentally filed away the lady's last name even as he made himself step back and release her. "I'm not bothering her." Okay, he had been.

The cop came even closer. His face was tight with suspicion, and it was a young face. The guy was in his early twenties and had ROOKIE written all over him.

"It *looked* like you were bothering her, so I'm gonna suggest that you keep walking now, buddy."

"It's all right." *Ms. Castille* put her hand on the cop's shoulder. "Thanks, Beau, it sure is nice to know you're looking out for me."

Beau smiled at her. Dean figured the cop's smile flashed because she'd just fired him that megawatt smile of hers, dimples included.

"Always here for you, ma'am," he told her, flushing a bit. Then he glanced back at Dean, and the cop's frown was back. "I'd like to see your ID, Mister."

Hell. But, whatever. Dean tossed the cop his wallet.

Beau pulled out his driver's license. Ms. Castille was right next to him as the cop read, "Dean Bannon, age thirty-six, from Atlanta, Georgia." Beau whistled. "Love me some Braves."

Dean waited.

"What brings you down to New Orleans?" the cop asked him.

"Keep looking in the wallet," Dean said.

The cop's brows scrunched when he pulled out one of Dean's cards. "LOST," he said, and his frown deepened. "I've . . . heard of that group." His gaze shot to Dean. "The LOST team caught that serial killer over on Dauphin Island awhile back!"

Yes, they had. And since Dauphin Island, Alabama, was just a few hours away, Dean wasn't real surprised that the cop had heard about the incident. "We didn't bring him in alive," Dean said. Because the Lady Killer hadn't given them that option.

"You stopped him," Beau said, sounding more than impressed. "That's good enough in my book."

LOST. The organization that Dean worked for was gaining more and more attention these days. *Last Option Search Team.* Dean's buddy Gabe Spencer had been the one to first put the team together. The ex-SEAL had wanted to bring in a group with varied backgrounds, a team that knew how to get the job done.

When local law enforcement gave up the hunt for the missing, when the families still needed hope, they turned to LOST.

Just like Ann Finney had. No one else had helped her to find Julia. Runaways disappeared every day. With Julia being an older teen, the cops hadn't spent a lot of time looking for her . . .

But Dean wasn't going to give up.

"There's a picture of a missing girl on *Ms. Castille's* table," Dean said. "We were just talking because I thought she might know where I could find Julia."

Beau tossed Dean's wallet back to him. Then the cop went to stare at the photo.

The woman didn't move, though. She kept her eyes on Dean. "I haven't seen Julia in over a week," she said, voice soft. "But I can tell you this . . . the last time that I did see her, she was scared."

His muscles locked. "How do you know that?"

The cop's radio crackled to life. Beau took a few steps away, turned his back, and pulled out the radio.

"Because I know what fear looks like." Her lips pressed together, then she said, "And I also know what bruises look like. She had bruises on her wrists. Someone had been hurting Julia."

He lunged toward her. "Why the hell didn't you tell me that before?"

She glanced over at Beau. He was on his radio, still staring down at that picture as he paced and talked. "Because you said you wanted to send her back home. Julia didn't want to go home. She was afraid of her family." Her eyes darkened with sadness. "There's a reason people run away, you know. If life were perfect, why would a girl like that leave?"

The cop was coming back toward them. He'd put up his radio. "You need to go down to the station," he told Dean. "You can check in with the detectives—"

"My partner is already at the station." While he hit the streets, Sarah Jacobs had wanted to check with the local authorities to see if they might have any leads. Dean wasn't exactly holding out much hope on that end. But, since he had a cop right in front of him, one who worked this beat, Dean asked, "Have *you* seen the girl, Officer?"

Beau shook his head. "She looks just like a hundred others I see every day. Sorry." His radio crackled to life once again. "Got to go. See you soon, Ms. Castille."

Thunder rumbled as the cop headed away. Dean looked up. There were a few dark clouds sprinkling over the sky.

"Storms come up fast down South. They rage hard, then they die away as quickly as they came." She turned away. Started shutting down her booth. "Good luck finding the girl."

Did she really think he was just going to walk away? "You're my best lead." So far, she was the *only* person who'd actually seen Julia.

Provided, of course, that she hadn't just been blowing smoke up his ass.

She pulled down her umbrella. "Bourbon Street."

His brows climbed.

"The last time I saw her, she was headed over there. But then, most folks wind up there, eventually, right?"

Dean pulled his card from his wallet. "If you remember anything else, call me."

She didn't take the card. "I won't remember anything."

He reached for her hand. Put the card in her palm. Stared at the faint scars. "They're defensive wounds," he told her, as another rumble of thunder sounded in the distance.

Her too-bright eyes held his.

"Someone attacked you with a knife. You raised your hands, and that someone—" A fucking bastard in his book. "Sliced you. The blade cut across your palm. It sliced into your forearm."

Her fingers closed around the card. "You left the FBI because you got tired of all the death."

He stiffened.

"You have scars hidden beneath your clothes. Scars on your skin. Scars *beneath* the skin." Her head gave a little shake. "You don't really think you'll find Julia alive. You don't think you'll find any of them alive."

What the hell?

"But at least you try." She backed away from him. Collected her bag. Her table. Started walking away. "Good-bye, Dean Bannon."

"Wait!" He hadn't meant to call out like that.

She glanced back at him.

"Do you . . . need help?" And why was he stuttering like some kid right then?

"I've never needed help." She turned away. Kept going. "I hope you find her."

Dean's legs had locked as he stared after her. He watched as she disappeared, not heading very far away at all but going toward a little shop on the corner. A small place that he almost hadn't even seen before.

A crystal shop.

I hope I find her, too.

And the sexy fortune-teller had been wrong. He did want to find Julia alive. He *needed* to find the missing . . . still alive.

Because he'd found too many dead already.

He tucked the picture of Julia back into his pocket. A drop of rain fell on him, but Dean didn't move. The dark-haired woman had vanished. There had been something familiar about her. Something that kept nagging at him.

Another raindrop fell.

Where have I seen you before, Ms. Castille?

And . . . *who the fuck hurt you?*

DEAN STRIPPED OFF his soaked shirt. Lightning flashed just outside his hotel room. For an instant, his gaze slid to the window. Being on the thirty-eighth floor gave him a killer view of the city. The river was below, dark and turbulent, and the clouds were swirling so close that it looked as if he could reach out and touch them.

Instead, he turned away from the window and reached for his laptop. In seconds, he had the thing booted up and was searching—for her.

Castille.

The name had struck a chord with him, stirring up memories of a case he'd heard about long ago.

He started tapping on the keyboard. Going through searches. Accessing records that most people didn't know about but that LOST operatives had managed to reach long ago.

Castille . . .

The memory of that name teased at him.

So he typed in . . . *Castille* . . . *psychic.*

The search results were immediate.

House of Death . . . *Psychic John Castille Arrives Too Late to Save Missing Teens* . . .

"I'll be damned," he muttered. He leaned forward as he read the first search article.

HE WAS BACK.

Emma kept staring at her client, nodding as the woman talked, but her focus was on the tall, dark, and far-too-dangerous man who stood a few feet away.

Dean Bannon.

He was wearing a different dress shirt today. A crisp white shirt in the ridiculous New Orleans heat. He'd rolled up his sleeves, like that was going to do much good. He was also wearing another pair of too-expensive pants.

Seriously, the guy was so out of place . . . and he just *looked* like a federal agent. How had he not expected her to tag him right away?

"Thank you so much, hon," Mrs. Jones was saying. Mrs. Jones was a weekly client. A sweet grandmother in her early seventies. "I love our talks."

Emma almost smiled at that. A real smile, but she caught herself just in time.

Mrs. Jones handed her a twenty. Emma reached for the money, but, instead of taking it, she leaned close to Mrs. Jones and caught her trembling hand. "I want you to see a doctor tomorrow."

Mrs. Jones's dark eyes widened. "Wh-why?"

Because she could feel the tremble in Mrs. Jones's hand. Because the woman's skin was paler than it had been the week before. Because her voice kept getting breathless when it shouldn't have. "Because you need to be checked out. It's been far too long since you've paid a visit to your doctor."

"I . . . *how did you know?*"

Emma stared into her eyes. "I'm worried about you, and I want you to go and see a doctor right away."

Dean inched closer. Eavesdropping? Sad. So sad.

"I-I think I'm fine . . ."

Emma pushed the money back at Mrs. Jones. "Have I ever steered you wrong?"

Mrs. Jones shook her head. "That's why I come to you."

No, Mrs. Jones came to her because she was lonely, and she just wanted to talk with someone who would listen to her.

"Then listen to me now. See a doctor."

Mrs. Jones nodded. Then she was off, hurrying away, and Dean Bannon was closing in. Great. Emma narrowed her eyes on the man. "You're terrible for business." Hadn't she told the guy the same thing yesterday?

He smiled, but it wasn't a real smile. Emma knew because she gave plenty of her own, fake smiles. Dean's smile just lifted his sensual lips, but the smile never lit his dark eyes. The man was handsome, in a too-polished sort of way. She'd like to see his hair longer, his tanned cheeks flushed more with fury or passion, and she'd like—

"You're not who you pretend to be."

Uh-oh.

Her gaze slowly swept over his face as Emma tried to figure out just what the guy could have learned about her. Unfortunately . . . *he could know too much*. In this Internet-filled world, secrets were just a search engine away.

Dean Bannon had closed in on her, his powerful body moving with a grace the guy shouldn't possess. He was controlled—*definitely controlled*. Everything about the guy screamed control, and Emma . . . well, she'd never had much use for control.

Emma let emotions rule her. She lived for passion, she lived for the moment.

Why live for anything else? Especially when nothing else was ever guaranteed. *The past is a nightmare. The future could vanish*. So why not live in that wonderful here and now?

Only the here and now wasn't always so wonderful.

His hair was cut a bit too short. His expression was too hard. That deliciously square jaw of his appeared to be clenched—again, and his eyes had locked on her as if he were a predator, and she were his prey.

"I didn't think psychics were supposed to tell bad fortunes."

Now he'd caught her by surprise. *I don't remember*

saying I was psychic. Emma always tried to choose her words very carefully. Whenever possible, she opted not to lie.

Her father had told too many lies. Emma had discovered that she didn't really have a taste for them. Even if she had inherited his . . . other . . . talents. Talents that weren't always savory. Talents that weren't exactly legal in some places. *Most places.*

"Were you trying to scare that woman?" he asked, voice sharp.

"I was trying to get her to see a doctor." Emma shrugged. "Horrible, I know, to want to make certain that a friend is in good health." Her eyes widened. "I guess that means I'm just a terrible, wretched person on the inside."

His frown got worse.

Emma sighed. "You'd be so much better-looking if you just smiled. Like, a real smile."

He blinked at her.

"Right, no smile." So she smiled brightly for them both. "To what do I owe the pleasure of your company today? Come for a reading, did you?"

Because she really didn't want to waste time talking with him. As it was, she'd spent most of the night staying up, thinking about Julia.

Now I have a name to go with her face.

And when sleep still hadn't come at midnight, Emma had slipped away. She'd gone to Bourbon Street, but there had been no sign of Julia.

He pulled out the folding chair she'd set up. The guy surprised her by tossing a twenty on the table and sitting down in front of her.

Intrigued now, Emma made herself comfortable in her chair, shifting a bit, as she kept her gaze on him.

"A reading . . ." he said. She almost shivered. The guy had one of those amazing voices that, once a woman heard it, she didn't forget. Deep and rumbly. A voice made for darkness.

And sex.

She'd detected no accent in his voice, and Emma was very good at recognizing accents. Accents, habits, behavior—she noticed them all.

Like the way Dean Bannon had a habit of rubbing his jaw with his index finger and thumb. He did that when he was thinking. When he was annoyed, she'd noticed that a muscle flexed along the left-hand side of his jaw. And—

"Your name is Emma Castille."

She leaned forward. "I can use the cards if you want. Some people like that part." She actually did know what all of the cards meant, so she could shuffle them and give a reading, no problem. But she preferred to work in other ways.

"You're not psychic."

Were they back to that?

She put her hands in her lap. Emma didn't believe in making nervous gestures. She didn't believe in giving away anything at all with her body language.

"What you are . . ." Ah, now he *did* smile. Her father would have called it a shit-eating grin. The more PC term was probably a Cheshire cat smile. Whatever the name, that smile annoyed her. "What you are, Ms. Castille . . . is a criminal. A fraud."

Maybe she should grab her chest and dramatically

gasp. She didn't. "Wonderful for you," Emma said. "You pulled up a background report on me." She let her eyes widen a bit. "It's amazing just what one can find if a person knows how to use a search engine."

A furrow appeared between his eyes.

"How about I say what . . . *you* are?" Emma asked him. "A washed-up FBI agent who snapped on the job. You held your control tight every single day, but the bad guys—they just didn't stop, did they? You hunted them, you stopped them, and more appeared. While you were fighting the system, they kept coming, and the bodies kept piling up on *your* watch."

He shot right back to his feet. The folding chair slammed down behind him.

"You and your father bilked desperate people," he accused. "You told them you were psychic, that you could help find their missing children. And you—"

"We found them." Two girls who'd vanished. They'd *found* them. "We just didn't get to them in time." And she would *not* go back to that place.

She motioned toward Manuel. He knew the signal meant he could take over her booth. There was no way, *no way,* that she was going to stay there with that prick while he slammed the most painful moments from her past in Emma's face.

Manuel, pale, tattooed, with piercings in his lips and eyebrows, quickly claimed her spot.

Emma jumped to her feet. Muttered her thanks, and fled right past the guy she was starting to think of as Agent Jackass.

She pushed through the crowd. Wasn't there always a crowd in Jackson Square? And that was why she loved the place. It was so easy to vanish in a crowd. To be anyone.

The crowd closed around her.

To be no one at all.

She hurried around the back of the cathedral. She knew the streets so well. Her home was close by. Emma would get inside and forget Agent Jackass.

I'm being followed.

Emma stilled at the intersection. A horse-drawn carriage rolled by her. Voices called out.

And he touched her.

Emma didn't flinch. Didn't scream. She looked down at the hand on her shoulder. "When a woman runs away from you, that means you need to stay the hell away from her."

His hold tightened on her. "You and I aren't done."

She looked up at his face. Had she really thought the man was handsome? Annoying, that was all Dean Bannon was.

"I need to find that girl, and you're the only lead I have so far."

"Then you're not a very good investigator."

Ah, that muscle flexed in his jaw. Lovely.

"You were heading to your apartment." He pointed across the street. "One block over, right? Seems like the perfect place for a chat."

My, my, but he had been busy. Only instead of spending all his time investigating her, he should have been looking for the missing girl.

Emma took a step forward. He, of course, followed right by her side. They didn't speak as they made their way to her apartment, a precious little gem that she adored. It was right over a clothing store, nestled up high, with a balcony view. She climbed the narrow flight of stairs that led to her room, then . . .

Emma stopped as her heartbeat increased. The pounding seemed to shake her entire body.

"What are you waiting for?" Dean demanded.

Emma shook her head. "Someone has been here." Her welcome mat had been moved. Moved over one tiny inch, as if it had been hit by a shoe. She could see the outline where the mat *should* have been. A bit of dirt, some dust. A marker that showed her something was wrong inside her place.

"How do you know?"

"The mat's in the wrong spot." Her hand reached for the knob, and it turned—far too easily beneath her hand. "And I never leave my door unlocked." With the things she'd seen in her life, Emma would never make that kind of mistake.

Never.

But the knob was turning easily in her hand. Far too easily. And as the door swung open, Emma sucked in a sharp breath.

The place was wrecked. Her mirrors were smashed. The furniture had been slashed. Cushion stuffing littered the floor.

Dean swore, and in the next moment, he grabbed Emma and pushed her behind him. "Stay back," he ordered. "The bastard could still be inside."

Then Dean was rushing inside. Going through the wreckage but being careful, she noted, not to actually touch anything. He searched the small place; the studio-style apartment didn't exactly cover a lot of square footage, so she could see most of her home from her nervous perch in the doorway.

But then Dean disappeared into the little attached room that she'd made into her bedroom. Emma realized that she was holding her breath, waiting for him to reappear. Only he didn't come out immediately.

She crept forward, and her right foot slid over the threshold of her home. She glanced down, and her eyes narrowed at the speck of red she saw there. Almost a dot.

Blood?

"He left something for you."

Her head whipped up.

"The house is clear." His voice was grim. "We need to call the cops right away. Maybe the guy left some evidence here." He motioned toward her. "Before they get to the scene, *you need to come here*."

She found herself walking toward him. A huge part of Emma was screaming that she needed to run the other way. To get the hell out of there. She didn't know much at all about Dean Bannon. For all she knew, he could have been the one to destroy her house. He'd known where she lived, after all.

And Emma stopped advancing.

Dean's eyes widened in surprise. "You're afraid of me."

Hell, yes, she was.

Emma took out her phone. Called nine-one-one. When the operator answered, Emma said, "Someone broke into my house. They've . . . *he* destroyed everything, and I-I think there's blood."

The operator's voice stayed calm as she asked for Emma's address.

"I'm not alone," Emma said quietly. Because she'd learned not to trust anyone. Not in this life. "A man named Dean Bannon is with me." She wanted his name on the record. Just in case . . . hell, just in case of what? That he decided to attack her before the cops arrived? Dean was making no move to come toward her. He was just standing there, watching her with those deep, dark eyes of his.

Emma gave the operator her address. "Get the cops to hurry, please." *Hurry.*

Emma lowered the phone and glanced around her apartment once more. *Gone.* She'd worked so hard to build this place—her sanctuary—and in one night, some bastard out there had destroyed everything.

"I won't hurt you." Dean's voice was low. She wanted to believe him. But she'd heard that particular lie from too many men before. "I didn't do this, Emma. I'm one of the good guys."

She laughed at that. "There's no such thing."

His lips thinned, then he glanced back over his shoulder, toward her bedroom. "You're going to need a guy like me in your life."

Goose bumps were on her arms. "I doubt that."

But Dean nodded, and said, "Come with me into the bedroom."

She shook her head.

"He left something you need to see."

Her gaze locked on the bedroom doorway, and Emma inched toward it. Dean backed up, but his shoulder brushed against her arm as she passed him. For some reason, that one brush against his body had her tensing. Heat seeped into her skin, and Emma hadn't even realized that she'd been cold. Not until that moment.

"The mirror," he told her. "Look there."

But her gaze was on the bed. It appeared as if someone had taken a knife to the mattresses and sliced them open. Feathers from her pillows littered the floor. Her clothes had been taken out of the dresser drawers, and they'd been slashed, too. Her shirts. Her skirts. Her bras. Her panties.

Her breath choked in as her gaze slowly rose to the mirror. It had been shattered. Long cracks covered the surface. As did . . .

Words. Words written in red spray paint.

You're next.

CHAPTER TWO

S HE WAS KEEPING SECRETS FROM HIM.
Dean crossed his arms over his chest and watched as Emma opened the door to the little crystal shop. "You're seriously going to stay here tonight?" he demanded.

Emma had shut down when the cops arrived at her place. She'd watched—her face totally devoid of emotion—as they started bagging and tagging potential pieces of evidence. When the cops had told her that the place was a crime scene and that Emma would have to sleep elsewhere that night, she'd just turned away from her home without a backward glance.

"There's a cot in the back." Her voice was low, too calm. "Don't worry your pretty head, DB, I've survived much worse."

His pretty head? DB? His brows climbed. "Shouldn't you be more upset? I mean, somebody just—"

"Destroyed everything I own? Threatened my life?" Now the calm veneer cracked a bit, but Dean didn't see fear in Emma's gaze. He saw rage. "Trust me, I'm plenty upset, and when I find the bastard who did this, he'll pay."

"You're planning to hunt him?" *What the hell?*

"No, I'm planning for him to come after me. I'm next, remember? So when he comes, I'll be ready."

Dean shut the door to the crystal shop. A little bell jingled overhead as he reached back and deliberately locked the door. "Emma Castille, I want your secrets."

She was near the counter. Emma turned with a laugh that sounded far too brittle. "And here I thought you already knew them. What did you call me? A criminal? A fraud?"

He stalked toward her. Put his hands on either side of her body and caged her. "Someone is trying to hurt you." That attack had been personal. Far too intimate. The rage had permeated her home. Emma should be terrified.

He'd seen other scenes like that. Too many scenes. *Fixation.*

The perp had planned an intimate attack on the prey he craved the most. He'd have to call his partner, Sarah Jacobs, and get her take on the situation. Sarah was the profiler for the team, and when it came to figuring out killers, the woman was top-notch. She'd be able to tell him—

"If you're not going to kiss me, then don't get this close."

His thoughts came to a crashing halt, and his gaze dropped to her lips.

"I'll find the man who did this. The man who jimmied my lock and didn't leave so much as a scratch on the door but left everything *inside* my home destroyed." Her delicate jaw lifted. "I'll find the bastard, I promise you that. I'm not going to be this jerk's victim," she snapped. "And I won't be *next*! Whatever the hell that means."

Her cheeks had flushed. Her eyes gleamed.

And he'd been right before . . . the woman was fucking beautiful.

She was also very dangerous.

He didn't move away from her, but Dean did lean in closer. The scent of jasmine filled his nostrils. That scent clung to her. "How do you know the SOB isn't watching you right now? What if he followed you here?"

Her eyelashes flickered. "I'll set the store's alarm. I'll be safe here." Her chin lifted, and she pushed against his chest. "I told you, dammit, don't be this close to me! Not unless—"

"I'm going to kiss you." He was more than tempted. To feel those lush, red lips beneath his. To taste her. Emma Castille seemed to bubble over with life and passion, and he bet that when she kissed—the woman went molten.

He'd sure love to find out.

But . . .

Never mix business and pleasure.

Dean backed away. One step. Two.

"Is it easy to always have that control?" Emma wrapped her arms around her body as she asked that question.

His eyes narrowed. If he didn't have control, then he had chaos.

"Time for you to leave, Dean Bannon," she murmured. "I think you can find your way back to the door."

"We're not done."

That bitter laughter came again. He'd expected her laughter to sound different—lighter, sweeter. Maybe her real laughter did sound that way. "Oh, I'd say we're done. I've had an intruder destroy pretty much everything I own. My night has gone straight to hell, and all I want to do now is crash."

She couldn't shut him out, not yet. He needed her too much. "You've got to tell me about Julia!"

Her face paled. There was a flash of something in her eyes then. Something that looked like fear, but she masked the emotion almost as quickly as it appeared.

"I haven't seen Julia in over a week, I told you that before."

"You told me to head over to Bourbon Street. I did. No one I spoke with there remembered her, but, hell, you know, the Bourbon Street crowd changes every night. *Hundreds* of people are there." Drunk men and women who weren't paying attention to a lost girl. "You're the one who saw her. The only one in this whole city who seems to remember her. Tell me which club she was heading toward. Tell me what she was wearing. Tell me *something*." He exhaled on a ragged breath. "I need to know anything that will help her."

Silence.

Then . . . "A long-sleeved blue blouse. It was too small, faded, and there were two holes on the right shoulder. She had on a pair of jeans, dark jeans, with a ripped right knee. Julia was wearing black flats that had scuff marks on the edges, and the heels were almost gone."

He frowned as he listened to her.

"Her hair was in a twist at her nape. Pulling her

hair back that way made her look older, so I think she was trying pass for at least twenty-one. She wore no makeup, no rings, no jewelry of any kind."

She was giving one very thorough description.

"I'd say Julia weighed about 110 pounds, and on her five-foot-eight frame, that was just too little." Her breath sighed out. "She was way too thin. I knew she'd been on the streets, and the fear clinging to her told me that Julia was running. I think . . ." Now her voice trailed away.

"Don't stop." Not now.

"She looked over her shoulder, and I think she saw someone who frightened her. She ran away then. I-I tried to go after her."

She had? His head cocked as he studied Emma. Her hands were still wrapped tightly around her stomach.

"I followed her down Bourbon. We were almost at Jean Lafitte's bar, and I-I lost her." She raised her right hand and stared down at her palm. "Blood."

"What?"

"There was blood on the wall. I know it was blood. On the bricks right outside of The Mask."

"The Mask? Is that a bar?" Because he didn't remember that place.

"It used to be, but it shut down last spring. Nothing is there now." Her voice lowered, and she repeated, "Nothing."

But he wasn't sure he bought her story. "A girl vanishes, you find blood on bricks, and you just—what? Walk away? Turn and go?"

"I called the cops. Told them everything." Her lips thinned. "But she was gone. They searched the area, they found nothing, and I'm—well, you know what I am, right?"

A criminal. A fraud.

You're next.

"I hope that you find her," Emma said, and her words were husky with emotion. "I hope like hell that you do because if you don't, I'm afraid that . . ."

"What are you afraid of?" Dean pressed when she trailed off.

"I'm afraid that Julia is dead." She shook her head. "And I don't want her to be dead. I want you to find her. I want her to be safe."

Dean reached out to her. He turned Emma in his arms so that she faced him. "I can't figure you out." On paper, she was a woman with a criminal past. As a teen, she'd been in near-constant scrapes with the law. She and her father had conned plenty of people.

But that had all changed one dark night, a little over ten years ago.

He caught her hands in his. Turned them over so that he stared at her palms and the faint scars there. His fingers smoothed over the marks.

"We wanted to help them, too," Emma whispered. "The cops wouldn't believe us, but we *knew* who the killer was. When they wouldn't listen, we went after him ourselves."

And her father had died in the attack. The police had blamed him for the whole nightmare scene.

Was there more to that story?

"You don't realize how very much you want to live until death tries to take you." Her words were soft, sad.

He was still holding her hands, and he couldn't look

away from her eyes. He'd never met anyone with eyes quite like Emma's. A man could probably lose his soul, staring into eyes like hers.

If he had a soul.

Emma smiled, but her dimples didn't flash. "You shouldn't look at me that way."

"What way?"

"Like you want to kiss me."

He did. No, actually, right in that moment, he could have fucking devoured her. His responses to Emma had been off from the very moment he'd seen her. He'd never looked at a woman, just stared in her eyes—and immediately wanted her naked, beneath him, screaming his name.

But he had with Emma.

So maybe she deserved the truth from him. "I could be dangerous to you."

Surprise flashed in that gorgeous gaze of hers. Then her smile stretched. "Not a man like you. A man like you is too used to walking the straight and narrow to ever be a threat to someone like me." Then she rose on her tiptoes and leaned toward him. He lowered his head, and her lips brushed against his ear, as she said, "But I could be very dangerous to you, DB. I could wreck you. Shatter that control you hold so dear . . . and then what would happen?"

He could already feel his control cracking because he wanted her sexy mouth under his. Wanted her, under him.

He felt the light lick of her tongue on his ear.

Fuck. His eyes closed.

"So maybe . . . maybe it's best if we just say our

good-byes now." She slid back down, moving away from him. "While there's still time."

Was there time? His eyes opened. Locked on her. "One thing first . . ."

Her brows climbed.

"This." Because, for once, he'd take something that he wanted. Dean pulled her fully into his arms, pressing her flush against him. His mouth crashed onto hers. His control was already cracked, so he kissed her harder, deeper, wilder than he normally would have—

And she kissed him back the same way. With a sensual abandon that punched him and had him holding her even tighter. His cock surged against Emma as arousal flooded through him. Too fast, too hard, the cracks in his control started to spread as his hold on her tightened.

When she gave a little moan in the throat, he lifted her up, pushing her to the edge of the counter, then sliding between her legs as—

He jerked his mouth away from hers. His hands slapped down on the counter, moving to either side of her body as he sucked in a desperate breath but just got—

Jasmine.

His heart thundered in his chest, and all he wanted— all he wanted was to put his hands under that flowing skirt of hers. To strip away her underwear and drive into Emma.

"Tried to tell you . . ." Her voice was a sensual temptation. "I'm not much for control."

He shoved away from the counter. She jumped down, and the skirt swirled around her legs. His gaze slowly rose up her body, sliding up her curves and up, up to her face. Her cheeks were flushed, her lips red and swollen from his mouth, and, if possible, her eyes seemed to shine even brighter.

If there was a woman to lose control for, it just might be her.

But Dean knew just how dangerous it would be for him to relax his guard. The last time he'd let himself go, death had followed.

He turned for the door because he wasn't sure what he should say to her. An apology wasn't coming from him because Dean wasn't sorry that he'd kissed her.

But he was sorry he'd stopped.

He unlocked the door and stepped out into the night. The bell jingled over his head.

"Good-bye, Dean," her soft voice followed him.

"ARE YOU AFRAID?"

The voice came out of the darkness, taunting her, terrifying her.

Julia Finney tensed. The ropes cut into her already bleeding and raw wrists, they sliced over her ankles, and a pain-filled moan slipped from her lips.

"I'll take that as a yes."

She felt his fingers on her cheek. Wiping away her tears. She couldn't see him, couldn't see anything but darkness in that place.

"Pl-please," Julia whispered. "I-I just want to go home . . ."

"I thought you hated home. You told me that you hated it, remember?"

The tears wouldn't stop.

"Don't worry, baby, I won't let them get you again." His fingers slid down to rest over her throat. Right over the frantic beat of her pulse. "I'll make sure that you never, *ever* have to go home again."

Then his fingers started to tighten around her neck.

HE WATCHED AS Emma slipped out of the little shop. It was far after one a.m., when she should have been in for the night. Safe.

But she was slipping away from safety.

She looked to the left. She looked to the right. Emma didn't see him because he was hiding in the shadows. Over the years, he'd grown far too used to the shadows. He could blend perfectly with them.

So when she started hurrying down the street, it was too easy for him to follow her. His steps made no sound as he gave chase, and Emma, oh, she was moving fast. There was no hesitation from her. Only determination.

When they reached Bourbon Street, the noise from the crowd was like a roar. The street was filled, overflowing. People were hanging over the sides of balconies. Men were vomiting in the street. Couples were making out in dark corners and under bright streetlights.

Emma ignored all of those people. She hurried away, moving down, down the street until the bars thinned. Until the noises dimmed.

Once, she glanced back over her shoulder.

But he was still covered by the shadows.

Her gaze swept over him, and she went right back to her path. And he went back to following her.

When she reached the boarded-up building, Emma hesitated. Her hand reached out and touched the bricks that lined the right wall.

The Mask. He looked up and saw the faded sign on the top of the building—two masks, not just one. A Mardi Gras mask that showed a big, wide smile, and one that showed a twisted frown.

She crept around to the back of the building. He watched as she yanked on the door, and when it didn't open for her, Emma retreated a bit and studied the old bar. The windows had been boarded up, but Emma grabbed one of those boards and yanked, hard. It popped loose. Then she used that board to smash the window. Glass shattered.

Breaking and entering? She kept surprising him.

Emma used her board to shove the broken shards of glass out of her way, then she climbed inside the building.

Well, well . . .

EMMA TURNED ON her small flashlight. Her heart sounded like a drumbeat in her ears as she crept forward. This was the right place, she knew it. The darkness was so thick, so cavernous, and yeah, okay, the place was also extremely creepy.

But if the girl was there . . . I have to find her.

"Hello?" Emma called out. She knew this wasn't her smartest move, but something had kept nagging at her as she'd lain on the cot in the back of the crystal shop. She'd been inside The Mask once before, right after the night she'd seen Julia. And she remembered . . .

Emma turned to the right. Her flashlight swept over the wall there. A wall that had already been marked by graffiti. Some random signs that meant nothing to her. A smiling face and—

You're next.

Her breath choked out when she saw those words. Yes, yes, dammit, they had been what she remembered as she lay in that too-small, too-uncomfortable cot in the shop's back room. She'd searched this place herself, after the cops had left, and she'd seen the graffiti then. She'd been intent on the girl, so when Julia hadn't showed up, Emma had dismissed all the graffiti.

She couldn't dismiss it now.

There was a faint rustle of sound behind her. Such a soft sound. One that could have been made by the wind, by the storm.

Or by *someone* else.

Emma's right hand slid into her pocket even as she kept shining the light with her left hand. If someone else was there, she'd already given away her position with that light.

But maybe, maybe that someone else was the missing girl. "Julia?" Emma's fingers curled around the weapon in her pocket.

No answer, but she could *feel* someone back there. Could almost hear the breaths of the person closing in on her.

Emma waited, her whole body tense.

The soft rustle came again. Emma yanked out her weapon, spinning around and shining her light into the darkness.

The light hit his face at the same instant that her knife came up, aiming for his chest—

But Dean caught her hand in a steely grip, a grip that quickly had her fingers going numb.

"After what you've been through," Dean rasped, "I would have thought the last weapon you'd use would be a knife."

He was so wrong. It was precisely *because* of her past that she always carried a knife. "I believe in facing what I fear." Not cowering in a corner. What? He thought because she'd barely survived an attack from a knife-wielding psycho that she would never touch a blade again?

So what if she'd vomited the first five times she'd tried to pick up a knife. She *had* picked it up.

He eased his grip, and feeling came back to her fingers in fast, hot pinpricks. But she didn't gasp at the pain. Emma was too accustomed to pain.

Her light spilled onto his face, but with all of the shadows around him, Dean looked even more danger-ous than usual. Predatory.

"You followed me," she accused.

"Guilty."

It was nice that he didn't deny it. She rather hated lies even if she'd learned—early in life—to tell them very well.

"Why are you here?" He leaned even closer to her. "In the dark, calling out for Julia?"

She could feel him all around her. Warmth seemed to flow from his body, flow *into* her. Emma found herself wanting to lean forward and touch him more. But, of course, that was ridiculous. Dean Bannon wasn't her kind of lover. She didn't want men who clung so tightly to their control. She liked her lovers wild. With a rough edge that couldn't be denied.

Dean was too controlled for her.

Right, keep telling yourself that.

"Emma." His voice held the unmistakable note of a command. "Why are you here? In the middle of the fucking night?"

"Why were you watching me," she threw back at him, "in the middle of the fucking night?" After that kiss, she'd expected him to run, not walk, away from her. She'd messed up his perfect, controlled world, pushed him too far—and she'd loved it.

But he'd backed away.

And she'd thought they were done.

But he followed me? Probably just because of the case. Of course, *just* because of the case. Why else would he trail her?

"I was worried about you."

Now that confession made her feel strange. Her stomach twisted, and she tugged her hand, needing some space between them. No one had worried about her in years.

Dean let her go.

And Emma started talking. Too quickly, yes, but she talked fast when she was nervous, and Dean had certainly managed to unsettle her. "When businesses like this one shut down, the homeless will move in." There were so many homeless people in the Big Easy. All ages, all races. Too many who made their lives on the streets.

Just like I did, once.

She slammed the door shut on that memory. "Julia was living on the streets. She was running that night, and I-I think she was trying to get back here." To the dark, cavernous space that she had called home?

"You didn't tell me that she was living here."

No, she hadn't. "I wasn't sure that she was. I just—"

"Knew psychically?"

She wanted to punch him. "I pay attention to what's around me. I never claimed to be psychic," Emma gritted out. *Asshole.* "I offer readings—I *read* people. I see what others don't, okay? I pay fucking attention."

Because that was what she'd been trained to do. Her father, yes, he'd claimed to be psychic, but the truth was that he'd just been good at reading people, too. Reading them, playing them. A con man to his core, he'd been able to ferret out people's secrets in an instant.

Mostly, he'd used his talents to earn some fast bucks.

But, sometimes, he'd tried to help people.

And look where that got him.

Emma's shoulders rolled back as she tried to push away the tension that was holding too tightly to her. "It was the message on my wall."

She still had her light shining right on him.

"You're next."

She shivered at his words. "Yes. I remembered seeing that message before." She turned around, and her light hit the wall. Skimmed over most of the graffiti, then locked on the letters that had been spray-painted in red. *You're next.* "I don't believe in coincidences," Emma said softly.

"Neither do I."

SOMEONE WAS IN his house. The house he'd claimed after he'd taken sweet Julia.

He could see the flash of the light from inside.

That was wrong. No one should be there. No one.

He slid around the back. His boot crunched on the broken glass, and he leaned forward, trying to listen carefully through that window.

"I don't believe in coincidences." A woman's voice. A voice that was familiar to him.

"Neither do I." A man.

His eyes narrowed as he listened to them.

"If Julia was here," the guy continued, "then there could be clues left behind. Something that tells us where she went—"

"Or who took her," the sweet, feminine voice finished.

No, no, no! He backed away, rage twisting through him. They weren't going to find anything. That was *his* house.

A growl broke from him. No one should be in his house. No one.

He bent and picked up a jagged chunk of glass that had fallen near the window.

Then he smiled.

It's my time now. Mine.

"WE NEED TO search this place," Dean said as he pulled out his own light. He'd already planned to hit The Mask at dawn, but when he'd seen Emma slipping away from the crystal shop, he'd followed her.

What the hell was I even doing there? Hanging outside that place? But he'd found himself lingering, strangely reluctant just to leave her in the shop. Time had slid past, and he'd found himself standing guard. Protecting her.

His flashlight swept to the left. Then back toward

the broken window he and Emma had used to gain entrance—

Someone was there. In front of the window.

He had a flash of the man, a tall guy, with a hat pulled low over his dirt-covered, grizzled face, and the guy screamed, *"Get out of my house!"*

Dean grabbed Emma and shoved her behind him even as the man let out a loud, enraged bellow and charged toward them. "Easy, buddy," Dean shouted. "You need to *stop*!"

But the guy wasn't stopping. He was running full speed ahead, and Dean's light glinted off the chunk of glass in the man's hand. Glass that was far sharper than Emma's small switchblade.

With a roar, the man lifted the glass.

Shit. Dean ran for him. The guy's hand was up, raised too high, so Dean went in straight for the guy's gut. His shoulders plowed into the guy, and Dean's tackle sent the attacker flying back toward the floor.

The glass flew out of his hand, but the man didn't stop. He was a big fellow, long, with thin limbs. His fists flew out and started pounding at Dean.

Dean pounded back. He had a general rule about fights . . . when some bastard threw the first punch—*or comes at me with damn glass*—he sure attacked back.

Dean drove his fist into the guy's stomach. He heard the groan of pain that escaped the fellow, and the man sagged beneath him.

Dean's hand stilled, poised over the guy.

"Call the cops," Dean ordered Emma. But he wasn't done. Long before those cops arrived, Dean planned to have his answers.

He jerked the now-moaning man to his feet even as he heard Emma calling for help on her phone.

"Where is she?" Dean demanded as he shoved the guy against the nearest wall.

"My house! You're in my house!" The guy's voice was a strangled cry.

"Where is *Julia*?"

"My house!" The guy tried to take another swing at him. He missed.

"You have her in your house?" Adrenaline pumped through Dean's body. "You bastard, if you've hurt her—"

"Get out of my house!" the man screamed as he struggled in Dean's grip.

"Stop!" That voice was Emma's. She touched Dean on the shoulder. "Seriously, *stop.*"

Was the woman insane? That bozo had just attacked them with glass sharp enough to kill.

"You're scaring him," Emma continued.

The fuck he was.

"He lives here, Dean." Emma's flashlight slid to the left. To the cardboard boxes, the assortment of men's clothes that were spread out on the floor. "We're in his house."

"My house!" the man screeched.

"Was Julia in your house?" Dean demanded. "Did you go after her the same way you came at us? Did you hurt Julia?"

The man started crying.

Emma's hand tightened on Dean's shoulder. "The cops will be here in less than five minutes. If you want answers from him . . . then let me talk to the guy. *Now.*"

Because she was going to get the guy to make sense when an ex–FBI agent couldn't? "Listen, Emma—"

"No, you listen," she fired back, her voice flat and hard. "If you want to find Julia, let me talk to him. Because all you've done is terrify him. I can do more."

Dean's back teeth ground together, but he moved away. Fine. If she wanted to have a stab at the guy, she could. But if that jerk made one move to hurt her, Dean would lay him out on the floor.

"Get out," the man muttered, his voice growling and desperate. "Out!"

"We'll leave," Emma said softly. "We were just looking for our friend."

The man's head was shaking frantically. Back and forth. Back and forth.

"You live here," Emma said.

The frantic shaking eased.

"We shouldn't have come into your house."

"Mine."

"Did you . . . share this house with anyone?"

"All mine!"

"We thought a girl lived here. That's why we came. A girl with blond hair and green eyes. She was young, a teenager."

The shaking stopped completely. "Left . . . with him."

Now Dean was the one who tensed. "With who?"

The guy's shaking started immediately. *"My house!"*

"Dammit, Dean, you're just setting him off!" Emma snapped. Then she sucked in a deep breath. "We'll leave your home if you just answer our questions."

Silence.

"Who took the girl? Did you see the person—"

"Only the c-car. Big black car. Put her . . . put her in the trunk."

What. The. Fuck? "You saw a girl getting tossed into the trunk of a car, and you didn't do a damn thing?" He wanted to punch the guy again.

But Emma was standing in front of the man.

Sirens screamed in the distance. The guy tensed.

"Did you notice anything else about the car?" Emma asked, voice soft.

"Big. Black."

Yeah, he'd already said that shit.

"Where did the car go?"

"Don't know! Don't know!"

"What was the girl doing when you saw her?"

"S-sleeping."

Dean's spine stiffened. Sleeping . . . or had she been dead?

He heard voices outside. Not the voices of the drunks celebrating on Bourbon Street but the cops who'd come in response to Emma's call.

"What's your name?" Emma asked the man.

But the cops were rushing inside then. They'd kicked in the door. Their lights hit Emma and Dean and their mystery man. The man cried out then. "My house!"

Dean's head turned, and he stared at the graffiti-covered wall.

You're next.

He knew he wasn't looking at a simple missing persons case anymore. Hell, were they ever simple? But this one . . . this one was darker. Far more sinister.

And he realized the case could be much bigger than

he'd originally thought. He would need to call in the whole team for this one.

"Hands up!" the cops shouted. Jaw locking, Dean lifted his hands.

DAWN HAD COME. The sun was peeking over the sky, lighting up the city as it slowly rose.

They were in front of the police station. It was a spot that Emma, rather unfortunately, felt she was becoming far too familiar with.

Dean was at her side, but he was silent. Big surprise there.

Emma knew she should walk away from him. If she had a stronger sense of self-preservation, she'd be fleeing the whole city right then. She was smart enough to know what she'd been caught up in.

But . . .

Julia's image flashed before her eyes. *Aren't you supposed to tell me that everything will be all right?*

Emma hadn't given her that lie.

Help me.

Was it too late to help the girl?

Emma glanced down at her palms and saw the scars that would always mark her. "Do you think she's dead?"

"I won't believe she's dead until I find the body."

It wasn't the answer she'd expected. He didn't strike her as the kind of man who held out a lot of hope. Emma glanced up at him.

"We don't give up at LOST. The people out there— the ones we are looking for—someone has to believe they're still alive."

"Do you always find them . . . alive?"

He shook his head. Sadness flashed in his dark eyes.

Her hand lifted. Light stubble coated that strong jaw of his. "You tried to play white knight." She wouldn't forget that. Sure, he'd followed her—not cool and a bit stalkerlike—but when danger had appeared, the guy had tried to shield her from the attack.

Sweet, in one of those good-guy sort of ways.

Not that she'd needed shielding. Not that she was particularly attracted to good guys.

But I am attracted to him.

"And you were playing detective."

His words had her brows lifting.

"You went out last night to try to find her, didn't you?"

Time for her confession. "Ah, Dean, I've gone out every night for the last week because I wanted to find her." But she hadn't, and now Emma knew why. Someone had taken Julia. The same person who'd broken into Emma's apartment and left her that dark threat.

"People vanish in this city all the time. Did you know that? The river is so close . . ." She could smell the river right then. "Bodies can vanish there. People disappear into the darkness, and the world just goes on, as if nothing has happened."

When something had happened. Someone's world had stopped.

Emma made her decision. "I want to help you find her." Her hand was still pressed against the stubble on his jaw. She liked the rough rasp beneath her touch.

Just as she'd liked the feel of his mouth against her own.

But Dean shook his head. "This isn't work for you."

And he stepped back, obviously dismissing her.

"My full team is flying down. We'll find Julia." He sounded so confident.

"I want to help!" Emma insisted. It was the first time she'd actually tried to help find someone since her father had died. She should have learned her lesson then, but . . . here she was. Trying again.

He shook his head. "It's dangerous for a civilian to get involved. You're playing out of your league."

Like she hadn't heard those words before. Actually, she'd heard those *exact* words before. Ten years ago. When she and her father had tried to do the right thing. The cops hadn't believed them.

"He's coming after me." She said this softly.

Dean's head jerked.

"We don't believe in coincidences, remember?" Emma gave a sad shake of her head. "*You're next.* Those words were written in Julia's home. They were written in mine. She's gone, and me . . . well, I'm right here." For now. "But he's coming."

"You don't know that."

"You saw what he did to my apartment." That place had been full of rage. A killing fury. "You really want to stand there and tell me that I'm not in danger?"

He didn't speak. Good. Maybe he didn't want to lie.

"You were outside that shop last night because you were afraid he'd come after me, weren't you?"

No answer. *Don't take the silence too far, DB.*

"That's what I thought," she whispered. It wasn't the first time a killer had put her in his sights. "He saw Julia talking with me that night." That was the only thing she could figure out. "Maybe he thinks I saw him, too. Maybe you're not the only one who has been watching me lately." And she should have noticed someone lurking around, dammit. Were her skills getting rusty? Her father had trained her over the years to always pay attention to her environment. *Always.* But she'd started to slack off. Started to feel a little too safe in New Orleans . . . where most people didn't glance at her twice.

Where she'd thought she had disappeared in the crowd.

She turned and started heading down the police station's stone steps. She'd only gone a few feet when Dean's hand wrapped around her arm. "What the hell do you want to do?" he demanded. "Offer yourself up as bait?"

A shiver slid over her but, yes . . . "That's exactly what I was thinking."

His eyes narrowed on her.

"But I was rather hoping you and your *team,* well, I was hoping that you'd have my back." Because the local cops hadn't exactly been cooperative. They'd kept the homeless man—a guy that they'd finally figured out was named Stan Tatum—for a psych evaluation because of the attack. But other than what Emma knew would be a cursory evaluation, the cops hadn't been exactly concerned or really buying the story that some mysterious man had kidnapped a sixteen-year-old runaway.

"You want protection," Dean said, as his fingers tightened around her arm. She looked down, her eyes falling to his hand. "Emma?"

"Why is it . . . that every time you touch me . . . I

feel warmer?" She looked up in time to see his eyelids flickering. "Never mind. Right. I want protection, and in return"— Emma exhaled—"I'll help you find Julia." She saw the doubt on his face, and that pissed her off. "I'm far more useful than you think." *And not just as bait.*

More silence. She was starting to think he was a master at the art of saying nothing. But he didn't let her go. He just kept staring at her, and, finally, Dean nodded.

Emma released the breath that she hadn't even realized she'd been holding.

"But we do this my way," Dean was quick to say. "You follow all my orders, understand?"

Oh, she was terrible, absolutely horrible at following orders.

"Emma?"

"I'll do whatever is necessary to find the girl." And to stop the man out there . . . the man who'd made the mistake of trying to target Emma, too.

The last man who'd tried to hurt her . . . the man who'd used his knife on her and attacked Emma's father . . .

She'd killed him.

CHAPTER THREE

"SO WHO THE HELL IS EMMA CASTILLE?"

Dean glanced up at the question, and his gaze met the old stare of Wade Monroe. Wade had been working at LOST from the very beginning—Dean had met the guy the very day they opened the doors to their new venture. Since that time, Dean had worked dozens of cases with the tough, ex–Atlanta homicide detective. Wade was a take-no-shit kind of guy, a man who didn't have much time for emotions but was more about action.

Dean liked the guy, he respected him . . . and he knew Wade's secrets.

But he doesn't know mine. Only one person at LOST did, and Gabe was a fucking vault. The man didn't share the secrets that his friends gave him.

"Want me to take that one?" This voice was softer, feminine and belonged to Dr. Sarah Jacobs. Sarah was petite, with dark chocolate eyes and jet-black hair. She was also the person on the team he normally avoided the most . . . since Sarah was the one who liked to screw with minds.

She was the shrink, the profiler who slid into killers'

minds far too easily. Mostly because that was a family skill.

"Emma Castille is twenty-five, self-employed, with no family in the New Orleans area," Sarah began.

Shit, so she'd been researching Emma. He shouldn't have been surprised. After all, he was the one who'd originally tipped Sarah off about Emma. And now that Emma thought she was joining their hunt . . . well, the whole team would need to know about her.

"She's a scam artist," Dean said. But then he frowned. Those words just felt wrong. He had a flash of Emma's bright eyes. Her winking dimples. He shook his head. "No." The word sounded like an angry growl coming from him, and he saw Sarah glance his way in surprise. "Her father was a con artist. About ten years ago, he said that he'd figured out who abducted the two Donovan twins . . ."

Twin girls who'd gone missing from a rich suburb in Dallas. The parents had been frantic. A ransom note had arrived, demanding $1 million. The ransom had been paid immediately, but the girls hadn't been returned. The days had stretched into weeks, and the Donovans had grown desperate.

The mother had started calling in psychics to help her find her daughter.

One of those so-called psychics had been John Castille . . . and his daughter, Emma. John had spent time at the family home. Talked with the twins' friends. And suddenly, he'd been saying that he knew where the girls were. That he knew who'd taken them.

"I remember that case," Wade said quietly as he gave a slow nod. "Castille pointed the finger at one of the twins' boyfriends, right? A kid named Phillip Trumane. Only the guy just happened to be the governor's nephew, so no one bought the story."

"No," Dean said as he rubbed the back of his neck. "No one bought it." They were in Jackson Square, seated at a bench under the sprawling branches of an oak tree. No one else was close by, and Dean figured this was the most privacy they were going to get right then.

"John Castille was right, though," Sarah said. Dean wasn't surprised that she'd found out all the details of the story. When it came to killers, Sarah was an expert. "He and his daughter located a property that belonged to the boy's family. They went out to the old cabin, and when they went in—"

"The boy attacked them." Because the kid had long since lost his grasp on reality. He'd been in that cabin, with the dead girls and the money, and he'd gone at John Castille with a knife.

"When the police finally arrived," Sarah continued as she stood and walked closer to the tree. "Only Emma and her father were still alive. He made it to the hospital, he backed up her story, and then he . . . he didn't make it out of surgery."

No, he hadn't. And Emma had been left alone.

Wade gave a low whistle. "And *that's* the woman we're protecting?"

Actually . . . Dean craned his head to the side. Emma was walking toward them at that moment. She was wearing a light blue skirt that floated around her hips and a white T-shirt that molded itself so very well to her—especially to her full breasts. Her dark hair was loose around her shoulders, and a pair of sunglasses covered her eyes. She was beautiful, too sexy, and *trouble*. "That's the woman."

Wade shot to his feet.

Sarah turned to face her, cocking her head as she studied Emma's approach.

Emma had left him a few hours earlier. She'd asked for his protection, then basically vanished. So much for a partnership. But she'd told him that she had loose ends to tie up . . . and that she'd needed to shop. Considering that all of her clothing had been slashed, he understood that part. But just going out on her own? How the hell had that made sense if she really thought she was being targeted by a killer?

Unless she was still trying to position herself as bait. Trying to draw the man's attention by showing him that she was out there, alone.

"Seriously," Emma said with a sigh as she closed in on them. "Could you and your team stick out more?" Her brilliant gaze was still hidden by her glasses as she turned to first study Sarah. "Guessing you're the shrink." Then she nodded to Wade. "Ah, a cop." Her head tilted a bit to the left as she seemed to consider him a bit more. "Ex-cop, with a whole lot of attitude."

"You told her about us?" Wade snapped.

And, no, he hadn't told Emma about them. He hadn't even mentioned Wade's name to her.

"Please." Now Emma sounded annoyed. "I tagged you as a cop five seconds after I saw you. Try changing your posture, maybe letting go of that battle-ready tension you've got. Stop looking at everyone in the park as if they're about to commit crimes. You might as well be flashing a neon sign." She took off her glasses and perched them on the top of her head. "Inconspicuous, you're not."

Wade stared into her eyes. Just stared.

Dean's own eyes narrowed.

"How'd you know I was the shrink?" Sarah asked, and for once, Sarah sounded curious. Sarah didn't usually show much emotion at all. Like Dean, she understood the value of control. But he knew that her reasons for reining in her emotions were a lot different from his own.

Sarah's father had been a serial killer, a real vicious bastard. Sarah had made it her life's goal to stop killers like him.

"I knew because you were standing away from the others. Studying them. Watching their body language, listening with your head cocked as you tried to look for deeper meanings in everything they said."

Sarah's eyes widened, and she took a step toward Emma. "You're not what I expected."

Emma shrugged. "I try not to be."

Sarah's gaze slid over Emma's shoulder. "You came in the entrance near the cathedral?"

"I was turning over my booth to my friend Lisa. She'd wanted the spot for a while."

Wade cleared his throat. "Your booth?"

"Emma gives readings," Dean said. He didn't like that Wade had moved closer to Emma. The guy had a reputation with the ladies—and the man did not need to be staring at Emma as if she were a new dessert on his menu.

"Like father, like daughter?" Wade asked, but then

his eyes widened in horror, and he glanced at Sarah. "Shit, I didn't mean—"

"I haven't asked about your family tree," Emma said, cutting through his words with an icy tone. "But I suspect I'll find plenty of skeletons there. I mean, there are two reasons men become cops. At least, in my book."

"What are those reasons?" It was Sarah who asked that question. Her face had paled at Wade's careless words. Sarah wasn't attacking, though, not like Emma. Sarah didn't attack, she withdrew.

Emma comes out fighting.

Dean crossed to Emma's side. His shoulder brushed hers.

"Men become cops because they want to be heroes, they want to save the day." Emma paused. "Or else they're trying to atone . . . for their own crimes." Her gaze swept over Wade. "I think I know why you picked up a shield, but the real question is . . . what made you put it down?"

Wade swore and backed up.

Emma flashed her smile. The one that showed her dimples. Her harmless, I'm-innocent smile. The smile that was so very deceptive.

And sexy.

Hell, he was starting to think that just breathing was sexy—when Emma was the one inhaling. *What the fuck is wrong with me?*

"Not what I expected at all," Sarah said again. She bit her lip, then asked, "How many men did you pass on the way to us?"

"Five," was Emma's immediate reply.

"How many couples?"

Dean's brows climbed. Was Sarah quizzing her? It sure sounded that way.

"Just one couple. College kids. She was a redhead from Alabama, and he was a surfer from California."

How the hell did she know that? Dean looked over his shoulder.

"He trained you." Sarah took another step toward Emma. "Taught you, didn't he?"

Emma nodded. "My father always said that if people just paid more attention to what was happening around them, they'd see a whole new world."

Sarah smiled. It was such a rare sight that Dean blinked. "I think you see the world very differently from everyone else," Sarah said, and her voice held a note that could have been relief.

But Emma's own smile vanished. "Don't you?"

Sarah gave a little nod. Then she offered Emma her hand. "It's nice to meet you, Emma Castille."

Emma's fingers curled around Sarah's. "I think you actually mean that."

"I do." A pause. "I'm Sarah Jacobs."

There was no recognition on Emma's face. Maybe she'd never heard about Sarah's father. He'd been incarcerated for the last fifteen years, but before then, he'd sure been splashed in the media plenty.

Emma inclined her head. "It's nice to meet you, too, Sarah."

Wade closed in, offered his hand to her, too. "I hear you're going to be working with us."

Dean didn't like the way the guy held so tightly to Emma's hand. And Wade held it for way too damn long. "If being your bait counts then, yes," Emma said, "I'm working with you."

Wade hadn't let her go yet. "Aren't you afraid?" Then he frowned and looked down at their joined hands. He pulled his fingers from hers but didn't let her go, not completely.

Dean knew the ex-cop was studying the scars on Emma's hand. Scars that crisscrossed her inner arm and were very clear in the bright sunlight.

"No," Emma replied softly. "I'm not afraid. I learned a long time ago that being afraid is a waste of energy." Her delicate shoulders rolled back. "When do we get started? That girl is out there, he has her, and I don't think Julia has a lot of time."

No, Dean didn't think that Julia had a lot of time on her side, either. The odds were against the abductor keeping Julia alive for this long. If the girl had just been a runaway, the situation would have been completely different.

But Dean believed someone *had* taken Julia. "We need to talk with Stan Tatum again. Maybe the guy has sobered up and can give us more information." Because that man was the last one to have seen Julia.

"Some perps do keep their victims alive for . . . longer periods of time." Sarah's voice was so soft that Dean had to strain in order to hear it.

Emma didn't speak.

"If the perp enjoys hurting his prey," Sarah continued, "he'll let her live longer."

Emma's shoulder brushed against Dean. He glanced over at her, surprised that she'd moved closer to him.

"I'll talk to Stan," Wade said. "The cops still have him down at the precinct."

Because they'd put him in the drunk tank. They'd said that they would send him for a psych evaluation, but Dean hadn't exactly been holding his breath on that part. The station had been full to bursting last night—and, he suspected—that was just a normal occurrence.

"I'll see what I can learn and get back with you two," Wade promised.

"I'll come with you," Sarah said.

Dean nodded. "Then Emma and I will head back to The Mask." Because he wanted to survey that place in the light of day. Maybe the perp had left something behind. A clue that could lead them to Julia.

"Then let's do this," Wade said, as his eyes narrowed. "Because Julia is out there . . . and she's waiting on us to bring her home."

SHE'D BEEN AFRAID to go home. Afraid of the pain that waited there.

But there was so much more to fear.

Julia didn't strain against the ropes any longer. What was the point? They'd already sliced deeply into her wrists, she'd bled and bled . . . and there was no escape.

So she just waited now. In the darkness. It was such a complete and total darkness. No matter how hard she strained her eyes, she couldn't see anything.

Just the dark.

He wasn't there any longer. He'd left her, but he'd promised to be back.

She believed his promises.

Her stomach growled loudly, and she felt the clench in her gut. Julia didn't know how long it had been since she'd eaten or drank anything. She'd screamed for a while, and that had just made her throat feel even more parched.

Screaming had done no good. He'd seemed to . . . like her screams.

He hadn't hurt her too much, though. Maybe he wouldn't. Maybe he was just some sick freak who liked to scare girls. Maybe he'd let her go when he came back. Maybe she'd be able to go home again.

Her mom might not be mad when she went back. Everything might be okay.

Julia heard the squeak of the door. At that soft sound, her heart thundered in her chest. *He's back.*

She licked her lips, but her mouth was so dry there was no moisture to spare. Her lips were chapped, cracked, and there was nothing she could do for them. "Please . . ." Julia whispered. "Let me go."

Silence. Maybe she'd imagined that squeak. Maybe he wasn't back. Had he been gone for hours? Or minutes? Julia wasn't sure.

She felt his fingers, brushing over her cheeks. "It's not time to let you go yet . . . you're not ready."

A sob built within her.

"But soon . . . so soon." Then his fingers were gone.

Her breath heaved out in frantic gasps.

"I have to make you ready first."

Then pain hit her. Sharp, stabbing. Deep. She screamed then, a high, frantic sound.

"Don't worry," he soothed her. "I didn't cut anything major."

He'd stabbed her. The psychotic bastard had stabbed her!

"You've brought someone to me. Someone I've been waiting for. *Payback* . . ."

The pain wasn't stopping. She could feel blood soaking her side. The knife was still in her side, and the pain rolled through her. Every breath she took just seemed to make the blood gush from her that much faster. "Please . . ."

"I should thank you, Julia. You've opened a whole new world to me."

The knife twisted. She shuddered in agony.

"So how about I give you a sporting chance, hmm?"

Did that mean . . . he was going to let her go?

"Let's just see what you can survive."

Julia whimpered.

BOURBON STREET WAS different during the day. Oh, there were still people out drinking. Still bars open. Emma knew that the bars stayed open twenty-four/seven. And with the all-day mimosas that so many places offered, drinks would always be on hand.

But the area was much quieter. Emptier.

The streets had already been cleaned. They were cleaned each day. And she could see the soapy residue draining away in the gutters.

She and Dean had walked over from the square, a walk that had been taken mostly in silence. When she'd passed her old booth, Lisa had already been at work. Lisa was one of the few people in the area Emma thought of as a friend. Like Emma, Lisa worked at the crystal shop. Lisa was sweet, open, a woman close to

Emma's own age and with dark hair that was nearly the same length as Emma's.

On the outside, Emma knew that she and Lisa shared a passing similarity, but on the inside . . .

We're night and day.

Lisa's past wasn't marked with darkness, not the way Emma's was. Lisa was happy, in love with a jazz performer. She was—

"Looks like the police roped the place off."

Dean's low voice drew Emma's gaze. A line of yellow police tape had been put up around The Mask. "Like that's going to stop us," she muttered. Tape? Really? That would stop *no one* in the area.

She headed toward the back of the old bar. The cops hadn't even repaired the door they'd kicked in. Emma slipped under the police tape and headed inside.

Faint lights spilled through the windows. Sure, the old owners had tried to board them up, but the glass wasn't completely covered. The furniture had been hauled out of the place, and it was obvious from all the scattered pieces of clothing and the trash on the floor that more than a few folks had made this old bar their home in the last few weeks.

People like Julia.

Like Stan.

Her gaze fell on the wall. On the bright graffiti there and on the words that appeared in dark red spray paint. *You're next.*

"You worked in the FBI," she said, as her gaze slid toward him. "Did you ever see anything like this back then? A guy telling his prey that he was coming after them?"

He shook his head.

Right. She inched closer to the wall. Her gaze slid over the letters. She thought of her own apartment. The police had said she could return to the place now, but . . .

I don't want to go back alone.

She'd lied to Dean before. She was afraid. Emma just didn't like admitting her fear. But this guy was targeting her, freaking obviously, and she didn't want to find herself—

Missing.

Lost.

Like Julia.

Dean was carefully studying the material left in the old bar.

"The clothes look like they belong to a man," he said. "Probably Stan's."

She shook her head. "When you're on the street, you take anything you can find." Just because the clothes were for a man, well, that didn't mean that a woman hadn't been using them. On the street, everything was unisex.

His gaze sharpened as he glanced up at her. *Oh, crap.* Had she just revealed too much? Emma quickly looked away from him. "But you don't leave your things behind. You *never* give up what's yours."

"Then the stuff *has* to be Stan's. He's the one who was here last night, ready to attack us."

He had been, but . . .

Emma went closer to the graffiti-covered wall. A few old newspapers were there. Cover? During the cold nights? The temperatures had dipped a bit after the bar closed. *Been there, done that, too.* She didn't want to think about those days. About the fear that had pumped through her. About all the nights when she hadn't been able to sleep for fear someone would get too close to her. That someone would hurt her.

Then she'd realized that there was a way out.

Her father had left her with talents. She just needed to use them.

She brushed aside the newspapers. Something glinted on the floor, catching her gaze. She bent and saw that a delicate chain had gotten stuck, right in the crack near the bottom of the wall. Emma tugged on the chain.

When it came free, Emma noticed that a locket was on one end. She opened it up and saw Julia's picture staring back at her. Only . . . Julia looked older. Her hair was darker.

Not Julia. Because there were *two* pictures inside. One was of the older version of Julia, the dark-haired girl. The other . . .

Young. Blond. Julia.

"What did you find?"

He was right behind her, but, then, she'd heard his soft footsteps, so Emma didn't jerk or gasp. She just stared at the locket and understood. "Julia lost her sister." Because the locket was a bit worn. As if it had been touched often. Stroked. She stared at those images. "That's why she ran away, isn't it?" Emma glanced over her shoulder at Dean.

He gave a grim nod. "It was a car accident. Julia and her sister . . . they were in the backseat."

She rose and offered him the locket. "Who was driving?"

"Julia's stepdad. He'd been . . . drinking."

Right. The pieces clicked into place for her. "And where is he now?"

"He's in jail."

Good.

"Julia is all her mother has left. She's desperate to find her daughter. The cops told her there was nothing she could do, so she—"

"Turned to you and your team," Emma finished. Her hands twisted in front of her.

He nodded.

She bit her lip, and said, "You know that Julia wouldn't have left that locket behind." The chain was broken, as if it had been torn from her neck. "She obviously looked at the pictures a lot. It appears to be the only thing that she brought with her from her former life. *She wouldn't have left it.*"

He pulled out a small, plastic bag from his pocket. *An evidence bag? My, isn't he the prepared one?* She bet that, back in the day, the guy had even been a Boy Scout.

"You think he ripped it off her neck," Emma said as she drew in a deep breath. The place reeked—piss, garbage. Blood? *I want to get out of here.*

Because it reminded her of another time. Of a dark cabin that had smelled of rot. Of a nightmare that had changed her world.

"If he did," Dean said, "then maybe some of his DNA is left behind. Maybe we can find the SOB that way."

They did another sweep of the bar. Found nothing else they could use. When they went back outside, Emma shielded her eyes against the light. The sun seemed too bright after the dim interior of The Mask.

She started to lower her hand and move forward, but Dean snagged her wrist. "Why do you talk about being homeless as if . . . as if you've . . . been there?"

Been there? Emma looked down at his hand. So strong and so much darker, tanner than her own. "What did you think would happen to a fifteen-year-old girl—a girl who didn't even have a driver's license or her high-school education—when her father died? When the only family she had was dead? Did you think folks would be lining up with job opportunities for that girl?"

"Emma . . ."

She pulled away from him. Pity was the last thing she wanted. From Dean or anyone else. "I survived." That was all she had to say. Emma started marching away from him. Her pace was fast because she wanted to be away from the place. She cleared the corner. Headed down another block. They should check in with some of the local bar owners and see what—

He grabbed her. Pushed her back against the wall of a nearby restaurant. "What the hell are you doing to me?"

"Nothing." She'd been trying to get away from him.

But Dean shook his head, and his eyes swept over her face. "Emma Castille." He said her name as if tasting it. "I have the feeling you keep a thousand secrets."

She did, on any given day.

"I'll learn them all."

No, he wouldn't.

His head came closer to hers. "And you will never, fucking *ever* live on the streets again." Then his mouth was on hers. Crushing down with a wild fury and passion that she hadn't expected. Her buttoned-down agent seemed to be on the very edge of his control.

I'll push him past the edge. If it's the last thing I do.

She licked the curve of his lower lip. Loved the way he growled against her mouth. When his tongue swept past her lips, she arched toward him.

There was no pity between them. Not then. Only white-hot desire consuming them both. Perfect passion.

Emma had never feared passion. Her hands were on his shoulders, her nails digging into the fabric of his shirt. She'd love to rip that fancy shirt away, and she would—just not there.

Not then.

Because he was already pulling back. Pulling back but staring down at her with a dark stare that seemed to burn with desire.

"What the fuck am I supposed to do with you?"

Whatever you want. No . . . *whatever I want.* "I guess we'll find out, won't we?"

He backed up a step and sucked in a deep breath.

"But first, let's talk to these bar owners before the crowds come back." She was impressed that her voice only trembled a little.

So did her knees.

A muscle flexed in his jaw.

And Emma smiled.

HE NEVER FORGOT a voice or a face. Especially not the face of a person who'd wrecked his world.

Special Agent Dean Bannon.

It had been years since he'd seen that bastard. Bannon's hair was shorter, his face harder, but he easily recognized the other man.

Last night, he'd thought it was him . . . thought that,

for an instant, he'd seen a ghost from his past when he peered inside The Mask.

But Bannon wasn't a ghost. Not yet.

You fucking will be.

Bannon had just been kissing the woman. Right there, on the street. And it was a woman that *he'd* already marked. The one who knew too much.

Does Bannon know I'm hunting here? Is that why he's in New Orleans? He'd hoped to lure in his prey, but Bannon had moved even faster than he'd anticipated.

Bannon and the woman—the lying fortune-teller—slipped into a bar. He eased back down the street, making sure to keep his head down. Now wasn't the time to attack. Not yet. He still had sweet Julia to take care of first.

Julia.

She wouldn't last much longer. She wasn't a fighter. But then, at the end, they never were. People had to fight for survival. They had to show that their lives meant something to them. If they didn't . . . *they died.*

But Julia had served her purpose for him. She'd brought Bannon back into his web, just as he'd wanted.

The time of reckoning is here.

His gaze slid back to the bar once more. He couldn't see Bannon any longer, but he knew where to find the man.

Wherever the woman is . . . he'll be close.

Because it sure seemed like Bannon was planning to fuck the dark-haired beauty.

But will you fuck her . . . before I kill her?

He whistled as he walked away.

CHAPTER FOUR

WHAT THE HELL? YOU SERIOUSLY JUST LET the guy walk away?" Wade Monroe demanded as he glared at the uniformed cop who was currently barring his way.

The fresh-faced kid lifted his chin. "There was no reason to hold Mr. Tatum. He was sober. He hadn't broken any laws—"

"What about trespassing?" Wade tossed out. "The guy had broken into that bar!" So had Dean, but Wade wasn't about to mention that fact right then. "And assault. He came after my teammate—"

"He's a homeless guy who got confused." Pity flashed on the cop's face. Right. The cop was so green that he didn't recognize how dangerous the "confused" people around him could be. "We sent him down to the shelter an hour ago. If you want to talk to Stan Tatum, find him there."

Dean spun away from the cop. He found Sarah watching him, one brow raised.

"What?" Dean growled as he stalked past her. Sarah didn't speak but followed on his heels. They'd passed the shelter on their way in, so he knew the place was just a few blocks away.

"Sometimes," Sarah said from behind him, "you could try finesse. Or charm."

He opened the door. Held it for her as she walked through. "Sweetheart, we both know I'm not heavy on charm."

Her shoulders stiffened, just a bit, as she glanced back at him.

Shit, a slip-up. Sarah hates it when anyone ever gets too close.

Wade cleared his throat. "You're the one who's supposed to play the mind games with people."

More silence. Sonofabitch. He could never say the right thing with her. Maybe there wasn't a right thing.

They were outside. Heading toward the shelter. Her silence was driving him insane, and—

"Is that what you think I do? Play mind games?" Her voice was soft, totally devoid of emotion.

But Sarah was good at keeping her emotions in check. Probably too good. "No, I think you do a whole lot more than that." He wanted to stop walking. To reach back. To touch her.

Touching Sarah was dangerous. Her skin was too soft. She smelled too good. She made him want too much.

So he kept walking. They didn't speak again until they reached the shelter. He tried really hard to use some *finesse* when he talked to the director. He tried because he didn't want Sarah to think he was a total jerk. But the director hadn't seen Stan Tatum. No one else there remembered him stopping by that day, either.

"There are lots of other shelters in the city," Sarah murmured.

Yes, there were. And he knew they'd be hitting them all, but his gut told him . . . "The guy is in the wind." Because Stan Tatum knew the city. He knew all of its dark spots—so he'd be able to disappear so very easily.

And if Stan had sobered up and realized that he'd watched a man abduct a woman . . . hell, yes, that guy would be wanting to hightail it out of there.

They might have just lost their best lead.

HER APARTMENT WAITED for her. Emma squared her shoulders and unlocked the door. She knew a disaster waited inside—cops weren't exactly big on cleaning up messes, and seeing the destruction in her place was like a punch right to her gut.

"You don't have to stay here."

She glanced back at Dean's low, rumbling voice. They'd pounded the pavement for most of the day, and they'd turned up nothing. The bar owners and workers on Bourbon Street hadn't remembered a sixteen-year-old girl named Julia. They saw too many people, every single day, for one blonde to stand out in their minds.

If they'd seen her, they'd forgotten Julia the minute she was out of sight.

Maybe that was the problem. Everyone was forgetting her.

Emma cleared her throat. "If I don't stay here, I think my only other option is the cot in the back of the crystal shop, and I've got to tell you, that cot is extremely uncomfortable." She could still feel the knots in her back.

"You could stay with me."

Oh, but temptation had never sounded so good.

"I mean, the point was for me to protect you, wasn't it?" Dean continued in his I'm-in-Control voice. "You think the killer is going to come after you . . . and you wanted me close."

Right. In other words, he wanted her near him because of the jackass out there. She paced toward her balcony—the balcony she loved so much—and headed outside. Voices and music drifted in the air, rising from the street.

Dean followed behind her. He was on that balcony, close enough to touch, but she'd noticed that the man had been working very hard to keep his hands away from her. Ever since that kiss.

"You should stay with me tonight," Emma said. *And not take us back to your place.* "Because I need to be here. If he's out there, watching, I need him to know—"

"That you're ready for him to take?"

Emma glanced at him. "But he doesn't get to take me, remember? That's why you're here. The big, strong agent. Ready to save the day." Just like a superhero.

He took another step toward her. "You'd better not be playing me."

She tried to look insulted. "What are you talking about?"

"You're smart, Emma Castille, probably a fucking genius."

She'd sure never been called that before. Lots of other names, of course, but never a genius. The guy was obviously trying to flatter her.

"Maybe you saw that writing on the wall at The Mask awhile back, and you thought you could use it.

You wrecked your place, you spray-painted your wall, you—"

"Wait! *Stop*." She shoved her hands against his chest and pushed, hard. "Just stop and get the hell out." Because his words had her seeing red.

He didn't back away. And her push had sent the man nowhere.

He just accused me? Seriously? "I offered to *help* you because I wanted to find that girl. And you think I'm what? Scamming you? Why the hell would I do that?"

Like father, like daughter . . .

Those had been Wade's words. Dean had better *not* be thinking the same thing.

"I don't know," Dean said softly as he stared down at her. "But then, there's a lot about you that I can't figure out."

Her hands were still flat against his chest. "Then let me clue you in on a few things. First, I want to find that girl. I close my eyes, and I see her. She's right in front of me, and she's scared, and when she runs away, I can't stop her." That *haunted* Emma. "I need to find her. I need to help her."

"Emma—"

"Second, I love this apartment. It's my home." The only real one she'd ever had. "I bought everything here with *my* money. Money that I scrimped and saved so I could have something. Maybe you don't know what it's like to have only the clothes on your back, but I do. This stuff isn't fancy, but it's mine, and I would *never* wreck it. The bastard who did this? He tried to destroy everything I had, and he left me a very clear message."

"You're next."

She nodded. "But I won't be. Julia won't be. We're going to stop him—you and I. So whether you trust me or not, well, screw it. We're working together, and we're going to find her." Her breath heaved out as she came to a fast decision. *No way are we staying in and playing it safe. We won't wait for the bastard to come—we'll hunt him down.* "We're going to keep looking tonight."

"Uh, we are? I thought we just got back."

They had . . . but this time they were headed out to a different location. *Yes, maybe I'm running from this wrecked apartment. I don't want to face it yet.* And so she wanted someone watching her back while she hunted, was that wrong? Hell, no, it was *smart*. The move of—as he'd astutely said—a genius. "I'm going to take you to the darker side of New Orleans"—the side most people would never see. "And we are going to find her."

He waited.

"Say something!" Emma snapped at him.

Dean blinked. "I thought there might be a 'third' coming in there. You were counting off, remember?"

Her eyes narrowed. "Don't push me."

His fingers rose and curled under her chin. "I could say the same to you." His mouth was too close to hers. *He* was too close. And she was suddenly far, far too aware of the long, hard length of his body. "You need to be careful with me," he said, his voice a rumble that had her breath coming a bit faster.

But he was wrong. With him, careful was the last thing she wanted to be. She stared up at him and thought about all that she *did* need.

"I think I want you . . . too much."

Her heart slammed into her chest. Jazz music was still playing down below. A soft, sultry tune. "Why do you say that like it's a bad thing?" She couldn't remember the last time she'd just let go with a lover. Just taken the pleasure and forgotten everything else. She wanted that fierce release.

Soon enough, with him, she'd have it.

"Because I'm dangerous when I'm out of control."

She didn't believe that nonsense. "I don't think you could be dangerous to me." So she leaned closer to him, pressing up on her tiptoes. His mouth was seriously sexy. "You're the good guy, remember?"

"Says who?"

But he didn't kiss her. She thought for sure that he would, but Dean backed away from her. Then he just watched her with that dark stare.

Her arms felt chilled. Ridiculous, of course, considering how hot it was.

"That was your last chance." His voice was flat. "I won't let you go again. Not if you stare at me that way."

"What way?"

"Like you want me to fuck you."

Well, she had. What was the point in denying it? "Oh, Dean . . ." His name was a sigh from her as she walked around him. "You're the one who was looking at me as if you couldn't wait to eat me alive." She headed back into her apartment.

"Oh, baby . . . if you only knew . . ."

His words made her glance back. There was no missing the sensual promise in his eyes.

"I won't back away again," he said.

Her chin lifted, and she hurried across the room. She

didn't waste time trying to clean things up then. Later, *later* she'd save what she could. When she was feeling strong enough to take on her broken home. But she quickly changed her clothes. Ditched her skirt and top. Put on the jeans she'd purchased earlier. Her new T-shirt. Her tennis shoes. She needed to be comfortable.

And I may need to run.

When you hunted in New Orleans, a girl never knew what she'd find.

LISA NYLE'S FINGERS closed around the deck of tarot cards. It was time to shut down for the night. The square always closed before sunset, the better for the city to keep out the large homeless population. Or, at least, that was the plan, anyway.

The others around Lisa had already packed up. But she'd lingered, wanting to stay. She'd raked in so much cash that day. An *amazing* day. She owed Emma for this one.

But it was time to leave. Her boyfriend had a gig in a few hours, and there was no way she'd miss his set. Her gaze drifted toward the St. Louis Cathedral. It was so freaking amazing. This city was great. She was going to bring in so much money, and she and Nate could get married by Christmas, and—

"You're not her."

She jumped because she hadn't heard the guy approach. A big guy, tall, with a wild tangle of dark hair.

"Thought you were her, all alone out here."

Lisa wasn't alone, though. There were plenty of tourists close by. She took a deep breath and tried to smile. Maybe the guy was acting a little weird, but he was still a customer, and she could fit him in before she had to close things down for the night.

"Your eyes are wrong. Not blue."

Her smile stretched a little. "You're looking for my friend, Emma." She shuffled the tarot cards. "I've taken over for her."

His gaze fell to the cards.

"Have a seat." She motioned to the chair in front of her little table. "I can do a reading for you." She leaned forward and lowered her voice conspiratorially. "And I'll even do it at a lower rate than Emma offered."

Emma didn't use the cards. As far as Lisa knew, Emma didn't use anything. She just talked to people. Or, she had. But Emma had gotten out of the business.

Her loss.

He sat down.

Lisa pointed to the sign. "Fifteen dollars."

He reached into his pocket. Pulled out a crumpled twenty. Tossed it to her.

Lisa put the cards in front of him. "Shuffle the deck."

His hands curled around the cards. His nails were dark. Red? Maybe he was a painter . . . she'd have to mention that when she started looking at the cards.

He shuffled the deck.

"Excellent." His hands were strong. *He* looked strong. Sure, his clothes were old, torn a bit, but the guy was in great health. And he was good-looking. Once you got past his glare and the dirt he seemed to wear like a second skin.

And the hair—it was bad. His hair seriously needed a cut. And he needed to shave the stubble on his jaw.

"Cut the deck. At any point you want." She paused.

"But as you cut, think of the question that brought you out here tonight. Focus on it."

The man's gaze held hers as he cut the deck.

"G-good." Okay, his stare was just creepy.

Since she was pressed for time, and the guy was giving her a serious creep-out, she decided to go straight for the three card spread. "Take three cards from your cut deck. Lay them out here . . . ." Her fingers feathered over her table. "Those cards will represent your past, your present, and your future." This spiel was standard.

Still looking straight at her, he took out three cards. He positioned them in front of her, but their faces were flat against the table.

Fine. Lisa licked her lips. "Pick one of the cards to turn over first. Pick the card that you can feel calling to you—"

He turned over the middle card. *Death*.

Her breath eased out. The Death card didn't mean the guy in front of her was dying. "This is a transformation card," she said quickly, hoping to reassure him because she didn't want the guy to panic on her. "It shows that change is coming to your life."

And he . . . laughed.

His laughter caught Lisa off guard. "Sir?"

He'd fallen forward, and his hand had slid inside his coat. A coat in September—how did that make sense?

"I'm changing . . ." He said, his words so low that she found herself leaning forward to hear him.

"You're—"

His hand flew up. A hand that held a knife.

She opened her mouth to scream, but he shoved the knife into her chest. There was no breath to scream then. Lisa could barely even gasp as she stared into his eyes.

"People are all around . . ." His voice was a low rasp. "And they're not even looking at you."

She wanted to scream. Wanted to so badly. Her mouth opened.

His hand pressed over her lips.

"Now they can't even see you if they did look." Because he surrounded her. Too big, too strong. "I'm going to stay just like this for a little while." And, she could have sworn that she actually felt him press a kiss to her temple. "Then I'll let you go. Poor lost soul . . . you weren't my prey tonight."

You're not her.

He'd said that when he first sat down.

Behind his hand, Lisa tried to whimper.

"People all around, and not one will help you. That's a lesson . . . you can't trust anyone. No fucking one. You think you can count on a friend, but you can't. In this world, it's just you. You come in alone. You go out the same way."

The shadows were lengthening. Her chest *burned*.

"I wanted to send a message with the death tonight . . . so I suppose you'll have to do."

She didn't want to die. *Please, I don't want to die. I don't!*

"I don't kill like this. Or, at least . . ." And his hand lifted. He wiped away the tears that were leaking from her eyes. She should scream.

But she could barely manage to breathe. The pain was so intense. Consuming.

"At least, I haven't. But I'm learning lots of new

things about myself. Things I never expected." He gave a low hum. "There's power in death. So much." Then, as if musing, he said, "You didn't even get to beg."

No, no, she hadn't.

"If I leave the knife in, you'll live longer." He whispered those words into her ear. "But if I take it out, you'll be gone in moments . . . all that blood will come rushing right out of you."

He started to withdraw the knife. She could feel the slow slide, and her hand lifted, it curled around his wrist, and she fought to keep his hand still. "Pl . . . please . . ."

"Ah, so I *did* get to hear you beg." He stopped pulling on the knife. "Live then, for a little longer. Maybe your friend Emma will come along, and she'll see what it's like . . . because she's next. Emma won't get away. I won't let her get away."

And then he was pushing her back, even deeper into her chair. He took off his coat. Covered her up so that no one could even see the knife in her chest. Her eyes were on him. Always, on him.

He bent and pressed a kiss to her lips. "You've been fun, fortune-teller. And, hey, I guess that death card was right after all."

Then he was backing away. Whistling.

"Pl . . . ease . . ." Lisa managed again. She was trying to call out to those around her. Those who were so close. Close enough to help her. But she didn't move because she was afraid to move. Afraid to dislodge the knife in her chest. "Pl . . . ease!"

But no one looked at her. If anything, people hurried away.

Her breath sawed in and out of her lungs. In and out . . .

"Please . . . help . . ."

EMMA HURRIED ALONG the broken sidewalk. The sidewalks in New Orleans were always their own obstacle courses. Her sneakered feet jumped easily along the cracks.

"Want to tell me where the hell we're going?"

"We're catching the trolley." Because she sure didn't want to take his fancy rental car to their destination. The thing would get stolen in seconds. "We'll cut through the square and head toward a station."

He snagged her wrist. "And after the trolley?"

She glanced back at him. They were just wasting time. "Look, sources are important in your business, aren't they? I mean, the FBI has to use tons—"

"I'm not an FBI agent any longer."

No, he wasn't. She got that. "But you're a LOST agent, and I'm betting you know just how important it is to get certain people to talk." She gave a nod. "Julia was surviving somehow in this city, and we're going to the people she might have . . . worked with."

The streetlight over them was broken, and in the growing darkness, it was hard for her to see his expression. "Sure seems like you have some interesting connections," he murmured.

"That's why I'm your partner on this one," she said. "You can thank me later."

Then she hurried forward, but he was right with her. Keeping hold of her wrist, and Emma found that she didn't mind his touch. Oddly, it was reassuring. Darkness was creeping over the city, and soon the faint streaks of light would be gone. She hurried toward the square, her gaze automatically sweeping toward her old booth—

It was still there. Lisa was still there. Slumped back beneath her umbrella. Some sort of cover or coat over her.

Emma froze. "Wrong."

Dean's fingers tightened around her wrist. "What?"

But she yanked away from him and ran toward her friend. "Lisa!"

And as she drew closer, Emma could see that Lisa's mouth was moving. She was whispering, "Pl . . . ease . . . please . . ."

"Lisa?" She reached for her because Lisa didn't seem to *see* Emma. Lisa shouldn't be there. She knew the rules. The square closed at seven. If she didn't get out, Lisa wouldn't be able to come back. The cops would make sure of it—

Emma knocked the coat off Lisa. A dark coat, black. A man's. Torn in places . . .

Familiar.

But she lost the thought as soon as she had it. Emma *lost* it because she could see the knife in her friend's chest.

"Pl . . . please . . ." Lisa whispered.

Emma's hand lifted.

"No!" Dean shoved Emma back. "Leave it the fuck in!" He yanked out his phone. Emma heard him demanding an ambulance, telling the person on the other end of the line that they had a stabbing victim, to get to Jackson Square right away.

"Lisa?" Emma said her friend's name softly. Lisa's

eyes had closed, and her head had sagged forward. Carefully, Emma curled her fingers under Lisa's chin. "Lisa, just keep hanging on, okay?"

A crowd had gathered around them now, people had finally noticed that Lisa had been attacked.

Lisa slumped forward, sliding right out of her chair—

Dean grabbed her. "The ambulance is coming. You need to stay with me, understand?"

Emma didn't think that Lisa was understanding anything right then.

He arranged her carefully, making sure that the knife wasn't moved. The knife was in Lisa's chest. There was so much blood on Lisa's clothing.

How is she still alive?

"Who did this to you?" Dean asked Lisa.

Emma peered down at her friend. The only wound was to Lisa's chest. There were no scratches on her arms. No slices on her hands. Emma clenched her own hands into fists, remembering how she'd fought when a knife came at her so long ago.

Lisa didn't have the chance to fight back. So he was close to her. Very, very close.

Her gaze slid over the ground even as an ambulance's siren wailed.

Cops were there, too, coming fast from the nearby precinct, running up to the scene and pushing Dean and Emma back as they tried to help Lisa.

Emma's shoe slid over a tarot card that had fallen to the ground. *Death.*

And she knew how the attacker had gotten close to Lisa. There was blood on that card.

He came to her for a reading. They were close, bend-

*ing together under the umbrella. It would have been so
easy for him to lean forward and attack.*

But—why? Had it been a robbery? Everyone knew
that the folks in the square were usually paid in cash.
The best time for a robbery *would* be the end of the day.

EMTs rushed by Emma. They carefully loaded Lisa
onto a stretcher. When they lifted her, Emma saw her
friend's purse—it was open and Lisa's wallet was right
there. Emma could see money hanging out of the wallet.

"What the hell happened here?" That was Beau's
voice, and she turned to see the uniformed cop staring
at her with worry in his eyes. "When I heard what had
gone down—I thought it was you, Ms. Castille."

But it hadn't been. Because Lisa had taken over her
space. Lisa . . . who looked so much like Emma.

Emma hurried to her friend's side, trying to reach
her before the EMTs loaded Lisa into the ambulance.
"Who did this?" Emma asked her. It was the same
question Dean had tried to get answered. The one that
mattered most.

Lisa's head moved, just a bit. It looked as if she were
trying to whisper something.

"Lisa?"

Beau wrapped his arms around Emma. "You have to
let them help her. Step back, Ms. Castille. Step—"

Lisa's lips moved. Emma couldn't hear her words.
She wasn't even sure that Lisa spoke at all. But the
movement of her friend's lips . . . it sure looked as if
Lisa were saying . . .

You're next.

The ambulance doors slammed shut, and the vehicle
raced away.

DEAN HAD NEVER liked hospitals. All too often, he'd just come to them when it was time to see the bodies—the broken bodies that had been left by killers.

Hospitals weren't a place of hope for him, and, as he watched Emma frantically pace back and forth across the small waiting room, he wondered if the place held much hope for her.

They'd talked to the cops. Spent far too long with the two detectives who'd come down to get their statements. From those cops, Dean had learned that no one at the square remembered seeing the attack on Lisa Nyle. No one had apparently even realized she was hurt, not until Emma came along.

The detectives were at the hospital, talking to the nurses, trying to find out what chance of survival Lisa Nyle had.

Emma stopped pacing. She turned and looked at Dean. "It was him."

He took a cautious step toward her. Emma had looked so damn breakable ever since she'd found her friend at the square. He'd called Wade and Sarah, gotten them to continue the search for Julia while he took Emma to the hospital—

"Did you hear me?" Emma charged toward him. Her cheeks were stained with red. "It was him!"

"Emma—"

"You're next. That's what she told me. What she tried to tell me."

He hadn't heard Lisa say anything.

"He told her that—he went after her. Hell, maybe he did it because he thought she was me. It was just like Beau said . . . at first, he thought it was me, too."

Her pain was palpable. Dean wanted to pull her into his arms and just hold her, and, hell, he'd never been the comforting type.

"He was right in front of us," Emma continued, her voice thickening with fury, "and I didn't see it. I think I'm so damn good at reading people—*and I didn't see it!*"

Now he was confused. "You saw the killer?"

"We both did." But she shouldered around him and marched toward the detectives. When they didn't turn toward her but kept talking with the nurse, Emma grabbed the arm of the cop nearest her. She swung him around to face her. "There was a coat at the scene. It was covering Lisa."

The detective—his name was Jonah Landry—frowned down at her. "The evidence team collected everything at the scene."

"That coat was the killer's."

Dean closed in on them.

Emma glanced back at him. "Didn't it look familiar to you?"

It had been a black coat, old, frayed.

"*He* was wearing it when he attacked us at The Mask. Only the guy was pretending to be crazy at the time, and I bought his act."

Dean stiffened. *Sonofabitch.*

"It's the same coat. It has the same frays. The same stains. It was the same size. It is *him*."

Now Landry was looking uncertain. "You know the killer, ma'am?"

"You had the bastard at the precinct. He was locked in your drunk tank last night." Her heart raced in her chest. "Only I didn't look past his surface. I knew to look past the surface, and I *didn't*."

Dean whipped out his phone. Dialed Sarah immediately.

"He was good," Emma muttered. "He had the clothes, he had the smell, he had the dirt on him . . . hell, he even acted the crazy part. A man who'd had everything taken from him and was desperate to keep the one thing that mattered."

His house.

"The guy was one fine actor. I've seen undercover cops who weren't as good as that guy. But he didn't go back for his things. That didn't fit." Emma was speaking so quickly. "When we were back at The Mask yesterday, that nagged at me. Especially when we found out that he'd been released from the drunk tank. Why didn't he go back for his possessions? They were all he had—you don't abandon what you have. You hold tight to it, no matter what."

Sarah answered her phone. "Dean? Is it the woman, Lisa?" He'd called her before and briefed her on the attack. "Did she—"

"Emma thinks she knows who we are looking for." And he believed her. Dammit, the bastard had been right *there*.

"Stan Tatum," Emma said quietly. "Though I don't think that is his real name. I think that's a name he gave us, maybe even the name of another victim. Get that coat checked." Her hands were fisted at her sides. "Maybe the blood of his victims is on there. Maybe we can find out if he had Julia . . . because I think he did. I think he's the bastard that we're looking for—and he was right in front of us this whole time!"

The operating-room doors swung open.

Emma whirled at the sound.

But one look at the grim expression on the doctor's face, and Dean knew the news wasn't good.

"Dean, Dean, what's happening?" Sarah demanded in his ear.

"Call you back." He shoved the phone into his pocket.

Emma hurried toward the doctor even as a young guy rushed into the waiting room. A guy with blond hair and worried eyes. A guy carrying a black instrument case.

"Is Lisa all right?" Emma asked the doctor.

The doctor shook his head. "I'm sorry, we weren't able to save her."

And Emma crumpled. She just—fell right there, sinking to her knees. Dean lunged toward her and wrapped his arms tightly around her.

"Lisa?" The blond man called behind Dean. "I-I was told my girlfriend was brought in here tonight . . ."

Emma's body shook as Dean held her, and he heard her whisper, "It should have been me."

HE HEADED BACK into the old house, a place that had stood in New Orleans for easily the last one hundred years. Storms had battered the house, the walls hadn't crumbled. He ran a hand over his jaw, feeling the faint stubble there. He'd have to get rid of that stubble soon. Clean up.

Hunt for his prey.

But first . . .

He entered the bedroom. Julia was still there. Still alive because quick kills really held no pleasure for him.

You have to fight to live.

He hadn't lied when he'd told the fortune-teller those words. Had she fought hard enough for survival? He doubted it.

Just as he doubted that Julia would survive.

She was still on the bed, her eyes closed, but he knew that she was awake. Her body was too stiff for her not to be.

"It's almost time," he told her. "When dawn comes, I'll take you home."

Oh, but *that* got her eyes open. Her eyelids flew up, and her cracked lips formed one word. "H-home?"

"Yes. You'll go home tomorrow."

She was trying to smile. That was sweet.

He leaned over her. Lifted his hand to touch her cheek and realized there was still blood on him. It was dry now. He stared at that blood for a moment. Was that blood from the woman at the square? Or from Julia?

Didn't matter.

He was used to having blood on his hands.

"If you can get out tomorrow . . ." he told Julia. "Then you'll be home free." Because he wouldn't kill her.

Not Julia.

In the end, life or death would be up to her. The way he liked for the choice to be. The way he'd learned that it should be.

You just have to make it out alive.

Hope was filling her face. Desperate, wild hope.

He wouldn't tell her that his last victim hadn't made it out alive. Why destroy that wonderful hope so soon?

She'd realize the truth soon enough.

CHAPTER FIVE

"L ET ME GET THIS STRAIGHT," SARAH SAID AS SHE stared at Emma. "A homeless man attacked your friend? And you think he's the same man who took Julia?"

They were in Dean's hotel room. A high-rise, too-fancy place that made Emma feel uncomfortable. *I don't belong here.* Her arms were wrapped tightly around her stomach, and chill bumps covered her arms. "He's not homeless. He just wanted us to think that he was." Talk about a great cover. The sneaky bastard. "That's probably how he got to Julia in the first place. She didn't think he was a threat, not until it was too late."

Dean had his shoulders propped up against the wall, and he was watching her with a too-intent gaze from across the room.

Wade sat next to Sarah, a little too close. Intimately close.

I have to start paying attention to everything. I was too rusty. If I'd been paying more attention back at The Mask, Lisa would still be alive.

She swiped her hand over her cheek when another tear

leaked from her eye. "What I don't understand is . . . why did he get so close to us at The Mask? Why come up and attack unless . . ." She didn't know. "He was checking us out?" Did that make sense?

No, no, it didn't make sense. The guy had taken a needless risk by exposing himself at The Mask.

She yanked a hand through her hair. "My father wouldn't have missed this. He would have caught a mistake the guy made. He would have *seen* right through him." But she'd been sloppy, and Lisa had paid for that with her life.

Hell! She'd seen through plenty of undercover cops when she'd been on the streets. She'd been able to take one look and tell if a woman really was a prostitute or if she was working vice. She'd pegged pretend-homeless guys in an instant when they were on stakeouts.

But I let him fool me. Why?

Her gaze slid to Dean. Had she been focused on him? On the strange awareness that he stirred in her?

No, don't blame him. This is all on you.

Sarah stood and headed toward Emma. The other woman reached out her hand, perhaps to offer comfort, but then Sarah hesitated, as if not sure what to do next.

"At least we know what the guy looks like now," Wade said. He hadn't moved from his position on the couch. Because they weren't just in a hotel room—the place was a suite. Giant, overlooking the glittering city below.

I so don't belong here. But after finding Lisa, after Lisa's death . . . she hadn't wanted to go back to her wrecked apartment.

But as far as knowing what the guy looked like . . .

Emma shook her head. "I doubt it. The guy will change his appearance before he comes at us again." She swallowed the lump in her throat. "He wanted us to know it was him—that's why he left the coat there. Like a taunt. He was right in front of me, and I let him go." That was going to haunt her forever. *I'm so sorry, Lisa.*

"He's a white male, probably in his late thirties, approximately six-foot-two . . ." Dean began, his voice flat.

"He wore clothes that were deliberately too big," Emma said, "to throw us off." So they wouldn't have a good indication of his weight. "He'll probably change his hair color and his eyes—he could've even been wearing contacts when we saw him." Hell, the guy could have even been using some of the costume makeup that was so popular with performers in New Orleans. She'd seen the prosthetic makeup applied to give a person a new nose, to change a jawline. Hell, one performer she knew gave himself horns so that he could look like a demon as he paraded around Bourbon Street.

With the right tools, a person could become anyone—anything—else.

Sarah's body was very tense. "A first-time killer isn't this organized."

Wade swore. "I was afraid you were going to say that."

Emma's temples were throbbing.

"He has a plan in place, an MO." Sarah's voice had grown thoughtful. "Maybe he warns all of his victims before he comes for them, almost like he's giving them a fighting chance."

Because she was staring right at Dean, Emma saw his eyes widen. As if . . . what? In recognition?

But he didn't speak. So Emma went to him. She stared up at him. "What aren't you telling me?"

His gaze met hers.

"Dean? Do you know something about this man?" He'd better not hold back on her, not with Lisa cold in a morgue.

But he glanced over at Wade. "You're heading back to the police station tonight?"

"Hell, yes, I want to see what the evidence team turns up on the coat. Landry promised to keep me in the loop."

Dean nodded. "Call me as soon as you learn anything."

Wade stood and made his way to the door. Sarah followed behind him. "I want to talk with the detectives, too. I need to find out if there are more girls like Julia who have gone missing in the last six months."

Emma already knew that Sarah thought there were far more victims out there. And Emma's hope for finding Julia alive? After Lisa's attack, that hope had faded.

She's already been gone too long.

Dean moved away from the wall, sliding around Emma. He leaned in close to Wade. Emma strained, trying to hear his words.

"FBI . . . compare the DNA there to my last active case . . ."

Her shoulders straightened when Wade nodded. The LOST agents *were* holding out on her. That just pissed her off. Wasn't she supposed to be working with them?

But she didn't speak again until Wade and Sarah

were gone. As soon as that door shut, and Dean flipped the lock—

"I'm the one who made the connection with the killer. *I* put the puzzle pieces together, and you're going to hold out on me?" Her words seethed with fury.

He turned toward her, staying close to the door. So she stalked toward him, and Emma jabbed her index finger into his chest. "We're working together! You don't hold out on a partner." God, but this night had been hell. Every time she closed her eyes, she saw Lisa, sitting beneath that umbrella and—

"You're not my partner, Emma."

The words hurt. They shouldn't have hurt, but they did.

"You're the woman I'm going to be watching fucking twenty-four/seven until this mess is sorted out. You called yourself the bait before, and you were right. This asshole took out your friend. He left a message in *your* apartment. Hell, yes, I think he's coming for you." Then he was the one to grab tightly to her arms and pull her up against him. Her toes skimmed over the floor. "And I'll be damned if I let him hurt you. I won't find you, covered in blood, the way—"

"Lisa was?" Emma whispered as pain rose within her once more. The pain seemed to choke her. Poor Nate had been devastated at the hospital. He'd kept saying, *"She's coming to my set. You're wrong . . . she's coming to my set."* As if the doctors were talking about the wrong woman.

"Like Lisa and too many others." His eyes blazed with emotion. "Too damn many others." His hands tightened around her, nearly bruising with their strength. "And you can't be next."

He sounded as if he cared. How sweet. But what a lie. He'd just met her. She was a pawn to him. She was a pawn to nearly everyone—the story of her life.

But Lisa, Lisa *had* mattered. She had a family that was grieving her. A boyfriend who'd lost it at the hospital.

Because of me. "I should have been at the square."

He shook his head.

"I should have been at that booth. He probably came looking for me. She didn't recognize him. She was caught in my place. It was *my* fault—"

He shook her then, hard enough for her head to whip back. "No."

Yes. "I would have fought. She didn't have the chance. She died when I should have—"

"No!" A low, dangerous snarl, and suddenly his mouth was on hers. Her body was plastered against his. She had tears on her cheeks because the pain of Lisa's death was eating her alive, and her emotions were flying all over the place. She was out of control, no going back, and he was *kissing her.*

Emma opened her mouth wider. She kissed him harder, wilder because the pain inside had to stop. It was too much. The pain and the grief were tearing her apart. It was just like before, when her father had died, when he'd died to protect her because she hadn't been careful enough.

For me, for me . . . when I didn't deserve it!

She could taste the salt of her own tears, and she hated that. Emma only wanted to taste him. Her body crushed to his. Their clothes were in the way. She needed him, skin to skin, needed the rush of pleasure to take the torment away.

Before she lost her mind.

His hands curled around her hips, and he lifted her up, holding her easily. Her legs wrapped around him, and Emma kept kissing him. Her heart was thundering in her ears, the beat far too loud and hard, and she didn't care.

He carried her to his bedroom. Her mouth slid from his, and she lifted her head when he lowered her onto the bed. The room was dark around her, but the blinds were open in there, letting the lights of the city spill inside.

He stood at the edge of the bed, watching her. He was a dark and dangerous shadow, and she needed him to touch her.

She needed him to make her forget.

"This isn't about forever," Emma said as she rose to her knees on that bed. She stripped off her T-shirt. Tossed away her bra. "This is about tonight. Just you and me." And because she wanted to be honest with him, Emma confessed, "I'm using you."

He came forward. His hand reached out, and his fingers curled over one taut nipple. The touch electrified her, and Emma gasped as liquid heat shot right to her sex.

"Maybe I'm using you, too," he told her, voice gruff. "You need to tell me to back away."

Adrenaline and pain were driving them both. Dangerous, so dangerous, she knew that, but Emma whispered, "I need you to fuck me." Not back away. She couldn't take it if he backed away then. Not when she had to have him.

The pain was too much. Drowning her. She had to take more—had to know more than the sorrow.

She had to take him.

His hand slid away from her breast. His fingers rose, and he started jerking at the buttons on that fancy shirt. Emma nearly stopped breathing then. *Hurry, hurry.* The chant was in her head. Desire was tight inside her, a need that had to be satisfied. Sex. Rough. Hard. Something to make her feel—feel *anything* but the guilt and the pain.

He threw the shirt to the floor. Ditched his shoes and socks. Then his pants and underwear. Her eyes had adjusted to the darkness, and she could see his outline as he stripped, and Emma could hear the faint rustle of his clothing as it hit the floor.

"I want you naked." His voice was a low growl that rolled over her.

She lay back on the bed. Kicked away her shoes and arched her hips when she pushed the jeans down her body.

He caught the jeans, jerked, and had them off her.

Her breathing seemed too loud in the darkness. And Dean—he wasn't touching her. Just standing at the edge of the bed, watching.

"What are you waiting for?" Emma asked him, her own voice far too husky as desire surged. Her whole body was bow-tight. So ready.

"I should let you go."

What?

"But I can't. I tried . . . *I can't.*" Then he caught her ankle and pulled her to the edge of the bed in a rough, sexy move that she hadn't expected. Not from the controlled Dean.

Her thighs spread, and he sank to his knees. Then he—

"Dean!"

He put his mouth on her sex. No foreplay. No games. He just put his mouth on her, and he tasted. Licking and kissing, and her body jerked—not to get away from him but to get closer. Her fingers sank into the thickness of his hair, and she cried out when the first wave of pleasure hit her. A wave that was rough and wild and just what she needed.

"More . . ." Her whisper.

And he was rising. Running his hands all over her body. Learning all the spots that made her gasp and quiver, and the pleasure was all she knew. The passion. His mouth closed over her breast. He sucked her nipple, and her hips slammed toward him. Emma could feel the long, hard length of his cock, and she wanted him *inside* her. That cock was sliding over the sensitive folds of her sex, a sex still quivering from her release, but he wasn't thrusting in her yet. She needed him inside.

She felt the score of his teeth on her body, and her nails sank into him. He growled then, and the animalistic sound was perfect. Greedy, demanding, just the way she felt. "I want . . ." Emma gasped out her words. "To taste you . . . too . . ."

"No, baby, first . . . you said you wanted to be fucked . . ."

The words were a rumble in the darkness, and the sensual promise made her even wetter. She hadn't expected her buttoned-down agent to be like this—

He pulled away from her.

"No!" Emma cried out.

But he was reaching into the nightstand drawer. Her eyes narrowed as she watched him. He was getting a condom. Sliding it on the long length of his cock.

She reached for him, and her fingers smoothed over his cock. "I could have done that." He was so thick beneath her touch. Long. Hard. Hot.

"Don't push too far . . ."

Oh, she'd push as far as she wanted. He was standing near the bed again, and Emma let her fingers slide up and over his chest. There was a rough ridge of scars near his heart. Her fingers lingered there, lightly tracing those scars. Such a severe wound. What had happened to him? Her head bent. Her mouth feathered over those marks.

"Emma . . ."

Then her mouth was on his nipple. She licked him, sucked that little nub, and gave him the same sensual torment that he'd just given her.

But then she found herself tumbling back on the bed, with Dean on top of her. He caught her hands, pinned them to the mattress, and his cock pushed between her legs.

She could feel him, right there, lodged at the entrance to her body, but he wasn't going in. "Dean! Now!"

"Be careful what you ask for . . ."

"I know exactly what I want."

"So do I." And he kissed her, thrusting his tongue past her lips even as his hips surged against her. His cock filled her, driving deep, and every muscle in her body seemed to quiver.

But the pleasure was just beginning.

His mouth was wild on hers, and his body—demanding. Driving faster, plunging deeper in a rhythm that left her quaking. She surged back up against him, moving just as fast, just as hard, and they rolled across the bed.

Emma found herself on top of him. He still had her hands in a tight grip, and she was straddling his hips. Her knees pushed down into the mattress, and she jerked against his hold.

He let her go, but she soon realized it was only so that his hand could slide over her clit. He stroked her even as he thrust into her, and Emma squeezed her eyes shut as the climax hit her. A climax that thundered through her, rolling again and again, and her head tipped forward, her hands slammed down on his chest as the pleasure tore through her.

Then he was rolling them once more. She was on her back, the pleasure still blasted her, and he said, "Not done, baby, not done." And he thrust even deeper. In a frantic rhythm that was beyond control. Beyond desire.

When he came inside her, she held him as tightly as she could. Her heart was a mad drumbeat, and sweat soaked her body.

He was above her, his body braced on his arms.

The sound of their panting breaths filled the air. The darkness cocooned them, and it held reality at bay for just a few moments longer. She didn't want to go back to reality. Didn't want to give up that moment.

Reality hurt too much.

"Knew it would . . . be a mistake."

The guy had better not be saying—

"Now I just want more . . ." And his head lowered as Dean kissed her again.

DEAN WAS ASLEEP. Her body was replete, pretty close to exhausted, but Emma's mind wouldn't shut off.

His arm was wrapped around her stomach. She

hadn't expected him to keep holding her, not in sleep. That seemed . . . too intimate. She knew it was an odd thought, especially after the sex they'd shared, but his touch—in slumber—still had her feeling unsettled.

Carefully, Emma lifted his hand. His breathing remained steady as she slipped away from him.

The bathroom was only ten steps away. She counted those steps carefully. Then she was inside. Emma shut the door behind her and flipped on the light.

Her stark reflection stared back at her. Naked. Body too pale but with faint red marks on her skin. On her breasts. Her neck. Her hips. Marks that had come from Dean's mouth and hands.

Her fingers locked around the countertop. She forced herself to look into her own eyes.

And then the tears came. Because the pleasure was gone, and the guilt . . . it was eating her alive.

I'm so sorry, Lisa.

DEAN'S EYES OPENED. *She's gone.* He jerked up in bed, his gaze flying around the narrow room. When he saw the faint light spilling from beneath the bathroom door, he released his breath on a sigh of relief.

Safe. Here. With me.

He rose from the bed, not giving a damn that he was naked. For an instant, he'd feared that Emma had gone out on her own. With that bastard out there, hunting, he'd been afraid that she'd walked right into a trap.

But she hadn't. Emma was there. Safe and sound.

He realized there was no noise coming from the bathroom. No running water. No rustles of movement. Nothing at all.

His hand lifted and he rapped lightly on the door. "Emma? Are you okay in there?"

Silence.

His hand dropped to the knob.

"I'm okay." But her voice was too soft.

Fuck. Had he hurt her? He turned the knob, but the door was locked. "Did I hurt you?" He'd tried to warn her that he shouldn't lose control, and hurting her was the *last* thing that he'd wanted. She'd given him enough pleasure to blow his mind, enough to have him nearly salivating for her again. But if he'd hurt her—

"You didn't." Again, her voice was too low.

Was she crying?

His shoulders stiffened. "Open the door, Emma." Because something was wrong. He could *feel* it. "Emma, come on. Open the door for me."

But she didn't. His jaw locked. Part of him wanted to break down that door. He wasn't supposed to do that, though. Not the thing a law-abiding agent would do.

I tried to warn her I wasn't the good guy she thought. "Emma—"

His phone rang then, the sound cutting through the room. He spun around, and his eyes narrowed on the phone. He didn't even remember tossing it onto the nightstand. He hurried across the room, his eyes focusing on the bedside clock. At 4:38 a.m., there could only be one reason he'd be getting a phone call.

Not Julia. Not her body. Don't have found her body.

The image on the screen showed Wade's picture. He picked up the device and slid his finger over the surface. "Is it the girl?"

"No . . . no word on her yet, but . . ." Wade exhaled. "This thing just got one hell of a lot bigger."

He turned to look back at the bathroom door. Still shut.

"You were right, man. You and Emma. The perp left that coat because he wanted us to know who he was. We found hair on that coat . . . hair that matched up to your last case with the FBI. Shit, I had to pull some serious strings, and Gabe had to throw his weight around to get a turnaround this fast . . . but *it's him*."

The door opened. Emma stood there, framed in the light. She looked delicate, far too breakable. Still nude.

So fucking beautiful.

"I thought he was dead," Wade continued grimly. "I know they never found the body, but a fall like that? Shit, he *shouldn't* have survived it."

"He excelled at survival." His words were flat. No emotion. Because there wasn't room for emotion, not now. The threat was too high. "Julia won't be the first, there's no way the guy has been dormant for this many years." He grabbed for his clothes, dressing quickly as he kept the phone pressed close to his ear. He didn't turn on the speaker because he didn't want Emma hearing this, not yet.

I don't want to tell her that a serial killer has targeted her. A sadistic prick who gets off on seeing just how long his prey can survive.

Emma had already faced off against one killer. She shouldn't have to fear another.

Too late.

"Sarah is accessing all of the FBI files on the guy

now. She's going to work up a new profile and figure out what kind of game this asshole is playing with us."

Yes, it was a game, all right. Because that was the way the man worked. But . . . hope stirred within Dean. It was a weak hope, but it was something. "He usually keeps his victims alive for a while. He gives them a fighting chance."

He heard Emma's sharp gasp.

"So Julia might not be dead yet." Not yet, not *yet*. "I'm on my way to the station. We need to call in the rest of our team, *now*." And get the other LOST members down there before the FBI swooped in and took over. Because with this development, hell, yes, they'd be coming.

He shoved the phone into his pocket and turned for the door.

But he found Emma in his path. Emma—who'd put on her shirt and nothing else. "What's happening?"

"We found out who the killer is." Or rather, who'd he been, five years before. Dean tried to slide around her.

She just sidestepped and blocked his path. "You already knew who he was. I saw it on your face earlier. When Sarah said it was like the killer wanted to give his victims a fighting chance, you knew then."

His back teeth clenched.

"You've . . . you've faced this man before, haven't you?"

"Yes," he bit out the word. "Look, I don't have time for this now. I thought she was dead—shit, I thought if he killed Lisa Nyle that fast, then Julia had to be dead, too. But that's not the way he worked back then. She could still be alive, and I don't have time to waste." So he just picked her up and moved her. "Keep the doors locked and stay here."

Then he made his way to the door. The past was all around him. A nightmare of blood and death that wouldn't stop. Only it wasn't the past. The past wasn't dead.

The bastard had made it out of that canyon.

He locked the hotel-room door behind him and hurried toward the elevator. The thick carpet swallowed the sound of his footsteps, and Dean jabbed his finger against the button for the elevator. It took forever for the elevator to arrive and the doors to open—probably because he was on the thirty-eighth floor—and then he stepped inside. The mirrored walls tossed his grim reflection right back at him.

He hit the button for the lobby. The doors started to close.

When there was just a few inches of space left, her hand shot through. The doors automatically slid back, and Emma was there, breathing hard and glaring at him. "You don't ditch your partner like that."

"We *aren't* partners, Emma."

She jumped into the elevator. "I say we are." She punched the button for the lobby and kept glaring at him. "And you were just going to leave me? Without even telling me what the hell is going on?"

"Julia is the priority." And he'd been screwing Emma while Julia was out there, fighting for life. "I can't waste any more time."

"Right. Got it. I'm a giant time waster."

He winced. "That's not what I—" He broke off because . . . he could see tear tracks on her cheeks. She had been crying in the bathroom.

"Who is he? How do you know him? Because it's obvious that you two share a past." She hesitated. "The . . . the scar on your chest." She reached out and touched his chest. Even through his shirt, her touch scorched him. "How did you get that scar? How did—"

His fingers curled around her wrist. "You were crying in the bathroom."

Her lashes lowered, shielding her eyes.

"I *did* hurt you."

"No." Her voice was so faint that he had to strain in order to hear it. "The pain only hit when the pleasure stopped. Reality came back then."

The elevator stopped. A little ding sounded, and the doors slid open.

Emma didn't move. "Don't leave me behind. Lisa was my friend. And Julia—I *need* to help her. Whatever is happening, I'm not scared. I can face him."

But he didn't want her facing this particular monster.

Emma pulled away from him. Walked out of the elevator. Waited. "I'm already in his sights. So either you tell me what's going on, or I'll find out another way."

He followed her. The lobby was deserted, and the faint drone from a vacuum reached him. "We have to get down to the station. Now that we know who we're dealing with, we need to organize a manhunt. There are certain places he'll use. Places that he'll take her to."

He caught Emma's hand and hurried for the door.

"We have to find her," Dean said, "before she gives up."

"Gives up?"

"He gives them a fighting chance. Or least, that's what the bastard did with me." After he'd carved into Dean's chest. The wound had been deep, but not a killing wound. If the SOB had wanted Dean dead immediately, then the knife would have sank hilt deep into his heart. But the killer had only wanted him weakened. He'd wanted to see just how much fight Dean truly had in him.

Plenty of fucking fight.

"Dean . . ."

"He'll hurt her," again and again, "but he won't kill her. If she can get away, she'll live. If she gives up . . ." They were outside now. The heat from New Orleans hit him hard. "Then she'll die."

HE WHISTLED AS he walked around the car. Long and black . . . just like he'd told Dean Bannon. Really, how much help did he have to give the bastard?

He popped the trunk, and Julia just . . . she didn't move at all. Didn't try to lunge away. Didn't try to fight him for her freedom.

"H-home?" Her voice was a broken rasp.

She seemed broken. Pity, he'd hoped she would have much more fight left in her.

"Yes, you're going home." He hauled her out of the car. Tossed her over his shoulder and started walking. She was so light, barely weighing anything at all. And she didn't even try to break away from him. Julia just lay in his grasp, limp.

In moments, he had her far away from the car. There was no sign of any other people. Just the chirp of insects and the croaks of frogs around them. The trees bent and swayed, and the murky water to the right was still. But when he glanced over, he saw eyes staring back at him, glinting in the night as a gator lifted its head and broke the murky surface.

The other hunters were already out.

He kept walking past them, his steps sure and certain. After all, he knew this area particularly well. He'd been there before, too many times.

It was his perfect spot.

He kept walking, kept whistling, and she just hung limply over his shoulder.

The swamp deepened around him. Cypress trees were soon on both sides of him, their branches weighed down by thick gray moss. There was no breeze blowing, just the thick, unrelenting heat, and the moss didn't sway on the trees. His shirt stuck to his back as he walked. One step. Another. Forward. Deeper into the swamp, then—

He dumped her on the ground. Julia groaned and rolled over. He stood in the darkness and watched her.

Julia stared up at the night sky. She didn't even try to look at him, not that she'd be able to see much in the dark. "Not . . . home . . ."

Her clothes were covered in blood. That scent would attract predators. Julia should be careful.

He backed away from her. "You have to get yourself home."

She slumped on the ground.

"Get yourself out of here, Julia. Get back to civilization, and you go home." Simple enough. He turned away from her, started walking. "Live or die, that choice is on you."

He always gave a choice, fast or slow, life or death. Because he understood how it had to work now.

His prey had to choose.

"W-wait!" Julia's trembling voice called after him. "Help me!"

His lips curved in a grim smile. She'd begged him to stop hurting her, and now—what? Was she about to beg him to stay?

How quickly the mind can shatter.

"D-don't leave me . . . here!"

He kept walking. But he did tell her, "I can kill you right now, if you want." *Her* choice.

That would probably be the more merciful choice. Because, left to her own devices, Julia wasn't going to escape. She just didn't have the willpower. She'd stay in that swamp, get lost—starve.

Die.

He'd seen it happen before.

"H-home!" Julia's voice was a rasp now, one that he had to strain in order to hear. "You promised me . . . home . . ."

He stopped then. Glanced back. She was trying to crawl in the dirt and grass. "Aw, sweetheart, what do you think death is? The final trip home."

She started crying then.

And he left her in the dirt.

CHAPTER SIX

THE BULLPEN AT THE NEW ORLEANS POLICE STA-
tion was filled with cops—detectives, uniforms,
men and women who appeared more than a bit
hesitant as they stared up at Dean.

Those cops knew they were in over their head. That
was why the FBI would—no doubt—be taking over
the case at the first available opportunity. But before
the FBI bigwig came in from Quantico and teamed
up with the branch agents, Dean knew that he had a
window of opportunity for action.

Because of his past—Dean's particular association
with the bastard they were after and because of the special connections that LOST had created within the law-
enforcement community—the police chief was willing
to let him steer the assembled officers.

Because time is of the essence. We have to find her.

"We believe that a serial killer is operating in the
New Orleans area." His voice was calm but clear, carrying easily across the room. "That individual's DNA
was found at a crime scene last night." And again, he
could only be grateful to be a part of LOST. Without
the organization's power behind him, there was no

damn way they would have gotten a DNA turnaround that fast.

He pulled in a deep breath, and, in that moment, Dean was far too conscious of the scars on his chest. "The perp's name is Jared Ricker, and, five years ago, he was responsible for the abduction and subsequent deaths of ten men and women along the Southeast coastline." He tapped a few buttons on his laptop, and Jared Ricker's face projected onto the screen behind him.

Sarah stepped forward. "This is the last picture we had of Jared Ricker. He is a thirty-seven-year-old Caucasian male, approximately six feet, two inches tall. At this time, his weight is undetermined, and we know that his appearance has altered since this image was taken."

Hell, yes, the guy's appearance had altered. "He's been passing himself off as a homeless man in the area, probably so that he can get better access to his prey and hunt undetected." Because if he'd been picking prey like Julia—runaways or other homeless individuals— who would have even noticed when they vanished? That bastard had found himself the perfect hunting ground. No one had noticed—no one had cared—when his victims vanished.

"He was in this police station," Sarah said, her voice carrying easily in the quiet room, "going under the name of Stan Tatum. He walked right out of the doors here, and no one had any clue who he really was."

"Because the guy is damn adept at blending," Dean added. "That's what made the guy so hard to catch five years ago. He would change his hair, use colored contacts, adopt new accents, new postures—he could

switch his identities easily in order to lure in new prey."
And to evade capture by the FBI.

His gaze swept the room. Emma stood near the back
wall, and Wade was at her side. Wade's arms were
crossed over his chest, and his gaze was focused on
the image of Ricker. Emma was also staring up at the
picture, her head cocked to the right and her eyes narrowed in concentration.

"Ah, sir?" A red-haired cop up in the front raised his
hand. "I thought Jared Ricker died five years ago. The
FBI task force caught him up in the Blue Ridge Mountains, right?"

The bastard should have died. "I was on that task
force." The fact that Ricker had gotten away—that
would always be on Dean's shoulders. "I tracked Ricker
to a mountain cabin. At the time, it was believed that
he was holding a twenty-five-year-old female named
Charlotte Brown." Dean hesitated. "Ms. Brown . . .
didn't make it off that mountain alive." He wouldn't
go into the grim details of her final moments, not right
then.

"Ricker's MO is unusual," Sarah explained in what
Dean thought of as her "clinical" voice. "He likes to
keep his victims, likes to weaken them through blood
loss or starvation, then he . . . lets them go."

There were murmurs from the crowd then.

Dean saw the furrow that appeared on Emma's brow.

"He lets them go?" It was Detective Landry who
asked this question. The guy's face reflected his confusion. "But I thought you just said he was a serial killer.
If he doesn't kill them, then how can—"

"Five years ago, he took his victims to isolated locations. He left them there, injured, with no food or water. The victims died in those spots. They weren't strong enough to survive. They couldn't find their way out, and Ricker . . . he'd watch them die." The bastard had confessed that to Dean. *When he thought I'd be dying, too.*

"Uh, yeah, our victim last night wasn't taken to any isolated location," Landry said again. "So how does that match up with Ricker?"

"When circumstances demand it, he changes his MO." Dean paced away from the laptop. "He could have killed Lisa Nyle in an instant. He didn't. He left the knife in her—" He saw Emma's face blanch with pain. "And he gave her—in his mind, anyway—the opportunity to live. It wasn't his usual hunting game, but he's worked that way at least one other time in the past."

Silence.

Dean cleared his throat. "He left a knife in my chest, too." He didn't look at Emma as he made that confession. "But I managed to survive. I shot Ricker—twice—and the perp went over the mountain's edge. He was presumed dead when his body wasn't recovered, but, obviously, he's still out there. Still hunting." Because Ricker's DNA had been found on the coat that covered Lisa's body.

Sarah started walking around the room, passing out files, maps. "Jared Ricker is a former Marine, he is a first-class outdoorsman. A survivalist. He would spend weeks in the wild, living off the land. He liked to pit himself against Nature . . . in the harshest of circumstances and see if he was strong enough to survive."

He risked a glance at Emma. She seemed paler.

"We believe that he is seeing just how strong Julia

Finney is right now," Sarah said, still with no emotion in her voice or on her face. "He took her and, we suspect he will soon be leaving Julia in the wild. If he hasn't already."

Dean thought the guy *had* already dropped Julia off in the wilderness. If he was already targeting new prey, then didn't it stand to reason the guy had already ditched his previous victim?

"He will leave her there with no supplies, he will leave her injured, and, unless we find her, he will leave her to die." She nodded toward the assembled police officers. "Based on his previous history, I've included locations that I think are possible drop sites for Ricker. The police chief is calling in representatives from Fish and Wildlife to be our guides in the field, and we're going to search as many of the areas as we can."

But they needed more manpower. "You have pictures of Julia Finney in those files. Talk to people—head to the parks and the swamps—the places that Sarah has listed. Talk to every person you see. Maybe someone saw Julia or Ricker. A hiker. A fisherman. Maybe someone out there can help us to save that girl's life."

He took more questions, only five minutes more, then Dean sent the officers out. It was barely seven a.m., and he didn't want to waste daylight.

He wanted eyes out there. Feet on the ground. They'd hit the state parks nearby, the swamps, the remote inlets near New Orleans. They'd search every space they could find.

And maybe we'll find her.

Maybe.

The officers went to work. Dean headed toward the back of the bullpen. He and Wade had already changed into their gear for the search, and Emma watched him with wide, worried eyes.

"I'm coming on the search," Emma said.

He'd figured that she'd say that. So Dean just nodded. "Then let's get the hell out there." Because there were so many areas to cover. Finding Julia Finney . . . hell, the odds were against them.

It was a good thing he'd never given a shit about the odds.

JULIA'S FINGERS SANK into the dirt, and she tried to drag her body forward. She couldn't stand up, she'd already tried again and again, but her legs wouldn't hold her. So she was crawling, moving so slowly, inch by desperate inch.

She'd tried to scream for help but . . . *things* . . . had just screamed back. She knew she was in a swamp, all of those hulking trees, those nonstop cries from the insects . . . they were all around her.

Mosquitoes kept swarming her, maybe drawn by her blood, and her arms were already swollen from all the bites.

Julia pulled herself forward another inch, and when her bloody fingers tightened on the chunk of grass that she'd grabbed, a long black snake shot by her hand. She would have screamed, but she didn't have any voice left. All she managed was a desperate gasp.

Then the snake was gone.

Would it come back?

Her head turned. She stared out at the dark water, water covered by heavy green algae, and in that water, she saw the head of an alligator peeking out.

The gator was still far out in the water. Still far away from her. But . . .

It started swimming closer.

Her bloody hands grabbed for another chunk of dirt and grass as Julia heaved herself forward.

Home . . . I want to go home . . .

Her mother was home. Her mother—her mother was all she had left.

TWISTING TREES AND heavy moss surrounded them on the left and on the right. Emma walked forward cautiously, her gaze scanning the area. Dean was up ahead of her, marching quickly, not hesitating.

They'd been out there for hours. Teams were searching all along the southeast tip of Louisiana, but . . . *there's too much ground to cover.*

And that was the problem.

They were on a trail right then. A parking lot was about two miles back. Sarah had told them that she believed Ricker would look for a spot accessible by car . . . that he'd drive to the scene, then hike out with Julia. Since he'd been in the city last night, Sarah thought the man had to be close—not staying out in a cabin, but right in the city.

Close enough to watch us.

Sweat was making tendrils of Emma's hair stick to her temples. Her T-shirt was sticking to her, too, and the heat was rising with the afternoon sun.

Sarah had been talking about the killer pretty much nonstop, saying all of the things he would do.

You don't keep the prey in an isolated cabin, not this time. You keep her where you want to see her . . . you

*keep her in the city. You don't take her out . . . you don't
take her out to the swamp until the very end. Because
that's when she has to fight.*

It was a little eerie the way Sarah was talking, all
those "You's," but Emma figured she wasn't exactly in
a position to judge anyone. And when it came to getting into the killer's head, well, that sure wasn't a place
Emma wanted to be. Sarah could just run with that.

But Emma was hesitant. There were plenty of places
to abandon a victim in New Orleans. The old factory
district, the empty houses outside of town, the shipping
sector . . . why go to the swamp? "Are you certain,"
Emma asked Sarah carefully, "that he would come all
the way out here?"

Sarah glanced over at her. Like Emma, Sarah was
also getting slick with sweat. "He's an outdoorsman,
always pitting himself against nature. So his prey has to
battle out here, too. This place . . ." She looked around.
"It's savage and it's beautiful. It's perfect for him."

Okay . . .

Emma kept walking forward. When they'd entered
the parking lot, she hadn't seen any signs of other cars.
If the guy liked to watch his prey make that last-minute
struggle for survival, shouldn't they have seen a car?
Something?

The team kept walking, cops and fish and wildlife
experts. So many people, now searching for a girl
who'd been right there, in the city, for so long.

Until the man named Ricker had taken her.

Emma eased closer to Sarah. "This man . . . he
really stabbed Dean?" She'd touched the scar, so she
shouldn't even be asking the question, but Emma felt as

if she was missing something. When Dean had spoken about the incident, his words had been too careful. *What didn't you tell us all?*

"Dean was the one who figured out where the guy was hiding. Dean thought . . ." Sarah's gaze was on Dean, and, for an instant, sadness whispered through her words. "He thought that he'd find the girl in time. But there was so much red tape. His superiors were worried about going in too strong and spooking Ricker, so they kept holding back the approach, and the girl—"

"She died," Emma said softly.

"Her neck had been broken. She'd fallen over the edge of the mountain and landed on a ledge."

Emma tensed.

"I-I read that in the report," Sarah said. "Dean didn't tell me. In case you haven't noticed, the guy isn't exactly big on sharing his secrets."

Emma's gaze slanted toward Sarah.

"I've consulted with the FBI many times. I have a . . . skill set that they find useful." Sarah's lips curved downward. "The FBI is very good at using people."

Those words held the note of a warning. Emma filed that away for future reference.

"He found her"—Sarah kept walking forward, her stare sweeping from the left to the right—"and when he was trying to help her, Ricker found him."

Trying to help her? "I thought you just said the victim had a broken neck."

Sarah stopped walking. "She did, but she didn't die instantly."

Oh, dear God.

"She couldn't move on that ledge. She could only

call out for help. Dean was leaning over, talking to her, trying to figure out a way to save her, when Ricker attacked him. Dean was distracted because his focus was on Charlotte, and Ricker came in hard and fast. They fought, and Ricker shoved his knife into Dean's chest."

"And he left the knife there," Emma said. And she had a flash of Lisa. The handle of that knife sticking from her chest. She'd reached for the weapon, and Dean's voice had cracked with a deep rage that she hadn't understood, not at the time.

"Ricker underestimated him. Because Dean wasn't ready to die, at least, not without taking Ricker out, too."

Emma brushed aside a hanging tree branch as she went forward. Her mind was filled with images right then. Dean, his chest bloody, fury twisting his face. Fighting for his survival.

"He had tried to get the FBI to do a full raid on the area, but they wouldn't give him the backup. If they had, then maybe Charlotte would have gotten out, or maybe Ricker would have been captured."

And maybe Dean wouldn't bottle so much of himself up inside.

"This . . . this didn't make it to the papers, but Charlotte Brown worked with the FBI. She'd been one of their informants, and when she first went missing, I think Dean's boss just thought the woman had cut out on them. He delayed the search for her. And, too late, they realized that she'd fallen into Ricker's hands."

Her gaze slid to Dean once more. *Too late.* Emma could understand all about the pain of being too late. She and her father had been too late to help those girls in Texas—they'd been too late for anything but death.

As she watched him, Emma saw Dean yank a phone from his pocket. He spoke quickly, his body tensing. She hurried toward him.

"Where? Yeah, yeah, that's about ten miles away. And you say a witness spotted a black car there this morning?" He seemed to listen intently, then he said, "Hell, yes, that could be him. Get the teams to focus there, *now.*" Dean shoved the phone back into his pocket, then he looked toward Sarah and Emma. "That was Wade. A fisherman out last night thought he saw a man carrying something through the swamp. The cops there just talked to someone else in the same area who swore he saw a long black car pull out after dawn."

A long black car . . . just like the one that "Stan" had described to them.

Dean was already running back toward his rental car, and Emma and Sarah followed closely behind. Hope was growing inside Emma, a wild, desperate hope.

Maybe this time, they'd get there in time.

DEAN JUMPED FROM his car and raced ahead. The narrow parking lot near the little pier was packed with cop cars. Emma rushed to his side, and they made their way straight to Wade.

"The search team is fanning out," Wade told them as he motioned to the swamp and woods that surrounded them. "There's a ton of space here, and we've got the K-9 unit to help us cover ground."

The sound of barking dogs drew Dean's attention. Hell, yes, it was about time the dogs arrived.

"We gave them the coat to use for tracking," one of

the canine handlers told him. "The dogs have a damn sight better chance of finding the girl than we do."

If she was there.

And, hell, if this was their lucky fucking day, they'd catch Ricker, too.

In seconds, the dogs were bounding away, moving with a quick, determined pace as the handlers rushed to keep up with them, and Dean was running right after them. He wasn't going to miss this. If Julia was out there, he was bringing her home.

The image of her mother flashed through his mind. She'd been so desperate when she walked into the LOST offices. The tears hadn't stopped flowing down her cheeks. She'd kept saying that it was her fault Julia was gone, that she'd made the wrong choice.

Her fault.

And she just wanted her daughter to come home.

THEY'D BROUGHT THE dogs. His head jerked when he heard the sound of their barking. Well, well . . . it looked as if someone had stepped up his game this time.

Dean Bannon hadn't come after him alone.

Learned your lesson?

It wouldn't matter, though. Bannon wasn't going to get him. He'd prepared too well.

So even as the dogs barked and snarled, he was backing away. Heading deeper into the swamp. Leaving his prey.

How much longer do you have, Julia?

He'd already moved his car—after he'd dumped Julia in the swamp, that had been his first order of business. He'd come back in via boat, and the old, wooden boat that he'd hidden after his arrival was just steps away. He pulled the boat from behind the bushes. Silently pushed it into the water. The boat tilted a bit when he climbed inside, but he steadied it easily, then reached for the wooden oars.

The oars didn't make a sound as they cut through the water. His grip was steady, his strokes sure. If he rushed, he'd make a mistake. Maybe give away his location. That couldn't happen.

He wasn't going to be caught by Bannon or anyone else. He was meant to be free. To hunt.

His choice.

The barking grew louder.

He kept paddling. In moments, he'd be long gone. He knew this area so very well. He would be out of there in plenty of time for the real fun to begin.

Because it's time for the next step. Time for Bannon to see that he's out of his league and headed straight to hell.

THE PATH AHEAD branched. As Dean bounded forward, he saw one of the dogs strain to the left.

The other surged to the right.

What the hell?

Their handlers were pulling the dogs back with sharp commands.

Two paths. The same scent on each path?

"Where do we go?" Emma asked as she reached them, breath heaving. Sarah and Wade were with her.

"We split up." He pointed to the left. He knew the water was heavier that way. *An escape path for Ricker?* "Half of us go this way. Half go right." Because they needed to cover as much ground as possible.

Wade and Sarah took off, with the cops going right.

Emma stuck with Dean. Two other officers came with him as they raced ahead. Running deeper and deeper into the swamp.

I'm coming, bastard. I'm coming for you.

SARAH RAN BEHIND the canine handler, a stitch in her side because it seemed like they were flying over the dank earth. She had to do some fast footwork to avoid tripping on the twisting roots that littered the ground, then she did her best to dodge the moss that hung heavily from the trees.

"Julia!" One of the cops called out, his voice seeming to echo back to them. "We're here to help you! *Julia!*"

But there was no answer. Maybe Julia couldn't answer. Maybe the dogs were confused—they'd tried to take them down two different paths, after all.

Only—

"I see her!"

Her head whipped to the left. The K-9 handler pulled his dog back, and Wade rushed forward. He fell to his knees beside a figure on the ground. A figure lying facedown and not moving at all.

Sarah staggered to a stop beside him.

She saw that Wade's fingers were trembling a bit as he reached out to the girl—a girl with damp, dirty blond hair. He was almost touching her—

The girl suddenly jerked away from him. She let out a long, hoarse cry and tried to kick out, to punch.

Wade didn't even attempt to deflect her attacks. He let her hit him. Again and again. "It's okay." His voice was low, soothing. "We're here to help you, Julia. We're here to take you home."

And she cried out again, another of those nearly soundless cries that still seemed to tear into Sarah's heart because it was so desperate and full of pain.

The girl's body was covered in blood, her clothes stained dark.

"Let m-me go," Julia whispered, and it *was* Julia. Sarah recognized her easily. "Please . . . I'll do anything . . ."

Sarah pushed Wade back. She needed Julia to see that it wasn't her tormenter who'd found her. Speaking softly, reassuringly, Sarah said, "We're here to help you, Julia."

Julia's body jerked again.

"You don't have to be afraid." Because fear was the emotion that Ricker used to control his prey. *Just like my father did. He used it on his victims and he used it on me.* "You're safe. We're going to get you out of here, and—"

Julia's head slammed into the ground. Her body wasn't just jerking. The girl was spasming.

Sarah grabbed for Julia's shoulders as she tried to stabilize the girl, and that was when she realized . . . Julia just might not make it out of that godforsaken swamp after all.

THE DOG STAGGERED to a stop at the end of a narrow, rickety pier. The pier spread from behind a cabin—or what was left of one. Only two walls were still fully standing for that cabin, and everything else had long since been reclaimed by the swamp.

"The trail ends here," the canine handler said, giving a grim shake of his head.

Dean hurried forward. His jaw was clenched with fury as he stared out at the water. The water was still and dark, showing no sign that anyone had passed over it recently, and he hadn't heard the telltale sound of a motor, but he knew Jared Ricker had been out there.

"There was a boat tied here."

He looked over at Emma's voice. She'd bent near the edge of the little pier and was pointing to the post.

"There are a few tendrils from the rope left, sticking in the wood. He probably paddled out, that's why we didn't hear him."

Because the guy had an escape plan. He would have stayed close to watch his prey—the bastard always liked to watch—but when the cops had started closing in, he'd fled.

The radio crackled on Dean's belt. Cell signals were shit out there, so they'd taken the precaution of bringing radios, too. He yanked the radio up even as his gaze swept the water. The problem was that the guy had too many options out on that water. It branched right up ahead, snaking in a half dozen different directions as it cut back through the swamp.

"We've got her!" Wade's sharp voice carried over the radio. "But we have to get her help—right now. He did a number on her, and the girl is seizing!"

Only one other person had ever escaped from Ricker.

But Ricker . . . that bastard always found a way to escape.

The girl is the priority. Save her. Get her out.

He glared out at the water. Search teams would be sent out there. The FBI would swoop in with more manpower, but the guy was already gone. A perfect hunter who'd slid into the darkness once more.

A hunter who would take another victim soon. Because Ricker never stopped. Like most serials, the guy *couldn't* stop. Killing was a compulsion for Ricker, one that would only end when he was caged or dead.

THE BLADES OF the helicopter spun overhead, their steady thud sounding much like a heartbeat. Emma watched the helicopter rise, taking away Julia Finney. The girl had been unconscious when she was loaded into the chopper. There'd been so much blood on her.

But she was alive. We found her. She made it out of this damn swamp.

Sarah had gone on the chopper with Julia. Emma knew that if the girl woke up and said anything about her abductor, Sarah wanted to be there.

If the girl woke up.

The chopper rose higher and higher, then vanished as it flew toward the hospital.

Wade slapped his hand on Dean's shoulder. "We found her, man."

Dean's body was too tense and hard. Locked down. He glanced over at Wade. "It's not over."

"No, hell, no, it won't be over until we bring in that bastard. But this is a win." Wade's voice deepened with intensity. "You're the only other person to escape him. You made it out. You got to Julia."

But Dean shook his head. "*We* did it." His stare cut to Emma. "*We* did it," he said once more.

She had to swallow the lump in her throat. When it came to hope, Emma hadn't exactly had a whole lot in her life. She'd desperately wanted to find Julia, but after Lisa . . . well, she'd thought they'd be too late to help the girl.

Just like she and her father had been too late that long-ago Texas night. Too late to do anything but find the bodies.

"He's long gone," Dean said softly. "As soon as Ricker heard the dogs, he was in his boat. The guy would have mapped out the area. Had a perfect escape route waiting."

Wade's hand tightened on Dean's shoulder. "So he runs, but we can find him. Come on. Let's get those dogs moving. *Let's stop the bastard!*"

Dean nodded grimly.

Emma reached for his hand. "Call the mother." *First.* Because that woman needed to know about Julia.

Dean pulled out his phone.

There has to be hope.

THE SWAMPS IN southeast Louisiana were a maze—no, they were hell. Hot, twisting, filled with snakes and gators. The swamps stretched for miles, and they probably had too many hiding spaces for their killer.

An hour later, Emma could feel the frustration rolling off Dean in waves. More men had come in to help with the search, more dogs, but, so far, they just weren't turning up anything.

"We need to get boats in the water," Dean said as he bent over a map. They'd set up a temporary base near the parking lot. "We'll cover more ground if we get the local fishermen to help us with the hunt. We can divide up and use their vessels to—"

Doors slammed. Voices rose and fell. Dean's head had lifted, and his gaze was focused right over Emma's shoulder. She heard the sound of approaching footsteps even as she watched Dean stiffen. *Uh-oh.* Emma looked back. Two men were there, one older, balding, with faint gray near his temples. The other was younger, fit, appearing close to Dean's age, but he had dark blond hair and a face that looked as if it had been etched in stone.

"Your job isn't to hunt killers," the older man said. He was wearing a white shirt that he'd rolled up to his elbows, and his sweat had already dampened the cloth. "Not anymore, Bannon."

It was the guy's tone. The authority there, a bit too much authority. And the clothes, of course. Dead giveaway. A glance downward showed Emma that both guys hadn't changed their shoes—*come on, you're wearing those in the swamp?*

The FBI had arrived, and from the look of things, they were about to take over.

Emma found herself edging closer to Dean.

"I don't think we've met," Wade said as he offered his hand to the older man. "You are . . . ?"

"Special Agent James Elroy," Dean supplied, as Elroy shook Wade's hand. "My former boss. I'm guessing he flew in from Quantico."

Wade's expression hardened—and Emma was pretty sure that his grip did, too. "Is that so . . ." His tone had gone arctic as he regarded the older man.

"When I got word that there been a hit on Jared

Ricker's DNA down here, I knew the cops would need me." Again, there was more than a touch of arrogance in the man's commanding voice. "Luckily, I had an agent I could trust already working close by in the Baton Rouge field office, and he can help run point for me."

Ah, and the agent the guy could trust . . .

That would be the blond fellow with him. The one who was watching Dean so carefully.

Wade glanced over at the blond.

"Kevin Cormack," the guy said, holding out his hand. "And I used to be Dean's partner."

She was missing a whole lot. Emma could feel the tension there, pulsing in the air between the men. She also thought that she caught a flash of what could have been guilt in Kevin's blue eyes.

"Didn't know you were still looking for Ricker," Elroy said as he crossed his arms over his chest and studied Dean. "That's a long time to hunt a supposed dead man."

"Obviously, he's not dead," Dean snapped back. "But, no, I wasn't hunting him. I was looking for the girl, Julia Finney."

Kevin nodded. "And you found her. Damn good work, man." He sounded impressed, sincere.

But the older guy was watching Dean with narrowed eyes. "We'll be taking over from here. The FBI is initiating a task force to hunt Ricker."

Dean surged toward him. "This isn't a pissing contest, Elroy. That bastard is a killer, and he's going to hunt again."

"Of course he is." Elroy's voice was flat. "That's what

serials do. They hunt. They're compelled to hunt. But the guy will have a cooling-off period—"

Dean was shaking his head.

"He won't take another victim right away," Elroy continued, voice hardening. "That gives us an edge. We can close in on him."

"Bullshit," Dean called. His hands were fisted. "He murdered Lisa Nyle while he still had Julia Finney. The guy isn't following any kind of timeline, and he doesn't understand the concept of a cooling-off period. I told you before, again and again, he hunts because he likes the thrill. The control. He always wants that feeling, and he's never going to stop."

Anger flashed across Elroy's face. "But he did stop, didn't he? For years . . ." He licked his lips. "Until now."

Now it was Emma's turn to step forward. "I'm sorry, but I don't think that's the case."

Elroy's slightly bushy brows rose as he glanced at her. "Excuse me?"

"I don't think he's stopped killing, and neither do you." Sure, she was no FBI agent, but she wasn't stupid. They weren't either, so why were those guys pretending?

"Who are you?" Elroy demanded, as his gaze swept over her.

Oh, what? Now he wanted a greeting from her? She'd been standing *right there* the whole time, but the guy hadn't reached for her hand in that little handshake ritual that the men had exchanged. "I'm the woman who knows you're lying," Emma told him. "You think he's been killing all this time, and now"—she gestured to the swamp around them—"you're wondering just how many bodies are out here, and if you'll ever even find them. Because you realize that he's probably been going for people who aren't missed by the rest of society. Runaways like Julia or even the homeless." Because the guy had played that role for a reason. "You've got a real shitstorm on your hands, and *that's* why you rushed down here so fast. Probably used a private plane to get down here before the press got the story. You're scrambling with your task force because you don't want this mess blowing up in your face." Her breath whispered out on a slow exhale. All of the men were staring straight at her. "Too late, because that's already happened."

Kevin's lips curved the faintest bit as he pointed at her. "The profiler. Sarah Jacobs. I heard about you."

"She's not Sarah Jacobs," Wade said as he came to her side. That was cute. Almost like a show of support. And here she'd thought that Wade wasn't exactly on the Emma bandwagon.

"You need to get as many cadaver dogs out here as you can," Dean said, his stare fixed on his old boss. "And your *task force* needs to start searching. Ricker was here. Maybe you can still catch his trail."

Then he reached for Emma's hand. His fingers curled around hers. Caught off guard, she glanced down.

"We're going to check on Julia. *She's* the reason I was out here," Dean said. "Her mother is desperate, and I want to make sure she knows her daughter has been found." Dean advanced, and Emma went with him, moving automatically.

But Elroy shifted to the right, blocking his path. "I want all the notes you have on this case. You need to turn them over to Kevin and me."

Was he serious?

"I don't know how you're working with your new team"—and his hard gaze darted between Wade and Emma—"but we both know you're too reckless. You risk too much—put innocents on the line—and I won't have you messing up this investigation."

Oh, the hell, no, he *hadn't* just said that to Dean.

Dean started to reply—

But Emma jerked away from him and jabbed her finger into Elroy's chest as she said, "Listen up, *Agent*. Dean Bannon and the LOST team just saved that girl's life. I didn't see you down here, looking for her. I didn't see *anyone* else looking. He knew the killer, he knew how to track him, and he saved her." Her voice sharpened with intensity as she said, "So if anyone can stop this guy, I think it's going to be Dean, and not your pompous ass."

Silence.

Dean's arm wrapped around Emma, and he pulled her back to his side. Then they walked away, with Wade close by. Emma wanted to turn around and glare at those FBI jerks. They really thought they could just ride in and take over? But she kept moving forward as she tried to control her fury.

They passed cops. A new search team that was coming in. Men and women she'd never seen before. Part of the task force? A force they were being shut right out of.

So much for cooperation. So much for teamwork. So much for fighting the real bad guy out there who'd killed her friend and tortured a teenage girl.

They neared the cars that were waiting for them. Fury

still pumped in Emma's body, and when Dean let her go for a moment, she found herself spinning around—

"Ease up there, fighter," Wade murmured. "I think you put that jerk in his place."

She could only hope, but Emma doubted it. Guys like that always thought they knew best. "There was an agent like him . . ." Her words came out in a rush, even surprising her. "When my father *knew* who'd taken those girls in Texas. He wouldn't listen. That agent was working with the cops, running the case. The guy thought he knew better than everyone else. When my father and I went into that cabin because no one else would help us, when my father died, that bastard came to me in the hospital and said that it was my father's fault, that a civilian should never have taken a risk like that." She'd wanted to attack that jerk. She'd been in the hospital bed, hurting—inside and out—and he'd stood there, cold. Hard. Telling her that the FBI and the local authorities weren't responsible for what had happened.

He should've left the case to the professionals.

"The professionals should have listened," she whispered. "Then he wouldn't have needed to die."

She was cold then, standing out in that Louisiana heat.

"I, um, I'll go check in with the cops. I'll make sure the contacts I have keep us updated," Wade muttered, and he quickly backed away.

Dean didn't back away. He positioned his body so that he was between Emma—and everyone else. "You defended me."

Her chin notched up as his words pulled her out of the past. "Of course I did." What had he expected her to do?

But he was staring at her in confusion, looking like he was the one lost.

"What do you think would have happened," Emma asked him, "if you hadn't found me in that square? If you hadn't come looking for Julia?"

His eyes narrowed on her.

"Wade was right. This is a win." *Please live, Julia. Please.* She'd been breathing when she was loaded onto that helicopter, and Emma was clinging to that knowledge. There couldn't be another death, not after Lisa. They needed hope. They needed life.

"You trust me." He seemed surprised.

Emma could only shake her head. "Do you really think I have sex with men I don't trust?" *Jeez, what the hell?*

Dean's hands rose, and he caged her between him and the rental car.

"You can find him," Emma said, certain of this. "You can stop him." Her heart was beating far too fast in her chest. "You *have* to stop him because we both know that FBI jerk is wrong. This Ricker guy is not going to cool off."

His body was so strong and hard against hers, and she could *almost* feel safe right next to him. Almost.

"Because if you don't stop him," Emma continued, and Julia's bloody image flashed through her mind, "we know who he'll take next."

Me.

But Dean gave a grim shake of his head. "That won't happen."

The fear was there, though, snaking inside her. She didn't want to be the person left, bloody and broken, in the swamp. Fighting for her survival.

"I'm not letting you go," Dean said, as his right hand lifted and curled under her chin. "He will *not* take you on my watch."

But he hadn't said Ricker wasn't going to come for her.

Dean's hand slid under the curtain of her hair. Then he leaned forward, and his mouth brushed lightly over hers.

Emma found herself leaning toward him. Wanting a deeper, longer kiss. But there were too many people there. Too many eyes watching them.

So she didn't push the kiss. Didn't hold too tightly to him.

Dean's mouth eased from hers. "Keep trusting me."

Odd words. Not what she'd expected at all.

"Whatever happens, *trust me*."

It almost sounded like a plea, and Emma didn't think he was the kind of man to ever make a plea. Slowly, she nodded.

His shoulders relaxed a bit, the only sign of his tension easing. "I'm not going to leave you. I won't let you be on your own with him out there. I found him once, and I will do it again."

He eased away from her and opened the car door. Before Emma slipped inside, she glanced back toward the swamp. The blond FBI agent stood there, watching them.

A shiver slid over Emma as she eased into the car. *The hunt is on.*

CHAPTER SEVEN

NIGHT WAS FALLING, A CREEPING DARKNESS that swept over the sky. They'd been at the hospital for hours, but Julia still hadn't woken up. She'd been taken to surgery, then kept in ICU.

LOST had arranged for Julia's mother to be flown down, and Ann was in ICU right then, crying as she held her daughter's limp hand.

Dean watched them for a moment. Ann had lost even more weight since the last time he'd seen her. Her body was far too frail now, her bones almost poking through the skin. She was rocking back and forth as she held Julia's hand.

The doctors were worried about an infection setting in with Julia. They'd stabilized her, done their best, but she'd had deep wounds—and they had no idea how long she'd been in that swamp.

"She just wanted to go home."

He turned and found Sarah edging closer. Sarah's eyes were on the mother and daughter. Dean and Sarah weren't allowed past the nurses' station in ICU, and Elroy had sent one of his men over to stand guard near Julia's bed. Dean didn't usually find many reasons to be grateful to that dick Elroy, but he was glad the man was trying to watch out for Julia.

"On the helicopter ride, she spoke, just a bit. She kept asking for her home." Sarah seemed sad. It was odd to hear any emotion coming from her, and when Dean studied her a bit more closely, he saw her blink quickly, as if she were trying to clear tears from her eyes. "But it's so hard to go back home after something like this. The rest of the world will expect her to be normal again, but every time she closes her eyes, she's going to see . . . *him*."

He'd wanted to question Sarah before, but he'd tried to respect her privacy. He knew she'd been through a hell that few could ever imagine.

When you close your eyes, Sarah, do you see your father?

"She's going to need extensive counseling. You can't just get over something like this. Surviving the swamp wasn't enough. Now she has to survive everything else that's coming."

He knew Sarah was speaking from her own personal experience.

Her gaze slid to his, and her cheeks flushed. Had she just realized how much of herself she'd revealed?

"I'll speak with the FBI and the local police—they need to understand just how delicate she will be—psychologically—when she comes back to us." Then she cleared her throat. Straightened her shoulders. "What's the status of the search for Ricker?"

She wanted to change the subject. Fine with him. He never wanted to push Sarah too much. He always felt like he needed to tread very carefully with her. He rubbed his neck, so much tension had gathered there, and he told her, "Wade found out that the cadaver dogs are in the swamp." Wade had a good contact in Detective Landry, and the guy was going to keep them apprised of the investigation. "And Victoria got into town a little while ago, so if they do find any bodies . . . maybe the FBI will let her examine the remains."

Because Victoria Palmer was one of the best forensic anthropologists in the United States. Gabe had convinced her to come to work for LOST a little over a year before. If anyone could unlock the secrets of the dead, it would be Victoria.

He inclined his head toward Sarah. "Do you think he's going to come for her again?"

Sarah's gaze had returned to Julia's still figure. "He didn't come for you."

No, he hadn't. "That's why I thought he was dead all these years." Because after what he'd done to Ricker, Dean had sure expected to be hunted. *If* the guy lived.

Sarah bit her bottom lip, an unusual sign of nervousness from her, and said, "There are a lot of rumors about what happened the night he attacked you."

Yeah, he knew that. "There are lots of rumors about you, too."

She nodded. "Only some of those rumors are true."

"So are some of my rumors."

They measured each other.

Finally, Sarah said, "It's a challenge to him. A game of survival. Right now, no one is sure *if* Julia has survived or not. The next few days are key for her."

Because maybe Ricker wouldn't have to come and finish her off at all. "You think he's just sitting back and waiting for her to die."

"The doctors said she would need to be a fighter to pull through."

Yes, he knew they had said that.

"We all have to wait and find out just how much Julia wants to live."

Dean rolled his shoulders, trying to push some of the tension away, but it wouldn't vanish. He kept seeing that damn muddy water in his mind. The bastard had been right there. *If I'd gotten there sooner, Ricker could be in jail.*

Now the guy was out in Louisiana somewhere. *But you aren't going to hurt Emma. I won't let you.*

"There's not much else we can do here tonight," Sarah said. "The guard is in position, and the nurses aren't going to let us near her anytime soon."

Not until Julia woke up. *If* she woke up.

"I need to take Emma home." Home. Where was home? Her apartment—the place that had been destroyed—or his hotel room?

"Are you using her as bait?"

The question pierced through him. Emma had offered herself as bait, but, hell, no, he didn't want her risked.

"Because we both know," Sarah continued quietly, "that he means to take her. The guy has developed a new ritual that he follows, that's obvious. He's building up to her abduction. He was probably going to do it in the square, but then he realized a new woman had taken her place there. *That* is the reason why he killed Lisa Nyle. Because his rage erupted. But he isn't going to stop, you know that. I know that."

He glanced toward the waiting room. Emma was out there, with Wade as her guard. "Emma knows that, too."

"Ah . . . so she's willing bait?"

There was a darker note in her voice. Dean focused on her once more.

"The FBI has taken over on this one, and we . . . we find the missing. No one is lost here."

Not yet.

"How long do you think the team will be able to stay down here? We have other cases. Other people out there who are waiting on us."

He knew. Dean was well aware of the fact that he was working against the clock.

"We can't protect her every moment."

We can try.

"I'm not giving up," Dean said simply. "Not yet. Ricker has taken too many lives, and I *know* him better than anyone else. I can bring him down."

She eased closer to him. "I know he's the reason you left the FBI. But, Dean, you need to be sure on this . . . are you doing what's best for Emma? Or are you letting the desire for revenge cloud your mind?"

"Revenge?" Now she had surprised him. "That's not what I want."

Her dark gaze held his. "He nearly killed you. You stayed in the hospital for weeks. After his case, you left the FBI—"

"That was *my* choice. I got sick of working with guys like Elroy, guys who would rather push papers around all day and bind you up in red tape instead of getting out there and trying to save a life." He fought to keep his voice steady and not let the rage sweep over him. "I've saved lives at LOST, not just buried the dead. Isn't that why you're at LOST? Because you want to help people?"

Her stare slid from his. "That's one of the reasons."

Sarah and her secrets.

"Are you taking Emma back to the hotel?" Sarah asked.

Her place was still a wreck, so, yeah, he'd planned to take her with him. His hotel would be home for the night.

"Is she safe with you?"

He didn't know what the hell kind of question that was. "Don't profile me, Sarah." It was a flat demand.

Because he knew that if she looked too deeply into him, Sarah wouldn't like what she discovered. No one ever did.

He marched back to the waiting room. Found Emma standing near the window, with Wade just a few feet away. Dean didn't slow down as he approached them. He just walked up to Emma and took her hand.

"Guess you're taking over guard duty," Wade murmured.

His curt nod was Dean's only response, but then he got a look at Emma's face. There were tears on her cheeks. "Emma?" Everything stopped then. Every fucking thing.

"I can't stop thinking about Lisa," Emma whispered. "She was here, in this hospital last night."

And he was a dumb asshole. He pulled her with him, leading her toward the elevator because he wanted her out of that place. He should have thought about Emma's reaction to being at the hospital again. Dean should have gotten Wade to watch her at the hotel. But he'd wanted her close, and he'd caused her pain.

I'm a selfish bastard.

The elevator doors slid shut on them, and he wrapped his arms around her, keeping her against his chest. "I'm sorry." He couldn't remember the last time he'd apologized to anyone, and the words felt rusty coming out. "I should have thought, I—"

"I wanted to check on Julia, too. I wanted to be here." She gazed up at him with those bright blue eyes, eyes that were wet from her tears, and he realized that the woman could take him to his knees.

His thumbs brushed over her cheeks as the elevator descended.

He hadn't thought much about tears before, but he knew that he never wanted to see Emma crying again.

Her hand lifted and pressed to his chest. "What happens now?"

"I take you back to my hotel. You'll be safe there, and—"

"I can't hide forever."

No, she couldn't. "For tonight, I'll know you're safe." Safe in his room, in his bed. Tomorrow, they'd start their attack.

"No one is ever really one hundred percent safe." The doors opened, but Emma stood there, in his arms. "You know that, don't you? No matter how hard you try, you can't protect everyone."

He leaned closer to her. His lips brushed over her ear as he told her, "I'm not trying to protect everyone. Just you." And he was surprised by how much he meant those words. He didn't form attachments easily but Emma . . . something about her was different. Something was pulling him in.

And demanding that he hold as tightly to her as he could.

LITTLE JULIA WAS alive, for the moment. Perhaps she was more of a fighter than he'd realized.

He stood across from the hospital, and he saw Dean Bannon exit the building. Dean's arm was around Emma Castille's shoulders. The man always seemed to be touching her, always staying close. The attachment that he'd formed was obvious.

Not that he blamed the man. Emma was very beautiful. But beauty was fleeting. It was weak. Beauty could be broken so easily.

Would Emma break easily?

Dean and Emma climbed into a car. Drove away.

It was almost time for him to find out. He'd warned Emma. Perhaps she should have tried to run. But instead, she'd decided to seek protection from Bannon.

Wrong move. He can't help you.

And just what would it do to Bannon when she vanished? When he lost Emma and was never able to find her again?

His lips curved as he enjoyed the idea. He'd originally wanted to take Emma because he feared she'd seen him that night with Julia. The more he'd watched Emma, watched her searching on her own, the more she'd appealed to him. Poor Emma, she was like his other prey, one of the "forgotten"—the term he gave for the people that you saw on the street. The people you spoke with, the people you smiled at, and the people you forgot.

People without families. Without close friends.

The homeless were forgotten. The runaways were forgotten. And women like Emma? Women who never let anyone get too close?

They vanished, too.

He hoped that Emma enjoyed her night with Bannon.

It would be her last good night, before she learned just how dark and dangerous life could be.

He'd teach her, the same way he'd taught Julia. The same way he'd taught so many others since he'd found his true calling.

And as a bonus, her disappearance would rip apart Bannon's world.

Rain began to fall then, a light spray that drifted over him. He turned up his collar and walked into the waiting night.

EMMA WASN'T USED to uncertainty. But she stood in the middle of Dean's swank hotel room, her hair wet from the rain, and she didn't know what she was supposed to do.

"You have to be exhausted," Dean said as he motioned toward the door on the right. The door that led to his bedroom. "You should get some sleep."

Yes, there was the uncertainty part. "I'm not tired." Well, okay, she was, but matters far more pressing than sleep were on her mind.

When you knew that a killer had you in his sights, sleep wasn't exactly high on your priority list. Staying alive? That was.

"You aren't going to stop hunting for Ricker, are you?" She needed to hear him say the words.

He was staring out the window, looking down at the city below. "No. Now that I know he's out there, I can't just walk away."

Good. Because she'd feared that the LOST team would be packing up and leaving the Big Easy. Running was certainly an option that had danced through her head when she'd first walked into her apartment and seen the wreckage, but Emma knew she couldn't just go now.

Because Lisa deserves better.

Emma had already hit her savings, the precious money that she'd fought so hard to keep over the years. She knew that Nate didn't have much money, and she wanted Lisa to have a nice funeral. So she'd contacted her bank and given Nate as much as she had.

"We're still partners," Emma told him.

He glanced over his shoulder. "Back to that, are we?"

Her hands twisted in front of her. "I can help you more than you realize." They'd never gotten to take their little trip the other night—because they'd found Lisa. But either with or without Dean, she'd be visiting her contacts at dawn. They could tell her far more than any cop ever could about what had been happening in New Orleans.

About just *who* else might have vanished.

And she'd only have to make a small deal with the devil in order to get that information. Some deals were worth it, though.

Dean turned to fully face her. There was tension in the long, hard lines of his body. Tension that seemed to cling in the air around him. "I'm not who you think I am."

Really? She was pretty sure he was the man she'd had mind-blowing sex with in that very hotel room. She also thought he was the too-uptight LOST agent who'd managed to galvanize a search for a missing girl. He was annoying, he was sexy, and he was probably going to drive her insane at some point.

"There are things I've done that no one else knows about. If you're going to stay with me, if he's coming for you, then you need to know about them."

She took one tentative step toward him. "You make your life sound so scary."

His jaw hardened even more.

"That bad?" Emma whispered.

"You met Elroy today. When I was working the Ricker case for the FBI, he was the agent in charge."

Yes, she'd already picked up all of that. Emma waited for him to continue.

"I thought I knew where Ricker was holding Charlotte. All of my intel was good. I knew we had to act."

She took another step toward him. "But he held you back."

"He wanted to wait for more confirmation. I didn't. So I took off on my own."

Emma found herself closing the distance between them, not stopping until they were just inches apart. She wanted to reach out and touch him, but she didn't, she waited. "You wanted to save her."

He gave a hard shake of his head. "That's the problem. For someone so good at reading people, you can't read me."

She thought she could read him pretty damn well.

"She was still alive when I got there, but before I could get help, he attacked me."

She couldn't wait any longer. Her hand lifted. Pressed to his chest. The shirt separated her palm from the scars that marked his chest.

"He didn't kill me outright. He stepped back. Watched me bleed. Left that knife in my chest."

Don't think of Lisa!

"Then he walked away. The SOB thought I'd just lie there while he got away." His hands fisted at his sides.

"He thought wrong. I had a backup weapon in my ankle holster. I went after him. I . . . shot him."

Did he expect her to be horrified by that? He had no clue who she was then. "You fired your weapon because you were trying to stay alive!"

"After the first shot, he lost his knife. The bullet slammed into his right shoulder, and his whole arm pretty much became useless. I could have stopped then. Taken him into custody."

She shook her head.

"Charlotte had fallen over the side of the mountain. Before he'd stabbed me, she'd been crying out. And after I shot him . . . by then, she wasn't anymore."

Emma hurt for him. Hurt for the woman called Charlotte.

"He told me that she wasn't suffering anymore. He *laughed,* and my control broke."

The precious control that he held so tightly. "Dean . . ."

"So I shot him again. I didn't aim for his heart or his head because I wanted those bullets to hurt him. I wanted *him* to suffer, just as his victims had suffered. Why should he get off scot-free? Why shouldn't he feel the same agony that he'd given to us?"

Her hand pressed harder to his chest.

"The FBI reports would say I was defending myself, but that was bull. I was attacking him. I wanted to *kill* him, and I thought I had. After the second shot, he went over the edge of that cliff. I looked, but I didn't see him. I believed he was dead. When the other agents finally arrived, they searched, too . . . a man shouldn't survive a drop like that."

"But he did," she whispered.

"It sure as fuck looks that way. We have his DNA here and, when Julia wakes up, she'll be able to give us a description of the man who took her."

Emma shook her head. "I don't know what you want me to think about you. He *attacked* you, Dean. You were definitely defending yourself." How could he think anything different?

But his face was still locked in that fierce mask. "There was a line there. When he lost his weapon. When I could have held him at gunpoint until backup arrived. But I didn't want to hold him. I wanted him to suffer, and I wanted him to die in agony."

It was there, then, creeping into his voice. A harder growl. A darkness. She could see the edge that clung to him.

"I left the FBI because I didn't want to play by their rules any longer. Didn't want to sit back and wait for some pencil pusher to tell me what to do. I wanted to act."

And he had. "And you really think this is going to scare me off?" Seriously, it was like he hadn't even met her. "So you've got some darkness inside. Do you think I don't?"

A faint frown appeared between his eyes.

She smiled at him. A slow twist of her lips. "Oh, Dean, maybe one day, I'll tell you some of my secrets." Because she carried more than her share. And when it came to the sins of the past . . . "Maybe we're more alike than you realize," Emma whispered as she rose onto her toes. Her lips feathered across his. "Maybe that's why you want me so much." She didn't even question why she wanted him. She just did. "And you do want me, don't you, Dean?" Emma could feel his arousal pressing against her. A long, hard bulge, and she wanted to strip away her clothes and be with him.

It wasn't just about fucking. Not just about hot sex though there was certainly a bonus there. After everything that had happened between them, to them, she wanted the elemental reaffirmation of sex. Of life.

Because there's too much death and evil around us.

She wanted to seize this moment with Dean. Seize the pleasure and not look back.

Her lips pressed to his. A light, sensual tease when she wanted much more.

"You should be afraid of me." His words were a low rasp.

Emma laughed at that. "You won't hurt me." She knew this to her core. He claimed not to be the good guy, but Dean didn't know the men she'd met in her life. She'd gotten quite used to looking *through* people and seeing the secrets they tried to hide.

Dean's big revelation hadn't scared her at all. It had just made her want him all the more. Because beneath that careful control, he was like her.

His hands curled around her shoulders. "I think I want you too much."

That didn't sound like a bad thing to her. "Prove it." And she kissed him again. Only this time, Emma's tongue slid over his lower lip. Then into his mouth. Oh, but she enjoyed his taste. She liked it when he—

Lifted her up. Held her too easily and had her pinned between his body and the wall in the next breath. And he took over the kiss. There was nothing soft or hesitant about Dean. His tongue plunged into her mouth.

He took. And she loved it. She kissed him back with a growing passion, the wildness barely held in check. He'd pushed between her thighs, and Emma wrapped her legs around him as she held on tightly. His cock pushed against her, and she arched against that powerful ridge, rubbing her sex against him. The clothes were in the way. She wanted him *in* her. Would the pleasure be as good this time? Would once be enough?

He pulled back just long enough to grasp her shirt, then he yanked it over her head. The shirt hit the ground, and he lifted her up. So strong. She kept forgetting how strong he was. He shoved her bra out of the way, and his mouth closed over her breast. Her head fell back against the wall as a moan broke from her. His tongue swirled around her nipple, and a streak of fire shot right to her core.

"Shouldn't want . . . this much . . ." His words were growled against her skin. "Shouldn't need . . ."

There was nothing wrong with need. Nothing wrong with a lust that consumed.

She'd squeezed her eyes shut. Emma opened them. Watched him. "Fuck me, Dean."

Something happened then. She could feel it in the sudden tenseness of his body. His muscles went rock hard against her. When his head lifted, and she stared into his eyes, his pupils had expanded. His gaze was so dark and deep. His cheeks were flushed. Desire, lust, was stamped on his face.

He slid her back to her feet.

"Dean?"

He reached down. His fingers brushed over her bare stomach as he yanked open her jeans. Then he was pushing the denim out of the way. It tangled around her feet, and Emma jumped, moving clumsily, to free herself, but then his hands were back on her. He was holding her there, keeping her still as his gaze swept over her.

She could feel that gaze like a touch. So hot, molten, then he *was* touching her. Not her breasts. Not her legs. His hand went right to her sex. His fingers—two—slid inside her, and Emma lost her breath.

"I'll fuck you until you can't think of anything else." The words were a dark promise.

But she already couldn't think of anything else. Her hips pressed down against his hand, moving helplessly because his thumb was right over her clit, and she loved the way his fingers were pushing in and out, in and out, and she'd be able to come soon if he'd just—

His fingers pulled away.

No!

He yanked open the fly of his pants. Didn't strip. Dean shoved on a condom as his eyes raked over her, then he was *in* her. Pinning her to the wall, pounding into her again and again, in a rhythm that was too wild to meet. Too strong to deny.

"Not . . . enough . . ." He rasped the words. Then he was pulling her even closer. Carrying her as he still thrust into her. Her breath came too fast. Her heart was about to jump right out of her chest.

Were they going to the bedroom?

But . . . no . . .

They fell onto the couch. He was still on top of her, but he moved her legs, opening her even wider for him, so that, impossibly it seemed, she took even more of him inside her. He was in so deep, filling her so completely, that Emma's body seemed more his than her own.

Deeper. Harder.

He put her legs over his shoulders. Drove into her. The position left her totally open to him, completely vulnerable, and she *loved it*.

He was growling her name. Telling her that she was "fucking perfect" and "fucking tight," and she wanted to speak but couldn't. Emma could only fight for her breath because the climax was there, piercing right through her, wave after wave that wouldn't stop. Too intense, too perfect, and, yes, even better than before.

And he was with her. His body jerked, and he held her in an unbreakable grip, nearly bruising. She squeezed her sex around him as he erupted inside her, and Emma held him as close as she could.

"Need more . . ." His words were so dark.

A shiver slid over her even as her legs fell limply back to the couch.

He'd told her that he needed his control. She knew that his control was long gone.

He was still hard in her, even though she knew he'd found his release. For an instant, their gazes held. There was a tangle of emotions in his stare. A need that seemed to consume.

Perfect. Just what I—

"I want more."

Her breath caught. She'd wondered if once would be enough this time. Her body was still humming with pleasure. Aftershocks still made her sex contract around him.

She wanted more, too.

He pulled from her slowly, a long glide.

"Don't move." His order. "We're not done."

Then he was heading to the bathroom. She heard the water running in there, and Emma didn't move, not because he'd ordered her to stay still but because she wasn't sure her knees would hold her if she tried to stand up.

She'd wanted him wild. She'd pushed him in order to get Dean's control to break. He only seemed to let go of that control when they were having sex. It was only then that he let what she thought of as his "real" side out. Because he wasn't the buttoned-down agent.

He was passion and fire and darkness.

She was naked on that couch. Spread out there, still feeling him inside of her.

And the lights were on. Glaring down at her.

Then . . .

Darkness.

Emma tensed. "Dean?" He'd done that, right? Turned off the lights?

The floor creaked. "I told you," he said, his voice seeming to come from that darkness. "We aren't done."

Another creak. This one closer. Her eyes were adjusting quickly because light still spilled from the window.

"Why do I want you so much?" His words rumbled to her.

She turned on the couch. Licked lips that seemed too dry. "That's not really a question that a man is supposed to ask a woman." Her hand rose. Curled around the length of his arousal. "You're just supposed to tell me . . ." Her head leaned toward him. Her breath blew over the length of his cock. "How much you do want me . . ."

"More than I've ever wanted another."

That stopped her. Surprised her.

"Y-you're just supposed to tell me . . ." She moved toward him again, sliding over the edge of the couch. Her lips brushed over the tip of his arousal. "What you'd do to have me."

Then she eased off the couch. Sank to her knees.

"Anything."

Her fingers were trembling faintly. He sounded like he meant what he was saying. Maybe in the heat of the moment, he did.

She kissed his aroused length once more, then took him into her mouth.

His fingers sank into her hair. "Emma!"

She stroked him with her hands and her mouth. She learned him, as he'd learned the secrets of her body the night before. He was thick and hot, long and hard, and when she licked the head of his cock, she could taste the saltiness of his arousal.

Like Dean, she wanted more.

So she took more, widening her mouth, moving her head as she found a rhythm. Her breasts brushed against his powerful thighs. Her nipples were tight, aching, and she couldn't stop tasting him. She wanted him at the edge again. Wanted him over that edge. With her, lost, with her.

"Emma!"

But he wasn't coming. He was pulling away from her. Staring down at her in the darkness, and she was still on her knees.

"Be careful . . ." A low growl. "I'm wanting you too much."

She shook her head. It wasn't possible to want someone too much.

Was it?

His hands reached for her. He pulled her to her feet, and her weak knees slid a bit. She thought they'd go to the bedroom, but they didn't. He just lifted her up, held her right there, and sank inside her.

No protection.

They were flesh to flesh, and Emma couldn't catch her breath. Her sex was swollen and slick from her climax, and he'd slid all the way inside her.

"D-Dean!"

"I'm . . . clean," he growled, "but I'll stop . . . I'll—"

"Don't." She locked her arms around him. Rose up. Pushed down. "Clean, too. Protected. On the pill." There was no risk of pregnancy.

And—

No stopping.

If she'd thought the rhythm before was wild, she'd been wrong. They were both out of control this time. Her nails scratched over his shoulders. His teeth scored her neck. He thrust into her, strokes long and perfect, and the pleasure wasn't just waiting, it was crashing into her.

"Yes!" His sharp words. "I can feel you . . . squeezing . . . *yes!*"

She lost her breath. Her heartbeat thudded into her ears, and she felt the hot splash of his release in her. Consuming. Completing.

Emma kept her eyes squeezed shut. She clung to the pleasure because it was too good to let go.

He carried her back to the bedroom. Slid her beneath the covers. Curled around her.

She still had her eyes closed. She was almost afraid to look at him. She was afraid of what she might see in his eyes. No, she was afraid of what he might see in her own eyes.

So Emma stayed silent, for once lost for words, and she stayed in his arms until sleep claimed her.

WADE HAD GONE back to the swamp. Night had fallen, and he was surprised that the cops hadn't halted their search for the day. But when he pulled up and saw the spotlights that had been set up, Wade knew that something had happened.

He approached Detective Landry. He was glad to see the guy there—because Landry had been sharing pretty freely with him since the FBI had come storming in. "What's happening?"

He could hear dogs barking in the distance.

Landry looked tired, the spotlights casting long shadows over his face. "One of the dogs found some remains near the edge of the river. We don't know yet if the remains are linked to the perp who took that girl, but . . ."

But it sure as hell wasn't a good sign.

He'd have to call the team and let them know. He thought Sarah was still at the hospital, and Dean—

"I figured some of the LOST team would be showing up again."

His shoulders stiffened at that voice, and he turned to see Kevin Cormack heading toward them. The guy had just parked his car, too. Had he gotten a call about the remains and rushed back to the scene?

"But I thought," Kevin continued, voice mild, "Dean would be the one to show first."

As Landry hurried away, Wade squared off with the FBI agent. "You found a body."

"No, we found 'remains' a few hours ago." Kevin's words were very careful. "We don't know yet if those remains belong to one of Ricker's victims or to some unfortunate fisherman who had an accident."

Right. This was where he could press his advantage. "And you won't know, not unless you get yourself one grade-A forensic anthropologist in here. Because if those remains have been out here for a while"—he was betting they had—"then the decomposition rate will make most methods of analysis useless."

Kevin rocked back on his heels. "I'm guessing LOST comes equipped with its own forensic anthropologist?"

"Victoria Palmer is the best." The simple truth. "The FBI has worked with her in the past, so it won't be a stretch bringing her on. She's already been vetted."

Kevin glanced toward the sound of barking dogs. "I've worked with Viki before."

His eyes narrowed at the familiar use of her name, but Wade said, "If you've worked with her, you know there's no one better. This asshole is out there, killing, and we need to move as fast as we can to stop him."

"Elroy isn't exactly known for moving fast," Kevin said softly, "but I'm betting Dean already told you all about that."

Actually, Dean hadn't. And Wade hadn't told the guy about his reasons for joining LOST. *We've all got demons. Live with them and move the hell on.*

"You can't move slowly with this perp," Wade said as he rolled back his shoulders. The cops seemed to be swarming—had they found another body? How many victims had Ricker taken out there? "Not when he already has another victim in his sights."

Now Kevin stepped toward him. "Another victim? How do you know that?"

"In the past, the guy never let one victim go, not until he had another lined up." That had been the way he worked. What, did the guy think no one had access to the old FBI profile on Ricker?

But Kevin was still advancing. "No, no, you're speaking specifically, aren't you? What does LOST know that we don't?"

Wade hesitated.

"If someone is in danger, we can help." Intensity thickened Kevin's voice. "Give me something here. I can go to Elroy. I can get him to cooperate with LOST . . . you just have to put your cards on the table."

But Dean hadn't told the guy. Why hadn't Dean told Kevin about Emma?

"Tell me what you know," Kevin said, "and I'll make absolutely certain that Victoria Palmer gets access to all remains found here."

That was the goal, wasn't it? Cooperation with the task force? He knew Dean wanted to take down Ricker. And their boss at LOST, Gabe Spencer, had given the guy the backup of the team, for a limited time.

I'll show you my cards, for now. "We think he's targeted the woman who was here with Dean earlier," he said softly. "Emma Castille."

"What?"

"Ricker broke into her apartment. Tagged her wall with a message saying she was next."

He could see that clicked right away with the FBI

agent. Kevin said, "The cops told us they found a tag like that in the old bar that Julia was using for a home."

So the guy *had* been briefed. *Only the cops didn't find that tag—Emma and Dean did.* "Our profiler thinks that Ricker has adjusted his MO. He's warning the victims about what's coming to build their fear, to give himself more power over them." With killers, it was always about power.

"Where is Emma Castille right now?" The agent's voice was strained. Too tense.

Wade thought the answer to that question should be obvious. "With Dean."

Kevin swore. "He's using her." Said so quickly. So flatly. And with total conviction. "He's going to risk her life to get Ricker."

When the guy started to whirl away, Wade grabbed his arm. "That's not the way that LOST works," Wade told him. They didn't risk innocents. Never had. Never would.

"That's the way *Dean Bannon* works," Kevin tossed back. "I worked side by side with the guy for years. I know him, and I know that Emma Castille isn't safe, not as long as she's with Dean."

Wade shook his head. No, no way would he buy that. Dean wasn't some renegade who'd risk an innocent woman's life.

"You don't know the guy as well as you think," Kevin muttered. "I thought I could trust him once, too. And you know how that ended? With a woman named Charlotte Brown being killed." Grief cracked through the man's voice. "I *trusted* him to save her, and Charlotte wound up in the ground."

DEAN TURNED HIS head. Emma was asleep in his arms. He could hear the soft sound of her breathing. Even. Deep.

She'd slipped easily into sleep, and she lay there, so trusting in his bed.

Emma was still naked, with the sheets lightly covering her body. He'd tried to warn her away, but she hadn't listened. She'd stayed, tempted him.

No one had ever tempted him the way she did. No one had ever made him ache so much.

It was dangerous. *She* was dangerous.

But he found himself leaning toward her. Pressing a kiss to her temple.

Trust. Such a delicate thing. She'd given him her trust, when she shouldn't have. Her trust, her body. Emma had held nothing back in those hot, passion-filled hours, and neither had he.

For the first time, he'd let go completely with a lover. Forgotten his control. Hadn't wanted it even for an instant. Emma didn't seem to mind the darkness that he carried. She wasn't scared of it—or him—at all.

Would that change with the coming days? When she saw just exactly what he had planned, would Emma turn from him?

His arm curled around her, and he pulled her closer to his side.

I can't let that happen. Emma, with all her mysteries, all her passion, was becoming too important. So important that Dean wasn't sure he'd ever be able to let her go.

CHAPTER EIGHT

EMMA TIPTOED TO THE HOTEL-ROOM DOOR. SHE'D dressed as soundlessly as she could, a pretty easy task since most of her clothes had been scattered in the sitting area, not the bedroom. Dawn was just about to break across the sky, and she planned to be out of there by the time the sun rose.

Her hand reached for the doorknob.

"Do you always sneak out of your lovers' beds?" His voice froze her. "Or am I special?"

There haven't been as many lovers as you might think. Emma pasted a bright smile on her face and turned toward Dean. "You're awake!" An incredibly obvious statement, but her mind was scrambling right then.

Wearing only a pair of his pants, he was propped against the doorframe, his arms crossed over his chest and one dark brow raised. "Going someplace?" A small pause. "Without me?"

Yes. She had been. Because when she'd woken, Emma had realized that she could probably get her contact to share a lot more if he spoke just with her and not with her new guard/partner.

"I thought we were working together, Emma."

She caught the edge of anger in his words. "We are." *Mostly.*

"He's out there, waiting, with you on his kill list, and you were just going out on your own?"

"I can't hide forever." *Not my style.*

He pushed away from the doorframe and stalked toward her. "Where were you going? Because he's probably watching your apartment."

"I-I wasn't going there." Not first, anyway. But a stop by that place was definitely in order. She'd meant what she said. Hiding forever wasn't on her to-do list.

His hair was tousled. From her fingers, she was pretty sure. And the guy's body—he had some serious six-pack action going on there. Emma forced her gaze off his sexy bod and back to his face. A face that was currently locked in some rather tense lines. If the guy knew that she liked it when he looked all dangerous and tough like that, well, he'd no doubt use the sex appeal to his advantage.

So she didn't move toward him. Didn't let her hands wander over those muscles. Emma kept her body stiff because she had a mission to accomplish.

And she'd realized that taking her current lover to see her *ex* . . . well, that wasn't the best plan ever.

His eyes narrowed, and it almost seemed as if he was trying to see into her mind. "Were you running from me?"

"No!" Her immediate answer. "I was just going out for a bit. I thought I'd be back before you woke up." That was only a half lie.

He leaned forward, and his hands flattened on the door behind her. "That's just insulting. You don't fuck a man one night and run away before dawn."

"You do when you're trying to stop a killer." Because

what was happening—this hell, this nightmare—she was going to help stop it. Lisa wasn't going to be put in the cemetery while that guy ran away and lived to kill another day. No way. So even if she had to face the ghosts in her past, Emma was going to do it.

"The dark side of town."

She jerked a bit but quickly controlled herself.

His gaze had turned thoughtful. "You were taking me there before we found Lisa. You thought you could learn something about Julia's abductor there."

She still thought that.

He leaned toward her. "Something you should know, baby."

Baby?

"You're not the only one who can read a person. You were trying to ditch me and go to that place on your own, but that's not happening. Too bad if you don't want me by your side, *partner,* because that's where I'm planning to be."

She held his gaze for a moment. Saw that he wasn't going to back down. And really, having backup wasn't the worst thing to ever happen. She'd just been alone for so long that getting used to someone else being there, someone else who wanted to watch out for her, well, it was different.

Not bad.

Different.

Her hand rose and pressed against that delicious chest. She could have sworn he scorched her. "Do me a favor though? Please, *please* try to look a little bit like you blend in. Leave the GQ look behind. I know you own a pair of jeans." He must.

He smiled at her, and Emma's breath caught. She didn't think she'd ever seen that particular slow and sexy smile cross his face before. It lit his eyes, warmed his face. Made her want to lick him. "Yeah, baby, I do." He backed away from her. "But how about you tell me just where we're going, *first*."

That was easy enough. "We're going to my old home. I still have some friends there." And an ex-lover. "They might be able to tell us if anyone else like Julia has gone missing."

He nodded, but then he cocked his head. "Old home?"

He'd see, soon enough.

"And maybe we should take a taxi or a trolley." So his ride didn't get, uh, borrowed.

But Dean shook his head. "The car will be faster."

"I hope you have insurance," she muttered. *'Cause you might need it.*

"EMMA, THIS ISN'T a home."

Dean looked around him, seeing the homeless men and women who clung in the shadows. The streaks of red and gold spreading across the sky told him that dawn had definitely come, and the people there were starting to slip away as the daylight spread.

"Not every home has walls." Emma was walking quickly down the street, a street in a run-down area that was far from safe. He looked to the left and saw the flash of cash exchange hands.

There were two scantily clad women to the right, edging toward what looked like some kind of bar. It was dark there, the lights turned off, but two motorcycles were in front of the place.

"It's going to close soon," Emma said, "so we have to hurry."

It? The bar? Okay, he'd keep going down this rabbit hole. He made sure to keep a perfect pace with Emma as they approached the place.

Not every home has walls. The woman had nearly gutted him with those words. He hated to think of her scared, alone, on the streets.

I'll never let it happen again, baby. I promise.

The women disappeared into the bar.

"Going someplace, buddy?" a rough, gravelly voice asked them, and Dean looked over to see a man with black hair and a snaking scar over his left eye. The guy had to be close to six-foot-five, and he was built like a tank.

Dean tensed at the guy's angry tone, knowing this wasn't going down well because—

"He's with me, Carlos."

She knew him?

A smile flashed across the guy's face. "Didn't see you, Em." Then he was shoving Dean out of his way and bringing her in for a quick hug. "Been too long."

Emma hugged him back. "You know why I stayed away."

He held her tight a bit longer, then slowly let her go. "Yet you're back here . . ." Carlos glanced toward the bar's door. "And you know he's inside."

Who the fuck was this "he" they were talking about? And was the guy going to get his hands off Emma anytime soon?

"I have to talk with Jax. Something's happening. Something bad."

Carlos's dark stare swept over him. "And you think it's smart to bring this guy with you?"

"A girl needs her protection." Her voice was soft. "I need that protection right now."

His brows flew up. "Someone's after you?"

She gave a small nod. "I need to talk with Jax," Emma repeated. She bit her lip. "You don't . . . you don't think he'll turn us away, do you?"

Carlos laughed, a rough, grating sound. "Just because you broke his heart?"

What. The. Fuck?

"Jax doesn't have a heart," Emma murmured. "Everyone knows that."

Carlos turned and opened the door to the bar. Dean realized that the guy had been out there, guarding the place. He'd let the women inside without question, but he'd stopped Dean and Emma.

A bouncer? The guy sure looked the part.

Emma and Dean followed Carlos into the bar. If the building had looked like a wreck from the outside, it was nothing compared to the way the place's interior looked. And smelled. Jesus—what was that scent? Piss and vomit?

There were some tables scattered around a small stage—and a stripper pole? Yep, definitely a stripper pole.

His gaze slid around the bar. The place was mostly deserted, probably typical for a joint like this one, especially near dawn. But, at the bar, counting out cash, he saw a blond-haired man. The guy's back was to Dean and Emma, but Dean could see the long lines of tattoos that covered his arms.

"You got company," Carlos called out.

The guy stopped counting his money. "Tell the company to fuck off." The women were near his side. He handed each of them some cash, and they hurried out without a word.

Carlos cleared his throat. "Not too sure you want her to vanish so fast, boss."

Emma's shoulder pumped against Dean's as she stepped forward. "I need a few minutes of your time, Jax."

The guy's hands slammed down on the bar top. *"Emma."*

When the man leapt up from his barstool and whirled toward Emma, Dean jumped in front of her. He didn't know what that jerk might be thinking, but he sure as shit hadn't liked the sound of his furious voice when the guy had said her name.

The blond lunged toward him. "Who the fuck are you?"

Like Dean hadn't been wondering the very same thing.

But the man's light blue stare quickly raked over him. Dismissed him. "Cop or FBI. Either way, your ass doesn't belong here." He tried to shove Dean aside.

Dean wasn't in the mood to be shoved. He caught Jax's hand and held it fast. "I belong wherever she is." Because he was getting the picture right then— especially since Jax's gaze kept trying to jump to Emma. *They were involved. Fucking intimately.*

Jax glanced down at Dean's hand. He shook his head, then glanced back up. "Let go, or I'll break your wrist," Jax told him, the words sounding matter-of-fact.

"Jax—" Emma began.

"You can try," Dean offered. "But prepare to have a

few things . . . broken . . . yourself." He wasn't about to let this jerk intimidate him. Dean would show the asshole just who the hell he was messing with, and—

"Stop it!" Emma shoved between them, while Carlos laughed. "I didn't come down here for this crap. Jax, stop acting like a dick for once and listen to me."

Jax glared at Carlos, and the other man's laughter turned into a coughing fit.

"Dean, show him the picture," Emma said.

"Dean?" Jax repeated. No, the guy mocked.

Dean pulled out the picture of Julia Finney and handed it to the asshole.

Jax's eyes swept over the picture. "I've seen her. So what?"

"You see most of the girls that come through here . . . if they're looking for jobs, if they're short on cash," Emma said. "You keep tabs of the people who stay near this block, *your* block."

"It's more than a block," Jax muttered, obviously insulted. "You know my territory is fucking bigger than that."

Emma didn't argue. She said, "That girl—Julia Finney—she went missing recently."

Jax's face tensed.

"Someone took her," Emma continued. "She was a sixteen-year-old girl living on the streets, and a man took her."

Dean caught the fast glance that Jax fired at Carlos.

"He held her, tortured her, and nearly killed her."

There was no emotion at all on Jax's face.

This was getting them nowhere. "The guy doesn't give a damn, Emma," Dean said. They were wasting their time. They should have gone down to the hospital, seen if Julia was awake. They could have—

"We're afraid he's taken others." Emma crept closer to Jax. The guy's posture changed as she neared. He leaned toward her. Even reached out as if he'd touch her, but, almost instantly, his hand fell back to his side. "Others," Emma continued, voice sad, "who he thought people wouldn't miss."

Jax glared at Dean. "And how does this bastard fit in?"

"He's the one who came looking for Julia. He wants to stop the man out there, a man who's hunting."

Carlos had moved behind the bar. He poured a fast tequila, downed it, then said, "We need to tell them, boss."

"Carlos." The name came as a snarl from Jax.

Emma reached out and caught his hand. "What do you know?"

He shook his head. "You run away, you *stay* away, and you think you can just came back now? To *my* bar? Walking in with that jerk"—his thumb shot toward Dean—"at your side? You think I'll help you?"

Dean stepped forward. That guy really needed to learn some manners, and if he kept talking to Emma with that hard edge in his voice—

"Yes, I think you'll help me. Because I believe people still matter to you. You know something, Carlos knows something, and I need you both to talk to me." Her voice rose when he just stared back at her. "Or are you really the cold-blooded bastard, straight to your core? Are you going to let that guy out there get away with hurting, killing? Julia is only sixteen. *Sixteen.*"

Jax glanced over at Dean. As he stared at Dean, fury flashed on his face. "You expect me to believe these people matter? People without homes, without money? People staying on the street—you expect me to think they matter to you?"

"They do," Dean fired back.

"He's picking them because he thinks no one notices when they vanish," Emma said, talking fast. "But . . . you notice, don't you Jax? You and Carlos noticed something happening."

His lips thinned, and Jax said, "Yeah, I noticed."

Emma's breath rushed out. "Talk to me. Please."

Dean didn't want her begging that guy. He didn't want her anyplace near him. But . . .

Maybe the SOB does know something we can use.

Emma's gaze was on Jax. "Dean works with a team who can find the guy. That's what they do. They find people," Emma told him.

LOST didn't usually find killers. They found victims. But this wasn't their usual case.

Jax wasn't speaking. Carlos had downed another shot of tequila.

Emma pulled her hand away from Jax. "Fine. Never mind. Don't care." She turned away from him and faced Dean once more. "This was a bad idea. Let's just go—"

Jax grabbed her arm—far too hard—and whirled her back around to face him. "Running away so fast, *again*?"

But Dean was already moving. He slammed his hand into Jax's chest and pushed the guy back against the bar, breaking the man's contact with Emma. "You don't grab her like that, do you understand?"

Jax laughed. "You have no idea who the fuck I am, do you?"

He didn't give a shit if the guy was the president. "You

have no idea who the fuck I am, either, so I'll clue you in," Dean said instead. "I'm the guy with Emma. The guy at her side *now*." Yeah, he was getting that this prick *knew* her. "And I'm the man who's making sure she doesn't get hurt. Not by you. Not by that bastard out there hunting."

Carlos slammed down his tequila bottle. The glass shattered, and the fellow started to lunge over that bar, broken bottle in hand.

Dean's head whipped up. "That'll be your last mistake."

"Stop, Carlos," Jax said half a second later.

Carlos—very wisely—stopped.

Jax smiled at Dean, and it wasn't a pretty sight. "You and I . . . we'll settle up later." It was a promise.

Damn straight, we will.

"But for now, I owe Emma." A muscle flexed along Jax's jaw. "So get your hands off me, and I'll talk."

Dean took his time dropping his hold on the guy. And he made sure that when he stepped back, Emma was at his side.

"Still have the same type, huh, Emma?" Jax asked with a flash of a shark's smile. "Never can play it safe, not even with the guys that *look* the part."

What?

"Six months ago," Jax said with a slow nod. "That's when I first noticed the missing."

Six months?

"I'd taken Wayne in, given him a job . . . not much, just cleaning tables. But the kid was starting to bust ass, he was trying, then"—Jax shrugged—"he vanished."

He felt Emma tense beside him.

"He had no other friends, no family in the area. He

slept in the back room because I told him he could crash there." Jax tapped his fingers along the edge of the bar. "Now maybe, if I hadn't just given the guy a chance at my place, I wouldn't have noticed when he disappeared. And that was the point, right? An ex-junkie, he disappears and you say . . . what the hell? Maybe he OD'd. Maybe he went to greener pastures. Who the fuck cares, and everyone moves on."

"That's what the cops thought," Carlos muttered as he put his broken bottle back on the bar top.

Dean's brows shot up. "You went to the cops?"

"Carlos did." Jax's voice hardened. "I knew they wouldn't do anything." His gaze slid to Emma. "For our kind, help's never really been too forthcoming, has it?"

"*You* looked for him," Emma said.

Jax inclined his head. "Turned up fucking nothing, but you know what I did see? In my back room, some dick had tagged the place."

"You're next." Emma's voice was certain. "That's what the tag said."

"Yeah, fucking prick move. When I saw that, I knew Wayne had been taken."

Just like Julia. So that made two victims . . . three, counting Lisa. *Emma can't be number four.* "Anyone else?"

"A stripper named Sandy Jamison. She owed me some cash, so when she didn't turn around for her payment, I went looking for her." His fingers stopped tapping on the bar. "Sandy spent most of her time in that little motel down the road, paying for a room each week. There was fresh paint on her motel-room wall when I got there . . . seems some kids had spray-painted the place. Or, at least, that was what the dumb-ass manager thought."

"But by then, you knew better," Dean said flatly. *Another victim.*

"The cops wouldn't even give Sandy's case a second glance. I mean, why would they? So a twenty-two-year-old stripper skips town. Big fucking deal." No emotion was in Jax's voice. "People disappear into this town every day."

"Only some days," Emma noted as she pushed back her hair, "they have help." Her voice was soft with sadness.

Jax held Dean's stare. "Sandy and Wayne are dead."

He was afraid they were. "The cops were searching the area where they found Julia, using cadaver dogs to see if any other remains were out there." And, according to the text that he'd gotten from Wade, they'd made a discovery. Just *who* they'd found, well, that wasn't known yet. They'd need Victoria for the identification.

"Someone has been hunting down here, in *your* territory," Emma told Jax.

"Yeah, I got that." Now anger clipped in his words. "But I've been watching, looking for folks who damn well don't belong." His brows lifted as he pointed toward Dean. "This asshole with you is the first one to stick out."

"That's because the man we're after doesn't stick out," Emma explained quickly with a shake of her head. "The first time we saw him, the guy was pretending to be a homeless man."

Jax gave a low whistle. "And you didn't nail him from first glance?" He took a step toward her. "What's happening, Em? Letting your talent slip? Once upon a time, you could've read a mark from a hundred feet away. You always let me know when the undercover cops were watching. One of your many . . . talents."

"I'm rusty, okay? I'll be more aware next time."

He grunted. "That's what happens when you spend your days in the square, telling people what they want to hear."

Her cheeks flushed. "Really, Jax?" Anger sparked, tinting her cheeks a faint red. "You're going to stand there and judge me?"

Another step had the tattooed jerk way too close to her. "Yeah, I fucking am. You know where you belonged, and you left. You walked out that door, and you didn't look back. Now you come around here, thinking I'm going to help you and this bastard"—his gaze cut toward Dean, then back to Emma—"this bastard who looks at you like you're his—"

She is. The thought—basic, primal—surged through Dean.

"Then think the hell again. I told you what I know. Now you can get out." He motioned toward the door. "Don't let it hit you on the ass."

The guy was such a prick.

He was also a waste of Dean's time. But maybe Carlos wasn't. Because he could see the rush of conflicted emotions on the other man's face. Dean pulled out his card. Put it on the bar near Carlos, and said, "If you think of anything else, call me. My team will look into these two disappearances, and we'll see what we can discover."

Jax's laughter was mocking. "Bull. You don't give a damn about Wayne or Sandy. You're just playing a part because you want in Em's pants."

What he wanted was to beat the hell out of that guy. With an effort, Dean kept his gaze on Carlos. "If he's hunted here before, he may be back. He'll blend, just like Emma said. Hell, he could even be someone you've seen before—a lot of times. You just didn't realize what he was doing." *Hunting.*

Carlos's hand reached out, and he grabbed the card.

"Let's go, Dean," Emma said, voice soft.

But he wasn't ready, not just yet.

He turned toward her and gave Emma a fast smile. "Give me just a second, baby." Yeah, that *baby* was deliberate. His hand brushed over her cheek. "I think there's one more thing left to cover."

Her eyes went wide. "You don't want to do this."

Sure, he did. Dean rolled his shoulders, preparing for what was to come. He might have to take a hit, but he'd be sure to give plenty of his own back. His head cocked as he glanced back over at a glaring Jax. "I think you need to apologize to Emma."

The fellow's jaw dropped. After a moment, Jax laughed, and said, "Are you shitting me?"

No, he wasn't shitting him. "She came here because she's worried that more victims are out there. The bastard tagged her wall, too, and left one of his 'You're next' signs—"

Jax lunged away from the bar. He grabbed Emma's shoulders and yanked her up against him. "He's coming after you?"

The guy was holding her too tightly. Again. Dean sighed. "This is why we're going to have a problem. You keep touching what you shouldn't. Keep saying what you shouldn't."

Jax ignored him and actually *shook* Emma. "He's after you?"

And that was it. Because Jax's fingers were digging too roughly into Emma's shoulders. Dean grabbed the man, yanked him back, and when Jax swung at him—*mistake, mistake*—Dean dodged and planted his fist in the guy's gut. Jax's pain-filled grunt filled the air, but the fellow didn't double over. He came up swinging again. Dean leapt back, dodging, then he went in for his own attack.

"No!" Emma yelled. "Stop it! Right now! Just *stop!*" And she was between them again. Not showing any fear, just flashing rage on her face. "We're here because people are missing. Not so you two can pound the crap out of each other."

Ah, but Emma had missed a very important point. Jax was still hung up on her. It was obvious in the way the guy kept giving her those too-possessive stares. And Dean had never been one to share. Especially not when he wanted something—someone—as much as he wanted her.

Jax swiped away the blood that dripped down his lip. "Always fun to see you, Em."

"Jax, listen, we want to help those people. And I don't want to end up missing." A harder edge entered her voice. "So put the past behind us, okay? We both made mistakes. We both—"

"I wasn't the one who walked away." A low growl.

"No." Her chin lifted. "You were just the one who made it impossible for me to stay."

Dean could tell her words had hit a nerve. Jax's stare jerked away.

"Carlos . . . Jax . . . if you have pictures of the missing,

please give them to us. If you've got family contacts—
anything that we can use, it would help," Emma pushed.

"They didn't have families. That's why they were
here." Jax's fingers were back to tapping on the bar.
"If we find pictures, fuck, yeah, I'll send them to your
guard over there." He nodded at Dean.

"Thank you," Emma whispered. Then she caught
Dean's hand. "Let's go."

His fingers curled around hers. He followed her,
making sure that his body stayed close to Emma's.

"Emma!" They were almost at the door when Jax's
voice called out after her.

Dean saw Emma's shoulders stiffen, as if she were
bracing herself, and when she turned back around, her
face reflected a bit of fear.

"You come to me, Em, if you think that bastard is
getting too close. If he's hunting you, if you're scared,
you come to me." Jax's voice was low and rumbling.
"No matter what happened before, I'd protect you."

Emma gave a quick nod, but she didn't speak. Then
they were outside. The sun was brighter, hotter, and the
people who'd been on that street before had already scattered. When they reached their car, it looked as if it was
still in one piece, and Dean opened the door for Emma.
When she slid inside, he caught her relieved sigh.

Then he was walking around the front of the car. He
looked back at the bar. Carlos was out there, watching
them.

Dean climbed in the vehicle and slammed the door
shut. As the engine growled, he demanded, "Want to
tell me what that was all about?"

"Why? You were the one throwing punches." Her

voice sounded tired. "I figured you knew more than I did."

He drove them the hell away from that bar. From the corner of his eye, he saw Emma lean her head against her window.

"Why didn't you go to him for protection?" She'd come to him, offering a deal, while Jax—

"Jax's protection comes with a price. I wasn't willing to pay that price."

His fingers tightened around the wheel. "You were lovers."

"A girl never forgets her first"—her tone was mocking—"even though she tries."

He braked. Dean recognized the emotion twisting his guts into knots. He hadn't been the jealous type before, but then he hadn't been with Emma before, either. "Why didn't you tell me?"

"Tell you what, exactly?" Her head rose and she gazed at him with glittering eyes. "That once upon a time, I was homeless, on the street, desperate? That the only thing standing between me and starvation . . . well, that was Jax? He'd just opened his bar, I'd just turned eighteen . . . I knew how dangerous he was, but I didn't care. I let him . . . protect me . . . then, is that what you want to hear?"

No, he really didn't want to hear another damn thing about the guy.

"I got tired of being hungry. Got tired of being scared. Jax offered me a roof. Money. Some time to get on my feet, but too late, I realized the strings that were attached." She glanced down at her hands. "Jax doesn't let go easily."

Neither do I.

"And in case you were wondering, most of the activities that go on in his bar aren't exactly legal."

Was he supposed to be shocked by that?

"Jax can hurt people, too easily. I don't . . . I don't like that. And I wanted to be *more*." She pushed back her hair. Pointed straight ahead. "The light's green, Dean."

Right. Hell. He shoved his foot down on the gas.

"I know you don't think much of my . . . readings. But I wasn't breaking any laws with them. I wasn't hurting anyone." Her shoulders rolled in a small shrug. "And I could look at myself in the mirror every day. I had my own place. My own money. Someone like you wouldn't understand what it was like for me."

There was hurt in her voice. She thought he was judging her. Had he? He reached out. Grabbed her hand. Brought her knuckles to his lips and pressed a quick kiss there.

"D-Dean?"

"I didn't like the way he looked at you." Like he'd had her and wanted her again. Endlessly.

The way I want her.

"Jax has a reach and power in this city that we can use. I needed to talk with him. We found out about the two missing—"

"Yeah, I know we had to see him." Knowing didn't mean he liked it. "But he's an asshole, and I don't trust him." Especially around Emma.

"That makes two of us." Her voice was so soft he had to strain to hear it. But then she cleared her throat, and said, "I do trust you."

His back teeth ground together.

"I don't trust many people, but you're different. You're not like Jax. Not like anyone else I've ever met. I think you really do want to help people and not just use them."

They drove in silence. Soon, more familiar parts of the city were coming into view.

"Does it change anything?"

He fired a quick glance her way.

"Knowing I was on the streets, knowing my past— does it change anything for you?"

He braked at another light. Turned to face her fully. Their gazes held. There was fear in her eyes, and he didn't like that. Not one bit. So she'd been homeless. So she'd had to con, had to lie. "It makes me want you more."

Surprise had her lips parting.

"You're a survivor, Emma. You're strong. You're determined. You're fucking sexy."

Her gaze fell.

A car horn honked behind him. The light had changed, but he didn't rush forward. Screw the honking car. He caught her chin in his hand and lifted her head back up. "Nothing about you is going to turn me off, do you understand that?" He wanted her so much that the need seemed to consume him. It wasn't natural, it wasn't safe, and he didn't care.

"Yes," she whispered.

"Good." Then he freed her. He drove forward, and Dean didn't mention that his protection came with a price, too.

I won't let her go.

Because when a man found something he needed as much as Dean needed Emma, he held tight.

THEY BRAKED IN front of Emma's apartment. She looked down and realized her hands were shaking. Yes, well, some trembling fingers were to be expected—especially after facing Jax again.

If the devil lived and breathed and walked the streets of the Big Easy, well, that devil would be Jax Fontaine.

Once upon a time, she'd mistakenly thought he was her hero. After living on her own for nearly three years, she'd found her way to New Orleans, only life there hadn't been any better for her . . . *Until Jax.*

She'd known him before the tattoos. Before he'd started crossing the line and *breaking* that line more and more.

Yes, once, she'd actually thought he was the man who was going to save the day for her. Too late, she'd realized he was trying to bring her down into hell with him.

So she'd left him. She'd saved herself.

One day at a time. Moment by moment.

Don't look back.

She opened the door before Dean could do it. Dean . . . so very different from Jax, no matter what her ex had been trying to imply.

Dean had called his team on the way over. Talked to someone named Gabe and given him all the details they had about Wayne and Sandy. Dean had checked in at the hospital, too, but there had been no change in Julia's condition.

Not yet.

She wasn't better, but she wasn't worse, either.

Emma hurried toward her building. "I need to get things cleaned up here. Sorted." Because she wasn't going to keep spending her nights at Dean's hotel, as tempting as that was. This place was her home, and she wouldn't lose it. "Go check in with Wade." Because she knew he wanted to see if the cops had learned anything else, and apparently, Wade was the connection to the New Orleans PD. "I'll keep my doors locked. I'll be totally safe until we meet up later."

He followed her into the building. On the stairs, she was reminded again of just how big the guy was. He seemed to surround her as they headed to her apartment. "I'm not leaving," he said from behind her, his words a rumble that rolled right over her skin, "not without doing a sweep at your place."

So he was definitely in guard mode. Fine by her. A sweep sounded good.

She inserted her key in the lock. Hesitated. Her mat was back in place. But it wasn't in the right place. The cops must have moved it a bit when they'd been doing their evidence collection.

"Emma? Is something wrong?"

Maybe. Maybe not. She opened the door, slowly, nervously.

And . . . the place was clean. New furniture. Shiny, too-expensive furniture. No wreckage on the floor. Some of her art, the pieces that hadn't been smashed beyond recognition, were even in place once more.

She hurried into her bedroom. The place smelled like fresh paint. And those stark, glaring words weren't on her wall any longer.

Emma whirled toward him. "You did this."

He shrugged. "LOST did it. I might have . . . borrowed your key, though."

The sneaky son of a gun. "When?"

"Last night. Don't worry. Every member of the cleaning team was thoroughly checked out, and I sent a guard to keep an eye on the place while they were here." His voice was too bland when he said, "It's not a big deal."

It was to her.

He shrugged again. Nervously? "There are special agencies that come in after crimes like this one. They just make it easier for people to get their lives back in order."

She glanced around her bedroom. There were new pillows. New covers. Covers that were the same dark blue shade she'd had before. "Who paid for this?"

When he didn't answer, her gaze zeroed in on him again.

He glanced toward her window. "LOST."

He was such a liar.

"You're working for LOST now, as a consultant, anyway, and Gabe wanted to show his appreciation."

"Gabe?" That was the name that she kept hearing pop up.

"Gabe Spencer is my boss. He's the man who founded LOST."

She filed that bit away for later. "Gabe didn't do this."

He took a step back. "I assure you—"

She reached out to him. Not to kiss, him but to hug him. "Thank you."

His hands settled—a bit slowly—around her shoulders. "You don't need to thank me for anything." Now his voice was gruff. "I told you, LOST did this."

When he lied, his voice went a bit deeper. He probably didn't realize he even had that tell. She wasn't about to reveal it to him. "Well, tell LOST I'm grateful." And if she hadn't drained her bank account, she'd be paying LOST back.

She eased away from him and stared up at his face. His expression was so hard to read right then. "Dean—"

A knock sounded at her door. Emma couldn't help it, she tensed. No one ever came to visit her there, mostly because she wasn't exactly the social sort.

Dean stalked toward her door.

"Hold on!" Emma called out as she tried to settle her nerves. Of course, it wasn't Ricker at the door. Bad guys didn't usually knock and wait politely while you opened the door.

Dean put his eye to her peephole and swore.

"Who is it?" Emma whispered as she tried to push the guy out of her way and get a look herself. And when she did get a look . . . "That's the FBI agent." Kevin Cormack. "And Wade's with him."

She fumbled with the lock and opened the door.

Kevin's expression was grim. "Ms. Castille? I'm afraid that I need you to come with me."

"What? Why?"

Wade flashed a look ripe with guilt over at Dean.

Kevin crossed her threshold. Kept his eyes on her. The guy managed to look—somehow—both determined and a bit apologetic. What was up with that? "We know the killer is targeting you, and for your own protection, you're going to be taken into federal custody."

Dean was ominously quiet beside her. That was fine. He could be quiet. She had plenty to say. And that plenty started with . . . "The hell I am."

CHAPTER NINE

SHE KNEW THE DEAD. MOST DAYS, VICTORIA Palmer thought that she understood the dead far more than she did the living.

Sure, the dead kept secrets. Just like the living did. But it was usually much, much easier to uncover the secrets the dead kept. The living were far too good at lying.

"I appreciate your cooperation on this case," FBI Agent James Elroy said as he stepped closer to the examination table. They were in the coroner's office—back in the exam rooms. The coroner had been fast to wave Victoria toward the remains. He'd looked a bit green when he did it.

And for something to make a coroner turn green . . . *this case isn't going to be easy.*

"I'm happy to help," Victoria said as she pushed up her glasses, just a bit. She hadn't gotten a good gauge on Agent Elroy yet. The guy was holding back, watching her with cold eyes and seeming to monitor her every move.

"We need to know the victim's identity." Elroy sounded a bit pompous, a little too bossy, but she knew that was the way with many FBI types. Sarah would, no doubt, be profiling the guy if she were there. But the dead, the remains—those weren't Sarah's department. Victoria was the forensic anthropologist, and when Gabe, her boss at LOST, had told her to hop a plane for the Big Easy . . .

Well, she hadn't exactly been expecting this.

We're looking for a serial killer? They didn't usually look for killers at LOST. They looked for the victims who'd been taken.

The coroner, a doctor who appeared to be in his mid-thirties and had identified himself as Dr. Bryce Armont, opened a vault and pulled out one of the slabs.

He started to unzip the black bag on that slab. Only . . .

That bag looked small.

"We have to see if this is one of Ricker's victims," Elroy continued. "We need the age, the sex . . . we need a damn name, so we can see what we're working with here."

Dr. Armont finished unzipping the bag. Yes, he was definitely green, and the guy's fingers were even shaking. When Victoria saw the remains on that table, she understood why.

It looked as if the animals had gotten to those remains. "There's not much to go on," she said, even as pity welled within her.

"You're supposed to be the best!"

Wait, had he just gone there? Victoria's hands rose to her hips, and she jerked her gaze up to meet his.

"Wade Monroe said you were the one we needed. I called my superiors at the FBI. They backed you."

Yes, well, she'd certainly worked enough cases with the FBI over the years. Enough to know . . . *I hate working with you guys.* What a bunch of arrogant asses—

"If you can't do it, then we need to get someone else

in here who can handle this job." He pointed toward Dr. Armont. "Seal it up, we'll get—"

She grabbed his hand. "There is no one else. I am the best."

He glared.

Victoria glared back. She knew better than to let a guy like him push her around. "I'll learn everything I can, but you need to stop expecting miracles. There's just not a lot to go on right here."

Through gritted teeth, Agent Elroy said, "I need to know if Ricker killed him, or if this is just some poor SOB who met his end some other way in that swamp." He leaned closer to her.

She wasn't even sure they were looking at a "him" just yet. "Let me do my job." *But don't expect miracles.* She'd been serious with that warning. There was only so much she could do.

"You're familiar with Ricker's work?"

She dropped his hand. "Familiar enough." Actually, after she'd met Dean, Victoria had made it a point to learn everything she could about Ricker. So maybe she shouldn't have pried in the lives of her friends, but she did. Mostly because she had a need to uncover secrets. Kind of a compulsion.

I have to trust the people I'm around. After what Victoria's father had done to her mother, she was always hesitant around people. Always worried she'd fall for a lie.

"I need this information yesterday, do you understand?"

She understood plenty. "Then you'd better let me get started," Victoria said as she reached for her gloves.

And she focused on the dead.

Unlike the living, the dead never lied to her.

THEY WERE TRYING to take her away from him.

Dean didn't move a muscle as he felt the anger surging inside him. He'd suspected this would be the FBI's move, and he'd tried to take steps to stop them.

"I'm not going anyplace with you," Emma said flatly.

His breath eased in and out slowly as he glanced over at Wade. The guy was looking seriously guilty. Hell. *What have you done, man?*

"Do you want to be taken by him?" Kevin asked Emma, his voice cold. "Because if the information I have is correct, it's only a matter of time. You need to realize Jared Ricker has killed over a dozen people. Their deaths weren't easy. He tortures his prey, enjoys their suffering."

Emma seemed to pale. Dean slid closer to her.

Kevin and Wade had stepped into her apartment and shut the door. And Kevin was inching a little too close to Emma right then.

"Has Dean told you about the other victims?" Kevin pressed. "About how we found them? About what Ricker did to them?"

He hadn't because he hadn't wanted to make Emma even more afraid than she already was.

"Ricker killed my friend, Lisa," Emma said quietly. Her hands had twisted in front of her. "He put a knife in her chest in the middle of a busy square. I found her. I think I can quite understand what he's capable of doing—"

"He was merciful with her." Kevin's statement curtly cut her off. "Probably because he never intended to focus on her. She was just in the way."

Emma went even paler then.

Dean surged forward. "Stop."

What could have been sympathy flashed across

Kevin's face. "You think I like reliving this shit? But she has a right to know what she's facing. *You* should have told her instead of trying to use her."

Use her? The hell he was. His hands fisted, but before he could say anything else, Wade was in his path.

"We made a deal, okay?" Wade was *definitely* looking guilty. "Victoria is down at the coroner's office right now. Our team is supposed to be cooperating fully with the FBI's task force."

And he was just learning about this shit *now*?

"We all want the same thing," Wade pushed. "To stop Ricker, right? To find him and to stop him *before* he hurts anyone else."

Yes, dammit, of course that was what he wanted. Did they seriously think he wanted something to happen to Emma?

"He drugs his victims first," Kevin said. The guy just wouldn't stop talking. "To make them weak, easier to manage. Then, when the drugs wear off, that's when he really gets started."

Emma backed up a step.

"He uses his knife. Slices them."

Emma glanced down at her hands. At her scars? And she immediately shoved her hands behind her back.

"He lets them bleed out for a while, he enjoys hearing them cry out." A stark pause. "At least, that's what the FBI profilers thought. Until Julia, we didn't have a victim—other than Dean there—who could tell us what hell those poor souls suffered."

"Enough," Dean snarled. The guy could stop terrorizing Emma.

"No, it's not enough," Kevin came toe-to-toe with

Dean. "Because I was there, remember? I saw you at
that cabin in the mountains. I know just how enraged
you were. I know how personal this is. You want Ricker
because that bastard nearly beat you. And you always
had to win, right?" His voice dropped. "Every case, you
had to prove that you were the best. That you could
catch the killers. But you didn't catch him, and I know
that's been eating you alive."

"You're one to talk," Dean gritted out. Because when
it came to the cases, Kevin had always been just like
him. Until the end.

"Rules are in place for a fucking reason," Kevin
snapped. "You didn't get that." He turned toward
Emma. "It's time to leave, Ms. Castille."

Emma shook her head. "I think you missed the part
where I said I wasn't coming with you."

Kevin's eyes narrowed on her. "And I think you
missed the part where I said you didn't have a choice."

"No." Dean caught the edge of fear in Emma's voice.
"You can't just . . . take me. I'm a U.S. citizen, I have
rights—"

"You're a material witness."

No, she wasn't.

"And you're being taken into federal custody." Kevin's hand curled around Emma's shoulders. "Later,
you'll thank me. This really is for your protection."

"Sorry, man," Wade muttered. "Didn't know it was
going down like this."

Kevin was leading Emma toward the door. She cast a
frantic glance toward him. "Dean!"

"Dean will be cooperating with the task force,"
Kevin assured her. "Once you're at a secure location,

I'll contact him. You'll see him again. Don't worry, that was part of the deal."

A deal that Dean had *never* agreed to. "Emma . . ."

Wade was still at his side. "If you want to stay in the FBI loop"—his words were low, warning—"we have to play ball. You know that."

But Emma was afraid. She was staring back at him with big, lost eyes. She'd just gotten back to her apartment. *And now she's being taken away?*

"We know the names of two others who were taken," Dean announced. Maybe if he shared, then Kevin would back the hell off. "They're our leads. We can track them and learn more about Ricker's activities in New Orleans."

Kevin and Emma were at the door. Kevin hesitated and glanced back. "You always were fast when it came to tracking."

"*Emma* is the reason I know about those two. She's working with us. She's not meant to be shoved in a safe house someplace!" They all needed her.

But Dean shook his head. "It's not my call to make." Elroy. Fuck.

"I'm not going." Emma backed up. "I'm not—"

"You can come out willingly," Kevin told her, "or you can come out in cuffs. There are two New Orleans police officers outside your building. They're waiting to make sure you leave with me."

And something happened then. As Dean stared at Emma, all of the emotion wiped from her face. Her gaze became shuttered, her expression completely unreadable.

Oh, hell. "Emma . . ."

She glanced at him. He missed the emotions in her stare. He missed—

Emma smiled, and her dimples flashed. "Don't worry. It's just for my protection."

No. That smile was *wrong*. It was her fake smile. One that said she was about to cause trouble. One that said danger in big, flashing letters.

"Don't take her." He grabbed Kevin's arm. "We can work something out. We'll all help you to find Ricker—"

"This isn't a damn debate!" Kevin's voice dropped. "I don't want it this way, either, but you know how Elroy gets. He's running the show. He wants her in custody. Brass is leaning on him, and he can't afford to lose her, not with the media attention that's going to be coming this way."

Dean knew the firestorm would ensue as soon as word spread that Ricker was back in action.

"I'll get her to one of the FBI's safe houses," Kevin continued gruffly, "and we can go from there. It's all part of the deal we worked out with LOST. She's covered, and we'll be working together."

A deal Dean hadn't brokered.

Kevin glanced back at Emma. "Are we doing this easy? Or hard?"

"Lead the way," was all she said. Such a change from her first words to Kevin.

The hell I am.

Dean knew she was just biding her time. If the FBI agents didn't watch her carefully, she'd vanish at the first opportunity. Then she'd be on her own out there, with Ricker waiting to attack. *And what would I do then?* "Keep a guard on her," Dean said, the words sounding too harsh to his own ears.

Her shoulders stiffened.

He hated to say it, but he had to protect her. "She's going to be a flight risk."

Her gaze cut to his. Still no emotion. Not a single drop in that bright gaze.

I'm sorry, Emma, but I want you alive. And until he could figure a way out of this mess, her FBI guards would have to keep her safe.

Her smile came again. Those perfect dimples winked. "Oh, Dean," she said with a sad shake of her head. "You don't know me as well as you'd like to think." She shook her head. "Lock up when you leave, would you? I'm rather tired of uninvited guests."

Then she left, with Kevin following closely behind her.

She left, and watching her walk away was one of the hardest things he'd ever done.

"Dean . . ." Wade sighed. "I'm sorry, man. We didn't have options. You'd told me that taking down Ricker was priority, and with your past, I know how much you want to see that bastard caught. I thought I was doing the best thing. For you. For her."

Don't punch your friend in the face. Don't punch your friend in the face. "I was keeping her safe." He had to get out of her apartment. Because everywhere he looked, Dean saw *her.*

He stormed out, with Wade following closely. Dean locked the door, just as she'd ordered. When she came back, the place would be perfect for her. She'd have her haven again.

Dean started down the stairs. Maybe he was going so fast because he wanted to see her, just once more, before Kevin took her away.

"He told me about Charlotte."

Charlotte. Not a place, a person. A woman that Dean had known so long ago. He whirled toward his friend. "Emma isn't her." He forced his back teeth to unclench as he said, "And I don't know what bullshit Kevin told you, but I didn't risk Charlotte." Her image flashed through his mind. Pretty, petite Charlotte Brown. She'd been an FBI informant, a woman who'd used her innocent looks to get close to a very dangerous crime family. When she'd wanted out, Charlotte had turned to the FBI. He and Kevin had been assigned to her case. And Kevin . . .

He'd fallen for Charlotte.

"She died."

"And I did everything I could to prevent that." He shook his head as he glared at Wade. "You know better than to believe any BS that you're told, even if that BS is delivered by the FBI."

"I didn't say I believed him . . . I said I had to get us an in with the task force. You're the one who said Ricker was the priority, or has that changed?"

He spun away. Hurried down the rest of the stairs. And he got to the street just as a cop car pulled away from the curb. Emma was in that car, in the backseat, like she was some kind of criminal.

This is wrong. "I have to get her back."

"You're a tracker, Dean. That's what you do best. You need to be out there, looking for Ricker. The FBI can protect her. It's win-win."

Not for Emma, it wasn't. He couldn't take his gaze off that car. "But we had a deal."

He and Emma. They were . . . partners.

"We had a deal," he said again, and Dean knew he *would* be getting her back.

"YOU'VE GOT QUITE an interesting history, Ms. Castille."

The FBI agent was with her in the back of that patrol car, sitting a bit too close and getting on Emma's nerves. But she didn't let him see her rising fury; instead, she turned her head, lifted her brows, and said, "Been researching me, have you?"

His gaze drifted over her face. Kevin Cormack was a handsome man even if his features were a little too rough. Maybe some women liked that dangerous edge. Maybe some women thought that his eyes were deep. Brooding.

She didn't give a crap about them. She just wanted out of the car. So even though she appeared to be staring at the agent, she was also taking careful note of her surroundings so she could see just where this safe house was going to be.

"I'm sorry about what happened to your father."

Ah, there was just the right amount of sympathy in his voice. If she hadn't been so furious, maybe she would have softened toward him.

But she didn't.

"And I know you thought siding with Dean Bannon was a good idea, but you put your trust in the wrong man. I'm just glad I was able to get to you in time."

The car turned right. "Excuse me?"

"Did Bannon tell you why he was forced out of the FBI?"

This was the first news she'd had about Dean being forced out of anyplace. "I know why he left."

"He's lucky that Elroy agreed to let him anywhere near the task force. You can't go all Lone Warrior when you're part of a team, and when people keep dying because of you . . ." His hands were fisted. ". . . then it's time for you to get out of the game."

The emotion that had just broken through the guy's words was real. "You don't care much for Dean."

"Once, he was my best friend."

Best friends could make for the most vicious enemies. Her gaze slid from his. They were nearing the cemetery, she could see the tall vaults rising over the stone wall on the left. Emma swallowed. "My . . . my friend Lisa is being put to rest today." She drew in a shaking breath as she glanced down at her watch. "The services will be starting soon, and I-I wanted to tell her good-bye. Before we left, before the safe house . . ." Emma reached for his hand. "Can we stop just a moment? Please?"

A tear slid down her cheek. It wasn't faked. She damn well hurt when she thought of Lisa, but she also wasn't about to be shoved into some safe house with guards she didn't know from Adam. The last time that an FBI agent had been close to her—well, her father had been in a body bag, and the agent had been blaming her father.

Dean was an FBI agent, too. A nagging voice had to remind her of that.

But Dean was different. Or at least, she'd thought he'd been different. *Ex-FBI.*

Kevin's gaze softened as he stared at her. "We'll stop, but just for a few moments, okay? I . . . heard about the attack. I can only imagine how hard it must have been, to find out that your friend died in your place."

She didn't just hurt. Emma felt as if a knife had been shoved straight into her heart. "Yes, it was hard." Her voice was wooden. She could only hope that the agent hadn't been fully briefed on Lisa—or rather, on her funeral arrangements. Because Lisa wasn't being buried there at all. The arrangements for Lisa were still being put in place.

"Pull up to the curb," Kevin directed the driver. "We're making a pit stop."

Emma drew in a shuddering breath. "Thank you." Once in the not-too-distant past, she'd done a stint as a tour guide at this particular cemetery. She knew all the twists and turns inside those walls.

She knew the perfect places to hide. Vanishing there wouldn't be hard at all.

Emma hurried from the car. The sun was glaring down on them, and she lifted her hand to shield her eyes. "Thank you," she told him again. "I'll only be a moment—"

He caught her wrist. "You don't think I'm letting you go alone?"

She'd hoped he would.

Kevin shook his head, the sun glinting off his blond hair. "We go together, Ms. Castille. That's the point of having FBI protection."

He was going to be a problem.

He bent near the driver's side window. "Keep an eye out, okay? I'll go in with her, and we'll be back in a bit."

That just wasn't going to work for her. Emma hunched her shoulders and headed through the old gates. As usual, there were plenty of people milling around in the cemetery, especially near the entrance, and that was good news for her. Maybe Cormack thought those folks weren't just tourists, maybe he'd believe they were there for the funeral service.

The funeral service that *wasn't* happening.

Emma hurried inside. With every step she took, Emma moved a bit faster, faster. She headed toward Marie Laveau's tomb. Once she got there, vanishing would be a snap.

But his hold on her wrist was unbreakable.

Too tenacious. She'd give the guy credit for that. But he hadn't counted on a woman like her.

People were up ahead, and the path narrowed. Excellent.

"Emma, where's your friend's tomb?"

Lisa doesn't have a tomb here.

"We're almost there," she lied without hesitation. "Her family's area is to the left." Bullshit, bullshit, *bullshit.* They were almost to the group of people on the path. Emma jerked hard to the left. There wasn't room for the agent over there with her, and if he kept holding her wrist, he'd block the others from passing by. She was hoping the guy's good manners would win the day.

Drop your hold. Let them pass. Drop your hold—

He did.

And Emma lunged between the crypts.

"Emma!" He roared her name, and she knew he was giving chase. Too bad for him. Too terribly bad because she knew this place better than she knew the back of her hand. She snaked to the left. To the right.

Rushed by another tour group, then—

There. The crypt that the tour guides had nicknamed the Vampire Den. It was an ancient place, with rusty chains in front of the door, a sad attempt to keep folks out. But with the height of vampire love a few years back, couples had started going in that place like crazy. If you just slipped under the chains . . .

Like I just did.

And grabbed the door, then pulled it *up* and *to the left* . . .

The door creaked as it opened, and Emma leapt inside.

The tour guides had grown used to pulling vamp-crazy teens and college kids out of that crypt. Nothing was in there any longer, not even a casket. Just cobwebs. Dust.

She pulled the crypt's door shut again, narrowing the small bit of light that spilled through. Emma didn't shut the door completely, though, because she didn't want to get sealed inside.

"Emma!" Agent Cormack's voice blasted from a few feet away. Emma tensed and barely dared to breathe. He was far too close. Right outside the crypt. Had he heard the creaking of the door?

"Emma, I was trying to help you!"

By taking her away from the life she knew?

"Emma!" But his voice didn't sound as close now. He was moving away. She finally took a deep breath for her oxygen-starved lungs.

Emma stared at that small crack of light. The idea of rushing back outside—oh, it was tempting. But he'd still be out there. She had to wait. Bide her time.

Slowly, carefully, she crouched until her knees touched the old, stone floor. When she inhaled, she could smell the dusty scent of the place and the faintest hint of . . . decay?

Emma sat down on that floor, her head falling forward. Her heart was racing far too fast in her chest, galloping like mad, and the burst of adrenaline in her body had her fingers shaking. She'd done it, though. She'd gotten away from the FBI. Now she just had to take a few minutes and figure out what the hell to do next . . .

Other than, of course, hide in a tomb all day long.

SONOFABITCH. KEVIN CORMACK whirled around. People were everywhere in the damn cemetery—slipping back and forth through the tombs. So many people, but where was *she*?

Because he couldn't lose Emma Castille. Elroy would have his head if Kevin didn't bring that woman back. Securing her had been priority one for him.

He ran ahead. Looked to the left. The right. Shit. This was bad. So bad. After the mess-up in Quantico, Kevin had been kicked back to a field office in Louisiana. This was his first chance at the big leagues again because Elroy had sent specifically for him. If he screwed up, there would be no second chances.

As quickly as he could, Kevin made his way back to the front of the cemetery. When he burst out of the place, he immediately saw the two uniformed cops. One was standing near the front fender of the patrol car, one was slumped inside. "Did you see her?" Kevin barked.

They jerked to attention.

"Emma Castille," he barked. "Did you see her come out?"

The two looked blankly at each other. "Uh, isn't she supposed to be with you?" the younger cop asked.

Such an asshole response. "If she were with me," he snarled back, "you'd freaking *see* her." He stabbed his finger toward them. "Don't let her pass, got it? She's in that cemetery. If she tries to come out, you stop her."

"Yes, sir!"

He nearly snarled again. Those two bozos weren't paying attention to anything. Emma could have already gotten out, and they wouldn't have known.

Kevin whirled around and rushed back into the cemetery. Hell, he'd made a rookie mistake, too. Just like them. He'd bought into the act that Emma fed him. She'd blinked those big, tear-filled eyes at him, and he'd done exactly what the woman wanted.

Gritting his teeth, Kevin yanked out his phone. Dialed Elroy. When the boss answered, Kevin told him, "We've got a problem."

EMMA INCHED TOWARD the faint beam of light. It was time. She needed to make a break for it and get the hell out of that cemetery before the agent wised up and started searching the tombs. Because if she didn't move soon, that place wouldn't just be a hiding spot for her.

It would be her prison.

As silently as possible, Emma rose. She'd already mentally plotted out her escape from the cemetery. She wouldn't make the mistake of going out the front gate, not with those cops there. But she knew of a crypt near the far right wall, one that had an angel statue near its base. She'd climb up that crypt and be able to jump over to the wall. Then she could climb down, piece of cake. She just had to *get* there first, undetected by Agent Cormack.

Step one . . . be prepared for your exit.

Agent Cormack would remember what she'd had on before. Lucky for Emma, she was wearing a light camisole under her shirt. She ditched the outer shirt and suddenly—*new outfit*. If someone was just scanning over her, for a fast instant, the change of clothes might fool the onlooker. Then she ripped her discarded shirt. Got just enough fabric for a tight, little strip, and used it as a makeshift ponytail holder. Again, it was just a small change. But a small change could fool a person . . . *for a few moments, anyway.*

Emma squared her shoulders. This was it. She'd have to walk fast. And luck would definitely need to be on her side.

Step two . . . get out of the crypt.

Her fingers curled around the door. She pushed it away from her, opening it a few more precious inches. Emma winced, sure that creaking sound was far too loud, but there was nothing she could do about it. Then she shimmied her body through that narrow opening. The sunlight hit her full force, and Emma had to blink quickly so her eyes could adjust.

Then she looked over to the right—

A boy was there. Maybe ten, eleven years old. He was staring at her, his mouth open in apparent shock. *Oh, right . . . a woman just walked out of a locked-up tomb.* No one else appeared to have noticed her. Just the boy. Emma put her index finger over her mouth in the universal sign for silence.

The boy's mouth snapped closed, and he hurriedly backed up. He bumped into his mother, and she glanced down at him. "Sweetie, what is it?"

Emma didn't wait around to hear the boy's explanation. She rushed through the maze of crypts, moving fast toward her destination.

Step three . . . don't get caught.

So far, she seemed to be home free. There was no sign of Agent Cormack. He wasn't—

There.

Emma jumped back and immediately flattened her body against the side of the nearest tomb. She counted to ten, and then, slowly, she peeked around the corner. He was gone. *Yes!*

So she shot away from the wall. A few more twists and turns, and she was in front of the little angel statue that she remembered so well.

Step four . . . use the statue to climb to the top of the crypt. Then get the hell out.

She put her foot on the statue. Grabbed for its head with her hand. *Sorry, angel!* Then she heaved herself up.

Hard hands locked around her stomach. "I don't think so . . ." The voice was low, grating.

Terrifying.

Emma tried to jerk away from that hold, but it was too strong. He yanked her back down, and she would have fallen straight to the ground if it hadn't been for his steely grip. Jeez. Agent Cormack was being too rough. So she'd tricked him, so she'd—

"Our fun is just about to begin," her captor rasped in her ears. *"Told you . . . you're next."*

She started fighting then, frantically struggling to turn around so that she could see the man who held her, but he now had his hand fisted in her hair. He lunged forward quickly, that one still hand in her hair while the other locked around her stomach, and he rammed her head into the stone wall of the crypt.

Emma didn't even have a chance to cry out.

The sickening thud of her head hitting that crypt was the last sound she heard.

CHAPTER TEN

W HAT THE FUCK DO YOU MEAN . . ." DEAN DE-
manded, his voice low and lethal as fury
surged inside of him, "you . . . *lost* her?"

Kevin's jaw was tightly clenched. "I mean just what I
said, okay? I lost her."

They were at a New Orleans police station, in a room
the FBI had taken over with its "task force." Elroy was
sitting at the conference table, like a king at his throne,
and Dean was about two seconds away from lunging
over and beating the hell out of Kevin. "You were supposed to keep her safe!" This couldn't be happening.

"If she'd cooperated, she would be safe." Kevin
started pacing. "She tricked me. Got me to stop at the
St. Louis Cemetery—"

"Which damn one?" Dean cut in.

Kevin stopped. Frowned. "What?"

Sarah cleared her throat. She'd been sitting at the
conference table, watching the others. "There are three
St. Louis cemeteries in New Orleans."

Kevin's eyes closed. "Look, she gave me this sob
story about her friend Lisa being buried. I knew that
was the woman Ricker killed in the square. I agreed to

stop by the cemetery for a few moments, so she could say her good-byes."

Rage was seriously about to choke Dean.

Victoria eased a bit closer to Kevin. She'd been working in the morgue but had come to join their little screwed up group a few minutes ago. "Lisa Nyle hasn't been released to her family yet. She's still in the morgue."

Elroy's hands slammed down on the table. "She was tricking you."

Kevin whirled toward him. "Yeah, I get that *now*. But I thought she was legit, and stopping by the cemetery for a few minutes didn't seem like too much trouble. I didn't know she'd pull some kind of Houdini on me and vanish."

He should have known. He should have fucking *known*. "Which St. Louis cemetery?" Dean demanded once more.

"It doesn't matter!" Kevin threw his hands up in the air. "I searched. The cops with me searched. That woman is gone. She's in the wind. Hell, she probably was on her way out of New Orleans five minutes after she cleared the cemetery."

He grabbed his ex-partner. Shoved him into the wall.

"Dean!" Sarah's sharp voice.

He didn't respond to Sarah's cry. Through clenched teeth, he gritted to Kevin, "You told me that you'd keep her safe. He's out there, after her. You were supposed to protect her."

"She *ran* away."

Because she hadn't wanted to be caged. And the FBI, oh, yes, they would have caged her.

"You should have left her with me. I was keeping her safe."

Kevin glared right back at him. Voice dropping, Kevin said, "The same way you kept Charlotte safe? Because you were supposed to *save* her, too, weren't you?"

He'd fucking tried.

Sarah's fingers curled around his shoulder. "Dean, let him go. This isn't the way a task force cooperates."

No, hell, no, it wasn't. He was no idiot, but Emma was *missing*. How could they not all be panicking? "He could have her already," Dean rasped. He hadn't let Kevin go.

Kevin shook his head. "She left on her own. Trust me, I know this."

That was the problem. Dean didn't trust him. And he knew Kevin felt the same way.

"Let him go, Bannon," Agent Elroy barked. "We don't have time for your shit right now."

And he didn't have time for theirs. Dean stepped back. "Where was the cemetery located?"

"Near the interstate, okay? It's the one with the voodoo queen." Kevin's cheeks flushed a dark red. "Look, I should have been more cautious, okay? Should have realized it was a scam, but I know Baton Rouge, not New Orleans. A woman is crying, telling me her friend is being buried at that place, so I felt sympathy, and I let her stop." He shook his head. "I didn't know she was going to run."

Dean spun on his heel, but he didn't get to go far because Sarah was in his path. Sarah with her intense stare and her carefully expressionless face.

"We need to compare notes," Sarah said. "I've been trying to work up a new profile on the killer."

"I'm finding Emma." Because *that* was what mattered right then. Guilt had been gnawing at him ever since she'd walked out of that apartment with Kevin. And, now, to find out that she was somewhere in that city, alone . . . *hell, no.*

The door opened. Dean glanced over Sarah's shoulder and saw Wade standing there. Wade, the guy who'd orchestrated this little task-force screwup. Yeah, Dean wanted to discover what data the FBI had, but . . .

Emma matters more. Knowing that she was safe. Finding her and getting rid of that terrible, pained betrayal that had been in her eyes. "They fucking *lost* her," he snarled to Wade.

Wade blinked, then frowned. "What?"

A chair squeaked behind him. "It's a good thing . . ." Elroy's snapping voice told him, "that your new job enables you to find the *lost*." That last part was sneered.

Dean glared at the guy.

Elroy waved to the door. "By all means, try to find a woman who chose to run away. See if you're really better than the FBI. And while you search aimlessly for her, we'll be here . . . or rather, we'll be hunting for the man who kidnapped and nearly killed a sixteen-year-old girl."

"You were supposed to protect her," Wade fired as he glared at Kevin. The same rage that Dean felt seemed to vibrate in his words. "That was the deal. I *told* you that she was on the killer's list. You were supposed to guard her—"

"You can't guard someone who runs away!" Kevin shouted.

Screw this. Until he could get some reassurance that Emma was all right, Dean knew he would be useless on the hunt for Ricker. He eased around Sarah. "I'm sorry," he murmured to her. "But I have to find Emma."

Because the twist in his gut was just getting worse.

He stalked out of the room, his mind spinning through search options. He'd start at the cemetery. See if there were any signs of her, then he'd—

"Maybe she doesn't want you to find her."

Wade's voice stopped him.

Dean glanced back over his shoulder. Wade was standing in front of the conference-room door. As Dean stared at his friend, two uniformed cops slipped into the room. They were all heading for the briefing, he knew that. Once upon a time, nothing would have kept him away from a briefing about that bastard Ricker.

But . . .

Emma.

"I saw the way she looked at you before she got in that patrol car, man," Wade said as he came closer. His expression was grim. "That woman was pissed at you. So after she gave old Kevin in there the slip, I sure don't see her rushing to call you."

"Because she thinks I turned my back on her."

"You didn't have a choice."

Dean's laugh was bitter. "We always have a choice." He'd just made the wrong one. He started walking again.

"So what are you going to do . . . search the whole cemetery? She's not there any longer."

He kept walking.

"If she's got friends in the area, you should check in with them first."

An image of Jax's face flashed through his mind.

"Maybe she turned to someone else, someone who could keep her safe."

I learned how to save myself.

"Dammit, Dean, I thought this was what you wanted! I know what he did to you. This is your chance for payback. Ricker is in the city. We have solid leads. The FBI is closing in."

Yes, once, he had wanted this. He'd wanted to see Ricker tossed in a cage and locked away for the rest of his miserable life.

But . . .

His hands fisted at his sides. "I want her more."

And that was all there was to say.

SHE HURT.

Groaning, Emma opened her eyes, but there was only darkness around her. A thick, complete darkness.

Pain rolled through her in waves so intense, she thought her head was going to explode. She lifted her hand, and when she touched the left side of her head, she felt the sticky wetness of blood.

"Dammit," she whispered. She was kind of foggy on a few things . . . like where the hell she was, but she remembered being in the cemetery. Trying to get *out* of the cemetery. But she hadn't made it out because someone had caught her.

She probed the wound at her head and hissed out a pain-filled breath. Yeah, someone had definitely caught her.

Her hand moved away from her wound. She was lying down, so she needed to get up and figure out where she was.

Emma sat up, moving slowly, and her head *hit* something before she'd even lifted more than a few inches.

"What the hell?" Now her hands were up. Patting the

area around her. Something hard was right above her. Like . . . stone.

Her breath heaved out faster. Her hand flew to her left side. Touched more rough, hard stone.

Emma knew she was lying on the stone, she could feel it beneath her, and, with fear knifing through her, she reached out to her right—

But she didn't touch stone then. She touched a soft cloth. She reached over a bit more. The fabric was around something. Something long and hard. Something that curved a bit in places. Fumbling in the dark, now both of her hands were flying over this new discovery. She reached out, touching blindly and felt—

Oh, God.

There were sharp edges beneath her fingers. When she moved her hand, she could have sworn that she was touching . . . teeth. Because there were several of them, very distinct, as if—as if she was touching a person's open mouth.

Long and hard. Fabric . . . fabric wrapped around . . . bones?

And my hand, my hand is in a mouth?

Emma screamed then, as loud as she could. She screamed because terror was clawing right through her.

Stone was all around her. A skeleton was beside her.

She'd been trying to get out of the cemetery, but the killer had caught her. She hadn't escaped, not at all.

He'd put her in one of the tombs and locked her inside with the dead.

THE BAR WASN'T empty this time. There weren't just two motorcycles in front of the place—there were easily twenty. Music pumped, filling the air, and bodies spilled outside the place.

Dean pushed his way through the crowd. A glance to the left showed a half-naked woman sliding up and down the stripper pole. A group of men were cheering her on.

To the right, he saw Carlos standing near a door marked "Private." Carlos had his arms crossed over his chest, and the fierce look on his face said he'd take no shit from anyone.

Good, cause Dean wasn't in the mood for shit.

He marched right toward Carlos. The guy saw him coming and stiffened.

"Where is he?" Dean demanded.

Carlos cast a quick glance toward that closed door. "He's in a meeting right now."

"I need to talk to him." Because if Emma hadn't come to that guy, then Dean didn't know where she could have gone.

Unless Ricker has her.

He slammed the door shut on that thought.

Dean had already wasted hours searching at the cemetery. Night had fallen, and he'd turned to this place— Emma's old haunt—hoping to find her.

Carlos put his hand on Dean's chest, blocking him from advancing. "You don't want to go in there now, amigo. Just sit at the bar. I'll send him to you soon."

"I don't have time to waste." Not when it came to Emma. "I'm looking for Emma."

And then . . . he saw it. The faint widening of the guy's pupils. A quick, guilty glance toward the closed door.

A dead giveaway.

She's in there.

"Move the hand," Dean ordered.

"You don't want to go in there—"

Too late, because Dean had already kicked in the door. The sight before him had Dean snarling and leaping forward.

A woman with long, dark hair leaned over Jax. She was naked from the waist up, and that hair—shit— "Emma!"

The woman laughed even as Jax swore.

Her laugh had Dean stumbling to a stop because . . . that wasn't Emma's laugh.

"We'll be done soon," she said, and she glanced back at him. Her face was similar to Emma's, but . . . rounder. And her eyes were smaller. A warm brown shade instead of Emma's brilliant blue. "But not . . . *too* soon."

Dean had to shake his head. This had better not be what the fuck it looked like.

It looks like the asshole gets off on screwing women who look like Emma.

"What the hell do you want?" Jax demanded. He still had his arms around the woman who was very much *not* Emma. "I'm busy."

"I'm looking for Emma."

Jax narrowed his eyes on Dean. "She's not here. Obvious-the-fuck-ly. Last time I saw Em, she was running out of here with you."

Dean whirled away and started pushing his way back through that crowd.

"Wait!"

No time for that. *Emma isn't here.*

He shoved the bar's door open and headed back outside. The moon was rising, a full moon that made the dark sky look all the more ominous. His heart was racing too fast and hard in his chest, and the uncomfortable knot in his chest—yeah, Dean knew that knot was fear.

Did you vanish on your own, Emma? Or did he take you?

Had Ricker been watching Emma's apartment? If he had, the guy could have followed her and Kevin to the cemetery. When Emma broke away from the FBI agent, Ricker could have seized his chance to take her.

"Stop, dammit!" Jax's voice blasted him about two seconds before the guy grabbed Dean's arm and spun him around. "Where is Emma?"

"If I knew," Dean threw back, "would I have come to you?"

Jax's eyes shot pure fury at Dean. "I thought you were keeping her safe."

"The FBI took her into protective custody." He should have stopped them. He *never* should have let her out of his sight.

Dean had worried about his control. He'd worried that Emma pushed him too close to the limits of that control.

He'd been wrong. Without Emma . . . hell, he had no self-control. With every moment that passed, his fear grew worse. His fear and his rage, and they were mixing in a deadly combination because he couldn't stop imagining her out there, hurting.

Being hurt.

Tortured.

While he did nothing to help her.

"If the FBI has her—"

"They don't." He rolled back his shoulders, but that did nothing to relieve the tension racing through him. "She gave the agent the slip in the St. Louis Cemetery. That was hours ago. Unless you're lying to me"—and he actually wanted the guy to be lying—"then no one has seen or heard from her since then."

Jax's face hardened. "You think that bastard hunting out there—you think he took her?"

Yes.

"What can I do?"

Dean shook his head. He didn't think he'd heard right—

"What? You think you're the only one she's ever gotten to? What. Can. I. Do?"

Dean swallowed. "We need to check with other friends she has in the area. See if she's contacted any of them. See if she's hiding with them."

"Emma doesn't have other friends. Just Lisa."

And she'd lost her.

"I already called the crystal-shop owner," Dean said. "She hadn't heard from Emma."

Carlos was walking up behind Jax. The guy's expression was grim, and Dean could see the worry in his eyes.

"You know Emma's old hangouts," Dean said. "Maybe . . . if she's running, she could be looking for someplace familiar. Maybe she's just pissed at me and trying to run to somewhere that makes her feel safe."

"Emma doesn't have places like that."

Yes, she did. *Her apartment.* Or she had felt safe there—before that bastard came in and wrecked the place. But Dean had tried to fix it all for her. Only

Emma hadn't gotten to enjoy her home, not before the FBI had swooped in.

"I don't know that Emma has ever felt safe." Jax looked down at his hands. "She sure didn't with me." When his hands clenched, the tattoos across the backs of his fingers seemed to darken even more. "But I'll send out my people. They'll hit every damn place I can remember her staying."

Dean nodded. "Thank you." Later, later he'd punch the guy's face in for that shit he'd seen in the back room. *The fixation on Emma has got to go.*

But right then, he needed Jax's help.

He needed all the freaking help he could get.

No ONE COULD hear her screams. That was obvious. She'd screamed until her throat hurt, and no one had come to help her.

Screaming wasn't helping. And . . . what if she only had a limited amount of air?

Emma was already close to hyperventilating as she lay trapped in the stone coffin—*is that what this is? Some kind of stone coffin? It feels that way.* She'd shoved up with her hands again and again, but she couldn't get the stone above her to move.

Emma tried to hold her body totally still. The sound of her breathing was far too labored around her. She had to calm down. She had to *think.*

Then she felt it. When she was totally still. The faintest stir of air near her left thigh. Emma reached down, slowly, tentatively. Her hand touched the stone and . . . the hole there. One that she could poke her fingers through.

She might have sobbed then. A hole meant air, right? She wasn't going to suffocate.

Of course, you're not going to suffocate. Ricker has you. And Agent Cormack said that Ricker keeps his victims alive. He tortures them.

She didn't want to be tortured. Emma didn't want to die. And Emma knew that if she didn't get out of that prison, she would die. Because Ricker had stashed her there, no doubt because too many tourists had been around. He'd thrown her in that tomb, and he'd left her . . . until he could come back. Probably in the middle of the night, when he thought no one would see him. He'd come back for her then. He'd take her away. Then the real hell would begin.

Her fingers fumbled in the hole again. He'd put her in that prison, so that meant there had to be a way out. She just had to find it. And she wasn't going to find it by panicking.

Emma pulled her hand back up. She shoved aside the skeleton. *Don't think about it! Don't!*

Then she tried to twist her body. Pushing with her arms hadn't helped, but she did some kickboxing at least twice a week. A girl had to stay in shape.

Emma lifted up her legs. She braced them against the stone over her head.

She shoved.

And not a damn thing happened.

So she shoved harder. With her hands. With her legs. She pushed on that stone.

And not a damn thing happened.

She screamed, but this time, the sound was filled more with fury than fear.

DEAN WAS BACK at the cemetery. The place was supposed to be closed for the night, but screw that shit. The cemetery was pretty much his only link to Emma. He was going to search that place. Again and again, because he would find her.

"Dean."

That was Sarah's voice. He wasn't particularly surprised to find that she'd tracked him. But when he glanced over, he saw she wasn't alone. Victoria was with her. Wade was there. And, hell, even Gabe Spencer was there.

He hadn't realized the LOST boss was in town.

"What can we do?" Gabe said simply.

Dean pointed to the cemetery. The gates were barred to them, but they'd just jump over those gates. "This is where Kevin saw her last."

And that was what the LOST team did. They retraced the steps of the missing. They searched. They found. They had to view Emma just as they viewed the others.

Someone they *would* find.

The cops weren't looking for Emma. The FBI wasn't looking. They thought she'd run away.

They also had believed that Julia had run away until the LOST team had found her.

"Ricker could have already taken her away," Sarah said as she turned on the flashlight she held, "but we can look for clues. There are always signs left behind."

The others turned on their lights. They'd all come prepared.

Dean glanced down at the flashlight in his hand. He didn't know what the fuck was happening to him. All he could think about was Emma. Getting her back.

Was this what it had been like for Gabe? He knew the other man had lost his sister. Amy had been taken from him, and Gabe had moved heaven and earth to find her when the cops had given up.

But Gabe had found her too late. He'd only recovered Amy's body.

Gabe's hand slapped down on Dean's shoulder. "You know Ricker doesn't kill his victims right away."

"He killed Lisa Nyle right away." And that hadn't fit. Not with the way Ricker worked. Or *had* worked. "He's changed." That change was obvious to Dean, and when he saw Sarah nod, he realized that she thought the same thing, too. They weren't facing the same killer. Ricker had evolved, transformed into something else.

"You have to keep hope," Gabe said. "Sometimes, it's the only thing you have."

And when you lost hope, what then?

The team moved forward. The locked gate was no impediment to them. In moments, they were inside the cemetery. Their lights swept over the area.

"Maybe he kept her here," Sarah said as she walked ahead of the group. Already thinking like a killer, that was Sarah. "He wouldn't have been able to drag her out, not in the middle of the day. This place would have been tourist central then."

Dean had thought the same thing. That was why he'd gone back and checked there first, only he'd turned up nothing.

Then he heard voices. Low. Muttering. Adrenaline spiked through him, and he shot forward. His light bobbed as he raced into the darkness, and—

Candles. Dozens of them. They surrounded a tomb

that was etched with red Xs. About five people were kneeling in front of that tomb, whispering still and ignoring Dean completely.

"Marie Laveau," Victoria said as she huffed to a stop behind Dean. "I heard her tomb was here though I'm not sure if the lady herself is actually buried there." Her light swept over the scene. "I think a lot of these old tombs are actually empty."

And that was *it*. He caught her hand in his. "Which ones?"

"Uh . . ."

"We need to figure out which ones are empty." Because if you were going to stash someone, wouldn't you put her in a place that *wouldn't* be visited by folks? A place that was empty?

"I-I don't know which ones are empty. I just . . . remember reading that online someplace." Victoria's voice was weak. "I'm sorry."

"We should look for older tombs," Sarah said, obviously catching Dean's suspicions. "Ones that haven't been kept up. Broken doors. Broken windows. Families would make repairs to places like that. Ones that have just fallen . . . well, those are the ones that might be empty. If no one is inside, then there is no family to care what the place looks like."

Now they were getting someplace.

"Wade, you come with me," Sarah said. "Dean, you and Victoria and Gabe can search one-half of the cemetery, and we'll take the other half. We can cover more ground that way."

The people in front of Marie Laveau's tomb were still muttering. Dean thought he saw one man push a coin forward, sending it near the base of the crypt. He reached out and touched the man's shoulder.

The guy whirled toward him.

Dean's flashlight hit the fellow's face. A college-aged kid, from the looks of him, with short, red hair and eyes that currently looked terrified.

"Have you all seen anyone else out here tonight?" Dean demanded.

The guy shook his head.

"Heard anything? Maybe from one of the crypts?"

The redhead laughed then. "Are you kidding me, man?"

Dean kept the light on him. The guy's laughter slowly faded away. "N-no, we haven't heard anyone."

Dean pushed him away.

The other LOST members were waiting for Dean. He knew he had to get a grip. He had to get the job done. Emma was out there, and she was counting on him. He couldn't let her down. Not again. He felt like he'd already failed her once before.

Not this time.

Old crypts. Broken doors. Broken windows. They'd search all night long. If she was there, they *would* find her. He wasn't going to give up on Emma.

"Let's do this."

And they got to work.

Dean knew the law. They all did. They couldn't just break into sealed tombs. But tombs with doors open . . . with windows that gave them access so their flashlights could sweep inside and look for Emma, hell yes, those places were all fair game.

He searched. His gaze swept into dark crevices, into

tombs covered by dust and time. He called for Emma. They all did. Their calls seemed to echo around him as he kept looking for her.

Emma had to be close.

At least, he hoped she was.

If Ricker had already taken Emma away . . .

IN THE MOVIES, people were always strong enough to get out of buried coffins. They were clever enough to escape from any prison or trap that the bad guy set up for them.

She wasn't in the movies.

And no matter how hard Emma strained, she couldn't get the stone to move. She was trapped there, with the skeleton. A prisoner, for however long that bastard Ricker wanted to keep her there.

Tears were on her cheeks. Her voice was hoarse from crying out. Since she'd found that small space for air, she'd been screaming again. If air could get in, then her voice could get out, right? Only . . . maybe there was no one out there to hear her screams. If night had fallen, the cemetery could be empty.

Smart folks knew to stay away from the cemetery at night. Criminals lurked in the shadows. And it wasn't like a man with robbery on his mind was going to come rushing to her rescue.

Emma pulled in a long, slow breath. *Focus.* She just had to think this through. There had to be a way out. Because she wasn't going to let Ricker win. Dean had escaped from him. She could, too.

Dean.

She'd thought of him too much in that darkness.

Where was he? Had Kevin told him that she'd escaped? Was Dean looking for her? He wouldn't just give up on her, would he?

She knew he was hunting Ricker, so surely—surely he'd be looking for her, too.

Or had everyone given up? Did they just think that she'd run away, vanished on her own?

In New Orleans, Ricker had picked prey that other people wouldn't miss. The invisible people on the outskirts of society. The homeless. Runaways.

Me.

She had no family. Her only friend was dead. Who would notice if she never showed up in New Orleans again? Who would grieve?

No one.

"Help . . ." Her voice came out too weak.

She'd saved herself before. When she'd gotten out of the life on the streets. When she'd worked to build a home. *"Help."* Her voice was a bit stronger. She couldn't give up. She wouldn't give up. Emma craned her body, twisting, until her mouth was right in front of that hole. *"Help!"* She'd scream until she had no voice left.

She'd fight until she was broken.

She would *not* give up.

"Help!"

DEAN PAUSED IN front of the statue. It was a white marble statue, of an angel bent over, with her wings curling near the ground. His light slid over her, then moved to the crypt right beside her. The crypt backed up close to the stone wall that surrounded the cemetery. If you wanted to, you could climb up on the angel, jump on the roof of that crypt, and make it right over the cemetery's wall.

If you wanted to . . .

But he wasn't looking for an escape path. He was looking for Emma.

Emma would have been trying to escape. She'd ditched Kevin, and she would have been attempting to get out of the cemetery. Only she wouldn't have gone back to the main gate. Kevin had been accompanied by two cops, and Dean figured those cops had been given guard duty at the front of the cemetery. So Emma wouldn't have fled that way. She would have tried to get out in a manner that wouldn't have caught the attention of the cops.

"I found something!"

Dean whirled, and his light hit Wade. Wade was holding up a blue shirt, soft, billowing.

Dean took two fast steps toward him. "Emma was wearing that shirt."

"Yes." Wade's voice was grim. "I thought she was. It's been ripped, torn, and—"

"Where did you find it?"

"In a crypt not too far from the voodoo queen's. I noticed the doors were open a bit. I pushed inside and found the shirt." Victoria stood silently behind him. "But nothing else was in there. Just this."

A torn shirt. No Emma.

His control splintered even more.

Emma!

His temples were pounding, the blood rushing too fast and hard through him. He had to find Emma. He needed—

"Help!"

Dean's whole body jerked at that cry, as if he'd been hit by lightning. Then he immediately surged to the left. Not back toward the crypt with the kneeling angel but the crypt beside it. A darkened crypt that appeared newer than the others. The front doors were immense, painted black, and, when he yanked on them, completely sealed shut.

They were supposed to be looking for crypts that had fallen into disrepair. But . . .

"Help . . ." That cry came again. Muted, distorted, but giving him so much wild hope.

He leapt back from the black doors. The others had fanned around the crypt. They'd all obviously heard that cry.

"The windows aren't broken. Everything seems sealed," Sarah said quietly.

"I think there are some loose bricks over here," Wade called out. "But I can't get in this way. There's not enough room."

The loose bricks had let them hear her call.

His eyes narrowed on the doors. "We're kicking the fucking doors in."

Wade and Gabe rushed back to his side.

Sarah and Victoria were right behind him.

They attacked that door. It had been locked, barred to them, but they were *getting* in.

The doors seemed to buckle beneath them, but they didn't open. So they hit it harder.

The doors flew open as the lock shattered.

"Help!"

Their lights swept the area. Dean saw a bench near the wall and a big, stone sarcophagus in the middle of the crypt. When his light fell on the sarcophagus, he saw . . . fingers poking out the side.

"Get it the fuck off her!" Dean snarled as he lunged forward. He grabbed the top of the sarcophagus and heaved. Wade, Gabe, Sarah, and Victoria all heaved too, and the stone flew up—then it hit the floor and shattered into fat chunks.

Then Emma was rising up, seeming to fly right out of that prison. The lights hit her, and Dean could see the blood and tear marks on her face. She was frantically trying to scramble out of the sarcophagus, and she was still saying, "Help, help, *help* . . ." Over and over, in a rasping voice.

Dean grabbed her. Held her tight. She was shaking in his arms. He was shaking. "It's okay," he whispered as he lifted her into his arms. "I've got you. You're safe."

"Help . . ."

She was breaking his heart. Odd, he hadn't even thought he'd had a heart to break. Not anymore. Not until her.

"I've got you," he told her again. *And I won't let you go.*

"Bastard locked her in with the dead," Wade said, voice packed with fury. "Twisted freak."

Emma shuddered in Dean's arms. "I'm getting her out of here," he said, aware that *his* voice was shaking. So were the hands that held Emma.

He looked back, down, and saw that one of the flashlights was aimed into the interior of that sarcophagus. The light glinted off the skeletal remains, stark white in tattered clothing.

He turned away from those remains. Held Emma as carefully as he could. Then they were out of that crypt.

The moon was above them, and Emma had a death grip on his neck.

"Dean!" She wasn't crying for help any more. She was back with him.

He kissed her. Soft. Light. Desperately. She'd just scared the ever-loving hell out of him, and he never wanted to go through that nightmare again.

"Emma, baby, I've got you." And he needed to get her to a hospital. He'd seen the blood dripping down from her head and sliding over her face. A doctor needed to check her out.

"I didn't see him." Emma's voice was hushed. "He caught me . . . right before I was going to leave the cemetery." Her hold tightened on him. "He shoved my head into the side of a crypt."

Fucking bastard.

"I-I woke up in there." Another long shudder shook her. Dean was already moving. Still holding her tightly and heading back toward the front of the cemetery. She was getting to that hospital, *now*. Sarah was a silent shadow beside him. The others were still in the crypt. They'd call in the cops, the FBI.

His priority was Emma.

That's my priority from now on.

Everything had changed for him. Every single thing. He rushed past the group still at Marie Laveau's tomb.

"S-someone was in there with me," Emma confessed. "In the stone coffin. He put me in there with someone."

One of the college kids at Marie's tomb screamed.

Dean ignored them. He and Sarah moved faster.

"I couldn't get out." Emma's voice was haunted. "No matter how hard I tried." Her voice was husky, so weak.

He kicked open the gate at the cemetery's entrance. Busted the lock. Didn't let her go.

Sarah hurried ahead and opened the passenger-side door of Dean's vehicle.

"I-I was going to . . . be like the others. He put me in there, and everyone was just going to f-forget I ever existed. No one was even going to . . . look for me."

He sat her down on the seat. The car's interior lights shone on her, and damn, but she probably had a concussion. The blood had matted in her beautiful hair, and her tear-filled eyes wrecked him. "I was looking. I wasn't going to stop." Not ever.

She wouldn't have been lost to him. He wouldn't have been able to handle losing her. As it was, Dean felt as if something had torn inside of him. Ripped open.

There is no control.

The darkness he'd always tried to keep in check was loose. Ricker had dared to attack Emma, to hurt the one person that Dean had come to need the most.

I just found her, and that bastard tried to take her away from me.

He hooked the seat belt around her. So carefully, not wanting to do *anything* that might hurt her. Emma wasn't moving. She was far too malleable, too listless. *Not* Emma. He caught her right hand. The knuckles were bruised, bleeding. A glance at her left showed they were the same way. *She tried to fight her way out of there.*

Dean brought her hand to his lips. He pressed a kiss to that delicate skin. "I would have looked forever." Because he never could have given up on Emma.

Her lips tried to lift then, curving the faintest bit. "Starting to . . . care?"

He wasn't starting to. He was in over his head. Drowning, and he never wanted to come up for air. He kissed her knuckles again, and said, "He's a dead man."

Dean wasn't going to let Ricker stay out there, hunting, waiting for another attempt on Emma's life. Emma wasn't going to be the next victim.

You are, Ricker.

Because Dean was going to hunt him. He wouldn't stop, not until he'd put the bastard in the ground.

VICTORIA STARED DOWN at the bones.

"What a nightmare," Gabe said from beside her. "You wake up and find yourself alone with . . . *that*."

Trapped in the darkness. For all purposes, buried with the dead. Yes, that was a nightmare. Torture at its core.

"He must have been planning to come back for her," Wade said. He was on the other side of the sarcophagus, and when Victoria glanced up, she saw that his gaze was locked on the bones. Her light showed the revulsion on his face. "He stashed her here, with *him*, and left her because he thought he'd be able to take her without anyone knowing."

Maybe . . .

Gabe backed away. "I can't get a signal in here," he said, "I'm going outside so I can call the cops and get Elroy's task force out here."

The task force that hadn't wanted to search for Emma.

"Ricker is one sick sonofabitch," Wade muttered.

Victoria bent over the remains. She didn't have her gloves with her, so she couldn't touch those remains but . . .

Something about this scene was nagging at her.

Sarah was the one who figured out the motivations for the killers.

Victoria—well, her job was the dead.

Something is off here.

Her light slid over the skeleton. It had been pushed, shoved to the side. No doubt by Emma during her struggles. "There are no flowers here," she said as she glanced around. "No flowers. No dust."

And there were plenty of tombs that Emma could have been put in but . . . *there weren't plenty that had a stone sarcophagus like that. A perfect one to keep her prisoner.*

The man who'd abducted Emma had specifically chosen this place. He'd specifically planned for her to be placed in that sarcophagus with those remains.

She leaned forward a bit more. Since the skeleton had been moved, she could see more of the actual bones— the old clothing had shifted a bit. Her eyes narrowed as she looked at the right shoulder bones. The markings there . . . on the humerus and the scapula . . . they looked like . . .

"He was shot." She'd have to examine more, but that wound appeared to have been close to his heart.

She let her light slide over more of the remains.

It looked as if he'd been wearing a green shirt, faded, but definitely a masculine cut. Brown pants. Hiking pants?

And those were definitely hiking boots at the bottom of that sarcophagus.

Her heart raced even faster in her chest.

"We need to get these remains examined." Her gaze

flew to Wade. *"Now."* Because her gut was clenching with a new suspicion, one that she wouldn't be able to confirm until she ran more tests but . . .

The left pant leg was torn. No, not torn. A hole was there, right at the knee. A very small, very specific sort of hole—the type she usually saw on clothing that had been penetrated by a bullet. *The dead man had been shot in the leg.*

"This body was staged." This wasn't some guy who'd been in there forever. The crypt itself was too new. And he damn well hadn't decomposed so fast that only bones were left behind.

It's all deliberate. The clothing. The bones. The tomb.

Emma.

"He wasn't coming back for her," Victoria said, and that part made her even sicker. If they hadn't found Emma, if someone hadn't heard her cries, would she have slowly starved to death? "He wanted us to find them, just like this."

Because the killer had wanted to send a message to them. No, not to the LOST group. Not to the FBI.

To Dean.

Wade came around the sarcophagus. His shoulder brushed against hers. "What are you seeing that I'm not?"

It was too early to say with certainty. She *couldn't* give voice to this suspicion until she'd done her tests but . . .

Victoria didn't think they needed to hunt for Ricker any longer.

She thought she was staring at the killer's remains.

CHAPTER ELEVEN

DEAN DIDN'T LEAVE HER SIDE. THE DOCTORS poked her, they probed her, they told Emma that she *had* to stay the night at the hospital and . . .

Dean stayed.

His jaw was clenched too tightly. His gaze looked too wild, and when he held her hand, his grip was too hard.

She didn't care. She wanted him there, wildness and all, because it was all Emma could do to hold herself together. Every time her eyes closed for even a moment, she found herself back in that stone coffin. Back with the bones. Screaming helplessly when she thought no one was coming.

They had to stitch her head. Shave a bit of her hair there and put in four stitches. The doctors kept telling her that the scar wouldn't be noticeable. She could just part her hair on the other side and *blah, blah, blah.*

Emma didn't care about scars. She cared about being alive.

And she cared about that bastard Ricker being caught.

"Okay, honey," the nurse—a bubbly woman who appeared to be in her late fifties—said as she patted

Emma's shoulder. "You're all set for the night." She pointed toward the remote on the nearby tray. "If you need me, you just hit the call button."

Emma nodded. She needed to be alone right then. No, not alone, but just with Dean. Because Emma was afraid she was close to shattering, and she didn't want to do that in front of anyone but him.

He'll understand.

She didn't even know why the hell she thought that.

He didn't give up. He found me.

The door closed behind the nurse.

Emma's lips were trembling, so she clamped them together.

"Don't." His order came out as a low growl. "Don't try to control anything. You want to yell? You want to cry? Then do it, baby. Do anything you need." He was right beside her bed. "I'm here, and if you want to pound my face for letting you go, if you want to do *anything* . . . please, just do it." He eased out a shuddering breath. "But don't hurt in silence. I-I can't handle that."

Then he bent, and he pressed his lips to her. No one had ever kissed her quite like that. As if she were breakable. As if she were infinitely precious.

"I couldn't find you fast enough. I'm so sorry."

A tear leaked down her cheek. "I didn't think anyone was going to look for me."

He pulled back then. The tenderness on his face seemed at war with the sudden anger in his eyes. "You thought I'd just let you vanish?"

"You let me go with the FBI."

He flinched, and she wanted to pull her words back. "I'm a fucking idiot. My priorities are in place now, you can count on that. From here on out . . ." His fingers squeezed hers. "You can count on me."

She wanted to smile for him, but she couldn't. Emma felt exhausted, bone-weary. She just wanted to close her eyes—but she was terrified to do so.

I don't want to go back to that place. I don't want to remember the feel of bone in my hand. Touching teeth in the dark.

"I was looking for you." His voice was so deep. "The LOST agents were looking. Jax—he had his people tearing up the town for you, too."

He'd pulled in Jax?

"And I need to call him," Dean muttered. "And let him know that you're safe." He pulled away from her. Reached for his phone.

He took two steps from the bed, seeming to head for the door.

"Don't." The desperate word slipped from her, and Emma hated that weakness, but it was there nonetheless. *Is this what he did to me?* "Don't leave me alone, not just yet."

More of that dark anger flared in his eyes. "Baby, I'm not leaving you again. Count on it." He came back to her. Squeezed her fingers lightly and held the phone to his ear with his left hand. She didn't even know when he'd gotten Jax's number. Those two must have sure gotten cozy while she—

No.

"She's at Midway Infirmary," Dean said. "She's concussed, but the doctors say she should be fine." His gaze cut away from hers. "No, we didn't find Ricker." A faint pause. "Hell, yes, that sounds good to me."

She wondered what sounded good. Jax and Dean working together? That sure shocked her.

Dean ended the call. "His men are going to keep searching. They're spreading the word about Ricker. The more people who know about the bastard, the better. The FBI is trying to keep this thing under wraps, but that can't happen. We need to shut down Ricker's escape avenues. Turn him into a wanted man, a man who doesn't have anyplace to run."

He spoke of Ricker with such hatred. Such rage. She didn't have the energy for her own rage just then. "Stay with me."

He pulled a chair closer to the bed. "Nothing would take me away."

That was sweet. She knew he didn't actually mean the words, but after everything that had happened, they were good to hear.

She turned her head on the pillow, so that she could study him better. "You seem different." Emma couldn't quite put her finger on what the change was, but *something* had altered him.

"Fear can change everything."

Her voice was a rasp when she said, "I didn't think you feared anything."

"I met you." Soft. "You changed a hell of a lot for me. More than I realized."

She should try to read him. See if he was lying . . . look for those little tells but . . . she didn't want to know that he was just saying what she needed to hear. Didn't want his words to be a careful falsehood designed just to get her through the bad moments.

She wanted him to be serious. She wanted him to

care about her. More than his job. More than his revenge. More than anything.

She'd never mattered that much to anyone but her father. Wouldn't it be great, wouldn't it be so wonderful, to have someone care that much again?

Her breath whispered out, and her lashes began to fall.

"No, YOU DAMN well *can't* talk to Emma now. She's resting!"

The angry growl of Dean's voice pushed through the fog that clouded Emma's mind. She blinked her eyes, and the room around her came into focus. The room was dark, with faint light shining through the blinds. For a moment, panic seemed to flood her, then she realized—

Hospital. I'm in the hospital.

"I talked to her, okay? I asked her what she remembered." Dean's voice was close and definitely angry. She turned her head. A white curtain was attached to the ceiling, and Dean was on the other side of the privacy curtain, talking to someone at her door. "She didn't see her attacker. Ricker came up from behind her. The SOB slammed her head into one of those crypts, then he put her in the sarcophagus. She can't tell you anything else about him—"

"She's a material witness."

Emma stiffened. That voice belonged to Agent Cormack. Kevin. *I won't go with him again.* Her fingers rose and curled around the bedsheet.

"She's a recovering victim, and you are to stay the hell away from her, do you understand?" Dean's voice was still low. Still obviously furious.

"We need a description of her attacker—"

Emma sat up in the bed. She was wearing one of those paper-thin hospital gowns, and the thing was sending a draft over her back as she tried to move to the edge of her mattress. She slid down and her feet hit the floor. A very icy, tiled floor.

"Ricker wore a disguise when we saw him before," Dean snapped. "Look, Julia is awake. Sarah told me the news not thirty minutes ago. Go talk to Julia. *She* can tell you what the guy looked like when he took her. Emma didn't see Ricker—"

"It's not Ricker."

Her knees almost buckled.

"At least, that's what *your* forensic anthropologist is saying."

Emma squinted as she stared at the clock on the wall. It was nearing seven a.m. She'd been out far longer than she'd thought. She'd been so sure she'd only closed her eyes for a few seconds.

"Jared Ricker is dead," Kevin said flatly. "He's the skeleton that was in the sarcophagus with your fortune-teller."

Her hand flew out and hit the bedside tray. The remote fell to the floor with a clatter, and Emma almost followed it down. Had the nurse drugged her? What the hell? Why was she so weak?

The curtain jerked back. Dean stared at her with wide eyes. "Emma!" He hurried forward and scooped her into his arms. Carefully, he put her back into the bed.

Had he missed that she was trying to get away from the bed? She'd wanted to find some clothes and get out of that place.

"I need to talk with you, Ms. Castille," Kevin said as he strode forward.

Dean spun toward him. "Get out. Now. Emma has been through enough."

"She was with the killer! A killer we *don't know at all!* We were all operating under the assumption that Ricker was behind the crimes because you found his DNA on the coat with Lisa Nyle, but he isn't the perp. The real killer was setting all of that up. Playing with us."

A wave of nausea rolled through Emma. She didn't know if it was caused by the blow to the head or by Kevin's news. "Are you sure about this?" Her voice was raspy.

"Victoria Palmer is sure. She's the forensic anthropologist that LOST sent in, the woman who is supposed to be the best. She saw the marks on the guy's bones." He pointed at Dean. "Marks you left when you shot him on that mountain. And then she realized that the fractures she was seeing all along the skeleton were consistent with a substantial fall. Jared Ricker didn't live to escape that day on the mountain. He plunged to his death. You killed him, Dean. And now . . . someone else is out there, hunting."

Someone who knew all about Ricker. All about Dean.

"She called me on the way here and told me that dental records confirmed the guy's identity. Ricker is now on a slab at the morgue. He won't hurt anyone ever again." Kevin huffed out a breath. "But it wasn't him that we have to worry about. Not this time."

Puzzle pieces were flying in Emma's mind. She'd been put in there with Ricker because . . . "He wanted you to find Ricker's body. He knew you'd look for me, and he wanted you to know . . ." Her breath felt cold in her lungs. "This is . . . it's all about you?"

She thought back. She'd found the message in her apartment . . . *after* she'd talked with Dean. She'd first met him the day before, when he'd come to the square and asked her about Julia. Dean had gotten intimately close that day, so close that Beau had to come to her aid, thinking that she'd been having a problem with a customer.

Then the next day, Dean had returned to her. They'd met again in the square. She and Dean had gone to her apartment together that day and found the wreckage.

Now she had to wonder, had the killer found her . . . *through* Dean?

"You search for the missing." She grabbed for the covers, feeling far too exposed in her hospital gown. "Julia . . . did the guy know that her mother would contact LOST? Was this all some big game to get you down here?"

Dean's eyes had narrowed. "That's not possible. There are too many variables . . ."

"Are there?" Kevin demanded. "Because the fact that Ricker's body was pretty much freaking bow-tied for us and left with your girlfriend, well, that makes me think this killer sure as hell wanted to send you some kind of personal message. I just don't know what that message is." He stalked toward Emma's hospital bed. "I need to know everything that happened."

"I don't remember much." She lifted her hand to the side of her head. The stitches felt tender, tugging lightly on the skin. "I was about to slip out of the cemetery, but he caught me from behind. H-he slammed my head forward, into the crypt wall, and I guess I passed out then." It was all so foggy in her mind. "When I woke up, I was in that place. With the skeleton."

"How do you know it was a he?" Kevin pounced. "If you didn't see your attacker . . ."

"I heard his voice. He told me that I was next." And she had been. "It was a man's voice. Low. Rasping. He also said something about . . . fun." She couldn't recall the exact words. "The fun was about to begin? Or maybe . . . time for the fun to start?" Emma shook her head. "I-I can't remember, not for sure."

Dean had turned to stone before her.

"Had you ever heard that voice before?" Kevin asked her.

Her hands locked around the covers. "He was disguising his voice, I think. It was too low for normal. So I-I don't know for certain if I'd heard it before." And that terrified her. What if the killer had been in her life, and she hadn't known it? He'd disguised himself before, so . . . *he could be anyone*.

"And he wasn't in the crypt when you woke up?"

"I don't know." She *hated* thinking about the crypt. "I was in the stone coffin when I woke up. I don't know where he was."

"But you—"

Dean pulled the guy away from the bed. "She doesn't know anything else. Give her some space."

Kevin shot another glance her way. "I don't know what the hell is going on," he told Dean, his voice lowering so that Emma had to strain in order to hear him. "This doesn't make sense. How the hell did Ricker's remains get all the way down to the Big Easy? Did this other killer find him in the mountains? I mean, shit, what is happening?" He raked his hand over his face. "Man, this is a serious clusterfuck."

Yes, it was. "Maybe . . ." Emma began.

Both men turned at her voice.

"Maybe there was never one killer," she said softly. "If someone *had* to take him out of the mountains, then maybe someone else was there all along. Someone who knew what Ricker had been doing. Someone who understood Ricker's connection to Dean." It made sense to her.

Kevin backed up a step. "There was never any sign of a partner."

But Dean shook his head. "Did we look hard enough? I mean, Ricker was there that night. He was the one attacking me with the knife. I never thought to even check to see if another killer could be there."

Kevin seemed to go pale. "Two of those bastards? This whole time? *Two?*"

Dean crossed his arms over his chest. "The docs told us Julia would be more aware soon. You should find out what she knows. Maybe the guy said or did something that can tip us off to his identity. I mean, she was there with him for days. She must have seen his face, right?"

Kevin nodded. "I'll get her to talk." But then he looked over at Emma. "We aren't done yet. I'll be back for you."

She shivered. "I'll be here."

She was in the hospital. Where the hell else could she go?

JULIA FINNEY KNEW that she was going to die.

Sure, the machines around her were beeping steadily, the nurse had just come in to tell her that her vitals were getting stronger, and her mother, well, her mother had told her at least a dozen times that everything would be okay.

They were wrong.

Nothing would ever be okay again. Especially not her.

Her mother had slipped away. Gone to call some relatives. People who'd never given a shit about Julia when she lived in Atlanta.

She'd learned a few things in the last few days. During all of that time, when that jerk had kept her, she'd learned . . .

You don't have anyone in this world but yourself.

Julia grabbed at the tube leading to her arm. She wasn't just going to stay in that hospital. What if he came back? He'd promised her she'd go home, but she knew now that his words were a lie.

She couldn't go home again. Couldn't live with the others and pretend to be normal.

It hurt when the IV came out. When she tried to stand, she fell on her face. But Julia crawled for the door.

She wouldn't let him catch her again.

Not ever again.

"IF HE'S GOING to talk with Julia, you should be there." Emma's voice was low.

Dean shook his head. "I'm not leaving you."

Her lips twisted, but the movement was too faint to be a smile. "Give me a guard. I suspect there are plenty of cops and FBI agents running around this place. Get someone to stay with me, then *go*."

"No."

Her fingers toyed with the covers. "I want to know

what she has to say, Dean. This man—we have to stop him. Go see what you can learn. You were the one looking for her. You were the one who learned the most about her life." The intensity in her voice deepened. "You can get her to talk. I don't think Kevin can."

His brows climbed.

"I sure wouldn't tell him anything," she added a bit darkly. Then she sighed. "Look, just go, okay? I'd be in there if I could, but my legs feel like jelly. Go to her. Explain what happened to me. Get her to help us to stop him."

He looked toward the door. Hesitated.

"We have to do it," Emma pressed. "I don't think the guy is ever going to stop on his own. I get the feeling that his game . . . it's really just getting started."

He feared the same thing. Dean pulled out his phone. Called one of the few men he trusted. Wade answered on the second ring. "Where are you?" Dean asked him.

"On my way to your lady's room."

Dean exhaled. Good. Wade would keep her safe.

"Should be there in just a few minutes," Wade added.

THE MACHINES IN Julia's room wouldn't stop beeping. As soon as she'd pulled out the IV, the beeping had gone crazy. So she moved as quickly as she could, crawling, twisting, shoving herself, and she managed to get out of the room just before the nurse hurried over.

Julia flattened herself near the closest wall as the nurse rushed by. They'd moved her to a private room earlier, and she'd tried to take note of her surroundings. Her mother had been crying and telling her how sorry she was . . .

I'm sorry too, Mom. Sorry that she couldn't be what her mother needed her to be.

Julia risked a glance around the corner, then . . . she saw him.

His back was to her as he paused at the nurses' station but he was familiar. Same broad shoulders. Same deep, rumbling voice.

He'd found her.

Her whole body shuddered as she backed away. No, no, this wasn't supposed to happen. He wasn't supposed to find her like this.

She didn't want him to use his knife on her again.

A moan slipped from her.

Then a doctor walked past, blocking her view of the man at the nurses' station. She strained, trying to see him, but . . .

He was gone.

She backed away. Her bare feet curled over the cold tile. Her gown gaped open.

"Miss?"

She whirled and found a nurse staring at her.

"Miss, are you all right?"

No, she wasn't.

"Can I help you?"

Julia looked back over her shoulder. He was gone. But he'd been *there*.

"You're bleeding," the nurse said.

Julia looked down at her arm. She was bleeding where the IV had been. And her gown was wet with blood, too. Had she broken some stitches when she fell in her room?

"Let me help you." The nurse tried to reach for her.

Julia screamed and punched her. Then she was running, running as fast as she could for the stairs. She'd seen the sign for them before, when they'd moved her to the private room. *The stairs.* They would get her out of there.

She hit the door that led into the stairwell. *Up or down . . . up or down . . .*

Julia went up.

Because she knew that she was going to die.

DEAN HEADED TOWARD Julia's room, only when he got there, Kevin and two nurses were running out.

"She's gone!" Kevin said. He glanced frantically around the area. "The girl took her IV out and left!"

Dean could hear crying. When he looked inside the hospital room, he saw Julia's mother, sitting in a chair near the bed, rocking back and forth, as tears slid down her cheek.

"I want the hospital locked down!" Kevin demanded. A security guard had just run up to him. "We need to find Julia Finney!"

Why had Julia disappeared? When the guard rushed away from Kevin, Dean joined the FBI agent.

"The girl ran into the stairwell!"

Dean whirled around and saw a nurse pointing to the left.

"I tried to stop her," she said, "but the girl was panicked! She wouldn't let me help her!"

Dean and Kevin both took off running for the stairs. Dean shot through the open door. He looked down and saw—Jax?

Yes, that was Jax rushing up the stairs.

The guy's thundering footsteps seemed to reverberate through the stairwell.

"Have you seen Julia Finney?" Dean demanded.

Jax froze on the stairs. "I thought we covered this shit. You found her, remember? I'm here because I want to see her and Emma."

Kevin swore and started running *up* the stairs. They were on the third floor, so Dean didn't understand why Julia would have gone up. If she'd been looking for escape, she would have run down to the first floor.

Unless . . .

Now Dean was swearing as he took off up the stairs. Jax called out after him, but Dean didn't stop. Not then.

They flew past the fourth floor.

The fifth.

The sixth.

Then Kevin burst out onto the roof. The door flew back as Kevin raced forward. "Julia Finney!" Kevin bellowed.

Dean rushed onto the roof after him. He looked to the left. Hurried forward. Peered right. "Julia! We want to help you!" He turned and saw Jax standing a few feet away. The guy had followed them up.

But Dean didn't see Julia.

Maybe he'd been wrong. Maybe she hadn't been running up to the roof. Maybe she'd gone into the stairwell, but when she'd heard Jax's footsteps, she'd panicked and run up a flight or two. They should go down and search the lower floors for her.

He swept to the left once more, rounding a corner.

And there she was.

Julia was standing on the edge of the roof, her hospital gown fluttering around her, her hair hanging down her back and blood dripping from her hand. Julia looked like an angel right then, one poised a step away from falling.

He didn't call out to her. Dean was afraid that if he did, she might panic and slip. Instead, he took slow, cautious steps toward her. From the corner of his eye, he saw Kevin jerk to attention, and he knew his ex-partner had just spotted Julia, too. Like Dean, Kevin didn't call out. He just started inching closer and closer to her.

"Julia!" But Jax called out. His voice loud and thundering.

At that shout, Julia's body trembled, and her right foot slipped, but she didn't fall, thank Christ. She stumbled and turned her body so that she could see them. The fear on her face made Dean's chest ache. No sixteen-year-old girl should look that terrified.

No one should ever be that afraid.

"St-stay back," Julia said, voice shaking as much as her body.

Dean froze. So did Kevin. Even Jax stopped advancing.

Dean knew they had to be careful with the way they handled this. One wrong word, one wrong step, and they'd lose her.

"I-I won't go back," Julia said, as her frantic gaze jerked between the men. "Do you hear me? You won't get me again!"

"No one's trying to get you," Dean told her. "Julia, you're safe here."

She inched ever closer to the edge. Her toes were just dangling over space now. "Liar!"

"No, Julia, I'm not lying. The hospital is safe." He kept his voice low and soothing. And he crept a step closer.

"You want to kill me! You want to torture me!" Julia's voice was growing louder with every word that she spoke. "It was all a lie! I was never going home!"

"You are going home," Kevin said. He took a step forward, too. "We just want you to tell us about the man who took you."

What the hell? Dean's stare snapped to Kevin. Now was not the time to be questioning her. The girl was a step away from suicide.

"You know," she accused, as her shoulders slumped, and she looked down at the ground below. "You know everything. You just want to keep hurting me."

It looked as if she were staring down at someone below. It was obvious the girl was confused. Probably from all the drugs the doctors had pumped into her system to help her deal with the tremendous pain her body had endured and help combat infection.

"I know what's going to happen. I know why you came for me."

"Julia . . ." Dean slid forward another step. She was still looking down at the street, her attention seemingly caught by something or someone down there, so he risked another step. Another. Kevin was mirroring his movements. "We came out here to help you." He was almost close enough to grab her.

Kevin crept forward even more.

Julia glanced back at him. Her smile was broken. "I can help myself."

Emma had said words like that once.

Julia's gaze jumped to Dean. To Jax. Back to the ground below her. "You won't hurt me again."

He knew what she was going to do. Dean lunged forward even as she jumped. *An angel falling.*

"No!" Kevin screamed, and his upper body flew over the edge of the roof as he tried to grab her. *Sonofabitch* Dean snagged Kevin's legs, held tight, and stopped the FBI agent from plummeting, too.

But . . .

"I've got her!" Kevin shouted. "Hold me—pull us up! *I've got her!*"

Dean and Jax started hauling them back. As he got a better grip on Kevin, Dean risked a glance over the side of the roof. Kevin had snagged Julia's left wrist. She was dangling there, staring down, and she screamed, "You're hurting me! You can't hurt me again! I won't go back!"

Dean knew the pressure of Kevin's grip could have easily dislocated Julia's left shoulder, but there was nothing they could do. Not then. First, they had to get her back on the roof.

"I can't lift her," Kevin panted out the words, "I-I can't—"

Because his shoulder would be feeling the pressure, too.

"Dammit, Julia!" Kevin snarled down at her. "Give me your other hand." He was trying to brace his legs now to get traction. Jax was helping to hold him in place.

Her right hand lifted, but . . . instead of grabbing his hand, her nails dug into Kevin's wrist. *"Let me go! I won't go back! You won't hurt me!"*

Kevin's hold on her seemed to slip. Her body was twisting and jerking as she fought to get free.

As she fought not to plummet to her death.

Dean leaned over the roof's edge. "Julia, calm down! No one is going to hurt you. We want to help you."

For an instant, she stopped struggling. Her head tipped back. She smiled at him. "I died . . . in that swamp . . ."

Then she yanked her left arm down, hard and fast, a move that had Dean roaring and grabbing for her because Kevin's grip had loosened too much.

But Dean missed her, and Julia—Julia fell. She didn't scream when she fell. Or when she hit. Then she just was on the ground, her body like a broken doll.

People were down there, staring in horror. Doctors and nurses in their scrubs were racing toward her.

"I couldn't hold on," Kevin said, voice thick. "I couldn't save her."

Dean kept staring below. A familiar figure was down there, someone who had been watching them the whole time. Agent James Elroy was about five feet away from Julia's prone body. He eased back when the doctors tried to work on her, then Elroy glanced up at Dean.

"I couldn't hold on," Kevin said again as he grabbed for his shoulder. "Dammit, I think I dislocated it. I *should* have been stronger. That girl—"

Was gone.

Dean swallowed and forced his gaze off Julia. Blood was seeping beneath her body, and Julia . . .

I died in that swamp.

No, she hadn't. But he knew she had just died in that hospital parking lot. Died, when he'd been helpless to save her.

SOMEONE SHOVED HER hospital-room door open. The door hit the wall with a thud and bounced back, and at that sound, Wade surged to his feet, dropping the magazine that he'd been flipping through and taking a fast, protective stance near her bed.

Emma saw a man's tall, strong shape behind the curtain, then that curtain was being shoved aside. Jax stood there, chest heaving, face locked in tense, angry lines. His gaze swept over Wade, then locked on Emma. Relief flared in his gaze, just for a moment, then he gave a grim nod. "We're getting out of here." He stepped toward Emma.

Wade moved into his path. "Want to start by telling me who the hell you are?"

Jax glanced at Emma. "You're not safe here. We need to leave, *now*."

Wade tensed. A battle-ready move if Emma had ever seen one. And Jax was always a little too eager to throw punches. "He's a . . . friend, Wade. You don't have to worry about Jax."

"Yes, he does," Jax snapped right back. "If the guy is going to try and get in my way, he definitely has to worry."

There was something about Jax's voice that was just off. A hardness, a . . . grief? But Jax didn't grieve anyone or anything, at least, not as far as she knew. Emma pulled her covers closer. "What happened?"

"What happened?" His eyes glittered. "I just watched a sixteen-year-old girl kill herself, that's what happened."

She jumped from the bed. This time, her knees held her as she reached out to Jax. She had to touch him. "Julia?" *No, not her . . . please, this can't be happening!*

"She was talking out of her head. Saying that she wouldn't be hurt again. That she'd died in the swamp. And she just jumped off the fucking roof."

Wade took a step back, and she saw his face go slack with shock. "Dean—"

"He and some other guy—a guy with FBI stamped all over him—were trying to pull her up." His chin lifted. "She didn't want to be saved. She only wanted death."

Emma hugged him. Jax had wound up on the street because his mother had committed suicide when he'd been just fifteen. He'd been the one to find her. The one who worked desperately to try to save her, but it had been too late.

Far too late.

I thought we'd saved Julia. I thought we'd helped someone.

"There's nothing for you here, Em," Jax whispered into her ear. "It's not safe here. They can't protect you. *I can.* I can get you out of here and keep you alive."

The door opened again. She looked up, and Dean was standing just beyond the curtain. Like Jax, deep lines were now bracketing his mouth. His eyes were too dark, too filled with surging emotion. Anger, grief.

They'd hoped that Julia could lead them to the killer's true identity. They'd thought that she was safe.

Why did you do it, Julia?

"Let's go, Em," Jax said as he tugged on her arm. "You don't belong here with them."

That was her problem. She'd never felt as if she belonged. And standing there, looking between Jax and Dean, she could feel their pain. Both men were hurting, *so much*. She wanted to help them, but she didn't know how.

"Julia isn't in any more pain," Dean said quietly.

Those words seemed to splinter something inside Emma.

She felt Jax shudder beside her.

"Oh, hell." Now Wade sounded like he was the one suffering. *"Why?"*

"I think . . ." Dean's voice was halting. "She believed he'd come after her again. She didn't want him to have the chance to hurt her. So she just took the only way out that she could."

Jax caught Emma's shoulder in a tight grip. His fingers squeezed around her, as he said, "You think he's just going to let you go, too? I don't know what screwed-up hell this guy has planned, but you have to get away. Come with me. I'll protect you."

But . . .

Wouldn't the killer just keep hunting? Keep killing? "I want to stop him." She didn't want to run. Emma backed away from Jax. "It's not about protecting me. It's about the others out there."

"I don't give a shit about the others." He jerked his thumb over his shoulder at Dean. "You think Dean over there does, either? Hell, no, he's thinking exactly what I am. We need to get you out of here. Get you someplace safe."

Now anger stirred within her. "Because that plan worked so well last time?" She shook her head. "No, I'm not running. I'm going to do everything I can to find this guy. He's not going to just—just get away with what he did to me." *Or what he did to Julia and Lisa.* Her voice lowered. "He locked me up in a tomb, buried me, Jax. You think I'm going to walk away from that?"

His face hardened even more. His right hand fisted, the tattoos stretching tautly.

"Would you?" she pushed.

He swore and whirled away from her. Jax stalked toward Dean. "If so much as a new bruise appears on her, I'll rip apart your whole LOST team."

Then he was gone.

Silence.

Wade whistled. "That's an interesting . . . friend."

Dean slowly closed the distance between him and Emma. "He's right, you know."

"Right that you want me to vanish into some safe house?"

His hand lifted, and his fingers slid down her cheek. "Right that you are the only thing that matters to me right now." His breath shuddered out. "Too much has happened. I can't lose you."

Her hand curled around his. "You won't." Did he think she was going down without a fight? "LOST is the best, right? We're going to find him. We're going to stop him."

For Lisa.

For Julia.

For everyone that he hurt.

For me, too. Because she wasn't going to let the man give her nightmares for the rest of her life. She wasn't always going to be looking over her shoulder, wondering if she was safe. Wondering if he would be coming after her once more.

"She was so scared that she wanted to die." He pulled her closer. His forehead pressed to hers. "Promise me that won't ever be you."

"It won't ever be me," she whispered.

"I wanted to save her. I could have *helped* her." She could feel the desperate tension in his body.

"Uh, I'll just give you two some privacy." Wade headed for the door.

"She wanted death more than she wanted anything else. Because of what he did to her." Dean's hold was desperate. "She was so sure he was coming back, coming to hurt her."

"Maybe he told her that he would," Emma said as her mind raced. "We don't know what threats he made to her." But a sixteen-year-old girl didn't choose death easily.

"I wanted her to live," Dean said. There was so much grief in his voice.

She wrapped her arms around him. "So did I."

SARAH SLAMMED HER car door shut, and the clang seemed to echo in the hospital's parking garage. She'd just gotten the call about Julia on her way there. Her insides were knotting, her hands shaking, and there was nothing Sarah could do to help anyone.

Another victim . . . gone.

"You should have told us if she needed to be on suicide watch!" The angry voice seemed to come out of nowhere.

Sarah spun around. Agent Elroy was there, glaring at her. It looked as if he'd just come from the hospital stairwell.

"We could've had better guards on her!"

Sarah's shoulders straightened. "I was under the impression that you *did* have a guard on her. For Julia's safety."

Nearby, the elevator dinged. The elevator's doors opened, and a man with blond hair strode out. Sarah glanced at him, her fast gaze taking in the hard edge of his face and the swirl of tattoos on his arms and hands. When her gaze met his blue stare, she stiffened even more.

Danger. Trouble. Back away.

That warning was instinctive, elemental.

"The guard left his post for just a few moments because he needed to report in."

And the guy couldn't have reported in *while* still watching Julia?

"He didn't know she was a flight risk," Elroy said with a glare. "You never told us that she would try to kill herself!"

The man from the elevator had lingered. Sarah risked another glance at him. Her gaze swept over the tattoos on his arms once more. So many of them. Beautiful, but . . . they added to his menacing appearance.

Sarah licked her lips and made herself meet Elroy's furious stare. "I never had the chance to talk with Julia. I told you, though, victims experience a broad range of emotions after attacks, especially vicious attacks like this one. I cautioned both Agent Cormack and the local police—I told them that she would need counseling and assistance from a qualified professional as soon as possible. She wasn't going to be able to just head back into a normal life." Sarah was hardly the best choice for a counselor. She had a harder time working with the victims, mostly because it was the killers that she understood too well.

"I just saw a sixteen-year-old girl plummet to her

death," Elroy snarled. "And as far as I'm concerned, this is on you and your LOST team."

Sarah stiffened.

"Stay out of the FBI's investigation, understand? Your group is *off* the task force—"

"You know . . ." It was the tattooed stranger who spoke, the man who'd decided to just make himself comfortable watching them from the shadows. "I don't think I like the way you're talking to the lady."

"I'm an FBI Special Agent, buddy—"

"I don't give a shit if you're Santa Claus," the guy drawled, the Louisiana rolling a bit in his voice. "And I'm not your buddy."

Elroy's gaze raked over him. "Do I know you?"

"You probably should. If you don't, well, that's because you're not that good at your job." He took a step closer to Elroy. "You were supposed to be keeping Emma Castille safe, but when she vanished—*on your watch*—you didn't send men after her. You didn't do anything."

"Who are you?"

"I'm the man you should fear."

"You can't threaten an FBI agent!"

"Just. Did." He paused. "And, for the record, my name's Jax Fontaine."

The name meant nothing to Sarah, but recognition flashed across Elroy's face. The agent even took a little step back.

"I'll remember what you did . . . or rather, didn't do for Ms. Castille." Now Jax's gaze cut to Sarah. "And I'll remember what LOST did, too."

Elroy huffed and stormed away. He jumped into his

car, a long black sedan, and Sarah watched as he drove away.

And the man called Jax moved closer to her. Sarah didn't stiffen at his approach. Didn't back away. She just waited.

She knew exactly how dangerous men worked.

"I've been doing some research on the LOST agents," Jax murmured. "Hello, Sarah Jacobs."

She let her brows climb. "You know you just pissed off an FBI agent."

"Like it's the first time." He gave a her slow smile, one with a wicked edge.

She knew his type all right. A man who thought he was his own law. A man who wasn't afraid of the darkness in the life.

A man who wasn't good.

A man who might just be . . . evil?

"Ah, see, when you look at me like that, you start to give me ideas, pretty Sarah."

Caught off guard by that comment, Sarah blinked. "I wasn't looking at you as if I wanted to have sex with you."

He laughed and came even closer. "No, you were just staring at me like you wanted to get in my head." Jax shook said head. "Trust me, that's no place you ever want to be."

She believed him. "You were involved with Emma Castille." That was the only thing that made sense to her. The way he was so angry that she'd been taken, his threats to Elroy.

"Part of Emma will always belong to me." His voice was so hard and deep. "You don't just get to walk away from your past." His smile came again, and she actually felt goose bumps rise on her arms. "But you know that, don't you, pretty Sarah? You know all about the darkness of the past. The way it can sneak into you, hold you tight, and never let you go."

She didn't like this man. He was unnerving her more than convicted murderers ever had. Sarah stepped around him, moving determinedly toward the elevator.

Following her, he said, "You know killers."

Her index finger stabbed the button for the elevator, and he . . . leaned toward her. Had he just *smelled* her? He was way too close, all in her space, and she should not be feeling that strange shiver of awareness with him.

But she was.

That's my problem. There is a darkness in me, and I want things—people—I shouldn't, Sarah tried so hard to play it safe, when there was such a big part of her that wanted to run fast and hard toward danger.

"Sarah, you know it's not that Ricker bastard, right? I'm sure you are quite in the loop. You probably heard before my . . . sources . . . told me."

She wondered what sources he had—cops?

"Looks like he got what he deserved."

She turned around. Found him close enough to touch.

"Who would you peg as the killer here?" Jax asked.

This man—this stranger—was trying to get her to profile for him? "Who the hell are you?"

He flashed that devilish grin again. "Told you . . . I'm Jax Fontaine. And that killer out there made the mistake of making me very, very angry."

"You should let the police handle this."

He laughed. Hard.

Why was the elevator being so slow?

"Who is he?" Jax leaned closer to her. "Tell me who to look for." His voice dropped even more. "Come on, tell me who to kill."

Her heart slammed into her chest.

"You know you want him dead. I sure do. If you'd just watched Julia get broken like I did, you'd be begging me to hunt down this man. You'd want me to break him, too."

The doors opened behind her.

"Sarah?" Wade's rough voice. Then he was pulling her back against him. Holding her a little too tightly. "What the hell is going on?"

Jax inclined his head toward her. "I know what you want, Sarah. I think I know a whole lot about you."

"Look, asshole," Wade blasted at the guy. "Emma isn't here to run interference for you, so you need to back the—"

Jax laughed again. "My Em knows what I am, too. And she knows what I'm going to do. Guess it's a race, huh? Let's see who gets to him first. If I get there, well, there won't be anything left of the killer for the LOST agents to find."

He turned away. Walked off as if he didn't have a care in the world.

Wade jabbed the button to close the elevator. "What the fuck, Sarah? It looked like you were making out with the guy!"

No. No, she hadn't been. But they had been standing close together. Almost touching. *Making out?* "He wanted me to profile for him."

"Profile? Is that what the hell we're calling it?" And he grabbed her. Locked his hand around her wrist and yanked her up against him.

He'd never been rough with her before. Never been anything but the perfect gentleman.

"I've been right here, and you're going to slip up with some guy like him?"

What?

But then Wade glanced down at her hand. At the wrist he'd squeezed too tightly. "What am I doing?" And he brought her wrist to his mouth. He massaged the faint red marks on her skin. "I-I didn't mean to. I'd never hurt you. I—" He let her go. Turned his back on her and jerked a hand through his hair. "This case is screwing with us all."

It wasn't just the case.

She'd known for a while that Wade wanted her. But Wade couldn't understand her. He thought she was like him.

Good and whole on the inside. Someone who wanted to help others. Someone who wanted to do the right thing.

He didn't realize that she battled her own monster every single day.

The elevator was rising.

Sarah squeezed her eyes shut and tried to shove her monster far back inside of herself because . . .

I do want that bastard dead. That was her problem. All too often, she thought of death.

CHAPTER TWELVE

Her apartment didn't feel like home anymore.

Emma stood just inside the entranceway.
Everything was as it had been before—well, the new-
and-improved everything, anyway. The doctors had
kept her in the hospital for twenty-four hours, their
"observation" period. She'd been about to go stir-crazy,
trapped in that small room.

"You should get some rest," Dean said as he shut the
door behind her. Emma heard the distinct click of the
lock. Then his hands were pressing lightly to her lower
back. "Why don't you go lie down for a bit?"

She glanced back at him. "You're kidding, right? You
have to be kidding." She'd been lying down for the last
day.

But his face looked completely serious.

Sighing, Emma turned to face him. "I got a bump on
my head. The docs stitched me up. I'm fine."

He still stared at her as if he expected her to shatter
any moment. They should have been past that point by
now. "I'm tougher than this, Dean, really. You don't
need to worry about me."

His hand eased away from her. "Is it wrong that I want to keep you safe?"

"It's not wrong, but I told you before, I'm not going to be locked up." Not even for him. "Now, screw that resting crap. Tell me what I can do to help you."

"Emma . . ."

"He's still in the city. He wanted your attention. He wanted you to know about Ricker." Since she'd been in that hospital room for so long, she'd had plenty of time to think. Sure, Emma was no profiler like Sarah, but things had added up in a way that sure made her nervous. "You said that Julia's mother was the one to contact your office in Atlanta. When she came there, did she specifically ask for you?"

A furrow appeared between his brows. "Yeah, she did. Ann said someone had sent her a clipping about me and my work at LOST. She thought I could help her." His lips thinned. "That didn't happen. I didn't help her. That poor woman is trapped in hell right now."

Emma swallowed. "What if the killer is the one who sent her that clipping? What if he was putting plans in motion so that you'd get sent down here to find Julia?"

Dean shook his head.

She grabbed his arm. "Just wait, okay? *Listen.* I think this is about you. Not me. Not Julia. Not even the other victims who have vanished." Her breath rushed out again. "Maybe he started taking people that wouldn't be missed, so he could test himself. If he wasn't the killer you hunted before—obviously, not," she muttered, "then he had to train, right? Had to get it all down? So he-he practiced." God, but that sounded cold. "And he got it all down pat. When he was ready to face you, he went after

Julia. A girl from Atlanta. A girl from *your* town. Then he got her mom to contact you. You flew down here and . . ." Emma shrugged. "Everything else fell into place for him then. His game went to the next level."

Dean just stared at her.

"*Say* something."

He paced away from her. Went to stand out on the balcony. She hurried to follow him, and the warm sunlight hit her. His fingers curled around the railing as he looked down at the street below them. "I wanted you from the first minute I saw you."

Now she was surprised. She definitely remembered the first time she'd seen him. Her out-of-place agent, walking around in that crisp shirt, sweating, and looking both sexy and dangerous. An intense edge had clung to him, and, as she'd watched him from beneath the shelter of her umbrella, she'd been compelled to call out to him.

"I thought you were the most beautiful thing I'd ever seen. You smelled so good. Looked so good." Now he did glance her way. "I wanted to fucking devour you."

Okay . . .

"But I was here on a case. I was supposed to stay focused on the case, on the missing girl, and not get caught up by a pair of the bluest eyes I'd ever seen. But once I'd met you, I couldn't just walk away. I pulled you into the investigation—"

"I volunteered." She moved closer to him.

"And I put you in his sights."

Emma shook her head. "That's not true! I was already searching for Julia!"

"But maybe he would have let you go. Maybe he wouldn't have marked you if I'd kept my hands off."

"Is that what you're having to tell yourself now? You trying to put all of this mess on your shoulders?" She caught his hands. Put them *on* her. "News flash. I wanted to work with LOST. I still do. And I wanted you." Emma rose up onto her toes. *"I still do."* And she pressed her mouth to his.

DEAN BANNON HAD learned nothing.

The man was up there on the balcony. Making out with Emma Castille. Acting as if she were the only thing that mattered in the whole fucking world.

I could have killed her in an instant.

He could have left her broken and lifeless body in that crypt. Then, when Dean had finally found her—with his precious LOST friends—death would have been all that waited.

But he'd been afraid of attracting too much attention. Eventually, yes, dammit, he'd planned for Emma to wind up in that tomb. *Only not that day.* He'd planned to take her to the cemetery later, but when she'd tried her escape attempt there, he just hadn't been able to pass up the opportunity to grab her.

Dean found her too fast.

That wouldn't happen next time.

Through his sunglasses, he watched the couple. The way Dean touched her so carefully, so tenderly, you could actually think the guy loved her.

Do you, Bannon? Can you love anyone?

It would be good if the guy cared for her. Not just wanted her but *cared*. That way, her death would gut him all the more.

Dean Bannon deserved pain. He deserved to suffer.

To have his reputation, his career destroyed . . . to lose everyone he cared about . . . and then, when nothing was left, absolutely nothing . . .

Dean would die.

He pulled his cap low and headed down the street.

"No, DON'T KISS me that way." Emma pulled back and glared at Dean. "Haven't we moved past this?"

Dean blinked. Emma sounded angry with him. Didn't she understand that he was trying to be a gentleman for her?

"I'm not asking you to fuck me right here," she said.

His cock jerked in his pants. *No, settle down. She just got out of the hospital.*

"That will come later. Right now, I want you to kiss me like you want me. Like I'm the woman you wanted to devour when we first met."

She'd just tossed his words right back at him. Only she didn't get it. He pretty much wanted to devour her twenty-four/seven. He couldn't be near her and not ache, not need.

But she'd just gotten out of the hospital. He was trying to take care of her. So, yes, his kiss had been tender. His hold on her was light. He—

She licked his lower lip. "Do you think he's watching us?"

Dean jerked away from Emma. His gaze automatically swept the busy street. It was teeming with people. So many tourists. College kids. Folks of all ages. Voices drifted in the air. A horn blasted. But as his gaze jerked to the left and the right, he didn't see anyone who seemed to be paying too much attention to him and Emma.

"Because I think he's watching," she added.

He grabbed her arm and hauled her right off that balcony and back inside her apartment. He slammed the door shut behind them. "You kissed me to rile him up?" He was starting to think she had a serious wild streak.

Emma shook her head. "I kissed you because I want you, always. If he was out there, then, yes, I wanted him to see that. I wanted him to see that he hadn't scared me. He hadn't driven any kind of wedge between us."

He rocked back on his heels. "You really think he was on the street."

"If you were the killer, wouldn't you be? I mean if he's after you, then it only stands to reason that he'd be seeing what *you're* doing." She gave a little shrug. "We talked about bait before—"

"I'd *never* use you as bait."

"I don't think I'm the right kind of bait. I think you are. I think we can use you to draw him out."

This was insane. "You're not an agent, Emma. You've never had any training. You can't handle a situation like this!"

She flinched but held her ground. "Why? What's the worst that could happen? I'd get caught, maybe thrown in a crypt with a skeleton? Been there, done that."

Two fast steps, and he was right in front of her again. "The worst that could happen is that you die!"

"Or you do." Her voice was soft. Her eyes seemed, if possible, even brighter. "Or have you not realized that could be this guy's end game? *You* dying. If he lured you down here, it's not because he wants you to live some long, happy life. It's because maybe, just maybe, *you're next*."

"Emma—"

"I was never an FBI agent, I don't have your precious training, but I can help, and I will help." She gave a hard nod. "I bet that while I was laid up in that hospital, your teammates were working on the case, weren't they?"

They'd pretty much been kicked off the case. Except for Victoria . . . she'd been allowed access to finish her examinations. Since Elroy needed her expertise, Dean figured the guy was content to keep using her.

"Victoria is down at the morgue right now."

Emma nodded. "Then what are we waiting for?" She spun and headed for her door.

Seriously? Part of him—a big part—admired her determination.

Another part wanted to grab her and run.

Emma was near the door when she stopped. "Oh, and Dean?"

"Yeah?"

"When you kiss me again, do it right. Kiss me hard and deep, kiss me like you need to have me that very minute. I didn't spend all this time working to get past your control so that we could go back to the beginning." Her gaze held his. "I want everything from you, and in return, well, everything is absolutely what I'll give you."

He had no words. Mostly because he was afraid he'd say the wrong thing to her. Emma kept him off-balance. With her, he just never knew what he was supposed to do.

"I won't break. I won't even bruise. I can take everything you've got—I want it all."

And he wanted all of her.

Dean followed her outside and waited while Emma

locked the door. They went down the narrow staircase and, right before they headed out onto the street, he caught her, pulled her back against him, and kissed her.

Deep.

Hard.

Like he needed her more than he needed anything else. Like he was so desperate for her that he couldn't hold himself in check.

His tongue thrust past her lips. He savored her taste. Demanded all that she had to give. When she moaned, the sound just drove him on. He pressed her up against the banister and knew that she had to feel the bulge of his arousal shoving against her.

She held him tighter. He felt the sting of her nails on his shoulders. Emma arched against him, and she sucked his tongue. That drove him *insane* when she did it.

He'd never wanted a woman the way he did her.

She licked his lower lip.

He thought about fucking her right there.

Concussion. She just got out of the hospital. Pull. Back.

His hands slapped against the banister, caging her there. Emma's breath rasped out, and her eyes had softened with desire. "Much better," she whispered.

Hell, yes, it had been.

Her hand slid between them. Pressed to his chest. "I'll be expecting more later."

He'd give her more.

EMMA HAD NEVER been inside a morgue before. Visiting one just hadn't been at the top of her to-do list.

So she was more than a little nervous when she followed Dean past the swinging doors and through the narrow office. When they entered the actual lab, the cold air blew over her, chilling her skin, and her gaze went—rather helplessly—to the line of lockers against the back wall.

Bodies were in those lockers. And those things made her think far too much about her own premature entombment at the cemetery.

She slid back a step, instinctively, but then Emma caught herself. Dean was already treating her with kid gloves. She didn't intend to give the guy any other reason to think she couldn't handle herself.

I have to prove to all of the LOST agents that I can deal with this. Because Emma had a plan. It was a plan that had developed shortly after she'd met Dean and learned about the work he did.

She didn't want to spend the rest of her days giving readings in the square. She wanted to do what she and her father had attempted so long ago—help people. She could *prove* that she had talents the team could use. She would prove herself to them all.

A redheaded woman bustled into the room. She was wearing scrubs and pulling on gloves, and a nervous energy seemed to cling to the air around her. "Great," she said as her gaze danced over Dean, then Emma. "You're here. I was worried you wouldn't arrive before Elroy came back for another update." She flashed a wide smile to Emma. "You probably don't remember meeting me before because you were, um, in a tomb."

"Jesus, Victoria," Dean muttered.

She winced, and her cheeks flushed. "Sorry. I have

been told that tact isn't so much my strong suit." Her smile had definitely dimmed. "I'm Victoria Palmer. The one who takes care of the dead."

Emma inclined her head. "Dean told me about you." The forensic anthropologist. For some reason, she'd expected someone older, but Victoria appeared to be in her late twenties, maybe early thirties. It was hard to tell for certain because she had smooth, pale skin and kept her hair pulled back in a ponytail. There was nothing hard or cold about the woman. She seemed to be spilling over with energy as she stood there, and her smile had certainly seemed genuine.

Even if her words had been a little off.

"I need to show you all what I found. Before Elroy figures out that you're here and freaks." She hurried toward the lockers. "I mean, really, what did you do to the guy, Dean? Agent Elroy can't stand you."

Emma saw Dean shrug. "The usual. Ignored his orders. Found the bad guy, got there too late to save the victim. Made Elroy look like an ass because if he'd just moved faster, everything would have been fine." Anger hummed in his words. "All in a day's work."

Dean blamed Elroy for what had happened . . . and Elroy blamed Dean. Talk about a recipe for disaster.

Victoria opened one of the lockers. "The regular coroner is on his break, a break I sent him on when I got the text that you were closing in. He's a nice guy, but Dr. Armont is way too keen on impressing the Bureau guys." She pulled out a slab. A slab that looked like it contained something . . . small.

Nausea rolled in Emma's stomach, and she had to look away.

"There wasn't a lot to go on here, at least not at first."

Emma's stomach churned harder. The smell of the place was starting to get to her. Antiseptic. Death.

"But during my exam of the leg, I realized the patient had gone through knee surgery." Victoria sounded pleased with herself. "There was a serial number on the screw that I discovered. I traced it and discovered that the remains belonged to a kid named Wayne Johnson. He'd had knee surgery after a car accident when he was seventeen." Sadness flashed over her face. "I was able to get hold of his medical records and it seems he developed an addiction to pain medication after that surgery. His parents were killed in the car accident, and I don't know, maybe the drugs made things easier for him." Her gaze seemed sad behind the lenses of her glasses. "I don't do so well at understanding the motives of the living. I can just tell you what the dead say."

Wayne. The name was clicking for Emma and making the churning in her stomach even worse. "Jax told us a boy named Wayne was missing." A boy who'd tried to get off drugs. Who'd tried to get clean.

Victoria's gloved fingers rose to the black body bag—a bag that could not possibly contain a full body.

"Don't," Emma said. The word came out sounding like a plea.

Victoria glanced over at her, eyes wide behind the small lenses of the glasses she wore.

"I have enough crap in my head. I don't want to see that, too," Emma said. So what if the confession made her sound weak? It was better than passing out at their feet.

Victoria flushed. "I'm sorry!" She immediately

jumped away from the bag. "I'm around them so much, I forget I'm not . . ." The flush deepened. "Normal."

The last part was whispered with shame.

Dean's shoulder brushed against Emma. "Are you okay?" His question was low, just for her.

Emma nodded. After clearing her throat, she said, "One of my contacts in the city told me that a boy named Wayne had gone missing. This all fits with what we know about him."

"Another victim. *Not* Ricker's kill," Dean said, "but one that SOB out there just tossed away like garbage."

Victoria pushed the slab back into the locker. She moved to the right but hesitated before she reached for the next locker. Her gaze darted toward Emma. "Do you want to wait outside? I really need to show Dean what I found on Ricker's skeleton."

Emma locked her knees together. She shouldn't have stopped the woman before. "I'm fine." *Just bones. Just bones . . .*

Dean's fingers caught Emma's and squeezed.

Victoria's worried stare swept over Emma's face. "They can't hurt you," she said. Then Victoria winced. "That sounded ridiculous, didn't it? I just . . . by the time they get to me, I figure they're the ones who've been hurt. I need to help them, in my way. Even people like Ricker. We have to find out what happened to them all, right?"

"I killed Ricker," Dean said, voice flat. "I shot him, and he fell off the side of that mountain. Kevin already told me that his body showed signs of broken bones and fractures—"

"Oh, yes, all of that *is* true. And when he called for an

update, I certainly shared that information with Agent Cormack. But there were a few things I held back." She unzipped the bag. Emma noticed that her fingers were shaking a bit. "There were certainly plenty of breaks. His left femur was broken in two places, his right tibia suffered a displaced fracture. His clavicle was also fractured. Four of his metacarpals were broken—"

"We get it," Dean said. "The guy's bones were wrecked."

That sure sounded like the result of a fall to Emma. When the bag opened, she made a point of not staring at the remains. Emma kept her gaze locked on Victoria.

The other woman nibbled on her lower lip. "You're on record saying that you shot him in the right shoulder and the left knee."

"Yes." Dean's voice held no emotion. "Then the bastard fell."

"You didn't shoot him anywhere else? You're absolutely certain?" She seemed to assess Dean. "It's just us here, and I hope you know that you can trust me."

Uh-oh. Emma had a feeling that the news coming next wasn't going to be good.

"I'm certain of where I hit him." Now Dean sounded annoyed. "I *know* what I did."

"Because I found evidence to suggest that he was shot a third time. With a gun that was similar in caliber to your own . . . actually . . . based on the marking that I found on his bones, I would say the gun used was exactly like your FBI-issued weapon, a Glock 22." She paused. "I believe that is the type of weapon you used that night, isn't it?"

"That's a standard gun for FBI agents."

"Yes," Victoria's voice was soft. "I thought it was."

"FBI agents," Dean continued. "And cops."

Victoria's hands hovered over the bones. "And anyone who wanted to put a killer out of his misery."

Don't look at the bones. Don't look.

"If he survived your shots, if he survived the fall but was incapacitated then perhaps that last shot wasn't intended to do anything but . . . take the man out of his misery. I mean, he wasn't close to help then, having fallen who knows how far. If he hadn't gotten help, he would have just slowly bled out."

Like his victims?

Victoria picked up the skull. Emma hadn't expected the move, and her gaze snapped right to it. For a moment, horror froze her.

Victoria turned the skull around. A hole was in the back of that skull. A perfect hole—a perfect entrance point for a bullet.

Dean's fingers tightened around Emma's.

"When Elroy comes in, he just looks at the front of the skull. He hasn't seen this particular wound because he hasn't stuck around to watch my actual examination." Victoria's shoulders hunched forward. "I will give him this bit of news. It will be in my report, but I wanted to talk to you first."

Emma couldn't look away from that skull.

With me, in the dark. Cold, hard bone . . .

"Hell, Viki, before you talked to Elroy, you wanted to make sure I hadn't gone up behind the bastard and shot him in the back of the head."

Emma shivered. She'd never heard that particular tone in Dean's voice before.

Worry flashed on Victoria's face, but she didn't deny his words. "He nearly killed you. You were defending yourself—"

"Not if I shot him in the back of the head."

Victoria swallowed. "No," her voice was low. "Not then." But her chin lifted. "That's why I think this was a mercy killing. He survived the fall, but he wasn't going to keep living much longer."

"I wouldn't have shown the bastard any mercy." Dean pulled away from Emma. Stalked toward the slab. Glared down at the remains. "I would have wanted him to suffer every moment he had left."

Emma had always known about the darkness in Dean. She'd felt it, brushing against his carefully controlled surface a few times. But right then, she could *see* it in him. His smile was slightly cruel, as Dean said, "He deserved the pain."

"Th-then someone else didn't think so," Victoria said. "Someone else put him out of his misery. Someone else moved his remains. Took care of the remains until . . ." She gestured to the slab. "Only the bones remained. Then that person gave Ricker a final resting place."

"A resting place in New Orleans." Emma turned away. She just couldn't keep looking at that skull. Dealing with the dead was commonplace for them, but not for her. Emma's hands were clammy, and her heartbeat was shaking her whole chest.

"No one was supposed to be in that crypt," Victoria said quickly. "Agent Cormack already did research on it. The family that owned it filed bankruptcy. They moved away—and the bank took control of their assets.

The crypt was just sitting there, waiting for the killer to find it."

The smell in the morgue seemed even worse. And why was it so dang cold in there?

She heard the *zip* of the bag being resealed. Her back snapped straight up at that sound.

"Sarah thought that whoever killed Ricker wanted to keep him close. Perhaps even wanted a place to go and visit him."

"There was a bench in that crypt." Dean's voice was halting. "But he put Emma in there. He wanted us to *find* them."

"Sarah doesn't think so." The metal locker clanged shut.

Emma glanced back. She was trying to focus on breathing. And not giving in to a sudden claustrophobic panic. *I'm not in the tomb. I'm not sealed up with the bones.*

"I mean, the guy isn't psychic, right?" Victoria continued.

That particular comment had Emma cutting her eyes back to the other woman.

"Crap." Victoria winced. "Wrong thing to say again, right?" She shook her head. "I just mean, what could the odds possibly be? How would he have known that Emma was going to try to slip away through the cemetery? I think he might have—I mean, *we,* Sarah and I—think he might have just put Emma in that crypt because he knew no one else was going in there. He thought it was safe." She gave a grim smile. "He was wrong. He messed up, and that gives us an advantage."

The main doors swung open then. Emma tensed,

expecting to see Elroy stride inside, but it was just Sarah.

"Good," Sarah murmured when she saw them. "The gang's all together."

"I was telling them about the new profile you're making."

Sarah motioned toward the door. "I'll tell you the rest, but we need to hurry. I saw Elroy on my way in here, but he didn't see me." Anger flashed in her eyes. "I told him earlier that the FBI's original profile was off, but he's not interested in listening to what I have to say. He made it clear that Victoria was the only one of us who was still supposed to have access on this case."

Dean marched toward Emma. "As soon as he gets Victoria's reports, he's going to push her aside, too."

"That's how the game works."

Emma and Dean followed Sarah out of the morgue. The farther they got from the place, the easier it became for Emma to breathe. And when they actually made it back to the sunlight, she felt a bit light-headed.

Emma's hand flew out and grabbed the railing near the building.

"Are you okay?" Sarah asked her, lightly touching Emma's shoulder.

After pulling in a few *very* deep breaths, Emma managed to say, "Never better." *I keep thinking that I'm being buried alive, but hey, that's totally normal, right? Nothing crazy there.*

"Is it your head?" Dean asked. "Dammit, this is my fault. I shouldn't have dragged you all the way down here."

"It's not my head." Well, maybe it was. But it wasn't

the concussion. It was the crap going on *in* her head. "I'm fine." She could lie with the best of them.

Emma straightened her shoulders and hurried across the street. Running into either Elroy or Cormack wasn't on her agenda, so she was glad to put some distance between herself and the morgue. *Never want to go back there.*

As soon as they were clear, Emma turned to confront Sarah. "Spill on the new profile."

Sarah's brows climbed, and it looked as if she almost smiled. "It's not perfect—"

But Dean shook his head. "Your profiles are usually pretty dead-on."

"Usually, but this guy is different. I think it's because the crimes that he's committed—well, it's more mimicry than anything else. He's been re-creating Ricker's attacks because he wanted us to think Ricker was involved." Her breath whispered out on a sigh. "That was the bait. He abducted those people—probably far more than we know about—and he killed them because he wanted to perfect his craft. He wanted to be able to kill the way Ricker had."

"Bait," Emma repeated. This was what had worried her the most. "Just who do you think he was trying to reel in?"

Sarah's gaze flickered to Dean.

"Me?" His brows climbed. "Why? Because I killed his damn partner, and he wants some payback? Well, then he needs to come after me, *me,* and not take Julia Finney or that kid Wayne or *Emma*—"

"I don't think they were partners."

Now Emma was surprised.

"A partner wouldn't have needed this practice time at perfecting his kills. A partner would have come after Dean much faster. This killer . . . he was slowly building up. Escalating. He's linked to Ricker, but I don't think he was killing with him before Dean shot the guy on the mountain."

The web just kept becoming more tangled for Emma. *So sort out that damn shit.*

She wasn't good at understanding motives. She couldn't psychoanalyze people she'd never met.

She needed to see people. To see places. To look for details.

Her eyes squeezed shut. "I have to go back to the crypt."

"The fuck you do," was Dean's instant denial.

That was so cute. Her eyes opened. "I get that you want to keep me safe."

"He *buried* you. Sure, you weren't under the ground, but he sealed you up there." He caught her shoulders and pulled her close. "Why would you ever want to go back there?"

"I don't want to go back, but I need to do it."

He was already shaking his head.

"I might see something there, okay! Something that others missed. Something that the cops didn't see. Something *you* didn't see because you were so worried about me." He had to give her that. "It's all I have to offer." Her voice dropped. "You were right. I don't have the training that you all have. I don't have a fistful of degrees like her." She pointed to a watchful Sarah. "I just have street smarts. I have a dad who taught me always to be aware of what was happening around me.

When I enter any restaurant, I automatically find all the exits. I count the number of booths. I do a sweep of the customers there." Did all of that sound crazy? Then fine, she was crazy. So what?

"Emma . . ."

She couldn't decipher the emotion in his voice, so she just kept talking, the words coming faster, as she said, "I might have let myself get a little rusty, but I can do this. I can prove that I belong on—"

Oh, hell. Was she oversharing or what?

Emma cleared her throat. "I can prove that I can help you."

Dean stared into her eyes. After a moment, he said, "Sarah, give us two hours, then get the team to meet us at Emma's apartment."

"Will do." Sarah hesitated, then said, "At least your dad taught you some good things, Emma. Some fathers just want their children to grow up and become nightmares. You should be grateful for the father you had."

What?

Before Emma could question her, Sarah hurried away.

"You don't need to prove yourself."

Uh-oh. Dean was sounding all pissed.

"Not to Sarah. Not to any of the LOST agents, and least of all to me."

"I'm not just some con woman."

He caught her chin. Tilted her head up so that she had to meet his eyes. "I know that, baby."

"My father was more, too." There it was. Stark pride came in her voice. "My mother cut out on us, and he did the best he could. I know he skirted the law. I know he wasn't perfect, far from it, but he loved me. And he died because he wanted to help those missing girls and because he wanted to save me."

Understanding flashed on his face. "And that's why you wanted to save Julia. Full circle, isn't it? Like father, like daughter."

Wade had said those words once, but they'd been mocking. When Dean said them, Emma thought the words sounded almost tender. "Is that so bad?" Emma asked. "To want to be like him?" Cars buzzed by on the street. "He would have loved the idea of LOST. I think he probably would have gotten your Gabe to give him a job in about five minutes flat." Her father had been able to talk his way into anything.

"What about you?" Dean asked her. "Is that why you've been so determined? Because you want . . . LOST?"

LOST was only the beginning of what she wanted. "We need to get to that cemetery."

"And you need to answer my question."

Fine. "I want you."

He blinked.

"I want to keep having wild sex with you."

An elderly man passing on the street stopped to cough. No, to choke. But he recovered fairly fast.

"I want to see what we have," she continued, voice a bit softer because *maybe* that other part she'd revealed had been too loud. "I want to see where it can take us."

"Emma—"

"And, yes, I might want to see if I can do more than just give readings. Is that wrong?"

He pressed a quick kiss to her lips. "Nothing about you is wrong. Not to me."

Ah, if only that were true. Emma knew she had plenty of dark places inside her. Her deepest secret was the one that her father had carried to his grave.

Ten years ago, she'd killed a man, and an act like that had to leave a mark on a person's soul. She was far too aware of that mark most days.

My father took the blame, but it was me. Always . . . me.

Dean had shared so much with her, and Emma didn't know why she still held back with him.

Because he was FBI for so long. Because the guy used to stand for truth and justice and all those things that matter.

"Let's get to that cemetery," she whispered.

He nodded.

WATCHING, WATCHING . . .

Dean Bannon had always been an arrogant SOB. To head right to the morgue, after he'd been told to stay off the case . . .

The guy never would learn. And that was all right. Lesson time was long over.

Payback. That was the only thing that mattered now.

He watched as Dean and Emma jumped into their car and raced away. Where were they off to now? Not that it mattered. They weren't going to catch him. He was in control now, of everything.

They would have to wait until he was ready to strike.

He'd be striking very, very soon.

But first he had to pay a visit to a certain lady in the morgue.

CHAPTER THIRTEEN

Y OU'RE A BADASS, I GET IT," DEAN DRAWLED AS he watched Emma slide under the police tape and creep right into the tomb. "You don't have to impress me."

She laughed, as he'd hoped, but the sound had a raw edge. She'd grown progressively paler as they traveled to the cemetery. He hated for her to be back in that place. Dean knew he'd never forget pulling her out of that sarcophagus. Not even if he lived to be a hundred years old.

"Impressing you is what I live for." But she wasn't looking at him. Her gaze was on the sarcophagus. Its top still lay on the floor, half-shattered. "I couldn't get that off. No matter how hard I tried." She glanced down at her hands. "That's why my knuckles are so bruised."

Fuck. She was gutting him.

"So we know we're looking for a man in his prime, strong, someone who could easily move that lid."

That fit with Sarah's profile.

"And there's the bench." Emma skirted around the sarcophagus toward the bench. "It's not dusty. No cobwebs at all."

No, there weren't any.

Emma spun back around. "What are we missing?"

Nothing. "Maybe there's just nothing here to find."

"I don't believe that. If he kept Ricker here, then the place is important."

Yes, it was.

"There has to be something else."

Dean went back to the sarcophagus. He studied the stone. Heavy and thick. When he hit against it with his fist, yeah, it was damn solid. He kicked the bottom.

Only that thunk wasn't solid.

Hollow?

"Dean?"

He'd already dropped to the ground. It *looked* like stone down there, but when he grabbed hold of the bottom, he found it was loose. A cheap veneer that had been put in place to cover the bottom five inches of that sarcophagus.

He yanked—and saw darkness.

But when he shoved his hand inside, he touched something familiar. The heavy weight of the gun was something he'd known before.

He jerked back almost instantly because he'd made the rookie mistake of putting his prints on that damn weapon. "I need a shirt or cloth or *something*."

Rip.

He glanced back. Emma had just ripped the bottom of her flowing skirt.

Okay.

He took the fabric. As carefully as he could, he pulled out the weapon. One look confirmed that he was staring at a Glock 22, an FBI-issued gun *just* like the one he'd had back in his Bureau days.

And Dean knew he was staring at the weapon that had been used to kill Jared Ricker.

VICTORIA'S EYES WERE narrowed in concentration as she stared down at the metacarpals of Jared Ricker's right hand. She had a magnifying glass gripped closely in her hand because she'd been going over every single inch of those remains. She didn't want to miss anything, not a mark, not even a tiny fleck of lint. Everything was vital on this case. *Everything*.

And . . .

"Got you," Victoria whispered. She pulled out her tweezers and very, very carefully bagged the hair that she'd just recovered, a small hair that had been stuck between Ricker's finger bones.

She zipped up the hair, keeping it secure in an evidence bag. Her fingers were trembling a bit. Yes, yes, the hair could turn out to be nothing. Maybe it could have been transferred to the bones when they'd all been at the cemetery or—

Maybe it's the killer's hair.

Victoria took off her gloves. Tossed them in the trash, then hurriedly texted Sarah. She had a meeting with Elroy scheduled soon. She told Sarah that she'd see her and the other LOST members as soon as she finished.

She didn't want to get their hopes up about the hair, not just yet. She'd do some tests and see what she could discover first. But she would be telling Elroy about the hair. Mostly because she wanted the FBI's resources to get her test results back faster.

Victoria stared down at the remains. She knew that

Dean viewed this man as the enemy, a person who deserved no sympathy. But what about justice? Did he deserve that?

The door opened behind her. *Right on time.*

Victoria reached for another pair of gloves. "We've got a lot to cover," she said, trying to keep her voice calm as she stared down at Ricker. But there was just no keeping the excitement at bay when she revealed, "I may have found a hair from the killer on the body, and—"

Something sharp pricked Victoria on her neck, as if a bee had just stung her. Her hand rose, and she automatically slapped at the spot.

Her fingers hit a syringe.

"You're right," a low, growling voice said into her ear. "We do have a lot to cover."

A heavy lethargy swept over her body. She tried to turn around, to see the man who held her, but her body wasn't listening to her mind's commands. Instead of turning and fighting, she sagged in his arms.

"That's good. Just relax, Doctor." He put her on the table. Right beside Ricker. The table was icy cold. Why hadn't she noticed just how cold it was before? "Now, you and I . . . we're going for a little trip."

Was he tying up her hands? If felt like he was.

Why? She tried to scream the question, but she couldn't speak.

"It's a good thing you like the dead," he said.

Her eyes were starting to sag closed. She hadn't been able to see his face. Not even once.

"Because you're going to be one of the dead soon, Doc . . ."

"YOU *TOUCHED* THE gun?" Gabe Spencer demanded as he paced in Emma's apartment. "Damn, man, what were you thinking?"

"Well, I wasn't thinking that I'd find a gun under there, that's for sure." But he *should* have been more careful. He'd been too on edge, too worried about Emma, and he'd screwed up. A plain and simple screwup. "Elroy knows my prints are going to be on the thing now, but maybe they'll turn up someone else's, too." The killer's.

Gabe stopped pacing. "Or maybe Elroy will claim *you* killed the guy because your prints were on the weapon."

What? *Shit.*

"It could happen." Sarah had her hands between her knees as she sat on Emma's new couch. "I mean, look at it this way, he could try to tell everyone that you had a breakdown after the Ricker case. You left the FBI, turned your back on your partner . . ."

No, Kevin had turned his back on Dean first. The guy had come to see Dean in the hospital just once. Dean had opened his eyes and found Kevin standing in his doorway. Kevin had told him, *"You fucking let her die."* Dean had said that he was sorry about Charlotte, over and over, but Kevin had walked away.

Dean had left the FBI after that, and he'd heard that Kevin had been transferred down to the Baton Rouge office. Elroy had even been demoted for a time—that would happen when the whole nation saw your screwup.

We all should have done things differently back then. Maybe if we had . . .

But they couldn't change the past.

"And maybe . . ." Sarah continued her voice jerking

his attention back to her, "because of what happened to you on that mountain, you became consumed with the idea of vengeance. Maybe you lost your grasp on what was right and wrong. You killed Ricker, and you started imitating his crimes down here."

Dean glared at her. "That is such bullshit."

Emma was silent beside him.

"Yeah," Wade growled. "It is bullshit. But it's the kind of bull I've seen the FBI pull off before. You need to watch your step. We all know that Elroy has a hard-on for you."

Emma surged to her feet. "You're all looking at this wrong. The gun is a solid lead! The killer screwed up. He left the weapon there, thinking no one would discover it, but we found it, and that puts us one step closer to solving this thing."

Gabe slanted a glance toward Dean. "I didn't expect her to be so positive."

His lips almost quirked.

"Yes, well, that's because you're a pessimist," Emma fired right back as she marched toward Gabe. "A guy who has something other than this case eating at him. I mean, seriously, you've looked at your phone seven times in the last twenty minutes."

"Seven?" Gabe repeated. "Thought it was just six . . ."

"*Seven.* And your gaze keeps darting to the balcony as if you're thinking about something or rather, *someone* else. Since your face softens when you do that, I'd say you were thinking about a lover. You're worried about her, and it's distracting you from finding this killer." She huffed out a breath. "We can't afford distractions right now."

Oh, hell. She had just gone after his boss. And she'd been damn sexy doing it.

"Positive and another head case," Gabe muttered.

Emma's mouth dropped open, but before she could attack, Dean grabbed her. He locked his arms around her stomach and pulled her back against him.

"Easy!" Gabe raised his hands. "I didn't mean *you* were a head case." He jerked his thumb toward Sarah. "I meant that you were like her. The two of you can get into someone else's head without even half trying."

Did Emma realize that was one of the biggest compliments that Gabe could give her?

"She's not like me," Sarah said quietly.

Now all eyes shifted to Sarah.

She shrugged. "I think she's better. I just figure out what sick, psychotic bastards have going on in their heads. She's able to figure out everyone else."

"She sure did a good job with me." Gabe inclined his head toward her. "I'm thinking about my fiancée. She's back in Atlanta, and I don't like being away from her. My head's not where it needs to be. Mostly because Julia Finney's death reminded me that I came far too close to losing my Eve a while back."

Dean had been there during those terrifying hours. He'd seen his friend nearly break apart. But Eve had survived. Both Eve and Gabe had battled their nightmares and won.

He glanced at Emma. When she'd been missing, terror had consumed him. It had grabbed tight to him, nearly suffocating him with its intensity.

He hadn't stopped to wonder why he was so afraid. He'd just reacted.

But now . . . now . . .

Shit . . . I went insane because I love her.

Impossible. They'd just met. They'd had fantastic sex. She'd gotten beneath his guard. She'd made him laugh. Made him share, actually *talk* about his life and his past. But . . . they had only been together for a few days. He couldn't love her.

Could he? Dean glanced at Emma.

I fucking do.

That meant they were both totally screwed.

"Victoria's text said that she had to catch a late meeting with Elroy." Sarah stood up. "I'll check in with her when she gets back to the hotel." She glanced over at Emma. "Are you sure you want to stay here tonight?"

"Absolutely."

Dean made sure he was at Emma's side. "She's not going to be alone."

"Damn straight," Wade agreed. "I'll be camped out close, keeping an eye on the place. If anything goes down tonight, we'll be ready."

"And I'll rotate with you," Gabe said.

When Emma frowned over at the LOST boss, he explained, "I took the liberty of renting out the space across the street. Since the bookshop closed down, the place is empty, and it will give us the perfect place to watch but not be seen."

Because they all seemed to think the killer would be circling back by . . . but whether the guy was coming for Emma or coming after Dean, well, that was the part they didn't know for sure.

You're not going to get either one of us.

He walked his friends to the door. This was a team

that he could count on. Dean knew that. They'd always had his back, from the first moment that he'd walked into the LOST offices in Atlanta.

It wasn't about red tape. Wasn't about some glory call. It was just about getting the job done.

Gabe hesitated before he left the apartment. "Your girl there . . . she's got some interesting talents."

Hell, yes, she did.

"Might be able to use someone like her at LOST."

Then he was gone.

Dean secured the door behind them. "You should get some sleep," he said, without glancing over at Emma. "The day has been hell." Talk about a serious damn understatement.

"I'm really not in the mood for sleep. Every time I close my eyes"—her laughter sounded too harsh, far too harsh for Emma—"let's just say I picture things that I'd rather not have in my head."

He turned toward her. "Nightmares can't hurt you." He knew that truth because he'd had his share.

Her smile was sad. "No, but they can sure scare the shit out of you."

He laughed. He shouldn't have laughed. There was just something about Emma . . .

"Your friends are watching across the street." She glanced toward her balcony. "Just how much will they be able to see?" Emma turned off the lights, plunging them into darkness. "Especially with the lights off."

Her hands pressed to his chest.

"Emma . . ."

"I need this, Dean. I need you. More than I can say."

How was he ever supposed to deny her? Dean didn't

think he could. He didn't think he'd ever be able to deny her a single thing.

"I don't want to be scared. When we're together, all I can do is feel pleasure. Please, give me that."

She didn't need to beg him for anything. *Never.*

Her scent teased him, and when she pushed against him, rising onto her toes, her mouth met his. She licked his lip. He *loved* it when she did that. Then she bit him. A light nip that sent a surge of arousal pounding right through him.

But he wasn't doing this her way. Oh, he'd give her the pleasure she craved, but tonight, his control would *not* break.

He lifted her into his arms. She gave a little gasp then, and he had to kiss her. He'd never get tired of feeling her luscious lips against his. He kept kissing her as he carried her into the bedroom.

Then he put her down on the bed. She reached for him, moving fast, but he caught her hands. "Careful."

"Careful?" Emma repeated. A lamp was on near her bed, throwing light over the covers. "Since when?"

Since you got a concussion. Since I realized I wanted to show you that you're far more than a fast, hard fuck in the dark.

"My rules tonight, Emma." *Your pleasure, but my rules.*

Her eyes narrowed. "We'll see . . ." A taunting whisper that seemed to stroke right over cock.

"Now, baby," he chided as he lowered her back onto the bed. "Don't make me have to tie you up."

"Promises, promises," she taunted.

He stiffened. Seriously, the woman was trying to

destroy his mind. His cock was about to burst right through his pants.

He positioned her hands back against the pillows. "Keep them there." *Or I will.* He'd already come too close to losing Emma. And now, now he desperately needed the reaffirmation of life with her. He wanted the wild flare of passion. He wanted the sensual release. But more than all that, he just wanted his Emma. He wanted to see her break apart in his arms, then come back together in the aftermath of her release.

He started with her shirt. Unbuttoned it, and left it hanging open. Then he went to her shoes, but before he could reach for them, Emma had kicked them away. She lifted her hips for him so he could remove her jeans, and since she was being so obligingly helpful, he slid off her panties, too.

"I don't want foreplay," Emma said, voice husky and so tempting. "I just want you."

And he wanted to fucking worship her.

So he did.

Dean slowly slid his hands up her legs, starting at her ankles, moving up, up, and caressing the silky expanse of her skin. What if he hadn't found her? What if he'd never touched Emma again?

He bent and pressed a kiss to her inner thigh. She trembled against him.

He'd have her doing more than just a little tremble soon.

He let his fingers rise. Emma, sweet Emma, parted her legs even more for him. And he touched her, caressing the delicate pink of her sex. Stroking her. Parting her folds. Pushing one finger into her and loving the way she arched up to his touch.

Slowly, with his eyes on her face—because he didn't want to miss a moment of her pleasure—he pushed a second finger into her. Deeper. A bit harder. And while those two fingers thrust into Emma, his thumb rubbed over the little button of her clit.

"Dean!"

She reached for him.

He pulled away from her. "Now, Emma, you know where your hands belong . . ."

"Tease!" she snapped at him, but Emma put her hands back up.

His muscles were locked and straining. Emma was wrong. This wasn't about teasing her. Not at all. It was about giving her as much pleasure as she could stand—and then sending her over the edge into oblivion.

And if she touched him, he was a goner. He wouldn't be able to hold on and do all the things he wanted with her delicious body.

Her hips lifted once more.

But he didn't put his hand on her, didn't put his fingers in her. Instead, he moved his body so that he was between her legs. "I missed your taste."

What if I hadn't found her?

He curled his hands around her hips and lifted her against his mouth. He didn't go slowly, didn't start with a tentative stroke of his tongue. He put his mouth on her, and he *took*.

She pushed against his mouth. Moaning and straining to get closer to him. He was watching when she came, watching that wild flush of pleasure that lit her cheeks. She didn't make the mistake of grabbing for him again. Instead, her fingers fisted on the pillow beneath her head. Her body went bow-tight as she called out his name.

He didn't stop. He kept licking her. Stroking her with his mouth and tongue. And she was perfect. He'd been right when he thought that he could get addicted to the taste of Emma's pleasure. He sure as hell could.

The second orgasm hit her, and she nearly came off the bed, but he had a strong grip on her hips, and Dean held her down easily.

So beautiful.

He licked her once more. Then he rose, crouching above her.

Emma's breath choked out. So did his. But . . .

He wasn't close to done. He'd kept his clothes on because that was another way to keep his control. His cock ached. The thing was rock hard, surging, and it probably had the impression of his zipper on it because his cock was about to burst out of his pants.

"Arch your back," he told her, and his own voice had turned into little more than a growl.

Emma arched for him. She also didn't let go of her grip on her pillow.

His hands slid under her back. He unhooked her bra. "Didn't think I'd forget these, did you?" A woman's orgasm could make her breasts even more sensitive, and he was counting on that sensitivity now.

He bent and blew lightly over her left nipple.

"D-Dean!"

Then he took that nipple into his mouth. He laved it with his tongue. He sucked it. He nipped it lightly.

Emma's body seemed to quake beneath him. Her hands stayed on her pillow, but her legs lifted and locked around his hips. Her sex was wet and hot, and he wanted to drive deep into her.

Not yet.

He kissed his way to her other breast. Her nipple was a tight, hard peak.

"T-too much," Emma gasped out when he sucked that nipple. "It feels . . ."

He sucked harder.

When she cried out, it wasn't in pain. Pleasure.

He deepened the pressure of his mouth. Scored her with his teeth.

Her body stiffened and, a second later, her hips were jerking against the front of his pants. She was riding him as much as possible, working her wet sex against him.

Did she just come again?

Fuck, he thought she might have, and that was the sexiest thing he'd ever seen. No, *she* was the sexiest thing.

He yanked open his pants. His cock sprang toward her, and her wet cream instantly coated the head.

"Now!" Emma demanded. "Now, now, *now*."

That same refrain was pounding through his head. He drove into her, and her sex clamped around her. So tight, so hot, so perfect.

He thrust, withdrew, thrust.

Her hips slammed up to meet his.

He grabbed for her hands. Their fingers linked, twined, and stayed there, right near her pillow. Her gaze held his as he drove into her, again and again.

Emma shook her head. "I-I can't . . ."

She could.

He'd make her.

He altered the angle of his thrusts, making sure that when he withdrew, his cock slid over her clit. Right . . . *there*.

Her moan was so sexy.

Again and again. The bed rocked into the wall.

His orgasm built, pressing down harder and harder. Closer and closer. But he wanted to feel Emma's release once more. Wanted her sex to squeeze him hard when she came.

He kissed her. Stroked with his tongue even as his cock sank into her. He couldn't hold back his climax much longer. Fuck, he'd wanted Emma with him when he exploded—

Her sex clamped around him, squeezing *hard*.

He didn't explode. It felt more like he imploded. His world shattered, and he held her in an iron grip as the pleasure pounded and pounded through him on waves that wouldn't end. That he *never* wanted to end.

Because he never wanted to be away from Emma. He wanted her with him, for every moment of every day that was to come.

Always, with him.

THE LIGHTS IN Emma's apartment had shut off.

Wade stared across the street. *Lucky bastard.* He had a real damn good idea of just what Dean was doing over there, and it wasn't pulling an all-night stakeout.

"I'll do a run on the streets," Gabe said. "You got things here?"

Wade glanced over at Gabe. Yeah, sure, Gabe was

the big boss at LOST, but the man was also Wade's best friend. He owed the man more than he could ever repay.

Will I ever be able to look at him without guilt eating me alive?

Because it was all Wade's fault. Gabe had been off fighting, protecting his country. The guy had asked Wade to do one thing. One fucking thing.

Keep an eye on my sister, will you? Gabe had smiled as he tossed out the question. *I mean, shouldn't be hard right?*

Because Gabe had known how Wade felt about Amy. He'd had a ridiculous crush on the woman for years, but he'd kept a strict hands-off policy with her. *Because she was my best friend's little sister.*

He'd kept his distance from the sexy nurse, and Amy had wound up with an asshole boyfriend. When Amy went missing . . . the cops had thought she was just with the boyfriend. They hadn't searched for her.

Gabe had been sent back home from battle, hurt, nearly broken, only to learn that his sister had disappeared.

Wade had been an Atlanta homicide cop then. He'd stepped on dozens of toes as he tried to search for Amy.

Too late, it had been Gabe and Wade who finally tracked down the man who'd taken her. They'd found her just days after her death.

Because the bastard didn't kill her right away. He tortured her. All that time, when I was supposed to be watching out for her . . .

"Shit, man, are you doing it again?" Gabe demanded.

Wade blinked.

"Guilt won't bring Amy back."

Wade looked away from him, glancing back over at Emma's darkened apartment. He'd left the force after they found Amy. And after . . . Amy's abductor had been killed.

"Do you think she'd want you doing this shit to yourself? Letting guilt eat at you to the point that you don't even have a normal life?"

A normal life. Happiness. Sex. A family?

Some dreams just seemed beyond him.

"I've watched you, man. You don't even try anymore. You don't flirt, you don't look for women, you just—hell, you pretend. Pretend that you're interested in Sarah because you know there's no chance there."

Wait, what? "We're on a stakeout," he muttered as he moved closer to the window. "Not on some bro-share night."

"Sarah's locked down, and you know it. With her past, she's not about to let anyone get close. And, hell, I don't blame her. But you . . . you used to be so different."

Wade shook his head.

"Don't try lying to your best friend."

He'd lied *for* his best friend. When the others had wanted to know how Amy's killer died . . .

Justice.

"LOST isn't about death, Wade. It's about hope. I want you to have some hope. Is that too much to ask?"

He didn't reply. Just because Gabe had found a woman to love, a woman to love him back, that didn't mean it worked out that way for everyone. Some people were just meant to be alone.

It was better that way. Safer.

Because when you opened yourself up to someone, you just asked for pain.

His gaze was still on Emma's dark apartment. "Dean let things get personal with her." And here he'd always thought the guy might have ice water in his veins. Cool and in control . . . that had been Dean, *before* the guy met Emma Castille.

"Sometimes, you don't have a choice." Gabe's footsteps were moving toward the door. "We can all get blindsided."

The door shut behind him. Wade didn't move. Blindsided.

But what happens when you lose the one you love?

The world shattered. That was what fucking happened.

SARAH PUSHED HER keycard into the lock on her hotel-room door. The light flashed green, and she quickly pushed open the door. Before it shut, she cast one last look behind her.

They never look back . . . that's why they don't see me coming. Her father's voice whispered through her mind.

Sarah threw the two locks into place, then she turned around. She was in a suite, one that had two connecting rooms, one for her, one for Victoria. The light in Victoria's room was on.

"Victoria?" Sarah called as she headed toward her friend's room.

A man appeared in Victoria's doorway.

Shit.

Sarah's whole body jerked.

It wasn't just any man. It was the guy from the hospital. Jax. Jax Fontaine. She'd done some research on him since that little meeting. A quick search online had revealed more than she wanted to know about the fellow.

"What the hell are you doing here?" Sarah demanded as she took a few fast-and-frantic steps back toward the main door. "And how did you get in?"

He lifted one brow as he studied her with his light blue eyes. "I came in through the door, of course."

He was mocking her. And he'd broken *in*. "The locked door." Terror was rushing through her. This wasn't right. The things she'd learned about him . . .

She turned and ran.

Her fingers fumbled with the locks. She always locked both of them. Because of her father. Because hotels weren't safe. She unlocked the top lock, reached for the second—

He caught her shaking fingers in his hand. "I'm not here to hurt you."

I'll hurt you. She drove back with her elbow. Heard a wonderful grunt of pain from him, but he didn't let her go. Fine. She'd *make* him drop his hold. Her foot slammed down on his. Her left hand—the hand he hadn't grabbed—fisted, and she snapped it back toward his face.

But her fist didn't break his nose. He'd spun her around and pinned her there, holding her with a strength that she *hated*.

"You are so full of surprises." His voice was admiring. "Just when I think I can't possibly like you any more, you have to do sexy shit like that."

He was *insane*.

And Sarah knew plenty about insanity. *So use it,* a voice in her head demanded. *Work him, get him to let you go.*

But it was as if her body didn't hear the voice's commands. Because she tried to kick him again.

He just took the blow.

Her nails went for his eyes.

He caught her wrists and pushed them back against the door. "Can't have that. I like seeing you too much."

His body pushed against hers, nearly suffocating her with its pressure, but he was making sure she couldn't get in another kick or punch or—

"Sarah . . ." His voice was low, soothing. "I really want to rip apart the bastard who put this terror into you—"

"You!" She managed to yell, and, what the hell was wrong with her? She should have yelled first. *"Help—"*

He kissed her.

She bit him. Tasted blood. Didn't care.

"Like you even more . . ." He whispered. Then, in a too-fast-to-follow move, he had her hands pinned above her head, held tight with one of his, and his other hand was over her mouth. "I think you've got more passion in you than anyone I've ever met." His smile flashed, but as his gaze swept over her face, that smile dimmed. "And more fear." His thumb began to lightly stroke her inner wrist. He didn't ease his grip, but the caress . . .

What is happening?

"I swear, I'm not here to hurt you. I would never hurt you."

She was supposed to believe him? A guy who'd been arrested a dozen times before he was eighteen? A guy who supposedly ran one of the most dangerous motor-cycle gangs in the South?

She wasn't an idiot.

But she was trapped.

You know crazy. Use it. Work it.

That little voice was finally making her body listen.

"I shouldn't have just come in, right? Yeah, I'm getting that," he murmured. "You're not the kind of woman who likes surprises."

What woman liked breaking and entering?

"What if I told you the door was open?"

She shook her head.

"It was, but I guess that doesn't matter. I came in because I was worried about you. I mean, first Em goes missing, then I—well, let's just say I wasn't too keen on the idea of something happening to you." He leaned forward, and his nose . . . nuzzled her hair.

She squirmed against him.

"Sorry!" He didn't sound it. Crazy, demented. "You just smell fucking delicious. A vanilla dream . . . good enough to eat."

She muttered behind his hand.

"I'm going to lift my hand, but I don't want you to scream. If you scream, then one of your hotel neigh-bors will just call security, and I'll probably get taken down to the precinct and have to bribe my way out of there." He gave a long-suffering sigh. "Again. And you don't want that, do you?"

Sarah nodded.

His smile—a true shark's smile—flashed at her once more. "There you go again, just making me want you more."

She stopped nodding.

"The door was open," he told her quietly. "I was concerned, so I came in. I did a search of the place, but nothing looks disturbed. You'll have to see for yourself if anything was taken."

Her gaze darted over his shoulder. A ridiculously broad shoulder.

"I mean, a maid could have accidentally left the door ajar, but in light of the case your group is working, I don't really buy that shit."

She didn't, either. Actually, Sarah wasn't sure if she bought his story at all.

"I came here because something has been nagging at me, and since you're the shrink, I thought I'd get your take on it." His brows lifted as he studied her. "Here's the deal, though, can we skip the whole screaming and cop-calling routine? Let me just tell you my piece, you do your shrink mojo, and I'll walk, leaving you untouched."

He was touching her plenty. She tried to say that behind his hand.

"Deal?"

If it got her free . . . Sarah nodded.

He dropped his hold and stepped back.

Sarah didn't move.

"You're not screaming."

Not on the outside. He had no idea that he'd pretty much just brought her past racing back to her. *Don't think about him. Don't.*

The monster who'd been her father.

"Sarah?"

Now this—this criminal was worried about her. Sarah's chin jutted up. "Say your . . ." What had he called it? "Say your piece and get out."

His gaze raked her. "I'm not as coldhearted as you might think. Or as the stories say."

The stories said he didn't have a heart. Just a reputation for danger and destruction.

"I was there when Julia decided to jump off that roof."

Don't flinch, don't.

He wouldn't know that she'd once nearly taken the same jump. A different roof, a different time. When she hadn't been able to handle the terror of her life any longer.

Everything had changed that night.

"I was there, that dick Dean was there . . ."

So he *hated* Dean, that much was clear in his voice.

"An FBI bozo named Cormack was there . . . he tried to interview me after, pushing for answers I didn't have."

She was listening . . .

"And, on the ground, I saw the FBI boss. Elroy." He lifted one shoulder. "I made a point to learn his name. When a man just watches a sixteen-year-old girl fall six stories, and he doesn't even move to check on her when she hits the ground . . ." His face hardens. "I make a point of learning who the hell he is."

Correction. He *hated* Elroy, and Jax just didn't seem to like Dean. She was learning a whole lot just from the way his voice roughened as he talked about each man.

"Julia was up there, and before she jumped, she kept saying . . . 'You.' Like . . . like she was talking to the killer."

She edged a bit closer to him. "Tell me her exact words."

He raked a hand through his hair. "When I first got there, she said, 'You won't get me again.'" He took a few hard, almost angry steps away from her. "It was weird, but I didn't think about it much then. I mean, she was on the edge. You don't have time for a whole lot of thinking right then."

No.

"But it bothered me. The whole time, she was acting like she was talking to the killer. 'You want to kill me.' She said that, too. 'You want to torture me.'"

Julia Finney had already been tortured, tortured to the point that her mind had broken. "Maybe she thought the killer *was* there," Sarah said softly. "Maybe he'd gotten to her so deeply, terrified her so completely, that she saw him in all aspects of her life. Everywhere she looked."

That had certainly been the case for Sarah . . .

No, focus on Julia.

That was the way she got through. By not thinking about her past. By trying to help the other victims out there.

"When Cormack told her that all he wanted was for her to tell him about the guy who'd abducted her, that she was free to go home, she told him, 'You know everything.'" Jax swung back toward her. "'You' again, the same way. Like she was talking to the killer."

Sarah took another tentative step away from the door. "But she wasn't. She was talking to Agent Cormack."

He stared back at her. "You're the shrink. I told you my piece, now you tell me what the words meant."

She didn't know. She knew the killers. They were so much easier to understand. Darkness and rage and evil, growing inside.

I understand . . . because I'm the same.

So many dark, evil parts, bubbling just beneath the surface.

"Had that poor girl's mind shattered?"

Her hands fisted.

"Or did she think her killer was on that roof or even down below? Because when she was dangling, when Cormack was trying to pull her back up, I saw her look down. And that's when she fought her hardest to fall."

Goose bumps were on her skin. "You want me to say one of the FBI agents did it."

The gun found at the crypt . . . it was just like the standard-issue FBI guns, only no record of that gun had turned up in the official system. Why? Because it had *never* been registered? Or because someone in power had erased the trail that would lead to the weapon?

"You want me to say that," she cocked her head as she studied him, "because you want to be free to go after one of them."

"Or both." He shrugged. "I'm an equal-hit kind of guy."

Yes, she rather imagined that he was. "When you're scared, when you're at the end of your rope, the things you say don't always make sense." He was asking her to go after federal agents. Surely, the guy realized just how—hell, how *hard* that was going to be. And if they attacked without evidence, LOST could find itself shut down. Scorned in the media, severed from all of its government ties. Ties they'd worked hard to cultivate over the years.

"And sometimes, when you've got nothing to lose, you say the things that make perfect sense." He gave her a tight nod. "Think about what I've told you. Then decide what you're going to do, and I'll figure out just what I'm doing."

Killing. She knew beyond a shadow of a doubt what he would be doing.

He started to stride past her. Sarah's hand lifted and grabbed his arm.

"Was that so hard?" His voice was a rough whisper.

She frowned at him.

"Touching me. It's the first time you've done it, without intent to damage." His lips quirked. "See, I don't bite. Unless, of course, you want me to."

"I don't understand you."

"Huh, and here I thought your deal was that you understood *everyone.*"

Not this guy. This guy who screamed death and danger but touched her so carefully. "Should I be afraid of you?" The question jumped from her.

He glanced down at her hand. "Everyone should be. But you . . . you're something different, something special. I could tell it the first time I saw you." He brought her hand up to his lips. Kissed her knuckles. "I'll be seeing you again."

The words were a sensual promise and a deliberate threat.

"Lock the door behind me."

Her eyes narrowed. She didn't need to be *told* that—

"Double-lock it, the way you like to do . . ." He

glanced back over his shoulder at her. "Then get on the phone and start calling your LOST friends. And you *might* not want to tell Dean you found me in your place."

"Because he hates you."

"Because I'd rather stop this killer first, *then* beat the shit out of Dean."

Now she laughed. "You're underestimating Dean." This she knew with utter certainty. "He might look like a suit, a guy who follows the rules, but there is plenty more beneath his surface." Dean was like her. "He's not about to let anyone hurt him."

"That's what I'm talking about," he murmured. "Do more looking beneath the surface because I think you're taking some folks at face value." His fingers curled around the doorknob. "Maybe Em can help you. She learned long ago that what you see is never what you get."

Then he was gone. As soon as the door shut behind him, Sarah lunged forward and flipped the locks. *Both* of them. Then she snatched her phone out of her bag. She dialed Victoria's number. The phone rang and rang and . . . rang.

Where are you, Victoria?

CHAPTER FOURTEEN

"No!" Emma shot straight up in bed, her fingers curled like claws as she raked at the covers above her. "Get me out!"

"Emma?"

She shoved the covers away and sucked in deep, heaving gulps of air.

"Emma?" Fingertips touched her shoulder, and she whirled, slashing out.

But he caught her hand. "It's just me, baby. You know I would never hurt you."

And the wild panic slowly faded. The dream— nightmare—slipped away. She was in her apartment. It wasn't pitch-black. Dean had left her bedside lamp on, and the soft light spilled over the covers. "S-sorry." Her voice sounded far too hoarse.

He pulled her close, holding her against his chest, and she could feel the frantic beat of his heart. It matched her own wild rhythm. "Bad dream?" he asked her, and he pressed a light kiss to her temple.

"Bad memory."

"You were back in the crypt." He held her tighter. "I'm so sorry, baby. If I could take that away—"

"No, no, I wasn't there." *Do it.* He'd bared his soul to her before. Why had she kept this hidden from him? *Because you're afraid he'll leave you.* But if she wanted to be with him—and she did, more than anything— then Emma knew she had to tell him the truth. What he did with that truth, well, that would be his call.

"I was back at the little cabin in Texas. With my father. With the bodies of those two sisters." And with the killer. The boy who'd been so close to her own age and who'd swung that knife so wildly. "I thought I was going to die then, too." Her soft confession. "And I didn't want to die."

Just as she hadn't wanted to die in that crypt.

"Memories can't hurt you. They're over. The past is dead."

Her laugh held a better edge. "It can hurt me. If the truth got out, it *would.*"

"Emma?"

She pulled away from him. Stood. She couldn't tell him this story when she was naked. Emma hurried to her closet. Opened it, and realized the guy had even bought her new clothes. A soft blue robe, just like the one she'd had before, was waiting for her on her little white hook.

He'd done so much for her.

She put the robe on with trembling fingers. "Why did you do all this?"

"All what?"

He was still in bed. Watching her. The faint light from her bedside lamp didn't illuminate much in the room, but she could easily feel the weight of his stare on her. "Fix my place. Buy all my stuff. You spent your own money on it all, didn't you? And don't try giving me that LOST bull—"

"I did."

"Why?" She needed some reassurance before she told him anything else. Before she revealed the secret that could wreck her life, she had to know . . . *how do you feel, Dean? This all can't just be on my side.*

"Because I didn't want that bastard to have taken everything from you."

She waited.

"Because I wanted you to be happy."

"Why does my happiness matter to you?"

"Because it's . . . you!" An angry snarl. "Now stop this and just come back to bed with me, okay?"

She walked to the edge of the bed but didn't climb back in with him. "I'm not exactly who you think I am."

"I know who you are." He sounded so confident.

She shook her head. "No, you don't. I lied to you." She'd never told another soul this story, not even Jax. And Jax wouldn't have judged her. She knew that. He would have backed her up completely. But this darkness was hers to carry, and she'd never wanted to share it, not until now. "I want you to know all of me. Good and bad." Even the parts that were all twisted together.

"Emma . . ."

"My father didn't kill Phillip Trumane." There, she'd done it, and once she made that confession, Emma found that she couldn't stop. "When we ran into that cabin, Phillip was waiting with the dead girls. He lunged out, and the first thing he did was drive his knife into my father's chest. He stabbed him four times before I could pull the guy off my dad." Because her dad had shoved her away when he saw the boy coming at him.

"My father hit the floor. His breath was wheezing out. He was begging me to run, to get out, to get help, but I didn't move." This was the darkest part. The hardest part. "I didn't stay because I was afraid. It wasn't like . . . fear froze me." Because she'd heard stories about that happening. People were so afraid, they couldn't move. "I wasn't afraid. I saw the bodies behind Phillip. I saw my father's blood on his knife, and I was furious. Enraged. I wasn't going to run because if I left, Phillip could get away. He would hurt someone else."

"You were so young."

Her age wasn't an excuse. "I knew exactly what I was doing. And I knew my father was dying." There'd been too much blood for her *not* to know. "He was the only one I had. The only one who ever took care of me. Wherever my father went, his whole life, he made sure I was there, too. He protected me, all the way to the very end, and I wasn't going to let that little bastard get away with what he'd done."

She bent and her hand moved down her body. "When I was thirteen, my dad told me to start carrying a knife on me." Her fingers fluttered around her ankle. He'd given her the ankle sheath as a birthday present. "He kept one on him, too. The places we went, they weren't always the best, and he wanted me safe." Her voice softened on that last word.

Dean rose from the bed. She backed up a fast step, but he made no move to touch her. *Finish it.* She just had to get these last words out, then the choice that followed, it would be his.

Stay with me. Turn me in. Walk away.

"I pulled out my knife. I don't think Phillip even saw it. His eyes—they just looked glazed. Wild. He was still talking about his girlfriend. About how no one would ever take her away. They were going to be together forever." Her breath seemed to chill her lungs. "I lunged at him. Too late, he seemed to realize what I was doing, but I had my knife in his chest by then." Her hands lifted. In the dim light, she couldn't see the marks there. "I'd never stabbed anyone before. I kind of thought that he'd just go down. He didn't. He attacked. Slicing and swinging, and I put my hands up to stop him."

Dean caught her hands. Held them tightly.

"Then I was afraid. I thought he'd kill me, too, and my hand flew out, and I grabbed my knife. I yanked it out of him." And that was when the blood had really flowed. "He was surprised," she remembered. "It was like he'd never felt the knife go into him, but he felt it come out. It sliced across his chest, cutting him so deep, when I yanked it back." How many times had she relived that terrible night? Some images would never fade from her mind. "He looked down, and blood soaked him. He fell after that. Fell, and tried to crawl over to his girlfriend's body."

While Emma had stood there, shaking, the knife in her hand.

"My father was still alive. He whispered for me to put the knife in his hands. For me to say it was *his* and to put his weapon in my ankle sheath." She'd been crying by then because her father's voice had grown so soft.

"Protecting me, always." Until the very end. "With his last breath, he said he was the one to kill Phillip, and the cops bought his story."

"Emma." His fingers tightened on hers. "You could have told them the truth. Your life was on the line in that cabin, you did what you had to do—"

"No. I killed him because I wanted that bastard to die." They needed to be clear on this. "I could have run. I was at the door. I could have left and gone for the cops. But I didn't want that jerk in *therapy* for years while my father was in a grave." *This* is what she needed him to understand. The darkness inside of her. When Jax had said that Emma had a type—this was what he'd meant. She went for men who could understand the evil that was out there . . . because she had evil in her. She had—

"You were a terrified teenager." He drew her closer to him. "That guy was a psychotic with a knife. If you'd tried to run, he probably would have stabbed you in the back. You were defending yourself."

She shook her head. Dean wasn't understanding. "I knew all about money and power. I knew that boy's parents would buy his way out of that mess. They would have said he was crazy, and he would have gone to some psychiatric facility. He never would have seen the inside of a prison. I wasn't going to let that happen. *I* was going to make him pay!"

And she had.

"What do you think this does?" His voice was a growl. So rough. So angry.

"I think it makes you see me for who I am."

"I already see you just fine." He tipped up her chin.

Stared into her eyes. "I told you what I did to Ricker. You think I'm going to stand here and judge you after that?"

"You didn't kill him . . ."

"When I find the bastard who took you, I *will* kill him." Said with absolute certainty. "What does that say about me? About who I am?"

Jax's words whispered through her mind. *Still have the same type, huh, Emma? Never can play it safe, not even with the guys that look the part.* But she shook her head. Dean was more than that, so much more. "You try to save the missing, you try to help—"

"I will fucking destroy anyone who hurts you. Don't you realize what's happening here? Between you and me?"

She was scared to hope.

"Then let's be clear." He kissed her. "I love you."

No. Emma shook her head.

"I. Love. You. And I don't care if it's too soon or too fast. You're the only one who has ever gotten this close to me. I think about you all the time. I want to make you smile. I want to give you the whole world. And when I lost you . . ." His voice roughened. "Everything went dark. *Everything.* I wasn't sane without you. I need you that much. So much that I don't want to think of a life without you. I can't."

"Dean?"

"Tell me you feel the same." The words were as close to a plea as she'd ever heard from him. "Tell me you need me. Hell, just let me know you feel *some* of the same desperation that I—"

Now she kissed *him*. Emma shot up onto her toes. Her arms locked around his neck, and she pulled him close for a hot, frantic kiss.

He didn't turn away. He heard my darkest secret, and he said he loves me! Me! Happiness poured through her.

And then the phone rang.

She kept kissing him. Whoever was on that phone could just wait awhile. This moment was more important than a call. Dean loved her. She had a high that was better than *anything* going on right then—

"It's my phone, Emma, and that particular ring sound means it's Sarah." His voice was gruff as he pulled away. "I have to check in with the team."

Right, right. His team. Emma put her hands behind her back.

He loves me.

Dean grabbed for his phone, but his left hand reached out, and he pulled Emma's right hand from behind her back. His fingers twined with hers. "Sarah, what's happening?"

Emma saw his body tense.

"Are you sure she's not there? And she's not answering her cell?"

Emma strained to hear Sarah's response.

"Have you checked in with Elroy? She had a meeting with him earlier today. She told us that she had to update him. Yeah, yeah, but that was *hours* ago, so maybe the guy put her to work on something else."

Silence.

Emma's bright glow of happiness had faded because there was worry in Dean's voice.

"I'm on my way down there. Screw what the FBI says, this is my *team*. I'll get the others to meet us." He put the phone down.

"Dean, what's happening?" Because lines of worry were etched onto his face.

"Sarah can't find Victoria anywhere."

And Emma remembered waking in a tomb.

SARAH PUT HER phone back down as she slowly turned around in the morgue. The room felt ice-cold to her, and, when she'd come in moments before, the place had been pitch-black.

The guy at the check-in desk on the first floor hadn't remembered seeing Victoria leave. He'd seemed confident she would still be working in the lab.

She wasn't.

Sarah walked slowly around the room. There weren't any signs of a struggle. Everything looked as if it were in place. *Where are you, Victoria?* She'd called her friend, over and over, but Victoria hadn't answered her cell.

A knot had formed in Sarah's gut. Ever since Jax had told her that he'd arrived to find her hotel-room door unlocked . . .

But there had been no sign of a struggle there, either. And if someone came for Victoria, the woman would fight.

If she had the chance.

The lab was too icy. And Sarah *hated* that smell. It stirred up too many memories from her past. A glance at those lockers, oh, *no,* but she did not want to go back there. She'd barely survived all that her father had done before.

She rushed forward. She'd wait for Dean and the others outside. She wasn't just going to stand around in there and—

Sarah shoved the swinging door open, and she nearly slammed straight into Elroy. His arms flew up and grabbed her. "What the hell? *Dr. Jacobs?*" His hands dropped almost instantly. "What are you doing here?" he demanded as he glared at her. "I told you before, you are off the task force. Only Victoria Palmer is clear to keep working with us."

Because you need her? You can't make the case without her?

Her gaze raked over his face. The lines there seemed deeper than before. A light shadow of gray stubble covered his jaw, and his clothes were rumpled.

When a man just watches a sixteen-year-old girl fall six stories, and he doesn't even check on her when she hits the ground . . . I make a point of learning who he is.

"Did you hear me, Dr. Jacobs?" He snarled as he took a menacing step forward. "I told you that—"

Her spine straightened. This guy wasn't going to bully her. *Try again, jackass. I've dealt with men far more dangerous than you.* "I'm here because I'm looking for Victoria. We had a meeting, and she never showed. She's also not answering her cell."

For an instant, uncertainty flashed across his face. "I . . . had a meeting with her today, too. When I went to talk with her, the lab was empty. I thought she'd just stepped out. I got busy with all the press conferences and the FBI brass breathing down my neck, so I didn't get to check back in."

He hadn't checked in again? *Am I supposed to buy that?* "She was running priority tests on the remains pertinent to your case, and you didn't even think of checking in again?"

His cheeks flushed.

"When Julia Finney fell to her death, why did you just stand there?"

The flush deepened. "What kind of question is that?"

"One that deserves an answer. I mean, shouldn't you have stepped forward, checked for a pulse, tried to stop the bleeding—"

"Her neck broke! She broke!" He grabbed her arm and started hauling Sarah down the hallway. "There was nothing I could do, and you, Dr. Jacobs, you are *done* here. I'm escorting you out, and I'm going to make absolutely certain you don't get any further access to this building."

His grip was on the verge of painful. She double-timed it to keep up with him, and when they saw the guard at the check-in desk, the guy shot to his feet.

"Dr. Jacobs is to be denied entry from this point forward," Elroy barked at him. "She is *not* a part of the task force and has no business in this building."

"My friend is missing!" Sarah snapped at him. This was ridiculous. The guy couldn't treat her like this. "I have a right to look for Victoria—"

"Sh-she checked out a few hours ago, ma'am," the guard said, sheepishly. "I went back through the sign-in log. She must have done it at the shift change, and I didn't notice."

Elroy propelled her outside and down the steps. The street was dark and dead silent. No cars were out. No pedestrians. The few streetlights there gave out only a weak light that spilled down—and, for some reason, the faint light just made the surrounding darkness seem all the more intense.

"See," Elroy huffed. "Victoria just cut out and left. You were trying to nose around my case—"

"Take your hands off her." A low snarl that came from that thick darkness.

A snarl Sarah recognized. One that Elroy apparently did, too, because the guy immediately dropped his hold on Sarah and backed up.

Jax stalked from the shadows. "You just keep making me dislike you, Elroy. That's such a fucking-bad thing to do." He offered his hand to Sarah. "Okay?"

Sarah didn't take his offered hand. She didn't move at all. "Fine."

Jax grunted. His hand dropped. And he turned on Elroy. "Kind of late for a trip to the morgue, isn't it?"

"Not when I'm working a case!" Elroy threw back.

"Or maybe not when you've been keeping eyes on Dr. Jacobs here, and those eyes tipped you off to the fact that she was coming in." Jax edged closer to the agent. "You had a tail on her. That tail told you she was coming over, and you rushed to intercept her."

Sarah shook her head. Jax was totally off base. The FBI wouldn't follow her. Would they?

"Maybe he figured LOST would crack the case first," Jax murmured, "and he wanted to use your team." Another step put him just inches away from Elroy. "Or maybe you wanted to keep track of her for another reason . . . Victoria is gone—"

He *knew* that now? Because he sure seemed to be speaking with utter certainty. She eyed Jax with suspicion.

"And it looked like you were trying to take Sarah away when I saw you hauling her from the building."

"No!" Elroy retreated up a frantic step. "I wasn't! I was just escorting her out!"

Elroy was obviously still afraid of Jax. Now that she knew more about the guy's past, that fear was understandable.

"How do you know he had a tail on me?" Sarah asked Jax as she tried to figure things out.

He shrugged. "Because I had someone watching you, too. My guy saw the agent watching you. That bastard Cormack."

"I didn't send Cormack after her!" Elroy blasted. "I just had a cop keeping tabs on her, that's all."

Jax had been spying on me?

"You!" Elroy shoved his finger at the guy. "You're the one with ties to this case. Every time I turn around, I'm finding links to you."

This was news to Sarah.

"You knew Wayne Johnson. You knew Julia Finney. So far, you're the only connection we have to both victims."

Car lights cut through the night. A few moments later, doors were slamming, and her LOST agents, plus Emma, were rushing toward them.

It got a bit easier for Sarah to breathe. Because for a bit there, in the darkness, panic had closed in on her.

I didn't feel safe with those two men. Not with either of them.

"What's happening here?" Wade demanded. He seemed to be turning most of his suspicion on Jax.

Elroy was aiming at the guy, too. Pointing his finger right at Jax. "I think we've got us a stalker here . . . because this man just confessed to watching Dr. Jacobs."

And he broke into my hotel room tonight. But she didn't say that, not at all. Because . . .

He didn't hurt me. If he wanted to hurt me, I would be dead right now, lying on the hotel-room floor.

"He knew the two victims—Julia and Wayne," Elroy continued, as if he had to bring the others up-to-date when he'd just been spouting about LOST not being involved in the investigation. "And he was romantically involved with you, Ms. Castille."

"That was a long time ago," Emma said, her voice clear and—Sarah was sure—carefully emotionless.

"When he found out that you and Dean were together, maybe that pushed him over the edge. Maybe he decided to get back at you. If he couldn't have you, then he'd lock you up and make sure that no one else could, either."

Jax laughed at that. "I don't work that way."

"Oh?" Elroy demanded. Now that there was more of an audience there, the guy appeared far more confident than he'd been moments before. "Then you're over Ms. Castille? Because according to the intel Agent Cormack acquired, you routinely engage in sexual behavior with a woman who looks just like her."

Dean started to lunge forward, but Emma caught his hand and held him back.

Jax just stood there. Then he laughed again. "You think you're pinning this on me."

Elroy lifted his hand, and, as if they'd been waiting

for just that signal, four uniformed cops burst out from the darkness. Sarah jerked, startled by them, and the cops ran to circle Jax.

"I needed to draw you out, Fontaine. I figured you'd show, sooner or later after that little encounter at the hospital. But this time, I was ready." His words held smug satisfaction. "Cuff the bastard."

When the cops swarmed him, Jax didn't resist. "What are the charges?"

"We'll start with threatening a federal officer and work our way up from there. Once I get you into inter-rogation, I'm sure you'll spill plenty about those poor victims you've been taking." He closed in on Jax. "But what I don't get is how you managed to bring Ricker's bones here. What the hell was that?"

Jax shook his head. The streetlight was behind him, and the faint illumination only served to make him look more ominous. "You know it's not me."

Sarah glanced between the two men.

"It's not him!" Emma shouted.

"We'll just see . . ." Elroy murmured.

THEY'D JUST TAKEN Jax away. Cuffed him. Mirandized him. *Taken him.*

"It's not Jax!" Emma said for what had to be the fifth time. Why were the LOST agents just standing there? "You know he couldn't have pulled Ricker's bones down here, and the guy would *not* have hurt me." Not physically, anyway. Locking a woman in a tomb wasn't Jax's style at all.

"He broke into my hotel room," Sarah said, voice soft, halting.

Emma's gaze flew to her. Sarah hadn't tried to stop Elroy from arresting Jax. She'd seemed to turn straight to stone during that bit of drama.

"He . . . he was waiting for me when I got back."

"And you didn't *call* us?" Wade exploded as he threw up his hands. "That guy is a psycho!"

Sarah flinched.

"No," Emma snapped back, "he's not."

Dean caught her fingers in his. She pulled away. "Jax is far from perfect, true. He's—"

"Been screwing a woman who looks just like you." Dean's voice was thick with fury. "That obsession needs to end."

Judging by the way the guy had seemed to stare at Sarah, Emma thought it was safe to say that Jax had moved on. "You're talking about Emma Grail, okay? They hooked up a few times before I ever came along." That was why Jax and Carlos had called her "Em"—to distinguish her from the other woman. "She has my hair color, nothing else. He doesn't *think* she's me. The guy just likes sex." Since when was that a crime?

Dean's tense posture said he wasn't convinced.

"Sounds to me like the guy needs to understand he has to back the fuck off," Gabe tossed in, voice sharp.

Emma wanted to scream. So she did. *"Where's Victoria?* Are you all overlooking the fact that she's gone?"

"Jax said he was trailing me." Sarah's voice was soft. "So maybe he'd been watching her, too."

Emma shook her head. "No."

"You don't know him as well as you think," Dean said.

Gabe nodded. "We never know anyone as well as we'd like to believe."

"I know him plenty well." This was insane! They were all just standing there, arguing amongst themselves. The cops had finally loaded up and left with Elroy, and—

"We're clear now," Sarah said softly as the lights from the patrol cars vanished.

Uh, clear?

Dean headed toward the morgue. "Then let's get inside and see what the fuck we can find."

Wait, what had just happened?

Wade's arm brushed Emma's. "We had to buy some time until they cleared out. Us having a fight seemed to work well enough."

They'd just been *stalling*? These people were about to drive her out of her mind.

"Jax didn't do it," Sarah said as she hurried forward. "He wouldn't have known about Ricker. He wouldn't have imitated the crimes, and he sure wouldn't have left Emma in the dark with those bones." Her steps quickened ever more. "But Elroy is sure looking for a scapegoat, and he's about to make Jax his sacrificial lamb."

No one sacrificed Jax. Elroy would learn that.

"Getting in will be hard," Sarah warned. "Elroy told the guard I was to be kept out."

Dean and Wade immediately shifted course. "So we go in the back way," Dean threw over his shoulder. A few minutes later, they were at the back of the building. The door was locked, but Wade leaned forward and got to work. She had to admire his skills because, about ten seconds later, the door opened, and an alarm didn't so much as beep because he quickly typed in a passcode.

"I might have picked that up earlier," he murmured. "Victoria, um, passed it along."

"One of the many things I love about Victoria," Gabe said with a nod.

Then they were hurrying inside. Going down to the lab, and the place was just as creepy as before.

Emma flipped on the lights. The lab felt way too much like a tomb.

And she realized everyone was looking at her.

"Do your thing," Sarah said with a wave at Emma.

Uh, her thing?

"I couldn't find any clues here. No sign of a struggle. Nothing." She nodded. "So do your thing. Find what I missed. Find *her*."

Oh, hell, talk about some serious pressure.

And they were all giving her that expectant, almost desperate stare. She wasn't a miracle worker. Emma backed up. "Look, I'm not—" *Giving readings in the park.* That was easy to do because there was no pressure. This was someone's life.

Dean's fingers brushed over her cheek. "Tell us what you see when you look around, baby. This is your specialty. The bastard screwed up. I know he did. You'll find his mistake."

Her heart was drumming too fast in her chest as she looked around that place. Everything seemed normal there. Nothing was tossed onto the floor. There was no sign of a struggle anywhere. The papers were stacked neatly on the desk. A pair of gloves were tossed onto the top of the garbage can. *Nothing* looked wrong.

Once you start looking beneath the surface, you'll be surprised at what you see. Her father's words whispered through her mind. *Most people never look that far, but we're not like everyone else.*

Wade wasn't waiting for her to do her mojo. He was riffling through papers on the desk. Sarah and Gabe went to help him.

And Emma found herself heading toward the lockers on the far back wall. Victoria had been planning to talk with Elroy, and, when Emma and Dean had left her last, she'd been in front of those lockers. *Did you keep working on the remains?*

She bent low and opened the locker that contained the remains of Wayne Johnson. Cold air rushed out to hit her, but the bag appeared undisturbed.

She started to reach for it, but hesitated. Ricker was the one in the middle of this puzzle.

So she closed that locker.

"Uh, yeah . . ." Wade said. "Just what are you thinking to find over there?"

Emma opened up the vault that had contained Ricker's remains. "I thought I'd find bones." She looked back at the others. "But they're gone."

"What?" Gabe demanded, then he surged toward her. Gabe grabbed the slab and pulled it out. The *empty* slab.

"He came back for Ricker," Sarah whispered. "I didn't even look in there—"

"Maybe there was evidence on the bones." Gabe was staring down at the slab. "Something he didn't want anyone else to see."

"Or maybe," Sarah said, clearing her throat, "he just wanted Ricker back."

Emma spun away from the locker. Her gaze darted

toward Dean. He looked as grim as everyone else. "The guy would have left carrying a body bag. That's not exactly easy to miss. *Two* bags," she amended as she considered the situation, and a dark suspicion took root in her mind, "because if he took Victoria with him, the easiest way to get her out would be to zip her up and act like she was a transfer being sent out."

"He put Viki in a body bag?" Wade snarled.

The lab's doors opened then. A man wearing a white lab coat sauntered in—it seemed to take him a moment to actually process the fact that other people were in the room. And when he did, he stopped, gasping. "What—what are you people doing in my lab? Where's Dr. Palmer?"

"That's what we're trying to find out," Gabe muttered.

But Emma had moved past him. Maybe the others had been right when they went to the desk before. She pushed aside papers and found the clipboard there. There was a sign-out sheet on the clipboard, with transfer orders. A scan showed her that most of the orders were signed with the same signature.

She spun back around. "Dr. Armont?"

"Yes." He gulped and took a step back. "I don't think you people are supposed to be here."

"And *you're* supposed to be here at this hour?" Emma threw back. "Or did you just come in to get the stash of pills that you keep in locker eight?"

He blanched. "How did you—"

"Your eyes are bloodshot, your fingers shake, and I'm betting the reason you work with the dead instead of the living is because your addiction got you into trouble in the past, and you got scared of hurting the living." She expelled her breath in a rush because she was taking some wild jumps, but the guy's body was stiffening with every word she spoke, and his eyes were flying nervously around the room—two sure signs that her words were hitting a target. So she plowed on, "Locker eight has a combination code on it. None of the others do. You didn't want anyone else to ever see what you kept in there."

He glanced over his shoulder. "Keep your voice down!"

"No." Her voice rose even more.

When the guy tried to retreat, Dean grabbed him.

Emma slapped the clipboard against his chest. "That's your name for the transfer at five p.m. today. You gave the okay."

"What?" His eyes bulged as he looked down. "No, no, I wasn't even here then. I was waiting for Dr. Palmer to leave, so I could—" His gaze darted guiltily to locker eight. "I was waiting for her to leave."

He was wasting their time. "Is that your signature?" Because she didn't think it was. It didn't match the others there, even if the name was the same.

He squinted, stared down at the scrawl, and shook his head. "I didn't give that transfer order. As far as I know, there weren't any remains scheduled to be removed today."

"But two were."

"One was Victoria? Is that what we're really saying?" Wade ran his hand over his face. "God, Viki."

Dr. Armont paled. "What's happening here? I-I don't understand."

Dean's grip tightened on the guy. "We think Dr. Palmer has been abducted. If you were here at five, then you very well might have been the last person to see her—"

"No, no, it wasn't me!" His eyes bulged. "I wasn't the last one! She was talking with that FBI agent—"

"Elroy?" Dean demanded.

"No, no, the younger one."

Emma's gaze met Dean's.

"She . . . she said that she'd recovered some trace evidence from the skeleton. Some sort of fabric that was caught in one of the broken metacarpals. She thought she could use it—" He broke off. "She was excited, okay? I heard her talking to him, and she sounded like she might be onto something."

"Elroy didn't mention this to us," Sarah said quietly.

"Maybe because Elroy doesn't know," Dean said.

In his gaze, Emma saw the same suspicion that she felt. She'd wondered how the killer had found her so easily in that cemetery. How he'd just . . . *been* there. She'd thought he'd been following her from her apartment, that he'd tailed her in that patrol car.

But now she realized that the killer had been at her side . . . in the patrol car, at the cemetery. He'd been the one hunting her, all along.

And he was the one who had Victoria.

Kevin Cormack.

CHAPTER FIFTEEN

I SWEAR, I WISH YOU'D JUST LEFT THINGS THE FUCK alone."

Victoria couldn't see the man who spoke.

"I mean, why the hell did you have to keep pushing? I didn't intend to involve you. You weren't on my list at all."

Her hands were tied together. Her ankles bound.

"But there's no going back now. Because you know what I won't do? Go down for this shit. I've got too much to lose."

She felt the knife shove into her side, and Victoria cried out in pain.

"I can be quick, if you want. If you tell me everything you learned and *exactly* what you shared with Dean and his little bitch when they came to see you at the morgue."

She shook her head as tears slid down her cheek. She was still partially in the body bag. He'd shoved a needle into her neck. When she'd woken up, she'd been in that bag. Gagged, feeling as if she were suffocating.

"I'm going to take the gag off so you can talk." The

knife sliced her again. "And you *will* talk. Because I've gotten to be very good at this. I can make you scream and beg. You'll be desperate to tell me anything just to make the pain stop." He paused. The blade ran lightly over her arm. "Or I can be fast, and you won't even feel death when it comes."

Why? Why? He was a federal agent! His job was to protect people. To lock up the bad guys. This shouldn't be happening, not at all.

He used the knife to cut away the gag. "What did you tell them?"

"N-nothing . . ." She hadn't even found that scrap—no more than a thread really—at that time. She'd been so hopeful when she made her discovery.

But he thought she'd found evidence to link him to the crime. *I didn't! I never suspected you!*

"Wrong answer." The knife pushed into her side.

The pain stole her breath, and tears leaked from her eyes. *No, no!*

"Now you're the one good at analyzing the dead, so you know I didn't hit an organ. *That* time."

"I-I told them about the gunshot at the back of the head."

He laughed. "That's right. *I* did that one. I'm the one who bagged Ricker, not Dean. Not fucking Dean Bannon. I'm the one who brought Ricker down!"

She couldn't see anything near her. Everything was too dark. But . . . she could hear insects. Dozens of them. They were chirping and seeming to cry out all around her.

He brought me to the swamp. He's going to leave me here.

Because he thought the swamp was so good at taking care of the dead.

And soon . . . I'll be dead. No wonder he left me in the body bag.

DEAN BURST INTO the task force's meeting room at the New Orleans PD. Elroy glanced up at him, face red. "What the hell are you doing?" Elroy demanded. "I'm interviewing a suspect."

"You're wasting your time, that's what you're doing," Jax muttered. He lifted his cuffed hands and waved at Sarah. "Good to see you, princess."

Dean ignored him. He could only deal with one asshole at a time. As he strode forward, he was aware of Gabe moving in perfect sync with him. This time, he had a boss who actually had his back. "Where is Kevin Cormack?"

"Get them out!" Elroy shouted to the two cops who were pretty much just standing there, looking confused as all hell.

Wade cut those two off before they could advance. "Wouldn't advise it, boys. You want to make sure you're playing for the right team here."

"What?" Elroy stalked toward Dean. "You're begging to get tossed in a jail cell—"

"Do you want to be known as the man who was blindsided by a killer?" Emma's quiet voice asked, cutting right through Elroy's fury. "Because I don't think you do. Beneath all that annoyingly cocky arrogance you carry, I suspect that, very far down, you might actually be a decent FBI agent."

Elroy's breath huffed out. "I don't risk lives. I play by the rules, and that's no mistake—"

"Cormack isn't playing by your rules," Dean told him flatly. He needed Elroy's help, so the bastard had to actually *listen* to him. "We believe he's the one who's been behind the killings."

Shock flashed on Elroy's face. "No, no, that's a lie!"

"Then call him." Dean slapped his hands down on the conference-room table. "Call him right now. Get his GPS location, get it from his phone because I know the FBI can do that. Get the location, and let's all go out there and see what he's doing." Fear and rage burned so brightly in him. "Because I think he has Victoria. I think the SOB took her out of the morgue in a body bag, I think he stole Ricker's remains because Victoria discovered evidence on them."

Elroy staggered back a step.

"And I think if we don't find Victoria—find her right now—he's going to kill her, and we may never find her body."

But Elroy was shaking his head. "You're wrong about him! After the blowup at Quantico, he got transferred down here, and he busted ass to prove himself again. Hell, he's the one who contacted me and tipped me off about Ricker's DNA being found on that coat and the hit turning up in the FBI database—"

"He tipped you off," Gabe told the guy in his fierce, no-shit-SEAL voice, "because he wanted you in his game."

"He blames you," Dean said softly, "just as much as he blames me."

Elroy stopped shaking his head.

"You wouldn't give the order to go in," Dean reminded the guy. *As if he needed that reminder.* "Back in North Carolina, it was your order that kept the other agents back."

"Protocol—"

"Kevin was sleeping with the victim. That woman up there—the victim that Ricker had taken last, Charlotte was his informant. He'd been with her for months."

"I knew about their relationship." Elroy's chin jerked up. "Why do you think I pulled him? I wouldn't let him partner with you on that case because of his emotional involvement—"

"I got there too late to save her," Dean said, "and he blames me for that. Most of all, I think he blamed Ricker. *That's* why he tracked the bastard down and put a bullet in the back of his head. But Kevin isn't done. He won't be done until he gets his revenge. On you. On me."

"You're wrong." Elroy's voice had gone hoarse.

The two police officers had frozen.

"He's an FBI agent," Elroy continued doggedly. "Not a killer."

"Then track his phone," Dean said because it was so simple. "Let's find out if I am wrong. Let's go find him. Dammit, Victoria is out there, and I can't arrive too late again. She needs us."

"Please," Sarah whispered.

But Elroy was still hesitating. "You have no proof! Nothing—"

"Dr. Armont said he overheard Agent Cormack talking with Victoria," Emma said. "Did the agent tell you about that meeting? Have you even spoken to him at all since five p.m. today? Because that's when he was with Victoria . . . that's when we think she was taken from the morgue."

"A lot can happen to a person in a few hours," Gabe added, voice hard. "Look, Elroy, don't believe us yet. Fine. But get the location of the guy's phone. We checked his hotel already—he wasn't there. Just do this. LOST can owe you a thousand damn favors, just . . . *do this*."

Elroy pulled out his phone. His fingers trembled. "He's not guilty."

Dean didn't say a word as Elroy contacted the FBI's tech team, a team that could find any phone . . . any-place.

"I'll prove he's not guilty, then you'll all still owe the FBI." Elroy waited a bit as his call connected, then he started making demands to whoever was on the other end of the line. A few moments later, Dean saw the guy's eyes widen and horror flicker over his face.

"Where is she?" Gabe demanded before Dean could speak.

"Th-the last cell tower that caught his phone pinging was . . . it was close to the site where we found Julia Finney." Elroy put his phone down on the table. "Why would he be out there, at this hour? There's no search going on . . ."

The chair squeaked as Jax leaned forward. "Face facts, man. He's out there because he's dumping a body. *He's dumping that woman.* Now move ass—and stop him."

Dean and Emma and their team were already flying for the door.

"DO YOU KNOW what it's like to lose the person you love?"

Victoria shook her head. She'd never been in love,

never been foolish enough to trust someone that much. Not after what had happened in her family.

"I loved Charlotte. She didn't love me, but I would have brought her around, eventually. I didn't get the chance. You see . . . Charlotte was walking such a fine line, selling out that mob family, telling me everything I wanted to know. But then *they* learned what she'd done, and they gave her to Ricker."

"Wh-what?"

"Oh, didn't I say that Ricker was a hired killer? No, sorry. Let me back up . . . you see, Dean never made that connection, either. Never realized that the sick fuck we were chasing actually got paid for his crimes. *I* figured that out. Me."

He sounded so proud of himself.

Crazy bastard.

"His victims had all pissed off the mob. And when the mob wanted someone to vanish, they gave 'em to old Ricker. The guy thought it was somehow more sporting to give his prey a fighting chance, though. Sick fuck."

You're the sick one. Victoria pulled at her ropes. Her bound ankles kicked inside the body bag.

"I found him in those woods. I knew he wasn't dead. Dean was in the hospital. Elroy was spouting off to the media, and *I* was the only one who kept looking. I found him, got him to confess . . . hell, Ricker even told me how much money he'd gotten for each kill. And he suffered during every single moment. He was so fucked up after the fall, there was no way he could fight back against me. When I was done, I shot him, but I guess you know that part, huh?"

Are you going to shoot me, too? Or will you keep using that knife on me? Victoria tried to block the pain that kept shuddering through her body.

"I couldn't let the body turn up, I figured I needed to get rid of the evidence, and shit, I thought I had. Do you know what a bitch it was to clean those bones?" He laughed. "Wait, of course, you do . . . forgot who I was talking with there."

But you slipped up and you left a hair stuck in his metacarpal.

"So what else did you tell Bannon?"

"N-nothing."

He sighed. "I am going to make you hurt."

Her mind raced frantically. Fine, if the truth wouldn't keep her alive, then maybe lies would. "I told him that I thought it was you!"

He tensed.

"I told him . . . to search your office, your home. To rip apart your life because I found your DNA on the skeleton."

"No!"

"Yes!" Her wounds throbbed. The wetness of her own blood soaked her shirt. "And I faxed my report to Elroy. He's going to be hunting you!"

"No . . ."

"We know about your victims. About Wayne Johnson . . ." She was definite on him. But Dean had told her the name of another would-be victim too . . . he'd called her . . . "Sandy . . ."

He laughed. "You have been busy." A dark pause. "And here I didn't think I'd left enough of Sandy for anyone to find."

Will there be enough of me for anyone to find? So many of the dead had crossed her table.

"Th-they know!" Victoria tried to sound strong, not terrified. "They're coming—you need to run. You need to—"

"You need to die, Dr. Palmer."

"No, no, *no*—"

He punched her in the face, and her screams stopped.

As SOON AS Dean's vehicle braked, Emma jumped out. The other members of LOST were already rushing into action, and she was—

"Keep the civilian back!" Elroy's voice bellowed.

Oh, he'd better not be talking about her. Didn't all of the LOST folks count as civilians, too?

But Elroy was running ahead with Sarah and Gabe while Dean and Wade split up to go with some cops—

You're not leaving me behind! She tried to lunge forward, but a fresh-faced cop locked his arm around her.

"Sorry, ma'am, you're supposed to stay here." The cop released her, but then he—and his equally young buddy—took up a protective stance beside her.

No way. "Dean!" she yelled.

He stopped. Right. He'd *better* stop. They'd been talking about search strategies during the drive there, and she knew his team was heading for the northern area and that search dogs were coming in to help, but she was definitely going on this hunt with him, too.

He loves me, he wouldn't leave me. He ran back to her, and Emma smiled in relief. "Good," she told him, "tell these guys to let me go—"

"Keep her safe," he told the two cops instead. Then

his hand sank into Emma's hair and he pulled her close. "I have to know you're all right."

"But—"

His mouth closed over hers. He kissed her hard and deep and fast, then he was running away. Leaving her behind.

What the hell, Dean? What. The. Hell.

"That's not the way it works," Emma whispered. Did he think he was the only one who was afraid? It sounded to her as if Kevin Cormack had planned for Dean's death all along. Did Dean really think she was just going to stand back while he faced the danger?

But he was running fast, not looking back.

She glanced at her guards. "There's too much ground for them to cover out here, you know that. Especially in the dark."

The cops glanced uneasily at each other. "More folks are coming. When the K-9 units get here, there will be more boots on the ground."

Ah, that one was ex-military. She could tell it by his lingo. "But what if Victoria Palmer doesn't have time for that extra help to arrive?" She could appeal to the guy's sense of honor, maybe his protective instincts. "We should go out and hunt right now. I mean, if I'm with you, then you *are* keeping me safe and—"

A twig snapped. The men whirled, moving swiftly as they tried to draw their guns, but they didn't have a chance to fire. There just wasn't enough time. Bullets blasted into them. One, two—perfect shots—and the men went down.

Emma didn't scream. She froze. If he'd wanted her dead, right then, a third bullet would have been fired.

A shadow ran toward her. Emma tilted her head back, and said, "Hello, Agent Cormack."

WHEN HE HEARD the gunshots, Dean froze. The blasts seemed to echo around him, then everything moved in slow motion as he tried to turn and head back to the cars. Back to Emma. Because those shots had come from that direction. Two gunshots. No screams. Just the gunfire.

He didn't roar her name. Didn't yell for her. Because he was too busy running. Praying. *Please let her be all right. Please don't take her. Don't take Emma.*

Wade was with him, breath coming in pants. And then Dean saw the bodies. His flashlight beam hit the two uniformed cops and the blood on the ground. Wade sank to his knees beside them. Checked for pulses.

"They're dead. Fast and clean shots, straight to their hearts."

Kevin had always been a good shot.

His light flew around, to the left, to the right, and—

"Emma." He whispered her name. His light had just hit her. She stood about twenty feet away, at the edge of the thickening swamp. Kevin had one hand around her neck, and the other hand held a gun to her temple.

Dean took a step toward her.

"No, I wouldn't do that." Kevin's voice rang out, carrying easily in the night.

He knew we were coming. The bastard heard our cars approach long before we arrived. Dean had known that was a risk, but they hadn't been given many options. In an area this isolated, there'd been no way to enter silently.

"If you take a step closer, I'll kill her."

Dean could hear the frantic thud of footsteps behind him. The sound of the shots would have been heard easily by Elroy, Gabe, and Sarah. They'd be coming, and he knew Elroy and his men would have their weapons drawn.

I can't let anyone hurt Emma.

"Victoria told you about me . . ." Kevin's voice was furious. "And you came hunting."

Victoria hadn't told him a damn thing, but Dean didn't deny Kevin's words. He kept his light on Emma. Beautiful Emma.

"You think I'm going in easily?" Kevin demanded, and he laughed. "You need to think again."

"Two men are already dead on the ground," Dean said. "There's nothing easy about this."

"Agent Cormack!" Elroy's voice barked. "What the hell are you doing? Put that weapon down and let the woman go."

Kevin laughed. "You really think you've got any authority over me? You're a joke, a fucking joke, and before I'm done, you're going to be choking on your own blood."

But Elroy stomped forward. "There's nowhere for you to run. You can't get out of here."

"Take one more step," Kevin warned him, "and I'll put a bullet in her brain. Try explaining that on tomorrow morning's news."

"You listen—"

Dean grabbed Elroy and shoved him back. "Not her life! You're not risking *her!*" He'd left her behind, left her furious and shaking, because he thought he'd been protecting her. *Wrong. Again. So wrong.* He whirled back around to face Kevin. "You want some payback because of Charlotte? Then come and get me." He tossed his gun to the ground but kept his flashlight on Emma. He had to keep seeing her.

Wade swore.

"I'm the one you wanted the revenge on, right?" Dean called. "Because I arrived too late?"

"You got credit for nothing!" Kevin snarled. "For letting her die—and they wanted to pin a medal on you! That bastard wouldn't let me anywhere near the case. I could have saved her!"

"Yes, you could have," Dean said, keeping his voice quiet with every ounce of strength that he had. "Her death was on me. It was all on me." And he wanted Kevin's rage on him, too.

"No, Dean," Sarah whispered.

"It wasn't Elroy. It wasn't the Bureau rules. It was me. I got there too late. I didn't save her."

"The mob put a hit on her," Kevin's voice broke. "That's what he did, man. He got paid for all those kills . . . only he enjoyed them, too. He laughed when he told me about them—laughed even as he bled and his bones were smashed to hell and back. I stopped that laughter, though."

"When you put a bullet in his skull," Dean said. *Emma, baby, hold on. We'll get out of this.*

"Yeah, that's when it stopped."

His hold was still tight on Emma. Dean could hear the soft rustles of sound in the air. He knew Gabe— with his SEAL training—would be going around to try to take the guy from behind. The cops would also be fanning out. They wouldn't let Kevin Cormack escape.

Dean wasn't worried about escape. He just wanted Emma to be all right. He swallowed back his fear, and asked, "Is Victoria alive?"

This time, Kevin was the one to laugh. "Not for long. Maybe you'll find her and maybe you won't."

"What did you do?"

"I made her talk . . . she said . . . The bitch told you all. Everything . . . no use hiding anymore." Now his words were coming out in hard pants. "Something . . . something just gave way in me when I saw Charlotte's body, all broken like that. She wasn't pretty anymore. Wasn't my girl. You, Elroy, and Ricker, you'd made Charlotte into something else."

"You're the one who's been killing!" Elroy shouted.

Oh, yeah, now he'd get on the Keven-Cormack-is-guilty boat. Once he saw the agent actually holding a gun to Emma's head.

"How many people did you kill down here in New Orleans?" Elroy asked. "How many more bodies are out in this swamp?"

"Guess you won't ever know," Kevin said, sounding damn pleased with himself. "You guys were all so fucking *blind*!" His laughter boomed again. "As blind as the victims. I changed my clothes, put on a wig, got contacts, used some of that costume makeup they sell on every corner in New Orleans and—just like that—I was someone new. I was someone who could get close to the victims. A homeless man who wasn't a threat. A man who could walk into an NOPD station and not have even one cop give me a second glance!"

"You were always good at undercover work," Dean said, trying to keep the guy talking. And the words were true. He remembered that Kevin had joined the FBI after working undercover vice down in Florida. The guy had even done a few undercover cases once he'd become an agent. He'd been able to easily adopt or lose an accent, change his posture, been able to slide almost seamlessly into any role.

I should have suspected him. How did we all miss this?

How had an FBI agent become such a brutal killer?

"When I saw you in The Mask that first night, I wanted to see if you'd recognize me . . . or if you'd be as blind as everyone fucking else." Kevin's voice boomed in the night. "You were—you only saw what I *wanted* you to . . . you were like a damn puppet on my string. You all were! I was in control! *Me!*"

Emma was holding her body so still as Kevin raged.

"I could come down here on the weekends," Kevin blasted, seemingly smug on his own power and wanting them to appreciate all the sick damn things he'd done. "Pick out my prey . . . become someone new while I hunted. Because if there's one thing the Bureau taught me, it's not to kill in your own backyard. That shit would have just brought attention. I didn't want the FBI seeing me, not until I was ready to take all you bastards down. Ready to make you pay!"

How many bodies? It was obvious to Dean that Kevin had been escalating with his attacks. He'd been driven more and more to the edge of reason with every kill.

"Are you watching, Dean?" Kevin asked him.

Dean still had his light on Emma.

"Because I need you to watch this next part very carefully."

"Dean," Sarah whispered. She'd angled closer to him. "Dean, he's not planning on going to jail. Not an FBI agent. He knows what they'd do to him in there."

Are you watching?

Dean turned off his flashlight. "Turn off all your fucking lights!" he yelled.

And . . . they did. One at a time, flickering off.

"No!" Kevin shouted.

Because the bastard had wanted Dean to watch him kill Emma. *That* was to be his punishment. To lose her, to break, just the way that Kevin had when Charlotte died.

Dean took off running, aiming straight for where Kevin and Emma had been just before those lights shut off. Every second, he was afraid he'd hear the blast of a gun. Every second—

He plowed into them. Their bodies crashed to the ground, and he grabbed out, desperately trying to find Emma. He caught her delicate wrist and tried to roll and pull her with him.

"You don't get to win."

Kevin fired his gun. The bullet burned across Dean's arm and he heard Emma gasp.

"You'll see what it's like!" Kevin screamed. "To lose what you value most! To have nothing! *Nothing!* When there's only a void left. Only the rage eating at you, making you hurt . . . hurt yourself, hurt anyone who gets close . . . *hurt* . . ."

Kevin fired again, but the shot was aimed behind Dean. A seemingly wild shot in the dark.

Dean caught Kevin's wrist in his grip. He slammed Kevin's hand back against the ground.

"Loved her," Kevin gasped out. "Loved her . . . after Charlotte, *gone . . . gone . . .*"

Dean felt the bones snap in Kevin's wrist. A light hit them again, shining down as the gun fell from Kevin's fingers. Dean looked up, and Gabe was there. Gabe and the cops hauled Kevin to his feet, but the guy wasn't fighting, not anymore. Sarah had said the guy wouldn't go willingly to prison, but he was just standing there, seemingly triumphant.

And that was when the terror nearly choked Dean.

He lunged for Emma. He'd felt the bullet slice over his arm, and that bullet—he'd pushed Emma away. She had to be okay, she had to be—

Emma was on the ground. He felt the blood soaking her shirt. "No . . ."

Lights were suddenly blinding him, and he heard the shout of "Medic! Get ambulances out here!"

But he didn't look up. He couldn't look away from Emma. There was so much blood on her shirt, and he couldn't even tell where the bullet had gone in.

"I'm . . . okay," she whispered. Her eyes were open. He couldn't see the bright blue, not right then, but her lips were trying to smile for him. "Okay . . ."

"No, she isn't," Kevin shouted. And he *laughed.* "You know I'm a good shot, so much better than you. *So much!* You wrecked my world, and I wrecked yours!"

"Get pressure on the wound!" That was Sarah's voice shouting, but . . . Sarah wasn't there. Her voice had come from a distance. She was talking about someone else. Someone else's wound? Who else had the bastard shot?

Dean remembered that last bullet, the one that had seemed to be a wild shot in the dark.

But Kevin never took wild shots. He was always the best at target practice.

"Say your good-byes," Kevin advised gleefully, as Gabe held him fast. "Because you're going to watch her die."

The hell he was.

He grabbed her shirt. Ripped the thing open. *Blood. Her blood.* It was on his fingers. Terrifying him.

"What will you do when she dies?" Kevin taunted.

"Shut him the fuck up!" Dean blasted. Then . . . "Emma, baby, just keep your eyes on me." Because her eyes were starting to sag closed. "You're all right, I've got you."

"Die in his arms!" Kevin was still shouting. "Go ahead . . . bleed out right there!"

"Shut him the *fuck up!*" Dean demanded once more.

He heard the thud of flesh hitting flesh, and Kevin finally stopped his yelling. Good. Dean could see the spot where the bullet had gone into her. Because he'd been pushing Emma at the time, the bullet had gone in at an angle. It hadn't gone straight into her heart. It looked like it had sliced into her chest, but, *thank Christ,* it had missed her heart.

Dean lifted her into his arms and started running.

"Where is Victoria?" he heard Gabe snarl behind him.

But there was no answer.

He rushed ahead . . . and saw that Sarah was on her knees, beside Elroy. *Fuck.* Sarah had her hands wrapped tightly around Elroy's neck. *Because Kevin had shot him in the throat.* And he remembered Kevin's words . . .

You'll be choking to death on your own blood.

It looked like Elroy was.

"Life flight is coming in!" one of the cops shouted. "We got them en route for Agent Elroy and your victim."

He wanted to jump in the car and drive as far and as fast as he could. But the chopper would be quicker, he knew that. The medics on the helicopter would be able to help her.

He put her on the backseat of the car, tried to make her comfortable. Until that scene was secured, the last thing he wanted was for her to be out in the open with Kevin. Dean curled his body over Emma's, and he kept his hand on her wound, applying pressure even as her blood soaked him. "Emma . . ." Her name was full of pain. "I love you."

He thought he heard her whisper . . . *I love you, too . . .*

But he couldn't be sure. Maybe he was just hoping too much. Because he needed her to stay alive. Needed her to stay with him.

He didn't want to think of a world without her.

VICTORIA DIDN'T WANT to die. She studied the dead. She didn't plan to *be* dead for a very, very long time.

So she crawled out of the body bag. Her hands sank into the earth, and she hauled herself forward. He'd slashed her, cut her with his knife, but he hadn't given her a killing blow. When the sound of approaching engines had reached them, he'd run fast, leaving her to the darkness.

She thought of Julia Finney. Of how the girl had crawled through this same swamp. Every sound she heard made her shudder. Snakes, alligators . . . they were out there, but she didn't fear them as much as she feared Kevin Cormack.

Because if he found her before *she* discovered help, Victoria would be a dead woman.

She'd heard the sound of gunfire. Hard, sharp blasts, and she was trying to crawl that way. If only she could stand, but whatever drug he'd pumped into her back at the morgue still had her too weak, and she hadn't even been able to untie the ropes that bound her.

Footsteps thudded, close . . . so close.

She started to cry out, but terror held her silent. What if that was Kevin, coming back to finish her off? She couldn't give away her location. She *couldn't*.

So she inched forward. Barely breathing.

"Victoria!" That bellow was familiar. Not Kevin. Not Kevin at all. Wade!

She opened her mouth to cry out but could only manage a weak gasp.

"Victoria!" It sounded as if he was moving farther away from her.

No! She swallowed frantically and tried again. "H-help!" It was like a frog's croak. But it *was* a cry. "Help!" This time, her voice was louder.

And his pounding footsteps were rushing toward her.

The beam of his flashlight fell on her. "Viki!" He scrambled toward her. Rolled her over. "Oh, Christ, Viki . . ."

"N-nothing vital . . ." she whispered, and caught his hand, holding him as tightly as she could. "He's . . . going to k-kill . . . Dean . . ."

"Gabe has him. He's not going to hurt anyone else."

He hefted her into his arms. "And I'm going to take care of you."

Her head slid down against his shoulder. She couldn't even put her arms up around his neck. "S-scared . . ." That whisper was a stark confession.

"So was I. So scared I wouldn't find you in time." He pulled her closer. There was a different note in his voice, one she hadn't heard before. "Sometimes, you don't know what you've got . . ."

What?

"Until it's too late." Then he was moving with her, running fast through the darkness, and Victoria knew there was something else she'd meant to tell him . . . She'd heard the sound of gunshots, but Kevin . . . Kevin liked to use his . . . "Kn-knife . . ."

CHAPTER SIXTEEN

D EAN COULD HEAR THE WHOOP-WHOOP OF THE approaching helicopter. It was a damn beautiful sound. "Help is here," Dean told Emma softly. "It's all right. You're going to be all right."

Her eyes were closed, and her pulse was thready. Dean feared that Emma might be going into shock. "It's all right," Dean said again as he pressed a kiss to her temple.

He glanced out of the car's back window and saw the helicopter landing. He pulled Emma into his arms, holding her carefully, and started running toward the chopper and the medics who'd just jumped from it.

They secured Emma quickly. Strapped her down. Checked her vitals. Went to work on her wound.

Elroy was loaded on board, but the guy wasn't moving at all.

"Wait!" Wade's voice cut through the night. *"Victoria!"*

Dean whirled and saw his friend running toward the chopper, with Victoria in his arms. "Can you fit three?" Dean demanded of the crew.

They hesitated.

"You're fitting three," Dean snapped at them. Then he was pulling Victoria from Wade's arms.

"Kn-knife . . ." she whispered to him.

Yes, that SOB had used his knife on her, and the sight of her injuries tore into Dean. She'd been pulled into his battle. Another innocent caught in the cross fire.

The crew secured her in the chopper. The blades started to whirl again. With so many victims loaded in, there wasn't room for Dean to go with them.

Emma's head turned. Her eyes were open. On him.

"I love you," he told her once more. It seemed like he couldn't say those words enough.

Then Sarah pulled him back. Dust and dirt swirled around him as the chopper rose, and all Dean could do was watch Emma leave.

I love you. He would tell her that a hundred times, a thousand times, every day for the rest of their lives. *Just don't leave me.*

For a time, all he could hear was the sound of the airborne chopper, the whir of the blades, then—

Laughter.

He turned. Uniformed cops had taken Kevin Cormack toward a patrol car. They'd put cuffs on the guy, they had their weapons trained on him, but Kevin was still laughing. Like the dead and wounded were just part of some sick game.

Dean surged toward him.

"Don't." Gabe caught him. Held him back. "He's trying to incite you. He wants you to attack. Hell, I think he may even want you to kill him."

Dean's gaze cut to a silent Sarah. She nodded.

And he remembered Victoria's whisper. *Knife.*

"Stop!" he yelled to the cops.

They froze. He broke free of Gabe's hold and ran to the man who'd once been his partner.

"Did your Emma die before they loaded her onto the chopper?" Kevin asked. "Because I think Elroy did. I know I hit his carotid. He was bleeding like a—"

"Did you search him?" Dean demanded of the uniformed officers.

The cops quickly nodded. "We patted him down, sir. No weapons."

"You checked in his boots?"

"He doesn't have any other weapons, sir," the cop on the right assured him.

But Dean wasn't convinced. "You were always good at having backups, weren't you, Kevin? Like the FBI gun you used to kill Ricker." Because back when they'd been partners, Kevin had always kept a second gun handy. *The gun we found at the crypt.*

And Kevin was still too triumphant for a man headed to jail. Dean bent and reached for Kevin's boots.

Kevin tried to kick out at him, but Wade and Gabe were there, too, helping to hold the guy down. At first, Dean didn't find anything in his search, and it looked as if the cops were right, no weapons, no—

Then he found the hidden lining in the interior of the boot. Tricky sonofabitch. He pulled out a knife from the right boot.

Then the left.

In the light, he could still see the blood on the knife that he'd taken from the left boot. Victoria's blood. He handed the weapons to the cop who rushed forward with an evidence bag.

"It's not going to be that easy for you," Dean told

Kevin as he rose and faced off against his old partner. "You don't get to escape into death. You have to stay here and pay for your crimes."

"No!" Kevin screamed, and he was fighting those who held him, fighting furiously.

"Lock him down," Dean advised the cops. "Keep your eyes on him at all times." Other FBI agents were joining them at the scene then—agents who'd have to deal with the fact that one of their own was a killer, and the K-9 unit had arrived. "Put him on suicide watch."

Then Dean headed for the line of cars. The bastard didn't matter any longer. He could rot in jail for the rest of his life. The person who mattered to Dean— Emma—he had to get to her.

"You'll turn out like me!" Kevin yelled after him. "You'll lose her, and you'll have nothing! *Nothing!* The darkness will eat you alive! You'll—"

Dean spun around. Once, that man had been his best friend. "I won't kill innocents. I won't hurt men and women just because I've been hurt, and I want to strike back at the world. How the fuck did you become like this? You used to be a good agent. You used to care about people."

Kevin didn't speak. He also stopped struggling.

"The badge you carried meant something. It should have, anyway. Or were you always like this?" And maybe that had been the case. "Were there signs I missed? Was the evil always rotting you from the inside, or were you something more once?"

Kevin didn't have an answer.

And Dean didn't care anymore.

He jumped into his car and raced away.

SURGERY WAS A bitch. Emma put it on her mental list of things that she never, ever wanted to do again.

Her eyes squinted as she stared at the white room around her. "I'm so . . ." Her voice came out hoarse. "Sick of hospitals."

Soft laughter. From the right. She turned her head, slowly, and Dean was there. His face was pale, his eyes were lined by dark shadows, but he had the biggest grin on his face that she'd ever seen.

He caught her hand and brought it to his lips. "Then how about"—his voice was almost as hoarse as her own had been—"we stay out of them for a while?"

"I-I like the sound of that." Why did her throat hurt so much? Oh, jeez, had they used a breathing tube on her?

Frantic now, she tried to look down at her chest.

"Only a little scar will be there. The bullet didn't hit your heart. You're going to be fine, soon. Better than ever."

Was he saying all that to convince her or himself?

Her gaze lifted to his face once more. "You don't . . . look so good." Had he been hit, too?

"That's because I thought"—he eased closer to her—"that I was losing my life."

Emma blinked.

"I don't know what I'd do without you, Emma. I just found you, and I want you to stay with me—always. To lose you—"

"St-stop."

He pulled in a deep breath.

"With me . . . without me . . ." Her voice seemed to grow stronger with each word she spoke. "You'll always be a . . . good man." He needed to see that. He was *nothing* like Kevin Cormack. And Kevin was an asshole to blame his madness on the death of his girl. Emma suspected the guy had been battling the evil inside for a very long time. "I just . . ." Now she smiled for him, a smile that she hoped flashed her dimples. "I make you . . . better."

Surprise had his eyes widening, then he laughed, and it was such a beautiful, amazing sound. A sound that she wanted to hear every day of her life.

Carefully, he eased into the bed with her. His arms wrapped around her, and he held her in the gentlest of embraces. As if she was the most important thing he'd ever touched. "Yes," Dean whispered, "you do. So much better."

Tears stung her eyes, and she knew those tears weren't from pain. Because she was too happy right then to feel pain. Dean was with her. They were safe, and—

"Victoria?" Emma asked. *Please let her be alive. Let her be safe.*

"She's stitched up and in the room next door. Wade is currently watching her like a very intent hawk."

Her breath came out on a relieved sigh.

"Agent Elroy didn't make it," Dean said, voice thickening a bit. "And the two cops with you . . ."

Sorrow filled her. "They were dead within moments."

He nodded.

Her lips pressed together. So much needless death. The happiness she'd felt a moment ago just seemed wrong when there was so much pain and sorrow. "What about Agent Cormack?"

"The NOPD has him in solitary confinement, on a

suicide watch. They're going to try to get him to reveal any other victims he might have killed. The dancer that Jax told us about? The police never found Sandy Jamison's body in the swamp, and we think there are more victims out there."

Many more. She thought the same thing. *Sandy Jamison.*

"Sarah's down there now, with Gabe, giving assistance during the interrogation."

So it was over. At least, the killing was. She hoped that Sarah could work her magic and find the rest of the victims.

"What happens next?" Emma asked. *No more death.* She didn't want to think of death and pain. She wanted life. She needed hope.

"Next . . . next I start convincing you that if you spend your life with me, I can make you happy. I can give you anything and everything that you could want."

Her gaze rose to meet his once more.

"Because *you* are everything that I want, Emma. Every dream I've ever had, dreams I didn't even know about. I look at you, and I want a future. I want a life with you. I can give you time. I can court you, I can do charm, I can do *anything* for you."

Emma studied him. She saw the slight tremble of his fingers and the shadow of fear in his eyes. The bruises on his knuckles showed his recent battle. The blood on his clothes showed the hell that he'd survived.

Dean wasn't an easy man to love. He was a man well acquainted with danger. A man who'd risk everything to protect those he loved. To protect the innocent.

"I don't need charm, Dean. I just . . . need you." That

was all it was for her. She looked at him, and Emma saw her future. A man who loved her. A man who understood her—even the dark parts of herself that she tried to hide from the rest of the world. Inside and out, he knew her.

She didn't have to pretend with him. Didn't have to lie. With Dean, everything was just right.

But she nodded, as if considering something important, and he watched her with a worried gaze. "Emma?"

"I do think, though, that you'll have to marry me."

"You want to marry me?"

"I want forever with you, Dean." Just so they were clear.

He held her tighter. "Yes. Marry me . . . *now*. Or, as soon as you're out of the hospital, or just—*be with me*."

Later, she'd tell him that, technically, she'd been the one to ask, and he'd said yes. But that part would come later.

So for now, Emma just smiled and tilted her head back. When he kissed her, Emma knew that everything was going to be all right. No matter what happened in the future, Dean would be with her.

And she'd be with him.

They weren't just lovers. They were partners . . . as she'd been trying to tell him from nearly the beginning.

Partners . . . forever.

EPILOGUE

"GOING IN FOR THE INTERROGATION, HUH?"

Sarah stopped on the stone steps that led up to the station where Kevin Cormack was being held. That dark voice . . . she glanced over and saw Jax Fontaine standing with his arms crossed over his chest, his back pressed to the side of the building.

She hesitated.

He lifted his hand and crooked his finger toward her. "I've got a secret . . ."

She slowly made her way to him. Gabe was waiting inside the building for her. She needed to get in there and find out just what Cormack had to say about his victims.

Jax's gaze raked her. "I was worried you might get caught in the cross fire." His lips thinned. "And since I was cuffed in jail, I couldn't exactly come and help you."

"I'm fine." She glanced toward the doors.

"Everything in there can wait, trust me."

She shook her head.

"Ah, no trust, not yet? Maybe one day."

Sarah squared her shoulders. "I need to get inside. I'm supposed to help with the interrogation."

"Because you're good at understanding killers."

"Something like that."

He laughed. A deep, strangely sexy sound. "Oh, princess, sometimes, killers just need to be put down. They don't need to be understood." Then he nodded toward her. "Do me a favor? Please tell Em that I still protect my friends. Always will." Then he was walking away. But he'd only taken two steps before he glanced back at her. "When you need me, come find me."

She didn't need him. She didn't need anyone.

But she watched him walk away. The guy just strolled down the New Orleans street as if he didn't have a care in the world.

"Sarah!"

She turned at the frantic call. Gabe had just burst out of the station and was running down the stairs toward her.

"I'm sorry that I'm late," she rushed to say. "I just—"

"Kevin Cormack is dead."

A chill skated down her spine.

"He tried to attack a guard on the way to the interrogation. The guard fired at him, and Kevin took the hit straight to the heart."

To the heart? That was the same shot that he'd tried to make on Emma Castille. A shot to the heart . . .

She looked over her shoulder. Her frantic gaze flew around the street, but Jax had vanished.

Please tell Em that I still protect my friends. Always will.

And she was suddenly very, very cold on that hot New Orleans street.

Don't miss the next sexy and suspenseful novel

featuring the LOST team

from *New York Times* best-selling author

CYNTHIA EDEN!

Read on for a sneak peek at

SHATTERED

Available in print and e-book October 2015!

MONSTERS WERE REAL, AND THEY USUALLY HID beneath the skin of men.

Dr. Sarah Jacobs had spent most of her adult life hunting monsters. She'd just finished her most recent case with LOST—Last Option Search Team—a recovery group that hunted the missing. They'd stopped the bad guy, but not before he'd killed.

More innocent lives had been lost.

No one is really innocent. Her father's voice whispered through Sarah's mind, and she hurried her steps as she walked down the busy New Orleans street. A few other members of her team were still in town, tying up the last of their loose ends. Before long, though, they'd all be packing things up and heading back to the main LOST office in Atlanta.

There would be another case waiting. There always was.

Sarah's footsteps quickened even more when she caught sight of her hotel. The doorman was outside, and a relieved smile spread across her face. She'd felt a bit odd in the last few days. As if she were being watched. She'd been taught never to ignore her instincts, but Sarah knew there was no reason for anyone to be following her. *Not now.*

She hurried past the doorman, mumbling a quick hello. Then she was in the bright hotel lobby. Her high heels clicked over that gleaming floor. She didn't slow down for a little pit-stop at the crowded bar. Sarah headed right for the elevator. She got lucky and was able to slip inside immediately. *Only me in here.* A quick exhale of relief escaped her as the doors started to close.

Then a hand appeared. A man's hand—strong, tan, and tattooed. Dark, swirling tattoos slid around his knuckles. He waved his hand, activating the elevator's door sensors and causing those doors to open wide for him.

Sarah pushed back against the wall of the elevator as Jax Fontaine stepped inside. She knew him by sight. Unfortunately. She also knew the man was trouble. The local authorities generally stayed out of his way. Unless she missed her guess, they were afraid of the guy.

And I don't blame them.

The word on the street was that Jax Fontaine was a very dangerous man. An enemy that most didn't want to have.

Thanks to her last case, she was now acquainted with him—and she knew that she'd attracted some unwelcome interest from the guy.

"Hello, pretty Sarah," he said. New Orleans drawled in his voice, just a hint of Creole rising and falling there. Jax smiled at her. *Right. Dangerous. Definitely dangerous.*

The elevator doors slid closed behind him.

Jax was tall, several inches over six feet, with broad shoulders and the kind of build that told her when he wasn't up to no good in the French Quarter, he had to spend some serious time working out.

The guy looked like a fallen angel—if fallen angels spent a whole lot of time scaring the hell out of people. His hair was blond, thick, and a little too long. His face—that face of his was eerily perfect. Almost too handsome. A strong, hard jaw, a long blade of a nose. He had sharp cheekbones and blue eyes that seemed to see right into her soul.

And the elevator isn't moving.

Probably because he'd leaned forward and pressed the stop button. *What. The. Hell?*

"I hear you're leaving town."

Her heartbeat spiked. When she was near him, that tended to happen. Her heart raced, her breathing came a little faster, and her stomach knotted.

Jax shook his head. "Leaving . . . and you weren't even going to come and tell me good-bye?"

Laughter came from her. Not real laughter. She couldn't remember what that felt like. Tight and mocking, the laugh pushed out from her. "It's not like we're friends, Jax." They'd been uneasy allies on the last case. Jax had known intel that she'd needed about the killer.

"Why just be friends? That's boring." His gaze slid over her. That light blue gaze seemed to heat as it lingered on Sarah's body. "We'd be much better lovers than we'd ever be friends."

Her hands were pressed to the wall behind her—only it wasn't a wall. A mirror. Mirrors lined that elevator. To be very clear, Sarah told him, "I don't date dangerous men."

Jax stepped toward her. He didn't move like other men. He stalked. He glided. Kind of like some big jungle cat—a beast hunting his prey. His hand lifted and his tattooed knuckles slid over her cheek.

His touch made her tense. Mostly because it seemed like an electric shock flowed straight through her body when his skin touched hers.

"Who said anything about dating?" Jax asked her. His smile flashed at her, showing his even, white teeth. "I thought we'd just spend the next seven hours fucking."

Fucking. Her chin lifted. "Start the elevator." Because she knew exactly what sort of huge mistake she'd be making if she got involved with a man like Jax. Sarah preferred to spend her time with men who were safe. *Law abiding.* Men who didn't thrive on danger and adrenaline. Men who had no idea about all of the darkness that existed in the world.

Safe men.

Jax wasn't safe. And if she wasn't careful, he'd see right through the mask that she wore.

When she inhaled, she could have sworn that she actually tasted him. He was so big, easily dwarfing her in that elevator, and his scent—masculine, rich— surrounded her.

Sarah pressed back against the mirror. "Start the elevator."

His blue gaze sharpened on her. "Are you afraid of me?"

"Aren't most people?" she dodged. Most smart people?

"Yes, but they have a reason to fear me." His knuckles fell away from her. "You don't. I wouldn't ever hurt you."

Right. Like she was just supposed to take him at his word. Once Jax had been drawn into LOST's investigation, Sarah had made it a top priority to learn as much about him as she could. Only it turned out that there wasn't a whole lot to discover. Most of his past was cloaked, little more than rumors and smoke. Sure, she'd seen his criminal record, but that had been all juvie stuff. The guy had been good at covering his tracks once he'd become legal.

He'd been on the streets since he was a teenager. Somehow, he'd clawed his way—quite literally—out of the gutter and become a force to be reckoned with in the area. He owned several businesses and had connections that stretched across the county. And the local police were sure that he was a criminal. They just hadn't been able to pin any serious crimes on him.

It's hard because he has money and power. And he's smart. She could see the intelligence in his eyes. The cunning. *He won't make mistakes easily.*

"I love it when your mind starts spinning," he murmured, his voice a deep rumble. "Tell me, Dr. Jacobs, are you profiling me right now?"

Her hands lifted and she shoved against his chest. He backed up, not because she'd been uber strong and knocked him back, but because . . . dammit, she suspected he moved for her.

To make her feel in control.

But he likes power.

And, hell, she *was* profiling him. "I don't understand the point of this little meeting. Stopping a woman in the elevator is hardly an appropriate pick-up routine—"

He laughed. His laughter actually sounded real. Warm and rough, it rolled right over her.

"How is anything about us appropriate?" Jax asked. That man's voice—so deep and rumbly—it was like pure sex. She was pretty sure, like one hundred percent so, that he normally had women tossing their panties at him on sight.

She wasn't one of those women. Or, rather, she was trying not to be one of those women.

Sarah hurried to the control panel and pressed the button to get that elevator moving again. "You're lucky security wasn't called in. You can't just stop an elevator." She was muttering. She was also not looking back at him. "Look, LOST appreciates your cooperation." Well, she didn't actually think her teammates did appreciate his cooperation. They pretty much thought Jax was trouble.

So right.

"But the case is over now," Sarah continued determinedly, "and your involvement with us . . ."

The doors opened. She breathed a fast sigh of relief and said, "That involvement is over, too." Sarah stepped out of the elevator, straightened her spine and made herself glance at him. Then she very firmly said, "Good-bye, Jax."

He caught her right hand. "You know we'd be dynamite together. We touch, and I pretty much implode."

Her whole body was trembling, but Sarah locked her knees. "That kind of desire is dangerous."

"Aw, pretty Sarah, that kind of desire is addictive."

Her room was just a few feet away. "Let go of my hand." This madness with him had to stop. And that was exactly what it was—madness. He wasn't the right kind of man for her. Not even for a night. He pushed her, made Sarah want to let go of her control, and she couldn't do that. She already walked a fine line as it was.

His index finger slid along her inner wrist. Her pulse jerked beneath his touch. He leaned toward her and his breath blew lightly against her ear as he asked, "What are you so afraid of?"

She'd never tell. "Good-bye, Jax."

He eased back from her. "When you change your mind, come and find me."

The guy's arrogance was too much.

"Did you really think I'd just jump on you when I saw you?" Her skin still felt warm where he'd touched her.

His mouth hitched into a half-smile. "A guy can only hope."

She shook her head. Then Sarah turned and marched away.

"That's not why I came tonight. Though fucking you would have been heaven."

Her steps slowed.

"I wanted to ask you about your business."

Her business? LOST?

"What makes your boss decide to take on a case?"

Curious now, she looked back at him. "Is someone missing?"

Jax just shrugged. "I did my research, too, you know."

She kept her expression still. If he'd been digging into the backgrounds of the LOST agents, then she realized that he knew all about the messed-up nightmare that was her past.

"LOST takes the cold cases, right? The ones that the cops have given up hope of solving."

Sarah inclined her head. Her boss, Gabe Spencer, had originally opened LOST because he wanted to make a difference. When his sister had vanished, the local cops had been no help. Gabe had found Amy on his own, but he'd found her too late. The man who'd been holding Amy had killed her right before Gabe got to the scene.

"There's no expiration date on your cases," he said. "Doesn't matter how much time has passed. You'll still take it?"

"We've taken cases where the person has been missing for over ten years." They were the *Last Option Search Team* for a reason. Most people who came to them had tried every other option available. Their efforts had turned up nothing. Desperate, at the end of their rope—yes, that was the way families were when they finally came to the LOST office in Atlanta. "But . . ." And he needed to know this, if he was looking for someone who'd been missing. "The longer a person is gone, the greater the likelihood is that you aren't going to find a . . . a live victim."

"Right." He pushed his hand through his hair. "I don't have to worry about that."

She stepped toward him. "Jax?" He'd made her curious now.

But he was backing into the elevator and shaking his head. "Forget it. I think it was a mistake." Then he flashed his broad grin at her. What she thought of as his panty-dropping grin. "Though seeing you is always a pleasure."

He was wearing a mask, one that hid his true emotions. In that moment, she was sure of it. For an instant, he'd let her glimpse behind the mask, but that instant was over.

"Have a safe trip back home. And who knows? Maybe our paths will cross again one day."

"Maybe." She was missing something there. She hesitated, then called, "Jax?"

But the elevator doors slid closed.

Sarah took a deep breath. Okay, so that had been unexpected. Pretty much everything about Jax Fontaine was unexpected. The last time she'd seen him—just days before—he'd told her, *"When you need me, come find me."*

Only he'd been the one to find her. Asking questions that had put her on edge.

The carpet swallowed her footsteps as she hurried to her room. Maybe it was because she was thinking so much about Jax or maybe she was just off her game, but it took Sarah a moment too long to realize that her door was ajar. She blinked, staring at it, then she tried to hurriedly back away.

But the door was yanked open. A man stood there. A man covered from head to toe in black. She whirled away from him, but he grabbed her and yanked Sarah back against him.

"Time to pay."

She opened her mouth to scream, but his gloved hand covered her lips.